KT-371-659

Aberdeenshire

3123487

EVA DOLAN

Long Way Home

ABERDEENSHIRE
LIBRARIES

WITHDRAWN
FROM LIBRARY

Harvill *Secker*

LONDON

Published by Harvill Secker 2014

10 9 8 7 6 5 4 3 2 1

Copyright © Eva Dolan 2014

Eva Dolan has asserted her right under the Copyright, Designs and
Patents Act 1988 to be identified as the author of this work

This novel is a work of fiction. Names and characters are the product
of the author's imagination and any resemblance to actual persons,
living or dead, is entirely coincidental.

This book is sold subject to the condition that it shall not, by way of trade
or otherwise, be lent, resold, hired out, or otherwise circulated without
the publisher's prior consent in any form of binding or cover other than
that in which it is published and without a similar condition including
this condition being imposed on the subsequent purchaser

First published in Great Britain in 2014 by
HARVILL SECKER
Random House
20 Vauxhall Bridge Road
London SW1V 2SA

www.rbooks.co.uk

Addresses for companies within The Random House Group Limited
can be found at: www.randomhouse.co.uk/offices.htm

The Random House Group Limited Reg. No. 954009

A CIP catalogue record for this book is available from the British Library

ISBN 9781846557798

The Random House Group Limited supports the Forest Stewardship
Council® (FSC®), the leading international forest-certification organisation.
Our books carrying the FSC label are printed on FSC®-certified paper. FSC
is the only forest-certification scheme supported by the leading environmental
organisations, including Greenpeace. Our paper procurement policy
can be found at www.randomhouse.co.uk/environment

Typeset in Charter ITC Std by Palimpsest Book Production Limited

Printed and bound in Great Britain by
Clays Ltd, St Ives plc

Long Way Home

ABERDEENSHIRE LIBRARIES	
3123487	
Bertrams	03/01/2014
MYS	£14.99

Prologue

The last thing he remembered was the pattern on the carpet, barbed strips of indigo and puce, like bruises inflicted by alien implements, then a steel toecap coming at his face. Now there was blood in his mouth, a seep not a flow, and when he probed with the tip of his tongue he found the splintered terrain of broken molars.

His hands were tied behind his back, feet bound with the laces out of his work boots. Through his jeans he felt the barn's concrete floor, cold and wet, a spray of broken glass under his right thigh. That was a distant and unimportant pain, nothing that would kill him. The pain in his head when he tried to focus on the barn door, that might.

He heard men's voices outside, shuffling feet, then the clang of a metal gate. They were moving the pigs, bringing them in to feed.

He had to get up. Get to his feet and get out. Now.

The blood was singing in his ears, running out of his broken nose down the back of his throat. This would not be the last thing he saw, this rank barn with its asbestos roof and barrels of dead chemicals. He would not die here. If they wanted to kill him they would have to catch him out there in the fields, in the darkness and the filth.

He rolled onto his back and brought his knees up to his chest, hooked his hands out from behind him, swearing as his flailing leg caught a metal butt and sent it ringing. The rope around his wrists was wet, the knots quickly tied, and he managed to pull his left hand free, skinning his knuckles. With shaking fingers he unpicked the laces knotted around his ankles.

Outside the voices were rising, not enough that he made out the words but he heard the tone change, the new belligerence. It made no difference, no one was arguing to spare his life.

The barn door shot back and he saw the floodlit yard.

'If you've not got the stomach for it, fuck off back to your old woman,' a man shouted.

His heart was thundering, deafening in the quiet of the barn, and ahead of him he watched his breath billowing hotly into the air, wondering how many more times that would happen before the last long one blew out of him.

He swore at himself. One on one he was as likely as anyone else to win a fight. That's why they had come for him in the middle of the night, knocked him out while he was sleeping, tied him up and gagged him. They were not the hard men they thought they were.

He moved into the shadows, hugging the wall.

The pigs were trotting in. Dozens of them, snuffling and snorting, huge pink beasts spotted with black, barging against the metal rails. He could smell them, saw the heat rising off their backs in the glare from the floodlights.

There was no way out, he realised. He would never get across the open yard unseen.

How many of them were there?

His brain lurched. Three men in the caravan was it? Two standing over the bed and a disembodied voice nearby? He remembered the walnut stock of a shotgun near his face as he fluxed in and out of consciousness, was sure he had smelled the oil on it.

The front third of the barn was lit now and he saw arcane machinery ranked up but rotting, blades blooming corrosion. There was nothing small enough to use as a weapon, nothing he could get his hands on without being seen.

He wanted to be at home. He wanted his warm bed and his warm girlfriend and the familiar glow of the street light coming through the curtains she had made him buy in Ikea. He wanted to close his eyes and roll over and press his face into her hair.

A rat darted across his foot, escaping from the pigpen. The

animals were rootling in the straw snorting, impatient for the food they couldn't find, knowing it was what they had been brought in for.

He stumbled, aware of voices now, loud, coming closer, and the sound of a rifle bolt ramming home.

Then he was running. Across the yard, heading for the unfamiliar woodland looming in the distance. He vaulted the post-and-rail fence as a gunshot rang out and dropped automatically onto his knees. Behind him dogs were snarling and he heard a barked command as they were released.

He ran across the uneven field, legs pumping and his heart hammering. He sucked down the night air, knowing he was crying, knowing the divine intervention he was begging for wouldn't come. He kept running, zigzagging as shots ripped past him.

The gibbous moon slipped behind a cloud and he ran on faster, knowing they would have night sights, that even in the woods he was as good as dead.

The field rose up to the margin of the wood and he threw himself across the narrow ditch at the perimeter. The dogs were almost on him, fifty or sixty yards away, he could see their eyes in the moonlight, two massive grey lurchers. Behind them a pickup was bouncing over the grassland, coming up slow enough that the man in the back could brace himself against the cab to shoot.

He moved into the woods, stumbling over the twisted roots, the rocks he couldn't see until he was on them.

This was it.

A bullet whistled past his head and he ducked behind a stump, dropping down onto his haunches. There was nowhere left to go now. They would hunt him down even if he reached the road. He could get to the village and it wouldn't matter. False dawn was falling, the streets would be deserted and no one came outside for gunshots in places like this. It would be rabbits or deer, some stupid bastard who probably deserved it.

He swore at the sky and pushed on.

WEDNESDAY

Four days earlier

I

Shreds of smoke lingered between the close-packed terraces on Highbury Street. Not much escaped from there; it was a narrow, congested road, cars parked both sides, barely enough room for the fire engine to squeeze between them. It was easing out as DI Zigic turned off Lincoln Road and his brakes bit a couple of inches from the high black bumper. The driver threw his hands up – *where am I going to go?*

Zigic backed onto a wedge of tarmac between the Hand & Heart pub and the garage next door, locked-down roller shutters emblazoned with a red English Nationalist League tag.

It was the third new one he'd seen this week. All within the few dozen streets which comprised New England, or as the locals were calling it these days Englandistan, a bustling suburb just north of the city centre, and home to the vast majority of Peterborough's migrant workers.

Highbury Street had been predominantly Polish five years ago, when he was first put in charge of the Hate Crimes Unit. Plenty of jobs around back then and the property market flooded with cheap money. The Poles moved up and on, bought houses in Paston and Westwood, gentrified the 1970s ghettos they were when he was a kid, opened supermarkets and beauty salons, turned the slums into suburbs. Now Highbury Street was more mixed, Bulgarians and Estonians, a Slovenian couple he knew from their son getting glassed on the embankment over Christmas. Nice kid, but the ones on the receiving end usually were.

Zigic got out of the car and buttoned his parka up to his chin, watching a woman retreat from the upstairs window of the house opposite, curtains a few inches too short swinging back into place. The house looked cheaply renovated and badly maintained, mismatched plastic windows packed out with bright yellow expanding foam, a front door showing the painted-over scars of old locks, busted and replaced.

The neighbours were more house-proud, neatly mown front lawn and primped hanging baskets on the porch. They had a St George's cross tacked up across the living-room window and somehow he didn't think it was there in readiness for the weekend's rugby.

There were a few English in the area still and the ones Zigic had run into operated under a siege mentality. Wouldn't be forced out; as if anyone was trying to.

They were the ones who squinted at his card, asked, 'Zygick? Zigick? Is that how you say it?' Then when he corrected them – *Zhigitch* – they got it wrong again. The ones who always wanted to know where he was from. No, really from.

Despite the Peterborough accent, burred with a fen edge he couldn't quite shift, they thought he was just off the bus. Taking some hard-working English copper's job.

They weren't entirely wrong. The ACC needed a foreign name to head up Hate Crimes and he wanted it attached to a third-generation body. Someone just different enough.

Zigic crossed Highbury Street between the cars, clocked an out-of-date tax disc in one, an empty vodka bottle on the dashboard of another. At the far end of the road a transporter van was unloading the night shift, another group waiting on the kerb to get in.

People were coming out of the houses, togged up against the early-morning chill in quilted coats and woollen hats, heading down towards the collection points strung along Lincoln Road. A couple of women with supermarket uniforms under their jackets grinned at Zigic as he stepped aside for them on the narrow path and he caught a fluttering of Latvian, recognised the shape of the words but couldn't translate them.

They had walked past number 63 without even glancing down

the driveway. Despite the police tape and the WPC standing guard with her hands tucked into the small of her back they hadn't let their curiosity get the better of them.

Zigic wondered where they learned that. What had been bad enough to override the hard-wired human instinct to look where you shouldn't?

Anywhere else the neighbours would be out in numbers but the group at the edge of the cordon was only four strong, an elderly couple in grubby anoraks and a young woman holding a squirmy toddler to her chest. None of them spoke. They hardly moved, only looked along the cracked tarmac driveway towards a pair of high wooden gates, which stood open a few inches, showing a sliver of metallic paintwork and the back window of an Astra van.

The house was 1930s, a pebble-dashed detached painted white, but not recently, with wooden windows done in the same expensively dingy green Anna had insisted they buy for their front door at home. It was still in the garage; Zigic told her you couldn't put it on while there was a risk of frost. He was hoping she'd come to her senses and let him paint it red.

'Morning, sir.'

The WPC lifted the perimeter tape for him and Zigic ducked under.

'Any trouble?'

'No, sir. Most of them are at work by now I reckon.'

'Has the doc been?'

'You just missed him.'

Zigic went through the gates into number 63's back garden, the smell of smoke hitting him full force, an unmistakable meatiness to it which snagged at the back of his throat. Flecks of black swirled in the air and he tried not to think what they had been part of as he picked one from his bottom lip.

The charred hulk of the shed was tucked into the far corner of the garden, against a run of old red-brick wall. It was a standard issue eight by twelve larch lap with a felt roof collapsed in on itself and a stable door smashed off its hinges. Inside Zigic saw a twist of blackened metal and springs which could only have been a sun-lounger, and a body caged by it, slumped in the middle. Only the head was clearly visible in a shaft of weak morning sun, scorched skin cracked and seamed red.

DS Ferreira was standing nearby with the fire officer, hands shoved into the pockets of her duffel coat.

'What have we got, Mel?'

'One lightly toasted corpse,' Ferreira said. 'Looks like he was in a sleeping bag.'

The fire officer nodded. 'I've dossed down worse places.'

'Me too.' Ferreira turned away. 'Expert witness says we've got accelerant.'

'Smells like kerosene,' the fire officer said, wiping his face with the front of his T-shirt. Neither were very clean. 'Reckon it might have been stored in the shed but you take a shufti in there, Inspector.'

He stepped back and Zigic looked beyond the remains of the sunlounger and the body which was bigger than he first thought, definitely a man and a well-built one at that, saw a few empty bottles next to a melted crate and a galvanised metal bucket which was somehow perfectly untouched. Other than that the shed was empty.

'Wish yours was that tidy, hey?' the fire officer said.

'It might've been an accident. He'd been putting some drink away by the look of him.'

'And it might've been spontaneous combustion, but there was a padlock on here heavy enough to hold down an elephant.'

'Inside?'

'Outside.'

'Where is it now?'

'Still on the door,' the fire officer said. 'Knew you'd want your people in here.'

The mobile on his belt sounded a plunging tone and he was

already moving as he checked it. 'I'll get my report over to you before five, Inspector. Mel – a pleasure as always.'

He jogged off towards the gates.

'God, he fancies himself,' Ferreira said. 'What is it with firemen?'

'I honestly couldn't tell you.'

'Man must be fifty.'

'Mel –'

'Just trying to lighten the mood.' The shed roof gave an ominous crack and she stepped away smartly, kicking up water onto Zigic's jeans. 'Sorry.'

'What do you think – a vagrant?'

'Maybe. Or a tenant.'

Peterborough had a high proportion of illegally converted sheds and garages. The rents were running at four hundred pounds a month and the planning department was having trouble keeping on top of them. For every one they cleared out, another three sprang up.

Highbury Street wasn't in their red zone though. Not yet.

Zigic looked to the back of the house, blinds drawn in every window, no lights on. There was a half-built conservatory poking out into the garden, brickwork up to knee height, a mound of water-logged sand on a plastic sheet. Half a dozen plastic signs advertising Barlow Property Maintenance were stacked against the fence, a mobile number but no landline, a small fish decal so you knew the owner was a good Christian; old folk liked to see that.

'Are they home?'

'Yeah. They're too shocked to answer any questions right now.' Amusement flicked around Ferreira's near-black eyes. 'At least that's what Mr Barlow's saying.'

'What about Mrs Barlow?'

'Puffy eyes, snotty nose . . . she didn't say much.'

'Which one of them called the fire engine?'

'Neither. Alec Lunka.' Ferreira pointed to the neighbouring house, a red-brick terrace with wind chimes jangling near the back door and three blue towels stiff on the washing line. 'He's Romanian. His English is pretty good though.'

'You talked to him?'

'Briefly – just wanted to keep him from going anywhere. I asked him to hang on until the boss got here. He's happy to cooperate.' She tucked her chin down into her plaid scarf. 'Thought I should try and get what I could out of the Barlows while they were still raw. So much for that. Didn't even get a cup of coffee.'

'Have you called forensics?'

'On their way.'

'Door-to-door?'

'Bobby's on it. He's got hold of a couple of off-duty CSOs. There's some new guy at London Road who speaks Hungarian – he's a techie or something but they're bringing him too.' She shrugged. 'It'll be a total washout this time of day, you know that? Anyone who might have seen anything will be at work now and anyone who's home now would have been on shift when this happened.'

'Lunka saw something.'

Zigic started for the gates. As he did, the kitchen door opened.

'Mrs Barlow, I'm –'

She slammed the door so hard that the wooden blinds clattered against the glass. The lock turned and a few seconds later turned back again but the door stayed firmly shut. Ferreira gave him a questioning glance and Zigic put a hand out to stop her. A man's voice cut sharply into the quiet and there was a sound like a stack of plates smashing, then another door slammed and the crying started.

'Try her now,' Zigic said.

2

Gemma Barlow was pale under her fudge-coloured spray tan and Ferreira guessed that without it she'd be just another blotchy pink lump of English womanhood. She made a lot of effort though – three different colours in her shoulder-length hair and a French manicure with half-inch tips. She was missing one on her thumb and she worried at the ragged stump while Ferreira gathered together the pieces of broken crockery.

'They just slipped out of my hands.'

'They're only plates, don't worry about it.' Ferreira dumped them into the bin and Gemma flinched at the sound like she'd been slapped. 'It must be a shock for you.'

'We didn't know he was in there.'

'You don't expect some guy to bed down in your shed, do you?'

Gemma took a packet of Silk Cut out of her cardigan pocket and lit up, the lighter flame wavering as her hand trembled. She wore a thick gold wedding band over a diamond chip, thin rings biting on two more fingers.

'We didn't even know there was anything wrong until we heard the sirens,' she said. 'Was it an accident?'

'It's still too early to say.'

Gemma nodded, took a deep drag. 'Sorry, do you want a cuppa or something?'

'Coffee if you've got it.'

'Instant alright?'

'Tea then.' Ferreira took a tobacco tin out of her handbag. 'You don't mind?'

'My grandad used to roll his own,' Gemma said. 'Cheaper, in't it?'

'I prefer the taste of them.'

Gemma leaned back against the worktop, eyes on Ferreira's hands as she rolled the tobacco between her fingertips, packing it tight inside a liquorice paper.

'You're not English, are you?'

'I was born in Portugal. We came over when I was seven.'

'No work over there, was it?'

'Not much opportunity.' She ran her tongue along the edge of the paper and twisted it into a slim torpedo. 'We went to Spalding first, then when my parents got enough money together they moved us here.'

'Do they work?'

'Yeah.' Ferreira lit up. 'They've got a pub.'

'They've done all right out of it then.'

Out of what, Ferreira wondered, grafting sixteen hours a day, seven days a week, Dad in the fields, Mum in freezing cold pack-houses, living in a caravan for two years, then a barely habitable pit for another five, four kids sharing two bedrooms; her and three younger brothers?

'They must be proud of you, getting into the police.'

'It was a pretty big deal, yeah.'

'They always send you when an immigrant gets killed?'

'What makes you think he was an immigrant?'

The skin around Gemma's small blue eyes tightened and Ferreira bumped her age from mid-twenties to early thirties.

'Well, you know, they're all foreign round here now.'

'You're not.'

She picked the kettle up before it hit the boil and poured water into their cups, sloshing some onto the fake terrazzo worktop.

'I just thought – who else'd be sleeping in our shed? No English person's going to do that, are they?'

'There're plenty of English people sleeping rough.'

'Not round here there's not.'

The kitchen door opened and Phil Barlow filled the gap, a

bulldozer of a man in badly cut jeans and a designer T-shirt. He was older than Gemma by ten years or so but he was wearing a lot of gold and Ferreira guessed that probably helped.

There was a smudge of yellowish bruising under his right eye.

'Making a brew, love?' he asked, holding his voice calm while he brushed one big hand over his bald head. 'Good idea. 'Spect you could use one too, Constable.'

'Sergeant.'

'Sorry, yeah, Sergeant.' He blew out a long breath. 'What happens now then?'

'We've got a forensics team on the way; they'll conduct a thorough search of the shed and your garden. When they're finished we'll take the body away –'

Gemma gasped and pressed her fist to her mouth.

Phil put his arm around her shoulders and she started to cry.

'Come on, love, come on, it's all going to be alright.' He gripped Gemma's forearm. 'She's a bit upset, that's all. Why don't you go in the front room? Have a sit-down. I'll talk to the sergeant.'

'I'll be alright in a minute.' Gemma wiped her eyes on the cuff of her cardigan. 'It reeks in here. The whole house reeks of it.'

Ferreira stubbed out her half-smoked cigarette, almost put the rest in her pocket but caught herself in time; old habits.

'Why don't we do this in the sitting room?' she suggested.

It was gloomy with the curtains drawn in the bay window, aubergine paint on three walls and gaudy damask paper on the fourth, not much of it on show between the huge black marble fireplace and the forty-six-inch flat screen hung above it. The smell was fainter in there, just an acrid hint under the bludgeoning sweetness of a magnolia room spray which puffed at Ferreira as she walked past it, going to a shelf of family photos, Phil and Gemma on holiday, beaches and swimming pools, toasting the camera inside a little hut with a banana-leaf roof. There were a few of a teenaged boy, chubby and freckled.

'Is your son here, Gemma?'

'He's my son,' Phil said. 'Craig. He stays with his mum during the week. We have him weekends.'

Gemma shifted her weight on the black leather sofa, punched her elbow into a cushion.

'I'll need to speak to her,' Ferreira said. 'Just to confirm.'

'He didn't set fire to the fucking shed.'

'It's routine, Mr Barlow, there's nothing to panic about.'

She took out her phone and entered the details he gave her; his ex still using his name, living in Woodston. Close enough for the boy to have come over on his bike in twenty minutes. If he felt like causing trouble. Close enough to disappear this morning too. It was still dark when the call came in, who'd notice him slip away?

'You two don't have kids?'

'We're trying,' Gemma said, a whole payload of want and frustration in her voice.

Phil sat down on the sofa next to her and took hold of her hand.

'What happened to your eye?' Ferreira asked.

He touched it quickly, glanced away.

'I was fitting a security light at a place over in Dogsthorpe, didn't have it hung right.'

'Looks nasty.'

'It's not that bad.'

'You're a builder? That right?'

'Property maintenance,' he said. 'Have to do a bit of everything.'

'You're multidisciplined.'

'Jack of all trades,' he said and gave a self-deprecating smile laced with bitterness. 'I was a kitchen fitter before, but the way the building is now . . . not many people want new kitchens when they can't afford the mortgage.'

'Looks like there're plenty of sites running around town,' Ferreira said.

'Can't get on them unless you're with an agency and you know what that's like, they're not going to pay me two hundred a day when they can get some Polack for sixty.'

16

'Just you, is it?'

'Same for everyone.'

'I meant, do you work alone?'

He nodded. 'I had an old boy with me last year but I had to let him go. He's working in Asda now, trained City & Guilds chippie and he's stacking fucking shelves. Way it is.'

Ferreira sat down on a fat leather footstool, moved aside a copy of *Grazia* with Cheryl Cole on the front cover.

'OK, so this morning . . . why don't you tell me what happened?'

Phil and Gemma Barlow looked at each other but he spoke.

'We don't know what happened. First we knew of it was sirens blaring out here.'

'We never thought anything of it,' Gemma said.

'There's always sirens round here. You ignore it.'

'Where's your bedroom?' Ferreira asked.

Phil Barlow pursed his lips for a moment. 'Over the kitchen.'

'So the shed's right outside your bedroom window and you didn't notice it was on fire?'

'We've got blackout blinds,' Gemma said.

'Which one of you's the light sleeper then?'

'Neither of us,' Phil said quickly.

'But you've got blackout blinds.'

They nodded in unison, didn't try a proper answer.

'When did you finally work out what was going on?'

'One of the firemen near battered our front door down. I got up then,' Phil said. 'I couldn't believe it.'

Ferreira's mobile vibrated and she went into the hallway to answer it, closed the living-room door behind her. The Barlows already had their story straight, no point letting them overhear what she was saying.

'What you got for me, Bobby?'

'They're all clean,' DC Wahlia said. 'The Lunkas and the Barlows.'

'What, nothing?'

'I know, what's the fucking world coming to?'

'I'd have laid money this arsehole had form.'

'Is he giving you shit?'

'Just the usual.' Ferreira checked the mail on the hall table, bills and circulars, the new Lakeland catalogue. Tucked behind the table was a hefty red crowbar. 'They're hiding something. The atmosphere's like cancer.'

A car pulled up outside the house, an insistent bass line pounding for a few seconds after the engine stopped. Forensics had arrived.

'What do you want me to do?' Wahlia asked.

'That's it for now. Unless you're going to come down here and beat some answers out of them.'

3

'You want coffee?' Alec Lunka asked, the pot already in his hand, a battered aluminium stovetop which looked like it had crossed continents.

'Black with one. Thank you.'

Lunka poured a shot of espresso into a mug and returned to the kitchen table while the kettle boiled. He picked up a bowl of milky porridge and tried to spoon some into his daughter's mouth. She was grizzly and stubborn though and turned her head away no matter how gently he coaxed her, twisting and dipping like she might escape the high chair at any moment.

'They're great at that age, aren't they?' Zigic said.

Lunka wiped her chin with her bib and she scowled at him.

'She only eat for Mama.' He said something to her in Romanian, his voice soft and hopeful, the tiny pink spoon held to her firmly closed mouth. 'You have children?'

'Two boys, five and three.'

'And they eat?' The kettle rattled to a boil just as the little girl opened her mouth. Lunka gestured away. 'You make.'

Zigic finished his coffee, added sugar from a canister and dropped the spoon into the washing-up bowl, checking the view out of the kitchen window. The Barlows' shed was less than thirty feet away, close enough to lay a sooty film across the glass. The inside was sparkling clean, like the rest of the small white kitchen.

At the table Lunka was making an elaborate display of trying the porridge; he mugged it up but the girl wasn't buying. Zigic remembered doing the same thing with Stefan; he was finicky, would eat something one day and not the next, refused it off a plastic spoon, had to be fed from the grown-ups' cutlery. Eventually they realised the only way to make him eat was giving the food to Milan first, then he'd scream and snatch at it.

Lunka sat back, defeated. 'They will feed she at nursery.'

Zigic sipped his coffee, the little girl watching him now, wondering who this strange man was.

'Can you tell me what happened this morning, Mr Lunka? Right from the beginning.'

He shrugged, frowning. 'I am in bed. I hear noise, wake up. I go to window, see fire in shed.' Another shrug. 'I call 999.'

'What noise woke you?'

'Some noise. A bang maybe.'

'Did you see anyone near the shed?'

'No.'

'But you knew there was someone inside,' Zigic said. 'You told the dispatcher that you thought there was a man in there.'

Lunka nodded.

'How did you know he was in there?'

'I hear, last evening. He come home, is drunk, singing.'

Zigic put his cup down. 'Came home? He lives there?'

'Some time, yes I think.'

'But not every night?'

'I am not policeman, stand at window watch neighbour. I see when I see,' Lunka said. 'If these people want make money for he to sleep in shed . . . plenty people do this. When I am come to Peterborough first I sleep in garage. Pay old woman fifty pounds week.'

'How long's he been there?'

'Two week. Three. I do not count.'

'Did you know him?'

'If is same man, yes.' Lunka picked up the tiny pink spoon and turned it between his fingers. 'He is . . . *cersetor* . . .' He cupped one hand at Zigic. '*Cersetor* . . . for money?'

'A beggar.'

'He come here, want money – I say fuck off. He want food. I say him leave or I get knife.'

Zigic nodded, waiting for Lunka to realise what he had just said to a police officer, but his expression remained neutral. It looked like innocence and Zigic decided to go with his gut unless the post-mortem uncovered a stab wound.

'Do you know his name?'

'No.'

'Is he Romanian?'

Lunka considered it for a moment, watching his daughter's fists close on air in front of her.

'Not Romanian. I think . . . Kosovan, maybe. He has nose like Kosovan.'

It would explain why he was dossing down in a shed. Illegal, no papers. It wouldn't be impossible to get work but it would be badly paid and precarious and if his bosses decided not to pay him at the end of shift what was he going to do about it?

'Have you had any other trouble from him?' Zigic asked. 'Other than the begging?'

'No. He sees I will not give nothing. What else is here?'

'Nothing's been stolen?'

Lunka shook his head. 'Is accident, this fire. Why questions now?'

'It's standard procedure, Mr Lunka, I can assure you.'

'I do right thing. Call for help. I am not criminal,' he snapped.

His daughter's face flushed and she let out a long, extravagant wail which drilled through Zigic's temples.

Lunka lifted her out of the high chair.

'You see. You do this.' He kissed the top of her head. '*Shhh, draga.*'

The little girl snuffled, gave a small, half-hearted mew and fell silent against Lunka's chest.

'You want ask question?' he said quietly. 'Ask why they no answer door when I knock? I ring bell. Five, ten minute I ring, shout through letter box, tell them is fire – no answer. They are in house. And no answer? Why is this?'

Zigic took a card out of his wallet. 'I'll need to speak to your wife at some point, Mr Lunka. Can you ask her to call me when she gets in?'

'She will call.'

'Thank you for your help, it's much appreciated.' They shook hands. 'I'll see myself out.'

The group in front of number 63 had moved on and the street was deserted now. Gone seven, everyone was where they needed to be. Some of the residents would be into their second hour of work, talking about the fire perhaps, but whatever they knew wouldn't come to light until the end of the day when they returned home and found the incident notice pushed through their letter box. Many would ignore it as another piece of junk mail and Zigic knew he would have to organise a fresh round of door-to-doors first thing tomorrow morning, catch them before they left for work.

He didn't hold out much hope for witnesses though. The countries these people came from, you didn't trust uniforms of any colour; play dumb, keep quiet, try to stay off the authorities' radar.

He couldn't blame them for thinking the situation was no better in England.

His grandparents had been here sixty years and they still spoke in hushed tones when they discussed money or politics, convinced that some shadowy state apparatus was waiting to swoop down and punish their dissent.

Along the street, half a dozen houses away, he saw a civilian support officer talking to a black-haired woman in a dressing gown. She was shaking her head, putting a defensive hand up as the CSO pointed to number 63. A loud *nic* rang out and the door closed with hard finality.

There were still a few Polish on Highbury Street then.

A scientific support van had arrived while he was in with Lunka and he saw Kate Jenkins's red Mini parked badly, half on the kerb, a couple of doors down. She was heading for the gates, her slight frame bent as she lugged a silver case two-handed, banging it against her thigh.

'You want some help with that?'

'It won't get the job done any quicker,' she said, but let him take it. 'Buggered my back up at the gym.'

Two of her team were already at work in the garden, androgynous figures in baggy blue plastic coveralls inching through the long grass where the shed's window had been blown out by the fire. In the doorway the photographer was squatting down, getting some good tight shots of the dead man's head.

'Is it safe for you to go in there?' Zigic asked.

Jenkins looked up at the clouds gathering overhead. 'If the wind picks up we could be in trouble. We'll throw a tent over it, hope for the best.'

'The roof's collapsed already.'

'That's something, I suppose.'

The photographer moved tentatively into the shed.

'Watch yourself, Tony,' Jenkins said.

'Yes, Mum.'

'If you were my son you wouldn't have that bolt through your nose.'

'But I could keep the one in my dick?'

Jenkins smiled faintly. 'I didn't need to know that, did you?'

'Not really,' Zigic said. 'Call me when you've got something?'

'Always do.'

He went round to the front of the house and rang the Barlows' doorbell, held it down and heard an amplifier echoing inside. Nobody could have slept through that.

Ferreira let him in and he followed her into the living room.

The Barlows sat close together on the sofa. Neither looked like they'd had enough sleep. There was thick grey stubble on his cheeks, bags under her eyes.

Phil Barlow stood up as Zigic went in.

'Are you in charge?'

'DI Zigic.' He stuck his hand out and Barlow hesitated a moment before he shook it with a strong grip. 'I'd like you both to come down to the station and give us a formal statement.'

'Can't we do it here?' Gemma said. 'I don't want to go to a police station.'

'We've done nothing. What d'you want statements from us for?'

'A man's died in your garden shed, Mr Barlow.'

Barlow drew himself up to his full five eight, six inches shorter than Zigic, but he was broad and powerfully built and Zigic knew he'd have to be quick if the man was stupid enough to throw his bulk around.

'I can't imagine any good reason why you wouldn't want to help.'

4

When Paolo first arrived here he would wake with a sense of dis-
location, a few seconds of confusion, thinking he was still at home,
expecting to look across the bed and see the familiar curve of Maria's
back, the dimples above her buttocks and the constellation of small
brown moles on her shoulder. Before he opened his eyes he would
reach for her and only then, when his hand found nothing but cold
air, would he finally realise he was alone.

Not alone, of course, he was never actually alone.

Three other men shared the caravan with him, one in this small
room, on an identical camp bed pushed hard against the opposite
wall, two of the new Chinese out in the main body of the van,
sleeping on the benches either side of the table they ate from.

The other man, Jakub, was less than a metre from him, close
enough that Paolo could smell the rot on his breath as he snored.
At night he talked in his sleep, speaking a language Paolo couldn't
understand, and so close he was forced to listen to every groan
in the darkness, every shuddering orgasm he brought himself to,
needing comfort or release as he thought of the woman he had left
behind.

Outside an alarm sounded, three shrill blasts from an air horn.

Jakub stretched and scratched his stomach, kicking off his duvet
cover. Paolo turned towards the wall, not wanting to watch the
other man rise from the mattress and dress himself in the small
space between their beds.

He stared at the wall, orange-and-brown paper in a floral pattern.
He found faces in it, gazing at each other and looking away, strange,
uneven profiles and eyes sitting askew.

He thought of the times lying on the beach with Maria, seeing faces in the clouds high above them, talking about the apartment they would buy when they had the money, kids and cars and holidays. She didn't want him to leave but she understood it was the only way they could make that future happen. They reassured each other that it would be worth it.

Jakub went out into the kitchenette and filled the kettle, whistled to himself as he waited for it to boil. Within a couple of minutes the other men were awake as well and the caravan juddered on its blocks as they moved around. One of the Chinese was coughing up the night before's cigarettes in the toilet, while he pissed noisily in fits and starts.

They had been here for a few days now. Paolo tried to speak to them but they had very little English and he wondered if he was the only person who had learned it before coming here.

Jakub poked his head in the room. 'Work now.'

Paolo dragged himself upright and pulled on the trousers he'd left on the floor. Put on a dirty T-shirt and an even dirtier sweater, dried concrete flaking off it, found his work boots and laced them with fingers numb from the cold.

In the kitchenette one of the Chinese handed him a cup of black tea and he thanked the man, got a small bow in return. There was a pan of beans bubbling on the two-ring electric stove and the man gestured towards it.

'You?'

Paolo shook his head.

Back in Portugal he had read of how the Chinese were smuggled into Europe. They scraped together the money from their families, borrowed the rest from gangsters, all for the promise of better paid work. They were dragged across mountainous borders in the snow, some froze to death, others starved, a few fell into ravines. The ones who survived considered themselves lucky.

The tea turned to dishwater in his mouth and Paolo forced himself to swallow it, didn't want to offend the kind Chinese man who didn't know him, had no reason to be nice to him, but had thought to make it.

Outside the second alarm sounded and the men left their breakfasts unfinished on the melamine table, grabbed their coats and hurried out of the door. Jakub trudged after them, eating a slice of stale white bread folded in half, and Paolo closed the door, pulling it up sharply to stop it blowing open again.

It was light now, and so cold he could see ice sparkling on the tarmac. A biting wind swirled around the yard, where the dogs were prowling, five vicious mutts in a pack. Paolo hurried to get inside the van away from them.

The gates opened automatically and the vans pulled out in convoy, four of them full of men, and this morning two went off to the left and two to the right, heading away to different jobs. That only meant one thing – they would work much harder than usual today.

Paolo shrank down in his seat and tucked his chin into his chest, hugging his arms to his body for warmth. Next to him Jakub radiated heat and he couldn't understand how the man was never cold. When it snowed he would work with no jacket and at the first sign of sun stripped down to bare skin, showing a broad back covered in acne scars and strap marks which became livid with exertion. Paolo had asked where he was from and when he couldn't make himself understood Jakub drew a crude map in the dirt with his finger.

Eastern Europe, Paolo guessed, one of those cold, grey countries run by gangsters and thugs.

He let his head fall against the window, watching the countryside swipe past, the fields shrouded by freezing fog. Saw the vapour trails of aeroplanes heading north, people flying away to new lives or maybe back to their old ones, freshly rich and full of plans.

He closed his eyes and imagined his own homecoming, finding Marla's smiling face among the crowd at arrivals, hurrying to her waiting arms and seeing the realisation light up her eyes as she felt the fatly packed money belt strapped around his middle. Later, in the bedroom, she would unfasten it and he would watch her count the cash into neat piles on the mattress, amazed by how much there was. Then he would spread it out, all that hard-earned money, and make love to her on it like they did in the movies.

5

Interview rooms had a way of deflating people, Zigic had noticed, and it started the moment the door opened and they saw the grey metal table and the four plastic chairs, two on either side, everything neatly squared.

He hung back and let Phil Barlow sit down first, curious which side of the table he would choose. Facing the camera or hiding from it?

He pulled a chair out and sat down.

'Other side please,' Zigic said.

'Why?'

He pointed to the camera mounted high in the corner of the white-walled room.

'Sorry, I never saw it.'

But he had. Clocked it the second he walked in.

Zigic took the seat opposite him and they sat in silence while Ferreira set up the recorder, running through the date and time in a brisk, businesslike tone. She prompted Barlow to state his name and his voice caught in his throat so that he coughed the words out.

The room was making him small already. Two minutes in there and his shoulders were hunched, chin tucked into his neck, hands clasped on the scarred tabletop with his forearms pressed together right up to the elbow.

It looked like guilt. Right away, without a single question asked, he looked like a guilty man.

Zigic gave him the benefit of the doubt though. He knew the room induced fear in the most innocent of people, something about its tight dimensions and the way the soundproofed walls

29

flattened every noise out. It changed your voice, made you sound alien to yourself, and once you couldn't trust your own voice what could you trust?

'Why did you lie to us, Mr Barlow?'

'What? I haven't.' He looked quickly between Ferreira and Zigic. 'What is this? You said you wanted a statement.' His foot scuffed the floor. 'This is a fucking interrogation.'

'When you're being interrogated you'll know about it,' Zigic said. 'This is your opportunity to tell us exactly what happened last night.'

'I don't know what happened, I was asleep.'

'Someone got into your garden and set fire to your shed – which is right outside your bedroom window – and you didn't wake up?'

'No.'

'And when Mr Lunka, your neighbour, shouted through your letter box to tell you your shed was on fire –'

'I never heard him.'

'What about when Mr Lunka rang your doorbell?' Zigic asked. 'And kept ringing it and ringing it and hammering on your front door?'

'That never happened.'

'Mr Lunka says it did.'

'Well, maybe Mr Lunka's a liar, you think of that?' Barlow said, throwing his chin up suddenly. 'Maybe Mr Lunka set fire to my shed.'

Zigic sat back in his chair, watched the lie develop on Barlow's drawn and stubbled face, a light coming into his eyes like inspiration.

'Why would he want to do that?'

'How'd I know? Bloke like that, could be anything. Maybe he don't like having English neighbours. Maybe one of his mates wants to buy my house, turn it into bedsits for two dozen fucking Albanians. You'll have to ask him.'

Zigic nodded, leaned across the table into Barlow's space.

'So – in your conception of things – Mr Lunka sets fire to your shed for an as yet unspecified reason and he lies about trying to raise the alarm because . . . why?'

30

'Shift the blame.'

'OK. There's a certain logic to that.'

Barlow was watching him carefully now, seeing if the lie was gaining traction.

'I mean, yeah, I can see how that might work,' Zigic said. '*If* Mr Lunka hadn't called the fire brigade. That would undermine his whole purpose, wouldn't it?'

A muscle twitched in Barlow's jaw.

'No,' Zigic said. 'I think Mr Lunka hammered on your front door and rang that klaxon of a bell you've got. Because he was worried, and rightly so – your shed's close to his house, the fire could easily have spread over there.'

'We heard nothing,' Barlow said firmly.

'I think you did. And you ignored it.' Zigic smiled at him. 'So we're back to my original question – why did you lie to us?'

Barlow fish-mouthed for a second, eyes darting around the room.

'Someone rings your bell in the middle of the night, you don't go and fucking answer, do you? It's not going to be anything good.'

'No, it's probably going to be an emergency. Like a fire or something.'

'I should have answered the door,' Barlow said. 'Alright. I should've and I didn't. That's not a crime. We've done nothing wrong.'

'You've lied to the police,' Ferreira said. 'That's an offence in itself.'

'And it tends to be habitual,' Zigic said. 'People tell us one lie and we catch them out, so they apologise and try to smooth it over. Then we catch them out in another one and another one and before you know it they're doing a life sentence.'

Barlow's foot struck the table leg and sent it ringing.

'That's your fight or flight response,' Zigic said. 'Your conscious mind understands you have to stay right where you are but your

31

reptilian brain knows you're in trouble and it wants to get you as far away as possible.'

'We've done nothing,' Barlow said wearily.

'You knew there was someone in your shed.'

'No.'

'Yes,' Zigic snapped. 'You knew there was someone in there because you were charging him to stay there.'

'What?'

'He'd been living there for weeks.'

Barlow's neck flushed bright red and he pressed his balled fists to his mouth. He closed his eyes and let out a string of half-formed denials.

'How much were you charging him?'

Barlow squeezed his eyes tighter shut.

'How much?'

'Nothing,' Barlow roared, slamming his hands down. 'We weren't charging him anything.'

'Very generous,' Ferreira said. 'The two of you must have been pretty tight.'

'What's his name?' Zigic asked.

'I don't know.'

'You let him live in your back garden and you don't know his name? That doesn't sound entirely truthful, Mr Barlow.'

'It is the truth.'

'Where's he from?'

'I don't know.'

'You didn't ask?'

'I never talked to him.'

The words were spoken at a whisper and Zigic felt the air in the room shift.

'So he was squatting in your shed?'

Barlow nodded.

'How did he get in?'

'He broke in about three weeks ago. We went away to

32

Gemma's parents for the weekend and when we come back he was in there.'

'Did you ask him to leave?'

'He didn't speak English.'

'Didn't you try to throw him out?' Ferreira asked.

Barlow shook his head.

'Try again,' Zigic said. 'That black eye looks a couple of weeks old to me.'

'I did it at work. A light hit me.'

It was a small lie, rooted in pride, and Zigic decided to let it go for the time being.

'Why didn't you call the police about him?'

'I called,' Barlow said with a bitter smile. 'Woman on the other end told me someone would call back about it. Nothing. I tried again, got an answerphone, left a message, never heard anything. So don't make out you'd have done something about it.'

'Sounds like your options were limited then,' Ferreira said. 'If you wanted a permanent solution to the problem.'

Barlow glared at her. 'I did not set fire to that shed.'

'If you believed it was empty at the time . . .' Zigic showed him open palms, an understanding face. 'We don't have to call it murder.'

'I want a solicitor.'

Zigic stood up and pushed the chair under the table. 'Interview terminated nine forty-four.'

6

Hate Crimes was shoved away on the third floor of Thorpe Wood Station, a claustrophobic beige office with a suspended ceiling six inches too low and arsenic-green lino studded with old cigarette burns. There were half a dozen desks paired up back to back. A run of battered grey filing cabinets lined one wall, whiteboards populated with their current investigations filled another, and on the third side a stretch of metal windows with flaking paint over-looked the bustle and shunt of Bretton Parkway. The engine drone leaked in, along with exhaust fumes and thin draughts which knifed you as you worked.

Even on sunny days it was gloomy. On an overcast February morning Zigic thought it felt like a side room in purgatory.

They'd been promised a refit eighteen months ago but he couldn't even get maintenance to come up and fix the radiators which never got above tepid and clanged like they were possessed.

'We've got a name,' DC Wahlia said. 'Door-to-door turned him up. Jaan Stepulov.'

Zigic went over to the whiteboard where Wahlia had plotted out the scant details beginning to filter through. They were very scant, just a map of the area with the Barlows' house highlighted in red and their names printed carefully in the suspects column.

'How do they know him?'

'The guy came over from Tallinn with Stepulov a couple of years ago,' Wahlia said. 'They weren't friends he reckons, just from the same village. You know how it works.'

Zigic nodded. You wanted to strike out west but you didn't want to go alone, so you asked around until somebody's cousin's friend said they were heading over too and you teamed up for the long, grey bus ride across Europe and the Channel, sleeping six inches away from each other, drinking and playing cards, talking about the pots of cash you were going to make, the house you'd buy, the car you wanted, building a fantasy to ward off the tugging in your gut as home fell further away.

Two days of that and you were blood brothers.

Until you got to England and found out your new kin didn't share your work ethic.

'He hadn't seen Stepulov for eighteen months or so. The guy's got a job at the hospital – he's clean by the looks of it.' Wahlia fetched a sheet of paper from the printer. 'Stepulov's got a couple of arrests. This is from the most recent. Fifteenth of December last year.'

Stepulov was a big man, six one by his mugshot, with mid-brown hair cropped close to his skull and a lean, square face all jaw and cheekbones under a patchy beard. Thirty-eight years old but he could have passed for forty-five when the photograph was taken.

'What's his record like?' Zigic asked.

'He went in for the aggressive begging in a big way,' Wahlia said. He perched on the corner of his desk, tucked the marker pen behind his ear. 'He was operating around the cathedral, bothering the tourists, got a couple of cautions.'

'Violence?'

'He was wanted over an aggravated burglary that sounds kind of borderline. Guy said he caught Stepulov trying to break into his house, went for him with a baseball bat and got on the wrong end of it. Stepulov broke the guy's arm and ran.' Wahlia shrugged. 'You could call it self-defence maybe. He didn't hang around to finish the job. Lot of people would have.'

'Why wasn't he arrested?'

'The doctor who treated the guy called it in – they got Stepulov's fingerprints off the bat, all the evidence is there – but he refused to press charges.'

'And CID were happy with that?' Zigic asked.

Wahlia flicked his fingers through his carefully styled hair, lifting the tufted spikes at the front. 'If the victim doesn't push it they're not going to break their arses looking for a vagrant are they?'

'Is the victim foreign?'

'Yeah – Andrus Tombak,' Wahlia said. 'Lives down Burmer Road.'

Zigic looked at the map of New England. Highbury Street and Burmer Road were half a mile apart, running parallel to each other, a couple more stretches of back-to-backs separating them, old railway workers' cottages and large semi-detached council houses carved up into bedsits at ninety pounds a week.

'Do you think Mr Tombak's got his cast off yet?'

Wahlia grinned. 'I'll find out.'

Ferreira came into the office, blowing on a cup of vending machine hot chocolate.

'Bobby's got a tentative ID on our corpse.' Zigic handed her the mugshot. 'Jaan Stepulov. Have you run into him before?'

She studied the photograph for a moment. 'Not bad-looking for a derelict, was he?'

'Your mother must cry herself to sleep at night,' Wahlia said.

She frowned. 'I'm not positive but I think I saw him at Fern House last time I was over there. You remember that Latvian guy who got queer-bashed down Rivergate? I'm sure this guy was in reception.'

'When was this?'

'First week of January. They were taking the Christmas tree down.'

'OK,' Zigic said, looking at the board, seeing how it fitted together.

The hostel was a five-minute walk away from Highbury Street, at the city-centre end of Lincoln Road, right in the heart of things. They would have given Stepulov a bed for as long as he needed it, clothed him and fed him, found him work if he wanted it and helped him get back to Estonia if he asked.

'Why the hell was he squatting in the Barlows' shed if he had a place at Fern House?'

'They're pretty strict about drugs,' Wahlia suggested.

'And they lock up at ten,' Ferreira said. 'Kind of limits your social life.'

'Five to one he's stolen something.'

'They're Christians,' Ferreira said. 'They wouldn't throw him out for that.'

Zigic half listened as they speculated but none of their ideas sounded credible.

'Let's talk to Gemma Barlow,' he said finally. 'Then you can go over and see why he left.'

'Why?' Ferreira kicked her desk drawer shut. 'We know who killed him.'

'Right now we don't even know for certain that he was murdered.'

'He didn't lock himself in there, did he?' Ferreira said, a hard edge coming into her voice. 'They wanted to burn him out. Come on. Bobby?'

Wahlia put his hands up and turned away. No help there.

Ferreira shook her head. 'Fine. But I'm right.'

7

The strip light was fizzing in interview 2, making the room judder intermittently.

Gemma Barlow sat slumped in her chair, an untouched cup of milky tea in front of her, next to a pile of shredded tissues. She looked washed out in the bluish light, every imperfection visible through her spray tan.

'Have you let Phil go?'

'Not yet.' Zigic took the seat opposite her and noticed a smear of dried blood on the back of her hand.

She gnawed on her lip and a fresh bead sprang up.

'Do I need a solicitor?'

'Do you want one?'

'I haven't done anything.'

'You're only here to give us a statement.'

'Then I can go?'

Zigic nodded.

Again Ferreira ran the litany and made the prompts. Gemma Barlow leaned forward to give her name, voice raised.

'Just speak naturally please,' Ferreira said.

Gemma glared at her and Zigic wondered if he should have brought Wahlia in with him instead. He was more subtle than Ferreira in these situations, had a way of handling people so gently they hardly noticed he was manipulating them. Women especially.

Ferreira was like sandpaper on shredded nerves some days. He should have realised in the office that today was one of them.

'I'd like you to take a look at a photograph for me, Gemma.' She stiffened as he opened the file with Stepulov's mugshot in and a panicked expression clenched her face. 'Is this the man who was living in your shed?'

'I –'

Zigic pushed the photograph across the table and she drew her hands away into her lap.

'His name was Jaan Stepulov. Do you recognise him?'

'We didn't know anyone was in there.'

'We've spoken to Phil,' Zigic said. 'He's explained the situation to us. This man Stepulov broke in while you were visiting your mum and dad.'

Gemma closed her eyes and a couple of quick tears ran down her cheeks.

'It's definitely him?'

She nodded.

'For the benefit of the tape Mrs Barlow is nodding,' Ferreira said.

Her eyes snapped open and she shot a pink-rimmed scowl at Ferreira.

Zigic nudged her leg under the table, telling her to rein it in.

'Had you had any contact with him before that?'

'No. We just came home Sunday morning and the shed door was open and he was sitting there on one of our sunloungers drinking. It wasn't even ten o'clock.'

'What did you do?'

'Phil asked him what he thought he was playing at and got a mouthful of abuse.'

'In English?'

'I don't know what he was speaking. I thought he was Polish.'

'Then he hit Phil?'

Gemma scrambled a fresh tissue out of the packet. 'Phil's a teddy bear. I know he looks hard but he's so sweet, really, he's never been in a fight in his life. This Stepavic –'

'Stepulov,' Ferreira said.

'This Stapolov just belted him. Out of nowhere.' She wiped her nose. 'I told Phil to stay away from him after that.'

'That must have been difficult with him out in your back garden,' Zigic said. 'Was he there all the time?'

'Oh my God, you don't – you can't –' Gemma broke down again, crying into the tissue, fat tears streaking her face and when she spoke again her voice was thick with emotion. 'Phil goes to work first thing, he'd got no idea what it was like for me in that fucking house on my own. I couldn't hang my washing out or go to the bin because he was out there. Every time I went in the kitchen he was out there. I was terrified. Do you understand?'

Zigic nodded, thinking that Phil Barlow wasn't much of a man to leave her alone like that. He'd let her endure weeks of it before he finally acted.

'I'd be washing up and he'd come and knock on the window. I didn't know what he wanted or if he was going to try and break in. He was shitting in the back garden and going through the bins like an animal.' She dragged her fingers through her hair, tugging at it as her eyes lost focus. Then she was back. Fresh disgust twisting her mouth. 'He had a woman in there last week. Some skanky Polish hooker. You believe it? He can't afford a bedsit but he could afford that. Jesus Christ, these fucking people. It's not right. Nobody should be living like that in this day and age.'

Ferreira leaned forward and propped her elbows on the table. 'If I was in your position – living under that kind of threat – I'd have burnt the shed down in a heartbeat.'

'Maybe where you come from that's how people behave, but we don't.'

Zigic stepped down lightly on Ferreira's toes and she pulled her foot away.

'We were going to demolish it,' Gemma said, looking back to Zigic. 'We'd decided to do it this weekend. I told Phil if we took it apart he'd have to leave.'

'Why this weekend?'

'He goes somewhere else at the weekend.' She laughed darkly. 'He's probably got a shed in someone's garden on the coast. His

40

holiday place.' Her face creased. 'I thought he'd left for good, the first time it happened. I was so relieved. I hadn't slept properly for days, you know, and then he was gone and it was all like some mad nightmare that never really happened. Monday morning I went to hang some towels out and he comes out the shed shouting. I ran back in the house.' She shook her head, couldn't look at them. 'He kept shouting and I realised he wasn't shouting at me, it was someone on the road. And then this other one turns up.'

'Did you recognise him?' Zigic asked.

'I don't know them,' Gemma said. 'Are you listening to anything I'm telling you?'

Zigic rested his chin on his fist. 'And then what happened?'

'They both went inside the shed. Could have been shagging each other's arses for all I know.'

'Did Stepulov have other visitors?'

'Oh yeah, he was popular,' Gemma said, an acid smile on her face. 'There'd be three or four of them some nights, out there singing and shouting at each other, pissed out of their heads.'

'Would you recognise any of them if we showed you some photos?'

'The young guy maybe.' Gemma nodded to herself. 'I did get a pretty good look at him the other day when they were arguing on the lawn.'

Ferreira sighed and Zigic felt it too, Gemma trying to turn their focus away from her and Phil.

'What did he look like?'

'Young, twenty probably, not much older.' She tipped her head back in a childlike thinking pose. 'He was tall.'

'Compared to who?' Ferreira asked. 'Stepulov? Your husband? You?'

'He was just tall. He was about the same as Stupulov.'

'Anything else? Hair? Was that the same as Stepulov's too?'

'He had short hair. Blondish. I think he was wearing an Adidas tracksuit. A blue one. And white trainers.'

41

She'd just described 70 per cent of the twenty-year-old men in Peterborough.

'Skin colour?' Ferreira asked.

'Lighter than you,' Gemma said.

'But not as orange as you?'

Zigic winced.

His mobile vibrated in his pocket; forensics.

'Interview suspended eleven fourteen.'

In the corridor he checked the message from Kate Jenkins while Ferreira muttered to herself in Portuguese. He recognised a few of the words, none of them were particularly complimentary.

'We've got a partial on the padlock,' he said.

'Which one of them is it?'

'Neither. It's Stepulov.'

'So he locks the shed up when he's not there and they use his padlock to seal him in.' Ferreira folded her arms. 'What does it prove? Any idiot knows to wear gloves if you're going to kill someone.'

'Go to Fern House and see if they know any of Stepulov's associates.'

'Christ, you didn't buy that, did you?' Ferreira stepped up close to him. 'We've got them and she knows it, so she's thrown up some bullshit argument with a non-existent person to try and deflect us.'

She started towards the interview-room door and Zigic blocked her off.

'Go to Fern House or go home.'

For a couple of beats she just looked at him, weighing the situation, then she smiled thinly and stalked off up the corridor.

8

The traffic was slow on Lincoln Road, an accident at the roundabout according to the radio, but all Ferreira could see was a white van with its side panel thrown back and a couple of uniforms milling about uselessly. A guy in orange council overalls was spinning a Stop/Go sign, letting through a dozen cars at a time.

She turned up the stereo and rapped her fingers against the steering wheel, the bass line from the tricked-out speakers pounding through her head and shaking her spine.

The cars inched forward and the song changed.

That fucking Barlow woman and her attitude. Zigic didn't see it, but why would he? He had the foreign name and the high Slavic cheekbones but he was still English.

Gemma Barlow was a racist. Out and out. Mispronouncing Stepulov's name like it was beneath her to get it right. Only the English thought it made them clever to be so ignorant.

She could have slapped her.

The driver behind her honked his horn and Ferreira saw the road empty ahead of her, the sign spun to Go.

The man beeped again and she counted five seconds before she pulled off.

If he wanted to follow her to Fern House and start something in the car park he was welcome to try it.

In her rear-view mirror she saw him turn across the traffic to get to the Booze and News, then she swung down Lime Tree Avenue and onto the short stretch of hard standing behind the hostel. There was fresh graffiti on the gates of the bed and breakfast opposite, Nigga and Paki in uneven black spray paint, and as she walked round to the front of the house she noticed the telltale acid-fade on the crumbling red bricks where a tag had been recently blasted off.

Two middle-aged men were sitting on the front wall drinking from cans; they eyed her as she went up to the door then returned to their conversation.

A buzzer sounded as Ferreira entered but nobody came to meet her.

The lobby was cluttered with softly stuffed big bags, the smell of unwashed clothes rising from them, overpowering the bunch of freesias sitting primly on a table pushed hard against the wipe-clean white walls. Above them a corkboard bore health notices and postcards, small signs in a dozen different languages for legal aid and taxi firms, a few job adverts among them and a comprehensive list of church services.

The door to Helen Adu's office was open and the phone was bleating on her unmanned desk. A cigarette was smouldering in the ashtray though, so she was about.

Late morning the place was always quiet. They turned the residents out at nine o'clock, didn't let them back in until eight, but somewhere nearby a woman was crying and Ferreira followed the noise through to the lounge. It was a large, high-ceilinged room done out with donated furniture, mismatched armchairs and a rag rug on the wooden floor, an ancient teak coffee table with old magazines in piles. Two small boys were sitting in front of the television, watching cartoons with the sound turned down low.

Joseph Adu squatted next to a mousy young woman, holding her hand between his as she cried into a tissue, speaking to her in heavily accented Polish. She looked at him with her big blue eyes shining, nodding, answering briefly, but even without understanding what she was saying Ferreira could see she didn't believe it.

Joseph moved onto the chair next to her and put his arm around her shoulder. She rolled into his chest and let the tears flow.

He still looked like a boxer and even approaching forty Ferreira could imagine him stepping into the ring, an ageing journeyman lacking his old speed but full of guile and unpredictable angles, giving some young prospect an education. If he hadn't got injured he'd probably be back in Bukom doing just that.

All it took was one bad fight to derail his career.

He'd told Ferreira about it the first time they met. They'd shaken hands and she'd noticed his knuckles, swollen up like ball bearings, asked what weight he fought at.

His manager had sent him over from Ghana, a late replacement in a middleweight title fight and he couldn't believe his luck, thanked the Lord for the opportunity which should have been another couple of years away at that point. It was a good belt too, he'd told her proudly, WBC, a Commonwealth title. He saw Las Vegas in his future and Madison Square Garden, thought he'd be the next Ike Quartey. All he had to do was put in a solid twelve rounds at Bethnal Green.

In the fourth he took a wild elbow to the left eye and the world jumped. He boxed on though and his corner, men he didn't know, supplied by the promoter, either didn't notice the injury or didn't care. He knew he should tell them but the boy in front of him was unskilled, had no chin, so he kept going and by the end of the fight he was ruined.

The promoter's men said they were taking him to hospital. Instead they put him on a northbound train, wanting the problem as far away from them as possible, and an hour after that a guard threw him off at Peterborough station. He had fifty pounds in his pocket, severe concussion and a detached retina.

'Sergeant Ferreira.' Helen Adu touched her elbow. '*Tudo bem?*'

'Fine, thanks. *E voce?*'

'It's the usual controlled chaos,' she said, forced brightness in her voice.

She looked tired out though, her pale skin desiccated and the wrinkles around her eyes deeper than usual. She fingered the chunky necklace she wore over a shapeless tunic and cast a worried glance towards the young Polish woman.

'She isn't your usual clientele,' Ferreira said.

'No. It's very sad. Her husband died a few days ago.'

'How did it happen?'

'He had an accident at work. It's horrific really, absolutely horrific.' Helen Adu lowered her voice. 'His arm was crushed by some machinery and he died of shock right there on the factory floor. He was only twenty-five.'

'What's going to happen to her now?' Ferreira asked.

Helen Adu checked her watch. 'She's taking his body back to Poland for the funeral. I don't think she'll want to come back to England after that. I'm driving her to the airport. We need to leave in a few minutes actually.'

'I thought you sent people home by bus.'

'I've managed to persuade the company to pay for the airfares,' Helen Adu said.

'Did you put a gun to their heads?'

'A metaphorical one,' she said with a grim smile. 'If there's one thing sure to bring out the benevolence in a capitalist it's the prospect of bad press. I thought the bastard was going to have a stroke when I told him how much it was going to cost to ship the body back but he found a few more drops of humanity. It was very reassuring.'

The telephone started ringing again in the office.

Helen Adu glanced towards the door but didn't move to answer it.

'Anyway, what can we do for you, Sergeant?'

'Jaan Stepulov.'

'Is he in trouble again?'

'I'm afraid it's a bit more serious this time. He's dead.'

Helen Adu pressed her hands to her chest. 'Oh my Lord, no? How?'

'There was a fire,' Ferreira said. 'He was dossing in a shed in someone's back garden.'

'Had he been drinking?'

46

'We're not sure yet. The post-mortem isn't scheduled until tomorrow morning. It looks like murder though.'

Helen Adu twisted her fingers into her necklace. 'I can't believe it. Why? He was such a lovely man.'

'The people whose house it was don't seem to think so.'

Helen Adu's watch beeped and she switched the alarm off quickly. 'I hate to be rude but I really do have to go, Sergeant, the traffic on the M11 is horrendous. Joseph knew Jaan quite well though, he can probably be of more use to you than I would.'

She gathered the woman and her children, picking up the smaller boy and holding him on her hip. The woman moved slowly, eyes down, like she didn't trust the ground under her feet any more, and when she stumbled Helen Adu caught her under the arm.

She mouthed a goodbye to her husband and nodded to Ferreira as they left.

The room felt airless, every breath sucked out of it by the woman's grief and overheated from the electric fire glowing in the corner. The television was still playing, bright cartoon animals and crunchy music absurd in that atmosphere.

'Sergeant Ferreira.' Joseph Adu shook her hand; the careful grip of a man well aware of his own strength. 'Are you looking for somebody?'

'No, I need to talk to you about Jaan Stepulov.'

'We have not seen him for several weeks now.'

'Did you ask him to leave?'

'No. Jaan was no trouble.' Joseph Adu spread his big hands wide. 'Of course he has some problems but I believe he is a decent man. It is easy to be perfect when you have everything, don't you agree, Sergeant?'

She did but it wasn't the time to get into that sort of discussion.

'Has he been arrested?'

'No, Mr Adu. Jaan was squatting in a shed over on Highbury Street,' Ferreira said. 'There was a fire there this morning –'

'Is he in hospital?'

'No. Sorry, but he's died.'

'Oh my Lord. So much death.' Joseph Adu sank into one of the armchairs, elbows on his knees and his eyes downcast. 'Are you sure it is Jaan?'

'We won't be certain until the DNA results are back. But it looks very likely.'

Ferreira took the chair next to him, the fusty smell of stale cigarettes rising from the draylon.

'When was the last time you saw him?'

'We have not seen him for almost three weeks.'

'Something must have made him leave.'

Joseph Adu rubbed his hands together slowly. 'A young man came here. He wanted to speak to Jaan.'

'Do you know what it was about?'

'No. I asked him to wait here while I fetched Jaan from the dining room and when he saw the man he ran out through the kitchen.'

'Did the man go after him?'

'He tried to.'

'But you stopped him?'

He nodded. 'I told him to leave.'

'And Jaan never came back?'

'No. We have been expecting him to return, but no.'

Ferreira thought of the argument Gemma Barlow claimed to have witnessed in her back garden. If it was the same man he could have tracked down Jaan Stepulov somehow. Three weeks between the two events, then the fire.

She felt a stab of annoyance, knowing that she was going to have to return to the station and admit the possibility that the Barlow woman was right.

'All of Jaan's things are still here,' Joseph Adu said.

'I need to see them.'

'Of course.'

Ferreira followed him up to the first floor, a thick, heavily

48

patterned carpet swallowing their footfalls. Doors stood open on either side of the corridor, showing rooms like prison cells, bunk beds on the left, lockers on the right. Pictures had been hung on the magnolia walls and there were blankets on the beds but the place felt transient and institutional, nothing genuinely personal anywhere.

They passed a bathroom where an elderly Ukrainian man, one of the hostel's long-termers, was scrubbing the toilet on his knees, singing under his breath.

Jaan Stepulov had bunked in the last room on the left. It had a narrow window overlooking Lime Tree Avenue, the fire escape of the B&B opposite all that constituted a view. The window was open a few inches and a stiff breeze blew through but it did little to shift the smell of contained bodies and dirty hair.

'Who's in here now?' Ferreira asked.

'This room is empty.'

Joseph Adu opened one of the lockers with a key from the bunch on his belt and stepped aside to let her examine Stepulov's possessions.

There wasn't much. An empty rucksack and a few items of clothing which were probably third-hand when Stepulov got them, a pair of jeans and some combats, a couple of wash-faded sweatshirts from Gap.

'The man who came looking for Jaan, can you describe him?'

'He was slim, the same height as me. Clean-shaven. I think he had blond hair but it was shaved very close. He had pale eyebrows I remember.'

'Was he Estonian too?'

'I could not say. He was wearing an Orthodox cross so I think he must be from Eastern Europe. He had a tattoo here,' Joseph Adu said, pointing to his own neck. 'Of a bird, I think.'

Ferreira turned Stepulov's washbag out onto the bottom bunk. The usual stuff inside it. She gathered it up again.

When you lived how Stepulov did, you kept the important things

49

on your person. Lockers got broken into, banks weren't to be trusted and you never knew when you'd have to make a quick exit. Anything they might have found useful would have been burned up inside his sleeping bag.

The buzzer at the front door sounded and Joseph excused himself to answer it.

Ferreira sat on the bunk and looked at the pathetic remains of Jaan Stepulov's existence stowed away in the locker. She wondered what he was expecting when he climbed onto the bus in Tallinn, leaving everything he knew behind him. Not this, surely. It was warm and dry but that was all you could say for the place, and as sympathetic as the Adus were it couldn't have been much consolation through the long, lonely nights and the days he would have spent wandering around Peterborough, trying to beg a few quid off strangers or find something worth stealing.

She closed the door behind her and went back downstairs.

Joseph Adu was in the office, signing for a parcel and she waited until the delivery man left before she asked why Stepulov wasn't working.

'His English was very rudimentary.'

'A lot of people get by without.'

'Jaan was not a worker by nature. We found him a job at the Gillette factory, packing the razor blades, but it did not last very long.'

'So what was he doing all day?'

'I think he was drinking,' Joseph Adu said, lowering his voice as if it were a damning admission. 'He was drunk most evenings when he came home. I saw him several times in Maloney's when I was taking people to the bus.'

'How do you think he was affording that?'

'A drunk will always find the money to feed the demon.'

There was more to it than that, Ferreira guessed. You didn't go into a pub when you could drink cheaper out of an off-licence.

Stepulov would have lifted what he wanted anyway, if it was just about getting alcohol inside him.

She thanked Joseph Adu for his help and assured him she would let them know if they could do anything else.

9

Maloney's was the last building standing on a patch of land opposite the city bus station. Four floors of gaudy Victoriana in exhaust-stained buff brick, with green tiles at street level and a sign declaring that they had Sky Sports.

Everything around it had been razed to the ground ready for the planned expansion of the Queensgate shopping centre across Westgate. They were going to build elevated glass walkways to link the new development to the old, put restaurants and clubs in there, a Debenhams which was supposed to draw the coach parties from far and wide, turn Queensgate into a destination.

The last time Ferreira went in there a quarter of the shops were shut down and she couldn't imagine where the money was going to come from to keep the new ones afloat. The whole city reeked of poverty since the crash, fewer cars on the road, fewer people out in the clubs at night. Gap was gone, Topshop was gone. The only new businesses opening up in the centre were pound stores and hole-in-the-wall gold dealers. Old-school fences given a gloss of legitimacy with a smart website and some cheap advertising space on Hereward FM.

She parked outside Cash Converters.

On a hunch she went in, got the manager, a dumpy middle-aged woman with bottle-black hair and a mouth like a straight razor. Yes she had seen Stepulov in there, no not lately. Of course they were happy to cooperate with the police but would you please get the fuck out, you're spooking our customers.

It was a logical process. Stepulov leaves the hostel on Lime Tree Avenue with empty pockets, robs something on his way through the city centre, cashes it in and two minutes later he's walking into Maloney's with his day's drinking sorted.

No wonder he didn't fancy twelve-hour packing shifts.

She went into Maloney's. Tail end of the lunch hour and the place was heaving but she knew it would have been just as busy at 10 a.m. Maloney's was always full. It was the first place you could get a drink off the train or out of the bus station, and the lot behind the pub was where coaches from all over Europe came to a final stop, ensuring a constant stream of euros. There were banners strung around the cavernous bar proclaiming 'Welcome to Peterborough' in eight different languages, flags lined up like a UN convention.

The landlord, Fintan Maloney, was holding court at a corner table and the three old Irish guys with him were probably the only people in there who hadn't been born somewhere east of the Channel. At the next table a group of young men were playing cards, a pile of matchsticks already in the pot, but their focused expressions made it clear that all debts would be met later in cash.

Ferreira went to the end of bar and waited to be served.

There were four woman working behind it, struggling to keep up with the demanding voices. It was a drinkers' pub and they didn't appreciate slow service, especially when they'd sunk a few already.

Ferreira eyed the replay of last night's Porto game on the big screen, saw Manchester City put a third goal in the net and turned away again. They weren't the same since Mourinho left, but who could blame him? You followed the money, no matter where it took you.

'Have you got the place surrounded, Sergeant Ferreira?' Maloney laughed lightly, always the same joke, and eased his bulk through the hatch. 'Haven't seen your bossman for a good while.'

'Guess you must be behaving yourself then.'

He winked at her and drained a dark rum off the optic.

'You'll be here about Stepulov,' he said, a twinkle in his eye.

'Bad news travels fast.'

'Fast? The man's been dead nigh on eight hours.'

'And we haven't released his name yet.'

'Sure if you want confidentiality you need to start paying those civilian support officers.' He poured himself a whiskey from a bottle of good stuff he kept under the counter.

Like a lot of what was on offer in there you had to know about it to get it. You wanted coke you went around to the service entrance and talked to the chef, you wanted a blow job you picked a waitress and asked her the price. False documents, blank credit cards, a gun with no history; it was all there if you knew which one of the customers to approach.

Maloney you went to for information and Ferreira knew several detectives had him on the pad, Zigic included, even though he behaved like a puritan.

'So what can you tell me?' she asked.

'He was a fine young lad.'

'Somebody didn't think so.'

'It wouldn't be anyone knew him well told you otherwise.'

He was right. All they had against Stepulov were the Barlows' statements and they were hardly unbiased.

'I'll tell you something about Stepi now. Round Christmas he was in here playing cards –'

'Was he any good?'

'I wouldn't have bet my bollock hair to bullion if I had quad kings against him.'

'So he cheated?'

'How he won is neither here nor there.' Maloney put his hand up. 'But there was a fella in here waiting for the coach back to Krakow. Real loudmouth piece of work he was, flashing his money around. Now he got into a game with Stepi and Stepi cleaned him out right down to his mobile phone – piece of shite that was too.'

Ferreira sipped her rum, waited for him to continue. Maloney liked to string things out when he had an audience for it.

'Your man had tears in his eyes, complaining how his ma was going to be so disappointed when he never came home for the holidays and his sister wouldn't be able to go back to university next year if he didn't give her the money.'

'Did he pay up?'

'Course he paid up. You lose your money, you pay your debts,' Maloney said. 'But Stepi was a proper gentleman about it, gave him his fare back and a few quid spending money. Even made sure he got on the coach safe and sound. He'd had a few, you know, man like that in that kind of mood, well, he was as likely to throw himself in the river as anything else.'

A shout went up from the corner of the pub.

'Łódź autobus – dziesiec minut.'

A few people stirred from the tables, gathering bags and draining their drinks. The driver ambled out again, none too steady-looking.

'That was the kind of man Stepi was. Salt of the earth.' Maloney topped his whiskey up from the bottle under the counter. 'Would I freshen yours, Sergeant?'

'I'm on duty.' She slid her glass away from his hand. 'Has anyone been in looking for Stepulov?'

Maloney smiled. 'You're a sharp one – already got a suspect in your sights.'

'Look, Maloney, I love an Irish accent as much as the next girl but get to the fucking point, hey?'

'Young fella came in here a couple of days back wanting Stepi. Said he was his son-in-law – gave me a load of old bollocks about his daughter being pregnant and nobody knew how to get in touch with him. Man wasn't even Estonian if you ask me.'

'What did he look like?'

'Long, tall streak of piss with a bird tattooed on his neck.' Maloney fingered the collar of his blue check shirt. 'Stepi wasn't in yet but the fella didn't want to wait around for him.'

'Has he been back since?'

'I've not seen him if he has,' Maloney said. 'I'll tell you something, he looked a nasty piece of work. I wouldn't proclaim to be an educated man but I know a thug when I see one.'

Ferreira drained her drink.

'If he comes in again I want you to call me right away.' She pushed her card across the bar. 'And if you hear anything. *Anything . . .*'

Maloney slipped her card into his breast pocket. 'You can rely on me, Sergeant.'

IO

Olga and Sofia were talking about the fire as they stacked the glass washer. It was all anyone had spoken of all morning, and Emilia tried not to listen, didn't want to think about what it must have been like inside that rickety little shed as the fire took hold.

It was easier not to think about it. Put it in a box and pretend it never happened.

There were many boxes in her head, all tightly locked and shoved away in the dark. Over time some of them fused and she was spared the memories she didn't want to face, but others corroded and leaked, snatches of conversations and strange faces swimming up unexpectedly, provoked by the smell of a certain tobacco or a snatch of music on the radio. Others snapped open without warning and slapped her between the eyes.

This box didn't want to be closed.

She pressed her lips together tightly and willed the images away.

The pub was busy now and that helped. She concentrated on taking orders into the kitchen, picking up plates of steak and pasta, the crockery burning the skin on her forearms through her thin white blouse.

The pain helped. She focused on that for a while.

But soon it became bundled up with other sensations and she couldn't escape the images which were so strong she felt she was there, feeling the heat on her own skin, breathing the thick, black smoke.

Maloney was at his regular table, laughing like a madman, wiping tears from his eyes.

She was sure he knew something.

When the policewoman left he came over and asked her to get him a sandwich, studied her carefully when she took it to his table and set it down in front of him. He never asked her to do things, always Olga. She was his favourite, the one he liked to serve him.

He would protect Olga from the police, but Emilia was sure she couldn't count on the same treatment.

When he asked if she was feeling alright she told him she was fine. Just a slight headache. She would take a pill in a moment.

He knew.

She could see it in his eyes. He was like a wolf, always prowling, always watching, and even when he smiled his eyes were dead.

'Serve this gentleman,' Olga said.

Emilia went to the end of the bar and opened a bottle of Beck's, took the man's money and gave him his change. Olga was watching her too, standing with her arms folded three feet away, a smirk on her red-painted lips.

Was she acting differently?

'I must go to toilet,' she said, and slipped past Olga, out from behind the bar, and she forced herself to walk naturally across the patterned blue carpet which made her eyes ache, not bolt through the door marked Staff Only.

Upstairs she locked herself in the bathroom. The sink was full of water, soap scum floating on the top and a damp flannel on the floor underneath it. The hamper was overflowing with dirty washing, the smell of it overpowered by recently sprayed deodorant, pink and sickly. A pair of seamed black stockings were drying on the towel rail and the sight of them made her stomach flip.

She rushed to the toilet and threw up, nothing in her but bile and it burned, making her eyes water.

She wouldn't cry. She couldn't go downstairs with puffy eyes. Couldn't afford the curiosity they would arouse and the questions she didn't trust herself to answer.

Emilia flushed the toilet and put the seat down, sat for a few minutes with her head in her hands, staring at the black-and-white chequerboard floor.

She used to play chess, but that was a long time ago. Another life. One without stockings and whores' baths, which existed only in one of those old, corroded boxes.

Now was not the time, she told herself.

She took out her mobile and dialled.

He answered immediately.

'The police have been here,' she said.

He swore. 'Did they question you?'

'No. She talked to Maloney.'

'They know about you.'

'They can't.'

'Why else would they come there? Think about it.'

'I don't know,' she said.

'They'd have arrested you if they had a witness.' His voice was smooth and consoling, the way it was when they were together, lying close in the darkness. 'But we need to work out what we're going to do.'

She nodded, as if he was there with her.

'Tonight, when you finish up, I'll come get you.'

'No.' The panic gripped her. 'Don't come here.'

'OK, your place then.' She heard him pacing around, then glass touching glass, liquid running. 'And don't call me again, Emilia. It's not safe.'

He rang off and she stared at the phone's black screen for a second. He was right, she had been stupid to call him. If the police came back for her this afternoon they would take her phone and crack its secrets.

There would be no lie good enough to get her out of trouble then.

She flicked through the photos she had taken; there weren't many. Almost nothing in her life was good enough to want to remember. A pair of shoes she wanted but couldn't afford, spiked gold leather things with straps around the ankle, a sunset which didn't look as beautiful as she remembered and a small white dog one of the regulars had brought into the pub, trying to find it a new owner. They were pathetic remnants of a life she felt coming to a close but they were not the ones she was worried about now.

Jaan, lying in bed with his hand under his head, smiling that hungry smile at her. Jaan showing off his muscles, posing like a star athlete. She kept deleting them, more photos of him than she remembered taking, and as they disappeared she wondered why she had bothered. He wanted her to take them, that was why. Was determined to have her prove how important he was to her.

She hesitated over the last one, their two faces pressed cheek to cheek, taken at arm's length, both smiling, but she saw her smile was not as deep as his and he looked a little drunk around the eyes.

She hit delete and it was like he never existed.

II

The report from forensics came through at three and Zigic took it into his office. Even with the lights on the room was small and dreary and nothing he'd done since he moved in made it any more comfortable. He'd bought a fancy leather chair with a lot of levers, put photographs of Anna and the boys on his desk, but it was still a windowless box with broom-cupboard dimensions and an acoustic tile ceiling splashed with old stains that looked like dried blood.

He opened the file onto a close-up shot of Jaan Stepulov's scorched head and reminded himself it could be worse.

The crime scene photos were extensive but they told him nothing he didn't know already. He shuffled them aside and picked out Kate Jenkins's preliminary findings. The post-mortem was scheduled for eleven o'clock tomorrow morning and until then they wouldn't know if the fire killed Stepulov or whether it was an attempt to eradicate evidence after the fact.

Tentatively Jenkins suggested the former was more likely.

Stepulov's body was stretched out on one of the Barlows' sunloungers and Jenkins had identified a high concentration of accelerant on his body and the concrete floor surrounding it – lighter fuel; she didn't have a brand yet but she was doing follow-up tests on the samples.

It was more reliable than vodka, more portable than petrol, all you had to do was squirt it around and drop a match.

They had found a brick, surrounded by broken glass, on the floor inside the shed, which suggested someone broke the window before the rest of it was blown out by the fire.

Zigic pictured the lawn, scattered with blackened shards . . . Stepulov's killer would have padlocked the shed door first, ensuring he couldn't get out, then smashed a pane of glass and sprayed lighter fuel into the confined space. The shed was small enough that hitting Stepulov would have been easily done, and even if they missed where was he going to escape to?

A wave of sympathetic claustrophobia seized Zigic but he pushed it away.

Could he imagine the Barlows doing that?

It was a coward's way to kill someone. Impersonal but with a high success rate. Phil Barlow might have been capable of walking outside at dawn with a can of lighter fuel, setting the fire then returning to his warm bed. He didn't seem like the type but under duress you discovered new corners of your soul and they were usually darker and colder than you believed possible.

There were photographs of the padlock, a weighty brass Chubb, fire-stained but new-looking. Stepulov's prints were the freshest, easy to identify, but there were others, smudged and older, which Jenkins was still working on. She had a thumbprint which might – she'd underlined that twice – might belong to Phil Barlow. A four-point match, not enough for the CPS but enough to raise some questions.

Like why wouldn't Barlow have worn gloves?

The padlock was on his shed though, and Zigic imagined himself in that situation, going out into his garden and testing the heft of the thing, wanting to smash it off the door, furious that someone had closed him out of his own property.

He scanned the rest of Jenkins's report. Empty bottles in the shed, a pair of heavily damaged work boots and the charred remains of a pickaxe handle. They'd found a handful of change in Stepulov's pocket, nothing else.

Zigic stared at the photograph of Stepulov's ruined head until it stopped being a person, wondering what he would have done in the Barlows' position. Could he leave Anna and the boys at home every day, knowing there was a drunk, aggressive man less than thirty feet away from his back door?

He couldn't and he knew he wouldn't have to. A phone call would bring a patrol car and as many bodies as necessary to swiftly evict the man.

The same was true for the Barlows, even if they had dismissed the possibility. Maybe they were just the kind of people who had little faith in the police. Or maybe things had gone further than they were prepared to admit on record and they wanted a more definite solution to the problem.

Ferreira opened the office door as she knocked on it.

'I thought you'd gone home.'

'I was in the pub.' She shoved both hands into the back pockets of her jeans. 'Think we might have another suspect. Some guy spooked Stepulov out of Fern House – that's what he was doing at the Barlows' by the look of it, lying low.'

'You get a name?'

She shook her head. 'But he was in Maloney's asking after him a couple of days ago as well. Might be nothing.'

They went back out into the main office. Wahlia was sitting with his feet up on the corner of the desk, phone cupped against his shoulder, hold music bleeding out of it. Zigic handed him the forensics report.

'Get that on the board when you're done.'

'They find anything good?' Ferreira asked.

He gave her a quick run-down.

'So what're you doing with the Barlows?'

'I've kicked them loose, we've not got enough to charge them with.'

Ferreira made a face.

'Is that alright with you?'

'I guess they're not going anywhere,' she said. 'Not like they're going to leave the country, is it? All those foreigners they'd have to deal with.'

Zigic picked up a marker pen. 'When did Stepulov leave Fern House?'

'Three weeks ago, bolted as soon as this guy showed up. He never went back. Then the same guy was at Maloney's a couple of days ago,' she said. 'So that would have been Monday. Stepulov hadn't been in there for a while though, and according to Maloney he was pretty much a fixture at the poker table.'

'Winning or losing?'

'Winning,' Ferreira said. 'With a bit of mechanical intervention. So we know what he was living off anyway.'

Zigic added the dates to the timeline, working back from Stepulov's murder.

'Did you get a description of this bloke?'

'Tall, skinny, pale. Tattoo of a bird on his neck.'

'Run that through the system and see if it hits,' Zigic said. In the suspects column he wrote the brief description. 'Sounds like it could be the man Gemma Barlow saw arguing with Stepulov.'

'He told Maloney he was Stepulov's son-in-law,' Ferreira said. 'Chances are he was lying but you never know, I guess. He knew Stepulov drank there and he knew to find him at Fern House so there's obviously a connection of some sort.'

'Is Stepulov old enough to have a grown-up daughter?'

'If he had her in his teens, but why would he run away from his son-in-law at Fern House?'

'Families can be weird,' Zigic said, going over to the coffee machine. He poured the last half-cup out of the pot and threw it down, felt the grounds grate the back of his throat. 'Stepulov had been living rough for almost three months, maybe there had been acrimony and he didn't want them to find him. You know as well I do there're a hundred good reasons to fall out with your family.'

12

The call Zigic was waiting for came in a few minutes after six, patched through from the patrol car he'd sent to Burmer Road, waiting outside Andrus Tombak's house.

'The van's just pulled in, sir. Should we take him?'

'No, wait for me.'

'He's looking over here,' the PC said, his voice rising with excitement. 'He's clocked us, sir, he's coming over.'

'Fob him off,' Zigic said. 'Don't make a move unless he looks like he's going to run. You got that?'

'Yes, sir.'

Twenty minutes later Zigic pulled up outside the halal butcher's on Burmer Road. Its shutters were down but the smell of stale blood rose from a wheelie bin on the pavement, and there were old crates piled up near the door, faded and stained. Across the street the patrol car sat with two wheels on the kerb, a small red dot flicking on and off as the driver smoked a crafty fag.

The street lights glowed orange, every other one dead; cost-cutting measures from the city council. There was road noise in the distance and the incessant, droning hum of the industrial estate, but the street felt strangely isolated and hunkered down.

'Which one is it?' Ferreira asked.

'With the green front door,' Zigic told her.

As he spoke it opened and a man came out, carrying a rubbish bag he dumped in a ragged patch of garden. There were a dozen or so already, tossed in among the docks and the thistles which stood chest-high and desiccated, scraps of paper snagged in their barbs, sheets of rotting newsprint and smashed bottles in the long grass.

The house was lit up behind papery blinds and as they crossed the road the door opened again. Eight men came out in single file, each holding the door for the next, and they moved without speaking, tired-looking with drawn faces and haunted eyes. They turned right and headed up Burmer Road where a van was parked under a street light, waiting for them.

Zigic caught the door as it swung closed and they went inside, Ferreira on his heels, radiating tension.

The smell of contained bodies hit him, the sour, sweaty odour of too many men crammed into close proximity, the whole house like a locker room after a losing game, that edge of fear and dejection. The linoleum floor was tracked with mud and sticky in places and up the uncarpeted stairs he heard somebody coughing, a deep, rattling hack like they were about to lose a lung. Footsteps trudged overhead, no energy in them.

'Don't wander,' he told Ferreira.

Doors stood closed on either side of them but the voices and the snores bled into the corridor, too many for such a small space.

Ferreira knocked on one of the doors and opened it without waiting for a reply.

The room was in darkness but in the dim light from the hallway they saw the entire floorspace was taken up with mattresses, three of them tucked tight together. The men slept doubled up on them, back to back, curled away from each other.

Ferreira closed the door quietly.

'Who are you?'

A man came downstairs to them, a grubby towel around his neck and the front of his grey vest spattered with water. He wore unlaced work boots thick with dried mud.

'We're looking for Andrus Tombak,' Zigic said.

'I do not know this name.'

'This is his house.'

'You are police?'

'Mr Tombak was attacked a few weeks ago,' Zigic said. 'His arm was broken.'

'I was not here,' the man said.

'We know who attacked him. We just need to speak to him about an identification.'

The man let out a rattling chain of Polish, told Zigic he didn't understand what he was saying, he spoke very little English, he would have to ask somebody else, and ducked quickly into the front room.

'He was scared,' Ferreira said.

'And he's not Polish,' Zigic told her. 'He speaks it pretty well but his accent's totally wrong.'

Cooking smells wafted along the hallway from the back of the house, garlic beginning to singe and a hit of spice. They followed it to a small kitchen with ancient palm-leaf wallpaper and a stripped concrete floor with a couple of thin rugs thrown down. It had a haphazard, scavenged look, white base units and wooden ones on the wall, some with missing handles. A washing machine was wheezing and creaking in the corner, a basket full of damp clothes on top of it. The kitchen was warm though, and steamy, two pans of water on a rolling boil and a fug of smoke sweetened with marijuana. After a sixteen-hour shift it would pass for homely, Zigic thought.

A fat man in a denim shirt and combats was stirring something in an old enamel casserole dish, holding the wooden spoon like a dagger, the movement made awkward by the cast on his left wrist. He didn't look up as they entered but the men sitting around the scrubbed pine table fell silent, their eyes fixing on the new arrivals.

Zigic felt their hostility and made himself straighten up.

'Andrus Tombak?'

One of the men nodded towards the chef then swiftly looked away, concentrating on his bottle of beer as if it was the most fascinating thing in the world.

Tombak glanced at Zigic.

'Who let you in?' he asked, picking up a cleaver from the worktop.

'The front door was open.'

'The door is never open.'

'We're police, Mr Tombak.' Zigic flashed his warrant card. 'DI Zigic, this is DS Ferreira, we'd like to talk to you about the man who broke your wrist.'

Tombak grunted and turned away, taking the cleaver to a cut of belly pork. The meat smelled high, an unhealthy bloom on it. As he sliced off thin strips, pinning it to the chopping board with the fingertips of his left hand, it bled greyish juices. He barked a brief command and the men rose obediently, went out into the back garden. Through the kitchen door Zigic noticed a large shed at the bottom of the garden. Dim light glowing through the newspaper tacked up across its windows.

How many men did Tombak have here? Six in the front room, perhaps six more in the room opposite that and the same again in each of the bedrooms. Three dozen men crammed into a space designed for the classic, four-person nuclear family of the 1970s. Each of them paying him ninety pounds a week and whatever extra he could squeeze out of them.

He didn't look rich but Zigic knew better than to make snap assumptions with men like Tombak. They lived close to their tenants so they could control them. They needed to watch them every hour of every day.

He hadn't expected this situation and he cursed himself for arriving unprepared.

'Can you tell us what happened, Mr Tombak?'

'I do not wish him to be arrested.' He threw a handful of pork into the pan. It sizzled as it hit the hot oil. 'I tell other police this.'

'He attacked you,' Zigic said. 'Broke your arm. Didn't you want him to be punished for that?'

'It was fair fight. He won.' More meat went into the pan. 'Is an English problem you have, say I lose fight this man must be punished. No. If I win is fair, if he wins is also fair. I make no complaint to this.' He turned away from the stove. 'Where is your woman?'

Ferreira was gone.

Tombak barrelled past, shouting in a language Zigic didn't understand. He flung open the first door he came to, catching a man standing naked at the foot of his mattress. He scrambled for his trousers but the door was closing already.

Zigic shouted to Ferreira, got no reply.

Tombak threw open another door, sleeping men, darkness, a radio playing at a low pitch. He swore in English, slammed the door again and made for the stairs. The whole house shook under the weight of his rage.

Upstairs a couple of men were queuing for the bathroom, each stripped to the waist and holding washbags. Tombak shouted at them and they averted their eyes, looking at their feet, shuffling where they stood. They were cowed and emaciated, like something from a famine zone.

A loft ladder blocked the landing and Tombak inched around it to get to the bedrooms. A tanned face with thick glasses and blunt, black hair appeared in the hatch for a split second and disappeared again with a crack of timber.

'You cannot search my house without warrant. I know my rights. I have lawyers,' Tombak snarled, opening another door. 'Where is she?'

Ferreira came out of the bathroom, smiled at Tombak.

'Sorry, sir, women's troubles.' She smoothed her hand over her abdomen, made a queasy face.

'How many men are living here?' Zigic asked.

'Eight.'

'I've seen at least a dozen.'

'They want bring friends home after work sometimes. I do not stop them.' Tombak folded his arms across his chest, nodded to himself. 'You want a bribe? Yes? To keep the council from visiting me?'

'We want some straight answers from you,' Zigic said. 'If we don't get them this place will be cleared by the end of the week.'

Tombak leaned against a rickety banister thick with layers of old gloss paint. It complained but held.

'I bribe you or I bribe them. Is all the same. Council man is cheaper than police.' He threw his hand up. 'Ask question then.'

Zigic gestured to the men waiting outside the bathroom.

'You're not worried about them hearing?'

'They speak no English. Stupid Bulgarians, only good for moving thing from here to there. Look – hey, Pyotr, you want to suck my cock?'

The man blinked, his eyes roving between the three of them. 'I speak no English.'

Tombak laughed. 'See. Ignorant Bulgarian peasant.'

'Where were you between three and six this morning?' Ferreira asked.

'I was here. I get up at five, get these animals up and ready for go to work.' He smiled with half his mouth. 'I have plenty witness. You see how many men I have. All tell you same thing. I am here. Go nowhere. Do nothing. I am here whole time.'

'Did you know the man who attacked you?' Zigic asked. 'Jaan Stepulov – he was an Estonian. Like you.'

'No.'

'Was he living here?'

'I say. I do not know him.'

'So you're saying he never stayed here?' Ferreira asked.

Zigic caught something in her tone and realised Tombak had too. What was she really doing in the bathroom? There was water running now and yet nobody had gone in or come out. She'd spoken to someone and covered for them when Tombak came charging after her.

'We know Stepulov was living here,' she said.

Tombak straightened. 'Who tells you this lie?'

'We have a positive identification, Mr Tombak,' she said. 'Who gave us it is none of your business. Not until the trial, then the CPS will hand over everything to your lawyers.'

'Get out of my house.'

Tombak grabbed Ferreira's arm and tried to bundle her towards the stairs but she twisted sharply, using his momentum, and slammed him into the banister, driving his broken wrist against the newel post. He dropped to his knees, a suppressed howl vibrating in his throat.

'Assaulting a police officer,' Zigic said. 'Think yourself lucky you're in England, Tombak, we're only going to arrest you for that.'

He took Tombak downstairs and out onto the street, handed him over to the uniforms waiting on the kerb. Before they pulled off he told them to have the doctor check him out, then called the station for more support.

All of those men in the house to question. Someone had spoken up about Stepulov already and he only needed one of them to be brave enough to break Tombak's alibi.

13

It was a long few hours of repetitive conversation in broken English and pidgin Polish, conducted in the back kitchen under a fizzing strip light with the smoke from dozens of counterfeit cigarettes thick in the air. After a while the meat Tombak had left cooking on the gas hob stuck and burned and one of the men threw the pan in the sink. He ran cold water on it but the stink of scorched flesh didn't go away, it just altered slightly, becoming even more like the smell of Stepulov, dead in the shed that morning, his body doused but still smouldering.

Zigic told one of the uniforms to open the window and thought, for the first time in years, of smoking a cigarette. Anything to smother that smell.

Most of the men were reluctant to speak, the presence of uniforms making them nervous and small even though every one of them was on legal papers and Zigic made sure they realised there would be no problems with immigration even if they weren't.

He just needed some facts on record and right then he would have given anything he had in order to get them.

The man Ferreira had spoken to in the bathroom changed his story once they took Tombak away and he looked terrified as she questioned him again, getting increasingly frustrated, colour rising in her cheeks. She kept repeating what he had told her and he kept denying it.

'Stepulov was here before Christmas,' she said. 'You were sharing a room with him.'

'No.'

'You told me you worked the same shifts.'

'No. I say nothing about this.'

In the end Zigic told him to go and Ferreira retreated to the back garden where some of the men were drinking beers and passing round a bottle of vodka. It was on her breath when she returned but she seemed calmer so he said nothing.

They had statements from four men confirming that Jaan Stepulov was living at the house when the fight between him and Tombak broke in December. They gave varying accounts of its cause but all agreed that Stepulov was in the right without being able to say why precisely.

Tombak wasn't just their landlord, Zigic discovered. He owned the house but he owned the men too, took money off them for board and food, controlled how and when their wages were paid and where they worked. The shifts were irregular and unpredictable, nobody staying at one place long enough to know exactly how much they should be earning. Tombak was getting rich off them and they resented it, but the situation was the same everywhere and Zigic felt their resignation heavy on him.

Stepulov wasn't prepared to stand for it, he suspected, and that was probably what they fought over.

The next man came into the kitchen. He was the oldest yet, late forties, sturdy and tanned with wavy black hair going to grey. He shook their hands with an air of stiff formality, his skin calloused and dry. He wore a narrow gold wedding ring and a couple of saints' medals on a thin chain which hung outside his T-shirt. He looked powerful around the arms but age was catching up with him and there was softness at his belly and ribs.

'DI Zigic. This is DS Ferreira.'

'Marco Perez.' He sat down at the table and turned towards Ferreira, started speaking to her in Portuguese.

'He says his English is bad.'

'OK, you do this,' Zigic said.

Their conversation proceeded at pace and Zigic watched without understanding more than an occasional word, noticing how Ferreira's voice mellowed when she spoke her native language, becoming higher and almost melodious.

'He knew Stepulov,' she said, and Perez kept talking, glancing once or twice at Zigic but always returning to her. His face was becoming more serious, drawing into a pained expression. 'He saw the fight . . . it was over a broken kettle?' she asked Perez again and he nodded, went on. 'Yeah, a kettle got broken and Tombak said Stepulov did it and he was going to take the money out of his wages.'

'Was that all there was to it?' Zigic asked.

Ferreira put her hand up. Perez leaned towards her, his voice dropping low, and he spoke in an uninterrupted stream for a minute or more. A light came into Ferreira's eyes and her mouth opened as if she wanted to say something but she didn't, only listened, and Zigic wanted to ask her what the man was saying but he looked so serious he decided not to.

'Stepulov's brother was here,' she said. 'Viktor.'

'When?'

'Last year. Late summer – they were harvesting strawberries. Jaan came here to look for Viktor. He told Mr Perez because he's been here longest – they were friends,' Ferreira said.

'How? He doesn't speak English.'

'He doesn't speak it well, he said.'

'But well enough for them to have a conversation about Viktor?' Zigic asked. He studied Perez's face, saw nothing which looked like dishonesty, but still it didn't make sense. 'What did Jaan tell you, Mr Perez?'

'His brother Viktor, he is not phoning home for two month,' Perez said, stumbling around the words. 'He comes here to see him but Viktor is already gone.'

'Did you know Viktor?'

Perez nodded and started to speak to Ferreira again, emotion thickening his voice. She reached across the table and put her hand on his shoulder, leaned her face into his. When she spoke he shook his head and talked over her, visibly agitated.

74

'What is it?'

'His cousin is missing,' Ferreira said. 'That's why Stepulov confided in him. Mr Perez's cousin disappeared early last year, he said he was going back to Lisbon but he never arrived and nobody's heard from him since. They think he must be dead.'

'Was he living here too?'

'He was in Peterborough but not here,' Ferreira said. 'He couldn't find work so Mr Perez gave him the money to get a bus back. That was it. Dropped off the edge of the earth.'

'Has he filed a missing persons report?'

Ferreira sat back, gave the man some space. 'I've told him to come in and I'll take care of it.'

'How did Stepulov know his brother had been here?'

She asked Perez.

'He doesn't know but the brother was only here for a few days.'

'Another fight with Tombak?' Zigic asked.

'He got offered a better job and he left to take it.'

'Does he know where?'

'*Onde ele va?*'

'*Eu nao sei.*'

Ferreira shook her head. 'He didn't say.'

'I bet Tombak knows,' Zigic said. 'And I'll bet he's still taking a cut off the top of his money too.'

Ferreira called in a PC with bad skin and too much product on his hair, told him to take Mr Perez to the station and fill out a missing persons report. It would be fruitless but she needed to feel like she was doing something for the man. He'd give them his cousin's details and they would disappear into the system, swallowed up among all of the other missing men who nobody looked for. The husbands who stormed out after an argument and never came back, the depressed and drunk and transient thousands who were old enough to take care of themselves until they were fished out of a river, bloated and unrecognisable.

Perez's cousin probably didn't want to be found, Zigic thought.

He'd come over here to work and it hadn't panned out how he expected. He was probably too ashamed to go home and admit the failure, have it rubbed in his face by family members who'd say 'I told you so'.

Ferreira heaved a huge sigh and started to roll a cigarette at the table, taking tobacco out of a battered tin with the Virgin Mary on the lid.

'How many more are there?' she asked.

'Just a couple.'

'Tombak's alibi's going to hold.'

Zigic was getting that impression himself. Even the people who hated Tombak agreed that he was here all morning, banging on doors and kicking anyone too slow to haul themselves out of bed.

'It doesn't mean he's not involved.'

'We need to find Viktor,' she said, sealing her cigarette. 'If he's still alive.'

14

Zigic's mobile rang as he pulled into the station car park; DCS Riggott.

'The press officer's after your balls, son. She had to shove young Bobby out on the steps for the hacks to play with.'

'He likes the camera,' Zigic said, climbing out of the car.

'And I like some rank on the teatime news. Show the civilians we're taking them seriously. You'll have a good excuse – and that's not a question – you *will* have a good excuse.'

'We've brought a suspect in.'

'Good. Come up and tell Daddy all about it.'

The night shift was ticking by in CID, nothing much to do yet, too early for the drinks to have kicked in. A young woman in a dark suit was stationed at his old desk, sitting with her legs tucked under herself, earphones in, eyes fixed on her Kindle, and he wondered if she was reading about fake crimes while she waited for a real one to break.

The desk outside Riggott's office was empty, his receptionist gone for the night, the dust cover slipped neatly over her computer and not a paper clip out of place.

Zigic knocked on the DCS's door and was told to come in.

Riggott's office had one of the best views in the station, windows on two sides overlooking the rolling parkland of Ferry Meadows, dark clusters of woodland and the river cutting through it. But not now.

It was dark out and the reflection of the office was superimposed over the view, cream walls and framed hunting prints like something from another century. Riggott fancied himself the country gent away from work and Zigic imagined it was an appealing idyll when you'd grown up in West Belfast, watching guns being put to their proper use. There was a pair of stuffed cock pheasants in a glass case on top of a filing cabinet and Riggott would inform anyone who asked, and many who didn't, that he'd bagged them on a shoot with the Chief Constable.

Zigic had told Anna about it, expecting her to laugh at his boss's pretensions, but she gave him a serious look and told him he should think about getting a shotgun licence.

Riggott had his feet up on the corner of his desk, handmade chestnut oxfords gleaming under the light from an anglepoise lamp, while he flipped through a copy of that night's *Evening Telegraph*.

'Well, they spelled your name right, Ziggy.' He threw the paper aside and gestured for him to sit down. 'Drink? Course you will.'

Riggott produced another tumbler from a drawer and poured a double measure of Connemara whiskey, pushed it across the desk. 'Twelve years old that, like licking peat off a witch's tit. *Sláinte*.'

'*Zivili*.' Zigic took a sip, tasted dirt and scorched wood and forced himself not to pull a face.

'So, you've released the racist householders and brought me what?'

Zigic debriefed him about the fight between Stepulov and Tombak, explained the situation at the house on Burmer Road and their clutch of unwilling informants.

'Break one of them and get him charged. We don't want this becoming politicised.' Riggott stared into his drink, a look of pure disgust on his raddled features. 'Press is already floating the ENL angle.'

'Where did they get that from?'

Riggott spread his hands wide, whiskey sloshing up the side of his glass. 'You're in charge of the investigation, Ziggy, I just sit here signing time sheets and adding up how much you spend on translators – which is down this month, by the way, gold star for you.'

'There's a lot of graffiti in the area.' Zigic took another sip of his drink. It was getting better. 'I don't see it though, they're more mouth than action.'

'You know who Peterborough are playing this weekend?' Riggott asked. 'We've got Luton at home. You'll have ENL wankstains coming up by the coachload. Better stamp on the possibility before their publicity department starts printing up flyers.'

Back in Hate Crimes Ferreira and Wahlia were standing smoking near the open window. The smell of Ferreira's rough tobacco had filled the room already, even with a breeze blowing through that was strong enough to lift the sheets of paper tacked to the murder board. Tombak's mugshot was up there now, promoted above the Barlows'.

Wahlia saw Zigic first and flicked his cigarette out of the window like a naughty schoolboy, nudged Ferreira who was talking in a low voice, her eyes fixed on the floor between her booted feet.

'Why have I just been asked about ENL?'

'Don't look at us,' Ferreira said. She took a final long drag on her roll-up and pitched the butt out of the window. 'There's graffiti at the top of Highbury Street – so they're active in the area.'

'Is there any chatter on the boards?'

'I haven't checked yet,' Ferreira said. 'I'd be surprised if they're not shouting about it already. I'll look if you want.'

Zigic glanced at the clock. Almost nine. He wanted to go home and wash the smell of dead fires and grinding poverty off his body.

'It can wait until tomorrow,' he said.

'What about Tombak?'

'He can wait too. We've got nothing to hit him with yet anyway. Go on, get off home the pair of you.'

'Pub?' Wahlia asked.

'Not tonight.'

Ferreira pulled on her coat, whipped her long black hair out of her collar. 'I could go for a quick one.'

Zigic caught a look pass between them but decided it was none of his business. If they wanted to save themselves a grim trawl through the bars by hooking up who was he to interfere? As long as they managed to maintain a professional distance at work he'd let it go.

He closed the window and switched the lights off as he left the office. In the stairwell he passed one of the regular cleaners, an ageless Latvian woman with hennaed hair and a lot of thin gold necklaces stacked on top of her tabard. Another cleaner was in reception as he went out, mopping up blood spots from the floor. The guilty party was sitting handcuffed on a chair, woozy-looking with a split lip weeping onto his pink silk tie. He touched his knuckles to his mouth and Zigic saw bone, very white, through the ripped skin.

He pulled out of the station car park onto Bretton Parkway, a knot of traffic at the roundabout but it cleared quickly, then he was through the dark cordon of Muckland Woods and into Castor, the village huddled in a shallow basin, two miles from the rough tumult of Bretton's mid-rise council blocks and 'problem families', but it felt like more as he passed the millionaires' houses on The Heights, then small limestone cottages all warmly lit and inviolate-looking, the Royal Oak with a fire up the chimney, the village hall hosting a movie night, which he remembered just then Anna had wanted to go to. Some Italian film they'd missed when it was on at the John Clare in Peterborough and missed somehow at Stamford Arts Centre too. He would buy a copy online later, get a good bottle of wine and cook her something special. Involtini. Maybe some of the veal saltimbocca she liked.

She was in the kitchen when he got home and he sat for a moment in the car watching her move in the lit window, unaware of him. He'd lost count of the number of times he'd told her to close the blinds at night but she never did and he knew it was this place, it felt so perfect and remote that it was difficult to believe anything bad could ever happen here.

She'd been to the hairdresser today and he noticed how differently she moved with her highlighted hair freshly styled and still bouncing, turning and catching sight of herself in the black glass.

He got out of the car and walked down through the side gate, let himself in through the back door and she was pouring him a glass of wine before he had even taken off his jacket. She held it away from him until he kissed her, then put it in his hand.

'Look at what that girl's done to my hair.'

'It looks perfect.'

'Maybe it'll be better when I wash it.'

'It's perfect.' He brushed it off her face, the spotlights glinting on the streaks of blonde. 'Where're the boys?'

'In bed.' She wrinkled her nose. 'Why don't you jump in the shower and I'll make some supper?'

Zigic trudged upstairs and stripped his smoke-stained clothes off, left them where they dropped on the bedroom floor and got the water running hot before he stepped into the shower. The cubicle filled with the smell of ashes and he turned his face into the jets, eyes closed, thinking of that house on Burmer Road and the one just like it he'd spent six months in, years ago now, out in Wisbech.

He'd done his gap year there – cutting vegetables in the unending black fields. His friends and family thought he was mad to do it and he still didn't know exactly why he'd gone himself. The money was pretty good and there was no question that he needed it if he was going to get through university without masses of debts, but there were easier ways.

At eighteen it held an allure which seemed ridiculous to him now and he realised it had been an act of solidarity as much as anything else. Mid-nineties and the first wave of new migrants were coming over in numbers, Polish and Portuguese, the Spanish who had been missed by the boom at home. There was a stirring sense of unrest locally, minor but vocal, and he began to notice that his name had gone from being exotic to problematic. People were surprised how good his English was suddenly, as if he'd choose this accent.

In retrospect it may have been an overreaction to throw himself into a situation like that, all for the sake of making a point it wasn't his place to argue.

He regretted it the second he closed the door of the room he was renting in the Wisbech backstreets, a ten by twelve cell with a bright red carpet which didn't quite fill the floor, and flock wallpaper imperfectly painted out in burnt orange. He had an air mattress which leaked the damp coming up through the uninsulated floor and a wardrobe with a broken door.

Nobody else complained about the place, though, so neither did he.

Two days in he got into his first fight and even though he'd been expecting the man to pull a knife it still surprised him to see one that large so close to his face. The English boy in him thought somebody would step in, hold the man back, but the Serb in him was already reacting, smashing the bottle he was drinking from against the side of the man's head.

There were no more fights for a while after that.

There was just work. Sixteen hours a day, unremitting grind. He got lean and hard during the summer, humping boxes in the fields, tanned a colour he had never achieved since. He started eating the black bread he refused at home, drank beer for breakfast with the other men, went for days without speaking English, getting by on the rudimentary Polish he was picking up.

Three weeks in he lost his virginity to a Spanish woman whose name he never knew. All he had of her now was a vague sense of bulk and heat moving above him as he stared drunkenly at her open mouth, thinking, I should remember this, I have to remember this.

The next morning, waiting for the van, his rudimentary Polish got augmented with a lot of language he'd not found much use for since, and he discovered that two of the men he shared the house with had been watching through the street window where he hadn't closed the curtains.

82

When he went home for Christmas everyone said he'd changed and he saw it himself. The boy was gone.

Walking back from midnight mass, holding his father upright and trying to keep him from singing, he realised for the first time that he was stronger than his old man, and the realisation drove the last of the drink out of his system, and what he did remember now, perfectly, was his father turning to him in the middle of Romany Gardens, his breath fogging when he said, 'It's made a man of you, Dushan.'

The water ran cold across his back and Zigic stepped out of the shower.

It was another life, but part of him missed it, and on days like this, mindless, repetitive work seemed very appealing. When you packed your last crate that was it, your errors didn't follow you home, you didn't obsess about missing vital clues or go to bed replaying interrogations, searching for some half-perceived nuance or allusion.

In the kitchen he took a bottle of Zubrowka from the freezer and poured a double shot while Anna told him about her day, relating the conversation she'd had with her hairdresser in forensic detail, the trouble she was having with her boyfriend and the new house they were buying on Hampton. He topped his glass up and nodded in what he hoped were the right places, thinking about the expression on Andrus Tombak's face when he shoved him into the back of the patrol car. Arrogance and contempt – what a guilty man looked like when he was sure of his alibi.

THURSDAY

15

It was like driving into oblivion this morning. The countryside a yawning grey maw on either side of the van, the headlights illuminating a narrow, winding road ahead of them, just two cones of weak light, no catseyes, no markings.

Paolo closed his eyes.

The heat of the van and the throaty rumble of the engine lulled him into light sleep and he was running across the beach towards Maria, feeling the warm sand between his toes and the sun beating down on his bare skin. She was smiling, standing with her arms open wide, wearing the spotted red dress he liked so much, the material stirring in the sea breeze. He could smell salt in the air and when he reached her, and buried his face in her neck, his brain recovered the scent of her skin and the sensation of her thick black hair as it tickled his nose.

His head struck the window and he came round again.

He slipped her photograph from his pocket – her twenty-third birthday and she was wearing the spotted red dress, standing on the balcony giving him *that* smile. He took other photos that afternoon, but this was the one he had printed up to keep close to him, and before he left she kissed the back of it, leaving a pillowy red O for him to remember her by.

It had been a long time since he pressed his lips to it. At some point, he couldn't say exactly when, he began to feel ridiculous doing it. Not the gesture – he always knew that was stupid and boyish of him – but what it implied. He kissed it knowing she was thinking of him and would kiss him back if she could.

The van passed through more small villages, red-brick cottages and white-painted houses with long front gardens, pubs and churches, post offices with old red telephone boxes outside and schools behind iron railings.

The sun was climbing slowly, throwing weak, grey light across the fields. In the distance he saw a bank of wind turbines turning lazy revolutions, dozens of them lined up in ranks and then they were gone and the van was slowing at a bump in the road, a sign flashing to warn the driver about his speed.

They passed a village shop where the same woman he had seen every morning this week was arranging boxes of fruit and vegetables on trestle tables. She had long blonde hair tied in a ponytail and gloves with no fingers. Then she was gone and they were crossing a river by a narrow metal bridge which clanked under the van's wheels, the sound brash enough to wake the man sitting next to him.

The site was only a few miles away now.

Paolo rubbed his hands together, feeling how rough his skin had become. No matter how often he washed them there was this dusty residue, crescents of dirt under his fingernails. He had always worked in bars before, kept himself clean and well groomed. He prided himself on having soft hands – just like a woman's, Maria joked – now they were cracked and scarred, filth ground into the creases. Would she still want them on her body?

He saw another man's hands running up her thighs, his fingers in her hair, on her neck. He saw another man unzip the spotted red dress and slip the straps from her shoulders as she gave him *that* smile.

The van turned off the main road onto a bumpy farm track. Ahead of them the weak sunlight hit the perimeter fence, glinting on the razor wire on top of it. Paolo pushed Maria away, rubbed his hands together again, feeling the roughness which would get a little worse today as he worked, and worse again tomorrow, and the day after that, until they were no longer his hands.

16

Phil Barlow was still in his dressing gown when he answered the front door but he'd shaved and showered, and there was smell of charred toast coming from the kitchen.

The television was playing loud, zingy breakfast voices bouncing around.

'Who is it?' Gemma called down from the bedroom.

'Inspector Zigic,' Phil shouted back, closing the door. 'When can we clear the rest of shed away?'

'Not yet,' Zigic told him. 'We might need to take another look at it.'

'Well, how long?'

'Mr Barlow, I don't think you understand the seriousness of this situation. A man has been murdered in that shed and you're talking about destroying evidence. Are you arrogant or just very stupid?'

Barlow's jaw tightened.

'If you are innocent –'

'We didn't have anything to do with it.'

'*If* you are innocent the last thing you'd want is for us to miss a vital piece of evidence which might lead to his killer.'

Barlow rubbed the back of his neck.

'We're just sick of the sight of it.'

Gemma appeared at the top of the stairs, her pink pyjama top buttoned wrong, sitting askew on her broad shoulders. 'What's going on?'

'I need you to take a look at something for me,' Zigic said.

She came down at a trudge, feet massive in a pair of shaggy white slippers.

Zigic took out Andrus Tombak's mugshot and handed it to Phil, who glanced at it for all of two seconds before he passed it to his wife.

'Who is he?'

'Don't you recognise him?'

'He looks familiar,' she said slowly. 'I reckon he might have been one of Stepulov's mates.'

Zigic showed her his best poker face.

'I reckon he was here once, yeah.'

'When?'

'I don't know. The Friday before last maybe.'

She was lying. Without question. But it was something to throw at Tombak.

He tucked the photograph back into his pocket as Phil closed the door on him, and walked down the short stretch of uneven path where a smashed bottle glinted under the street light, its label in Cyrillic, a deep Fabergé blue.

At six thirty Highbury Street was all bustle and he realised how close they had come the day before, no more than fifteen or twenty minutes too late to ask their questions.

Dawn was still little more than a smudge of pink on the horizon beyond the Eastern Industrial Estate but almost every house was lit up, showers to be taken, lunches to be packed. A woman in a silver people carrier was doing her own door-to-door routine, collecting kids from their doorsteps, a sleeping baby she carried out to her car wrapped up in a blanket.

Zigic went over to her as she was strapping the baby into a carrycot on the passenger seat and showed her the photograph of Jaan Stepulov, then another of Tombak. She tilted them into the light and studied them for a few seconds before she shook her head and passed them back to him, told him sorry, no, in Polish, then again in English is case he didn't understand.

It was becoming a theme of the operation. No, *nic, niet, nem.*

One door after another slammed and the occupants of Highbury

Street walked away, down to the transporter vans waiting at the collection points on Lincoln Road, which would take them east into the wide black fenland fields, or to one of the factory units dotted around the city where they'd pack shampoo or bagels or engine parts for twelve hours, welded to the spot, only their hands moving as the conveyor belt hummed and squeaked, going slightly too fast for comfort.

At the far end of Highbury Street he saw a CSO in a high-visibility vest step across the low garden wall between two terraced houses and heard Ferreira shout at him, telling the man to go round, have some fucking respect for people's property.

Three or four more and that was it. An hour and a half and they had nothing new. Nobody had seen Tombak or the man with the tattooed neck, nobody admitted to knowing Stepulov. Zigic hadn't expected much but he'd been hoping for something. Stepulov was one of them and he was dead and yet nobody wanted to help.

Phil Barlow backed out of the driveway of number 63 and left his van ticking over at the kerb while he closed and bolted the high wooden gates at the side of the house.

Less than a day had passed and he was returning to work.

Part of Zigic understood the necessity, he had bills, a mortgage, the same demands as everyone else, but a larger part of him wondered if an innocent man under threat of rearrest could manage it. He thought of the old saw, passed on to each new generation of coppers: only a guilty man slept while he was in custody, the innocent were too scared. Barlow was out of custody but he was very far from free.

'That's it then,' Ferreira said. 'Big fat nada. Could have had a lie-in.'

'Maybe we'll get something from the information line. Nobody likes to be seen grassing.'

'Maybe.' She nodded towards Barlow's receding van. 'He's up and about very early for someone who does property maintenance, don't you think?'

'Commuting?'

'Tension in the home?' Ferreira punched her hands into her pockets, shoulders rounding against the wind. 'You want to get some breakfast before we go back in?'

'Go on then.'

He gathered the uniforms and dismissed them back to their regular duties, then got into Ferreira's gleaming red Golf. It smelled of cigarettes and musky perfume, a hint of coffee from the takeaway carton scrunched into a cup holder between the seats. There was an empty condom wrapper in the footwell and a brief image of her and Wahlia flashed in front of his eyes. He dragged the wrapper under the chair with his heel, hoping she wouldn't realise he'd noticed.

She did.

'There's nothing going on, you know.'

'Sorry?'

'Me and Bobby.'

'I never thought there was. But if there ever is –'

'I'm not his type,' she said, her eyebrow flicking up.

Zigic smiled, 'Come on, Bobby's not gay.'

'No, he's not. But he only likes white girls.'

Her words hung in the air for a few seconds and Zigic tried to decide if it was regret in her voice or a more general disapproval of Wahlia's sexual prejudices. To be so close to someone and find out your skin colour was unattractive to them; he was surprised they were still friends, especially with Ferreira's hair trigger for racial slights.

'I thought they'd be more helpful around here,' he said, as she nosed out into the pre-rush-hour traffic on Lincoln Road. 'He's one of them. They should want to help.'

'He isn't one of them though, is he?' Ferreira braked sharply as the car in front stopped to let a rangy black woman cross. She moved slowly, weighed down with shopping bags, a girl of three or four hanging onto the hem of her coat. 'Blokes like Stepulov are an embarrassment. They all go to work, pay their taxes, knuckle down.

And he's out there on the rob, begging. As far as they're concerned he's giving them all a bad name.'

Ferreira headed north on Lincoln Road, the traffic at a slow, shunting pace now as buses pulled in and out of the stops and agency vans parked up wherever to make their collections. They passed a Polish grocer's with a few men sitting outside at the tables, beers in front of them, winding down off shift. The door was thrown open but one roller shutter was still locked in place, a red ENL tag, two foot wide, filling it.

Was that another new one? Or had he just missed it before?

They'd marched through Peterborough in January, three hundred of them with banners and placards, hollering the length of London Road, chanting and singing, just a lot of angry noise which didn't even faze the police horses. Then they reached the embankment and ran into the counter-demonstration, a loose conglomeration of anti-fascists, local Muslims and a few shoppers who'd wandered over from the city centre to see what would happen.

Fifty arrests, a few small fines and some community service, followed by a six-figure bill which the council could ill afford. The press reported 'clashes', the police that 'no significant incidents occurred' and the ENL boards were aflutter for weeks about the great victory they had scored.

Ferreira punched the horn as a motorbike shot across the street in front of her.

'Ruining my fucking paint job because he's suicidal.'

She went over the lights on amber and passed her parents' pub, a big white stucco building with a throng of smokers near the door and an 'All Day Breakfast' sign screwed to the front wall. Maybe she was going to double back.

Her mother cooked an amazing ham and red-pepper frittata, spiced with smoked paprika, and they had the best coffee Zigic had tasted. He'd begged her for the method but even after she told him he couldn't replicate the effect. He suspected she'd lied just to shut him up.

Ferreira pulled onto the kerb without indicating, stopping outside a Polish greasy spoon with one of its front windows boarded over.

'What's this?' Zigic asked, but she was already gone.

An electric bell chimed as they went in and the sound barely registered above the babble of voices and the radio playing Lite FM at a deafening pitch. The tables near the broken window were cordoned off, plastic chairs stacked on top of them, and there was hardly a free seat anywhere. A piece of broken glass crunched to powder under his heel as he followed Ferreira to the long silver counter at the back of the cafe.

She ordered a bacon butty and a coffee and Zigic eyed the full English for a moment before choosing the same.

'Ooh, table.' Ferreira darted off as a couple of men in GPO uniforms left and Zigic paid the woman behind the counter.

'What happened to your window?'

'It was smashed last night.' She handed over his change. 'Some drunk.'

'Did you see them?'

'We see nothing, only hear glass.'

'Have you reported it?'

The woman smiled. 'We have number for insurance. What else is there to do now but clean up mess?'

She loaded their order onto a tray and Zigic carried it over to the spot in the window Ferreira had snagged.

'I thought we were going to your place,' he said. 'I could have killed for one of your mum's frittatas this morning.'

'And I'd have been expected to go in the kitchen and cook it for you.'

He smiled.

'It isn't funny. They roped me in to doing a shift last night.'

'I thought you and Bobby went out last night.'

'We did. This was when I got back.' She opened up her butty and smothered the bacon in brown sauce. 'I was stuck in that kitchen for two hours cleaning fucking plates.'

'Tell them you've been at work all day and you're knackered.'

'You don't understand. If I'm there I have to help out.'

'So get your own place.'

'I can't afford it.'

Zigic sipped his coffee; it was somehow bitter and weak at the same time.

'Mel, I know what you earn.'

She glanced away as men's voices rose sharply at a nearby table. There were empty beer bottles in front of them, a couple of tumblers holding short measures of brandy. They had the local paper open to the jobs page.

'I haven't even paid off my student loans yet,' she said. 'And I owe Dad, like, God, eight grand or something. It's probably more.'

He almost asked what she was wasting her money on, but then he remembered the shopping trip to New York before Christmas and the three weeks she spent in Cuba over the summer. Then there was the car, a Golf GTi loaded with extras, and the clothes she obviously didn't scrimp on. He'd flicked through enough of Anna's magazines to realise those little leather jackets and fat handbags didn't come cheap. At work she was always the first one to go out for lunch, or get a pizza delivered if they were staying late, and unless the money was pressed on her she'd just pay for it herself.

It was a consequence of living at home, he guessed, that complete disregard for money. She would only learn the value of it when she started paying her own bills.

By the time he made sergeant he was married to Anna, saddled with a full complement of pension plans and life insurances to go with the mortgage on the two-bed stone cottage in Wansford she thought was so cute and such a bargain, exactly the kind of place where she might be able to get pregnant. A year after they moved in Milan was born and she decided the cottage wasn't cute any more, it was draughty and damp and those stairs were so narrow somebody was going to fall and break their neck on them.

She had to wait for the next move though, and Zigic felt the full force of her annoyance on a daily basis until it came. It was the best motivation to get promoted he could have asked for.

'There's a bad vibe around this,' Ferreira said.

'We're making progress.'

'Say this tattooed guy is who we want –' she sucked brown sauce off her thumb. 'He could be long gone by now.'

'Someone knows who he is.'

'Well, they're not saying.'

Zigic took a mouthful of his bacon butty. The meat was smoky and salty, cooked to a perfect crisp. He thought of Stepulov's body in the shed and forced himself to swallow. He put the rest of the butty down on the plate and swilled his mouth with the bad coffee.

'Maybe we should fit the Barlows up,' Ferreira suggested with a mischievous grin.

'So you think they're innocent now?'

'You let them go, who am I to argue?' She pointed at his plate. 'Aren't you going to eat that?'

'No, take it.' He pushed it across the table. 'I don't think the Barlows did it. Logically, you look at that situation and they should be guilty as hell. But I just don't think either of them are capable.'

Ferreira squeezed more sauce into the half-eaten butty. 'You bought that about them preparing to demolish the shed?'

'Phil told us the same thing when we interviewed him.'

'They had plenty of time to work out their story.' She took a bite and held her hand over her mouth when she spoke again. 'And if they were really going to do that why didn't he tell us when we interviewed him the first time?'

'That's partly why I think they're innocent. It's such a good excuse he should have shoved it at us right from the off. That's what you do when you're nervous and guilty, you get your best lie and run with it.'

'It's not much when you weigh it against the whole means, motive, opportunity thing,' Ferreira said.

'It's immaterial. We haven't got enough for the CPS unless one of them cracks and if they didn't do it yesterday when they were under pressure they sure as hell won't do it now.'

'The post-mortem might throw up some leverage.'

'Jenkins is pretty sure the fire was set through the window. Whoever did that wanted to make damn sure they didn't leave any physical evidence behind.'

Ferreira wiped her fingers on a paper napkin and shoved her plate aside.

'Tombak's capable,' she said. 'Stepulov rocks up at the house looking for his brother . . . we've got to assume Tombak knows where he is, don't we?'

'It's more likely they were arguing about that than a few quid for a broken kettle,' Zigic said.

'Maybe the agency knows where the brother moved on to. Perez said they did a couple of shifts at one of the big fruit farms out near Spalding.'

'Did he say which one?'

'No, but Pickman Nye run most of the labour over that way,' Ferreira said. 'You want another coffee?'

'No, come on. The stuff in the office is better.'

In the car he began to think back through the previous year's caseload. They had the lowest conviction rate in the station but it wasn't for lack of suspects or evidence. When you were dealing with a transient population timing was everything; a witness not followed up quickly enough or a forensic report delayed and your window snapped shut. The person you wanted, whose guilt you could prove incontrovertibly, would be gone.

Twenty-four hours since Stepulov's death . . . his killer could be anywhere on mainland Europe by now and they didn't even have a name for Interpol.

17

Pickman Nye's offices were located in a three-storey Georgian town house within sight of Peterborough Cathedral's western front and if it wasn't for the steady stream of foreign workers coming through the place it would have looked more like a chamber of law than an employment agency. Austere black gloss doors stood at the top of four weathered steps and the windows were tall and slim with shutters folded back inside. The name plate was small, brass, gave away nothing.

They were the largest agency in the county though, and Zigic supposed they didn't need to advertise any more, not when they were running nine thousand workers on a margin of a pound an hour.

Fifteen years ago they were a two-man outfit operating out of a rancid office above a tanning salon down Cowgate. The street door was kicked in twice a week and more than one employee had found themselves in A&E when the money in the envelope didn't match the work done in the fields. Back then they were PN Employment Solutions, supplying contract cleaners and farmhands at rates which dipped well below minimum wage once their 'overheads' had been taken into account.

A tax investigation and a tactical bankruptcy later they re-established themselves on Priestgate, moving one street over and a few rungs up the ladder. They expanded into medical personnel, added a lucrative fifty-thousand-pound-plus head-hunting service, and slowly the reputation for worker exploitation and casual brutality went away.

The gangmasters were now recruitment consultants, the business became discreet, the charity work ostentatious, Mr Pickman earned himself an MBE and retired to Malta. Mrs Nye took them into the cathedral precincts.

Zigic went up the concave stone steps and through the door which was standing open, into a tiled lobby and through a second, toughened-glass door, into the reception area like a doctor's waiting room, uncomfortable chairs tightly packed, a table with old magazines and leaflets in different languages. There were half a dozen people waiting to be seen, mostly in a tolerant silence, but two of the men were talking across the narrow aisle, speaking Polish, discussing a friend's cousin who was working as a prostitute from a bedsit in Woodston; her brother would kill her when he found out.

The receptionist – Euan – glanced up from his computer as Zigic approached the curved blond-wood counter. The woman at the other end kept working, her fingers flying across the keyboard, eyes on a sheet of paper filled with indecipherable handwriting.

'Inspector Zigic, good morning.' Euan flashed a bleached smile. 'Is there something I can help you with?'

'Is Mr Harrington available?'

'I'm sure he is.'

Zigic followed Euan through another toughened-glass door into a second waiting room identical to the first, everything bland and functional, conveyor-belt abstracts on the cream walls, the carpet brown marl, stained here and there and with a defined pathway which they followed to Patrick Harrington's office.

Euan knocked, poked his head around the door. 'Detective Inspector Zigic for you.'

'Well, let him in then.'

Harrington's office was large and dark, despite the optic-white walls and the chrome lights hanging from the distant ceiling, decorated as if he wanted to be in a Docklands warehouse conversion rather than a nineteenth-century town house, with Eames chairs he probably couldn't fit in and copper venetian blinds at the deep windows, which overlooked a brick wall where an extractor fan pumped out the salty, spicy smell of the takeaway noodle place behind the office.

'Ignore the mess,' Harrington said, hefting his bulk up to shake Zigic's hand across the broad glass desk, cluttered with paperwork. 'You'd think this'd all be on computer by now, wouldn't you? What can I do for you?'

'We need some information on a couple of your employees. Addresses, work records, everything you've got.'

'OK,' Harrington said slowly. 'Have they done something they shouldn't?'

'It's an ongoing investigation, I can't go into details.'

'Have you got a warrant?'

'I can get one.'

Harrington cracked a sly smile. 'Pulling your leg, Inspector. You know we're always happy to help.' He dragged the keyboard towards him. 'What're the names?'

'Stepulov,' Zigic said and spelled it. 'Jaan and Viktor.'

Harrington frowned at the computer display. It was a common occurrence, judging by the deep trenches cut either side of his mouth. The air of joviality was reserved for clients and coppers, Zigic imagined.

'Alright, here we are.'

'Did they give you a next of kin?'

'We ask but if they don't want to that's their business. Neither of these two have. It's not unusual.' Harrington leaned back in his chair, swivelled it from side to side. 'I don't know how useful this is going to be to you, Inspector, we haven't had any contact with either of them since last year. Looks like they moved on. Or went home. That's a sight more common than it was.'

'Did you struggle to place either of them?' Zigic asked.

'I wouldn't have dealt with them,' Harrington told him, straightening up as he spoke. 'They're both down here as D1 – that's our basic class. Poor language skills, no qualifications. There're plenty of posts about for blokes like that but a lot of them think they should have something better. You know, they all come over expecting big wages and the big wages aren't there any more.' Harrington shrugged. 'Problem is the recruiters back in old country don't tell them we've got a recession on. Fact is they're as well off at home now, what with the cost of living and that.'

The printer on Harrington's desk started to purr, working quickly, spitting out time sheets and copies of passports, tax documents, various internal forms.

'This wouldn't be to do with that death over New England, would it?'

'We're still waiting on a positive ID,' Zigic told him. 'But yes.'

'Bad business. You reckon it's a racial thing?'

'Why do you say that?'

Harrington reached into his pocket, took out a mint. 'A lot of our workers get hassle off the locals. Minor stuff, nothing they'd bother you lot with, but it's persistent. I've been saying to Euan for years, it's only a matter of time before one of them gets done over by some nutter – doesn't take much, does it? Headcase loses his job, sees it go to a migrant . . . you don't know how that sort thinks. Torched his doss, didn't they?'

'That's right.'

'Hell of a way to go,' Harrington said, shaking his head. 'You wouldn't wish it on your worst enemy.'

He gathered the papers from the printer, squared them up with a couple of sharp taps against the desk and slipped them into an envelope.

'Hope that's of some use to you.' Harrington stood up to hand it over, smoothed his gold silk tie as he did, and Zigic stayed seated. Reluctantly Harrington sat again. 'Would a reward help? If he was one of our workers I'm sure Mrs Nye would be more than happy to put a few grand up. Might get someone to come through for you.'

More conspicuous charity, Zigic thought. A few grand they could set against their tax bill and what would it achieve? They'd get a lot of time wasters hunting the reward, more dead leads to run down, and if by some miracle it brought out a useful line of inquiry the eventual prosecution would be undermined when the defence flagged the financial motive. He'd seen it before, didn't want his case compromising like that.

'I'll discuss it with the higher-ups,' he said. 'They don't let lowly DIs make those kind of decisions.'

'Well, like I say, I'm sure she'd like to help however she can. We take the welfare of our workers very seriously.'

'And what about their living conditions?'

'If we'd have had any idea he was sleeping rough like that we'd have found him a room,' Harrington said, piqued now.

'With Andrus Tombak?'

Harrington didn't reply. Held his breath, waited.

'Did you know Tombak had a run-in with Jaan Stepulov?'

Harrington cleared his throat. 'It happens.'

'Tombak attacked one of my officers when we went to talk to him.'

'Is he alright?'

'She's fine. Thankfully. But we'll be charging him with assault, so if I were you, for the sake of your company's good name, I wouldn't get involved with his defence.'

'I don't know what Tombak's told you but he doesn't work for us in that kind of capacity. He brings men in, we fix them up when we can. He's a free agent.'

'Does he bring you workers very often?'

'Offhand, I couldn't say.'

'Maybe you should check your records,' Zigic said.

For a long moment they stared at each other and he saw the wheels turning behind Harrington's serious grey eyes, weighing up the pros and cons of refusing. Did he want to look involved? Was Tombak worth enough to them?

He must have been expendable because Harrington took another pass at his keyboard.

'I can give you a list of men registered to his address, but that's all we'll have on file.'

'It's much appreciated, sir.'

Zigic took the list and went back out through reception. A gang of men had come in, one doing all of the talking, his tone stern as Euan stood bored and implacable, hands on his hips. Until the man jabbed a stiff finger at his chest, then he snapped.

'Look, I've told you we don't pay for overtime if it isn't signed off. You don't have the dockets so you don't get paid.'

'You pay these men.'

'Bring the dockets.'

'I bring last week.'

'We don't have them.'

'I give you myself,' the man said.

'Are you calling me a liar?'

Euan's face was tight and he seemed taller and broader suddenly, nothing like the man who had shown Zigic into Harrington's office.

'No dockets, no pay. You understand that?'

Outside the sun was shining on the cathedral green, glimmering across the stained-glass windows and picking out the specks where the yew trees were coming into bud. A group of tourists came into the precincts through the Western Gate, the Gothic facade looming up ahead of them, blasted and weathered, the saints and patrons indistinguishable from one another. There were a few people taking photographs from the grass, more of them sitting outside the cafeteria in the breezy winter sunshine, an elephantine American woman filling the air with her opinion on how quaint it was, how absolutely darling. But the rest of the place? *My Lawd* . . .

This cloistered little corner of Peterborough was not the city though, and Zigic imagined the ones who'd come here because they'd seen it in *Barchester Chronicles* must have been disappointed by the brutal sixties architecture of the centre and the closed-down shops. They'd head on to Stamford maybe, see where *Pride and Prejudice* was filmed and feel they had found something infinitely more English at last. Some authenticity.

18

Ferreira started a fresh pot of coffee while her computer booted up.

Wahlia was trying to get hold of Stepulov's medical records, hoping to trace his next of kin from them, but it sounded like he was running into resistance. Hold music bled out of the phone and she saw a familiar moue of annoyance on his face. He tugged on the gold stud through his left lobe and snapped to attention as the music cut dead.

Obviously he'd got a woman this time. His voice deepened and he smiled while he talked, telling her it was OK, he understood how it was.

'The name's Stepulov, Jaan,' he said, and gave her the date of birth from his file.

Ferreira slipped into her seat and started opening up the pages she had bookmarked under 'Fascistas' – the BNP, National Front, Combat 18 – starting with the English Nationalist League's website, then their Facebook page and the main boards for the local chapters. East Anglia and the West Midlands were growing factions; over the last year she'd watched their membership rise steadily with sudden spikes after the Wootton Bassett fracas and the clashes in Luton. A big one when news broke in Bradford of Muslim men grooming young white girls for sex. Every time the *Daily Mail* ran an inflammatory piece about migration or unemployment, or some English company lost a contract to a foreign competitor, a few more disillusioned bigots joined up.

She clicked a link to the English Patriot Party site, the ENL's unofficial parent organisation. On the front page was a reminder to their members that *Newsnight* would be featuring their leader next week. They took it as a sign of greater acceptance that Paxman was prepared to lock horns with him.

Ferreira thought of the performance Tommy Robinson gave on *Newsnight* and wondered if Richard Shotton would do any better.

He'd put himself forward for the Police and Crime Commissioner elections in Cambridgeshire last year, causing a brief stirring of concern which increased as the low turnout was announced, but in the end he took less than 10 per cent of the vote. He responded by stating his intention of running for Parliament.

'Mel, where's your mug?'

She found it sitting empty in the top drawer of her desk and gave it to Wahlia.

A few minutes later he placed a cup of hot, strong coffee next to her hand and it went cold, untouched as she scanned the boards, barely blinking, sitting still with her chin propped on her fist, tapping at the keyboard to take her deeper in.

There was no specific mention of Stepulov's death but plenty of vitriol aimed at migrant workers; they were parasites and scum, living off benefits and jumping to the top of the council housing list.

Ferreira hadn't come across a migrant worker yet who was living in council accommodation. It didn't work like that. You came over with just enough to get yourself established, or, more usually, the gangmaster who employed you provided some run-down bedsit and charged it against your wages at a premium rate. There were thousands of Andrus Tombaks out there, putting people in the kind of accommodation these people wouldn't tolerate in a million years.

She felt her face flushing with anger as she read on and knew she should leave it. She was weeks before Stepulov's death now and nothing anyone said was going to help the inquiry, but she couldn't stop scrolling down. It was a kind of masochism, like picking at a scab, the need to know just how much people like her were hated.

Not that she needed these websites to show her it.

In Spalding, growing up, the Portuguese and Polish kids were treated like filth. The first year at school there were only three of them, Mel and two other girls, and they formed a tight gang despite not particularly liking each other. It was necessity, stand together or be picked off individually by the clique of blonde princesses.

Mel's mother went to the charity shop on the high street for her clothes. Mel, tall for age, was sent to school in old women's trousers from M&S and misshapen jumpers with badly darned moth holes.

One Saturday her mother came home with a new winter coat, jewel red with a fur-lined hood and huge buttons. It was too big on the shoulders and it smelled faintly of damp but not so badly that it couldn't be aired on the washing line. Monday she walked through the school gates in it and one of the blondes – Becky Deere, she still remembered the bitch's name – said it was one of her sister's cast-offs. Her friends started laughing and Mel lashed out, dragged her to the ground and beat her around the head, using all the moves she'd learned fighting with her brothers. Becky Deere lost two front teeth and the tip of her tongue.

The bullying didn't stop though, not right away, and it was only when more foreign kids joined the school and they had numbers behind them that things changed. Then the parents started getting involved, saying their kids were being held back while the teachers concentrated on basic language skills. It wasn't racism, it was concern for their little darlings' educational development.

A couple of years out of university, while she was still in uniform, Mel pulled Becky Deere over on a country road between Peterborough and Spalding. She'd put on weight, dyed her blonde hair black and been sprayed a deep mahogany, and Mel smiled to herself, thinking how desperately she'd wanted to be pale and blonde when they were kids.

Becky pretended not to recognise her, played the innocent. She was three times over the limit but just for good measure Mel took out her baton and smashed the car's offside brake light. Becky complained but Mel's partner backed her up and she lost her licence for two years.

It was a small, petty pleasure, but she felt she deserved it.

'Hey, Mel.' Wahlia's hand came down on her shoulder. 'Can I borrow your lighter?'

'Yeah, hold on.' She stood up, her legs stiff and numb from sitting in the same position so long. 'Where's Zigic?'

'Gone on to the post-mortem.'

'I've been doing this for two hours?'

'You looked like you were in the zone.'

'Is that why I didn't get another cup of coffee?' She worked her lighter out of her back pocket. 'What're you doing?'

'Checking out the recently released arsonists.'

'Anything?'

He cracked open one of the long metal windows before he lit up. 'Some kid who's just been released from Claire Lodge – he burned down his foster-parents' house in Fletton. That was personal, I guess – it was his first offence anyway. And a guy who tried to torch his girlfriend's place.'

'Unlikely suspects then.'

'Yeah, but –'

'Hold on, gotta pee.'

Mel grabbed her handbag and went downstairs to the Ladies, striding the tightness out of her legs. She needed to get back into the gym but by the time they knocked off she couldn't face it. Maybe in a few weeks, when the clocks changed and the evenings were lighter. She missed running on the road, that feeling of eating up the miles, the wind streaming past her face. Charging full pelt at a wall which never moved just didn't match it. Especially when there was some idiot on the next treadmill who didn't understand the gym etiquette of 'earphones in; I'm ignoring you'.

When she went back to the office Wahlia put her Porto mug in her hand, gave a small, ironic bow and returned to his side of the desk.

She took a sip of coffee, it was hot and bitter, an aftertaste of tobacco. 'Suspects then?'

He snatched up a mugshot from his cluttered desk.

'Recognise him?'

'Yeah,' Ferreira said slowly, but she didn't know why or where from.

He was a grubby-looking white guy with large green eyes under thick brows cut with old scars. He wore a few days' worth of stubble and his shaved head showed the shadow of an unevenly receding hairline. Mid-forties, Ferreira guessed, or younger maybe if he'd had a hard life. The prison tattoos on his neck suggested he had, a string of nonsensical letters and a crude Britannia figure.

'This can't be the guy Adu and Maloney mentioned, can it?' she said. 'No one's going to mistake those tattoos for a bird.'

'It's Clinton Renfrew.'

She stood sharply. 'He's not out already? Didn't they give ten years?'

'Ten years, yeah, knocked down to five. They let him out just before Christmas,' Wahlia said. 'Must have been a model prisoner.'

He stuck the photograph up in the suspects column of Stepulov's murder board. Clinton Renfrew looked made for it.

'Where is he now?' Ferreira asked.

'I'm waiting on a call from Littlehey.'

'You think he's come back to Peterborough, after what he did?'

'Where else is he going to go?' Wahlia said, folding his arms across his chest. 'He's a fucking hick. Blokes like him always come home.'

Ferreira started to roll a cigarette, thinking of the last time she saw Renfrew; Peterborough Crown Court, the public gallery packed and more people waiting in the corridor outside. The jury took less than an hour to deliberate and when they returned to the stuffy courtroom the crowd broke into furious whispers which took minutes to subside, despite the judge banging his gavel and threatening to clear them out.

Renfrew stood stone-faced as they found him guilty, threw his chin up in the air and weathered the fury coming from the public gallery. It was easy to ignore when he couldn't understand what the largely Portuguese crowd were shouting.

Ferreira lit up and typed Renfrew's name into Google.

The first ten results were old news items, archived pages from the *Evening Telegraph* and the *Citizen*, heavy on local colour; a couple of the nationals had picked it up too and they used the incident as launch pad into the larger issue of immigration and a lack of social cohesion, making Peterborough a microcosm for the rest of the country.

She stopped.

'Clinton Renfrew is on Facebook.'

'Of course he is.'

His timeline was headed by a St George's cross and she saw familiar names in his friend list, local ENL activists and BNP members, affiliates of the various, smaller right-wing groups which came and went.

Wahlia's phone rang and he listened for a long time to the person at the other end, writing fast notes on a scrap of paper.

Ferreira leaned back from the computer screen and smoked her cigarette, watching Wahlia's expression harden. His hand froze.

'Yeah, we know it.' He grinned at Ferreira. 'Yeah, thanks, John . . . yeah yeah, definitely. I owe you one.'

He ended the call and walked over to the murder board, uncapping a red marker pen.

'Come on then, where is he?'

Wahlia marked a circle on the map of New England.

Ferreira grabbed her keys, already dialling Zigic's number. 'Call Littlehey back, get everything they can give you. And find out who his probation officer is and call them –'

'I know.' Wahlia waved her out of the office. 'Go, I'm on it.'

19

'Late to the party again, Inspector,' Dr Irwin said, pulling his latex gloves off in a puff of chalk. 'Anyone would think you were squeamish.'

It's just meat, Zigic told himself, looking at the wrecked remains of Jaan Stepulov laid out on a gleaming stainless-steel table. Thin pink juices dripped into the drain below, the sound intermittent but resonating around the white-tiled mortuary, percussive against the medley of humming freezers and a droning light which flickered at an epileptic rate, making his eyeballs throb.

It's just man-shaped meat.

The burnt ones didn't usually bother him. His first corpse was the victim of a house fire in Paston, an elderly woman murdered by her grandson for the savings she kept hidden between the yellowing pages of her Mills & Boon novels. The house was alight for hours before they managed to bring the fire under control, fuelled by piles of old newspapers and magazines she'd hoarded over the years, and by the time her body was recovered it was nothing more than a jumble of brittle black sticks.

Everyone expected him to throw up but the body was so unlike a person that he didn't react.

Jaan Stepulov was still identifiably human though. Alive he had been lean and fit, and even with the lighter fuel as an accelerant the fire hadn't done as much damage as Zigic expected. His face was still a face despite the blasted flesh and the empty eye sockets, an arrow of deeper black where his nose had been. His clothes had insulated him well and his body was only superficially burnt. It still had bulk and a terrible solidity.

'So, what's the verdict?' Zigic said, dragging his eyes up from the corpse.

'The victim was definitely alive when the fire was set,' Irwin said, coming round the table to stand by the Y-incision, which stood out vivid pink against Stepulov's charred skin. 'There was extensive damage to his respiratory system consistent with smoke inhalation.'

It sounded bad but Zigic knew it was an understatement. Stepulov would have breathed fire as tried to free himself from the sleeping bag, blinded first by the lighter fuel then by the flames, which would have turned his eyeballs to liquid. He would have screamed and thrashed but there was nowhere to go and the only saving grace was the more he panicked, the deeper he inhaled and the faster the carbon monoxide would have knocked him out.

'Any signs of trauma?'

'He'd been in a fight by the look of things. Hairline fracture to a couple of ribs, some broken teeth, nothing fatal,' Irwin said. He spread his hands wide. 'It's exactly what it looks like, Inspector. Somebody doused him in lighter fluid and set fire to him. I'll email my full report over to you this afternoon but that's about the size of it.'

Zigic thanked him and left the mortuary.

In the windowless grey corridor he passed a porter bringing down another body. It was small and insubstantial under the white sheet, no avoiding the fact that it was a child. The man nodded to him and kept walking, the squeak of wheels receding and finally stopping on the other side of the swing doors.

He went up the stairwell and passed through reception into the fresh air. A few people were milling around outside the main doors, waiting for taxis to whisk them away or delaying going in for a few extra seconds, trying to find a happy face for their terminally ill. A man on a drip was smoking in the lee of the wall and he looked freezing in his thin pyjamas, nothing on his feet but a pair of hospital-issue paper slippers.

As Zigic reached the car his mobile rang and he put it on speaker, not wanting to hang around there a second longer than he had to.

'Clinton Renfrew's out,' Ferreira said, her voice echoing.

'When did that happen?'

'Christmas.' Her feet slapped the stairs. 'He served five years, can you believe that?'

Zigic backed out of his parking space, two cars waiting for it and he left them to fight it out.

'I know what you're thinking, Mel, but it isn't Renfrew's MO.'

'He's dossing at Fern House,' she said. 'Don't you think that's a bit too much of a coincidence for us to ignore?'

'I'll check it out.'

'I'm on my way now.' He heard the peep of her remote locking and the car door slammed. 'I'll meet you there.'

She ended the call and he pulled out onto Thorpe Park Road, swearing under his breath. The lunch-hour traffic was heavy across the Crescent Bridge, two lanes cut down into one where they were reinforcing the metal superstructure and it took five minutes to get across and onto the roundabout at the shopping centre. As he passed he noticed how empty the car park was, even though half of it was cordoned off for maintenance. Everything in the city seemed to be crumbling.

He cut down Deacon Street, stamping on the brakes as a coach pulled out of the lot behind Maloney's pub, bound for Krakow or Łódź, packed full of travellers. There were three more parked up waiting, groups of people standing around nearby, bags at their feet.

He turned onto Cromwell Road, heading for New England. The street was busy, kids who should have been at school and women in hijabs carrying bags of shopping. One of the tightly set terraced houses was being renovated and a skip half blocked the road, a cordon of orange tape around it so you couldn't say you didn't see it when you lost your wing mirror. A load of smashed plasterboard hit the bottom of the skip as he passed, throwing up dust and a sound like a gunshot.

His grandparents' first house was on Cromwell Road back in the late fifties and it had been a mix of Italians, Slavs and West Indians then. Peterborough needed their labour but it didn't want them as neighbours so they were shoved away in the soot-stained ex-railway houses. No heating, no indoor toilets, walls which sweated condensation.

By the eighties they had moved on and the area was firmly Indian and Pakistani, men brought in to do the heavy work at the brickyards in Fletton. Within ten years the yards were in decline thanks to cheap imports from Belgium and asset stripping by the new bosses. The company was wound down to a skeleton staff, the pits were turned into rubbish dumps and finally deemed fit to build on.

Now Cromwell Road was shifting again with the new influx from Southern and Eastern Europe. The builder's van belonged to a Polish construction firm and on the crossroads with Russell Street a madrasa faced off with a Portuguese club retrofitted into an old double-fronted house. There were tables and chairs out on the pavement, a couple of men sitting drinking beers.

Hidden behind the houses was a warren of garages and illegally constructed outbuildings catering to migrant workers who couldn't afford a shared room. Officially the council disapproved but there was a tacit agreement to let them remain, he guessed. Much cheaper to ignore the problem than provide accommodation out of the public purse. Never mind that people were getting ripped off and living in unsafe conditions.

The one-way system took him along Gladstone Street, past the mosque. A *trompe l'oeil* mural filled the end wall of the house opposite it, a multicultural street scene which didn't look as fresh as it once had. Faces had been blasted off, others grafittied, and again, springing up like melanoma, there was a red ENL tag over a figure in a burka.

He kept driving, caught behind a guy on a bike who was weaving drunkenly between the cars. He shouldn't have come this way.

It was slow and winding, but when he reached the junction with Cobden Street he realised what had drawn him off the main road.

The man on the bike pulled away and disappeared and Zigic sat, hunched over the wheel, looking at the block of recently finished flats which filled the corner plot. A couple had To Let boards screwed up and the developer's sign was still standing out front. It had taken time to get planning permission, he supposed. The building sat uncomfortably on the street, huge and blocky against the terraced houses, but it was better than what was there before, the burnt-out shell of a takeaway place, decaying behind security fencing, its yard full of debris and overrun with rats.

Clinton Renfrew was known to the police long before he burned the takeaway down. An arsonist for hire, his name linked to a handful of gutted factories around the city. He'd been clever though, always had a rock-solid alibi, never splashed the cash about, and if it was just a matter of property damage he might have got away with that one too. But whether Renfrew knew it or not a man had been asleep in the storeroom the night he turned up to torch the place.

Ferreira was right, five years wasn't enough.

A few minutes later Zigic pulled up around the back of Fern House. Ferreira was already there, sitting on the bonnet of her car with a cigarette going, talking to someone on her mobile.

'All evening? You're positive?' she asked, nodding to him as he crossed the road, '. . . no, I can appreciate that.' She dropped her spent butt and scrubbed it out with the toe of her boot. 'Thank you, that's it right now. We'll be in touch if there's anything else.'

'Who was that?' Zigic asked, as she ended the call.

'The first Mrs Barlow. Craig was at home like they said. She doesn't let him go out on school nights apparently.' Ferreira rolled her eyes. 'And I got the distinct impression she doesn't like him going to his dad's at all. There was some snark for Gemma.'

'About what you'd expect from the ex,' Zigic said, buttoning up his parka. 'How did you get here so quick anyway?'

'I don't drive like a pensioner.' She slipped her mobile into the back pocket of her jeans. 'And I got an update from Bobby – looks like Renfrew was radicalised in Littlehey. He celled with Lee Poulter.'

'Refresh my memory.'

'Ex-BNP fucktard. He kicked that Pakistani kid to death in Cambridge a few years ago – you remember?' Zigic nodded. 'I've been on Renfrew's Facebook page. He's dropped in pretty tight with the ENL set-up here. He's only been out a couple of months so they're probably connections he made inside.'

They walked up Lime Tree Avenue, around to the front of Fern House.

The door was open and the sharp scent of lemon cleaning fluid filled the air. An elderly man in worn jeans and a holey jumper was cleaning the tiled floor.

'Is Helen here?' Ferreira asked.

'Mrs Adu is not home.'

'What about Mr Adu?'

Joseph came out of the lounge, clutching a bundle of newspapers to his chest.

'Inspector Zigic, have you found the man who was looking for Jaan?'

'Not yet. He's proving very elusive,' Zigic said. 'We need to speak to Clinton Renfrew, I understand he's staying here.'

'No, Mr Renfrew was only here for a week or so.' Joseph Adu put the newspapers down on the hall table. 'You do not think he was responsible for Jaan's death?'

'We just need to talk to him.'

'Did they know each other?' Ferreira asked.

'I do not believe they were well acquainted but Mr Renfrew did arrive whilst Jaan was still with us, yes.'

'Was there any trouble between them?'

'No. Mr Renfrew was very self-contained.'

'Did you know he'd just been released from prison?' Ferreira asked. 'He firebombed a takeaway place on Gladstone Street – a man died.'

Joseph Adu gave her a look of sad indulgence. 'I spoke to Mr Renfrew about this. He is profoundly aware of the cost of his actions. He told me he met the young man's mother during his incarceration and begged her forgiveness.'

It explained why his sentence was shortened, Zigic thought. Show contrition, beg if you have to, weep if that's what they want to see.

'I do not believe he would murder a man in cold blood,' Adu said. 'He does not want to go back to prison. He told me he has missed enough of his children's lives already.'

'He's making some very ill-advised friends if he wants to stay out of trouble,' Ferreira said.

Adu gave her a questioning look and Zigic cut in before she could explain; there was nothing to gain from exposing Adu's misconceptions.

'Do you have an address for Mr Renfrew?'

Adu nodded slowly.

'We need it.'

'He is living with his brother,' Adu said, going into the office, where a printer was methodically throwing out flyers. He checked a book and wrote the address on a sheet of headed paper. 'But I think you are wrong about Mr Renfrew, he is a good man.'

Ferreira started to speak and Zigic touched her elbow.

'Thank you, Mr Adu.'

20

They went to the address in Old Fletton where Renfrew's brother lived, a 1930s semi-detached built in the shadow of Peterborough United's south stand. Neither man was home but his sister-in-law, a meaty blonde in pink Juicy Couture tracksuit and a fistful of gold, told them Clinton was at work.

'Some garage over near that pikey site on Eastern Industrial Estate.'

Mid-afternoon and the road was clear under a darkening sky. Ferreira dropped her car off at the station and they cut back across town, neither speaking, the silence growing charged as Zigic accelerated along the parkway. Ferreira wanted it to be Renfrew but Zigic was unconvinced, sure the man's history was affecting her judgement.

'Barlow didn't have the balls to tackle Stepulov,' she said. 'Paying Renfrew to get rid of him makes perfect sense.'

'Perfect?' Zigic asked. 'Really? How would they know each other?'

She shrugged, recrossed her legs. 'They're living a few streets apart, maybe they drink in the same pub, I don't know.'

She didn't know and that was a constant problem with Ferreira. She was too confident of her instincts, too willing to dismiss the evidence that contradicted them.

'Renfrew must need money,' she said. 'And setting fires is pretty much his only marketable skill.'

'There's a world of difference between burning out commercial properties to order and setting fire to a shed where you know someone's sleeping.'

'He's killed one person. Maybe he found out it doesn't bother him.'

Zigic took the slip road off Paston Parkway, cut back under it and headed into the Eastern Industrial Estate, its plastic and corrugated buildings sprawling away into fenland, the low skyline broken in places by occasional wind turbines attached to factory units and the ugly bulk of the green power station which filled the air with a sickly sweet odour like rotting fruit and mouldering grass clippings.

They passed the travellers' site, several acres of mobile homes and steel lock-ups, kids playing at fighting and women standing around in the gateway, waiting for the older ones to get off a bus pulled up across the road. A monolithic apartment block rose behind the site, clad in cedar and stretches of very white plaster. Beyond that the tops of pylons, strung along wasteland, followed the curve of the River Nene as it ran away towards the Wash.

Zigic pulled into the forecourt of a garage advertising £40 MOTs and tyres while you wait. A fast-food van was doing a brisk trade in the lay-by, half a dozen white vans parked up, and the smell of it flipped his stomach as he got out, frying meat and onions caramelising. He realised he hadn't eaten anything since breakfast but it would have to wait.

Ferreira strode away towards the garage. Its front was open, two bays both in action, a red BMW ramped up with a couple of men in grease-stained overalls trying to figure out what was wrong under it, and a temporarily forgotten Subaru with its alloys off.

One of the men elbowed his mate and they both turned to Ferreira as she entered the workshop.

'Alright, darling, want me to check your points?'

Ferreira shoved her warrant card in his face. 'Where's Clinton Renfrew?'

The man backed away, giving her an unpleasant smile. 'Clint, mate, copper here wants to talk to you.'

Renfrew came out of a small glass-walled office at the back of the garage, wiping his hands on a rag. He was short and lean inside the overalls he wore folded down to his waist, bare arms dirty and heavily tattooed. His right arm was bandaged from the elbow to the wrist, the dressing fresh-looking, and as he came closer Zigic noticed a smear of dried blood on the front of his khaki vest.

'What do you want?'

'See they didn't teach you any manners in Littlehey,' Ferreira said. 'Jaan Stepulov, friend of yours?'

Renfrew nodded, gave a tight, pained smile. 'I get you. The dead bloke from over Highbury Street.'

'That a yes?'

'He was in the hostel the same time as me. Wouldn't have said we were mates but he seemed alright.'

'For a foreigner?'

'I've got no issue with people coming over here to work, Constable.'

'Sergeant.'

Renfrew looked past her at Zigic. 'Right terrier you got yourself there, boss.'

'Stepulov wasn't working,' Ferreira said. 'He was on the scrounge.'

'Sure he was looking. Not much work around at the moment, what with the economy the way it is.'

'You think your lot could do better?'

'I wouldn't vote for any of the bastards.' Renfrew picked up a can of Coke left open on a stack of tyres with unevenly worn treads. 'This some new approach they're teaching you now? Political discourse? Want to ask my opinion of the common agricultural policy?'

'Taught you some long words in the nick anyway,' Ferreira said. 'You know how Stepulov died?'

'I've seen the news.'

A compressor screamed across the garage and Ferreira flinched at the sound.

'You get used to that,' Renfrew said. He slipped his arms back into his overalls and began buttoning them up again. 'Some fucker set fire to the shed he was kipping in. You arrested the people whose house it was, didn't you?'

'The Barlows.'

'That's it.'

'They're helping us with our inquiries,' Zigic said. 'You and Mr Barlow go way back he tells us.'

Zigic caught a flicker of panic in Renfrew's eyes, but he blinked it away, shook his head.

'No. He never told you that.'

'You think he's worried about dropping you in it?' Ferreira asked. 'Man's facing life. You remember what that feels like, don't you, Clinton?'

Renfrew's jaw hardened. 'He never told you because I don't know the cunt.'

The two mechanics standing under the BMW were paying full attention now, and Zigic noticed a third man coming round the other side of the Subaru. A solid lump of aggro with a wrench in his hand.

'Where were you between four and six on Wednesday morning?' Zigic asked.

Renfrew dragged his eyes away from Ferreira. 'At home, where d'you fucking think? Ask my brother.'

'Your brother isn't much of an alibi.'

'I was at home,' Renfrew said firmly. His feet shifted on the concrete floor, getting ready to run or fight, Zigic wasn't sure which. 'Look, I've done my time and I am never going back in that fucking place again. I hardly knew Stepulov or whatever his name was. Why would I want to kill him?'

'You tell us.'

'This is harassment.'

'It's a murder investigation,' Zigic said, taking a step towards Renfrew. 'And when we see a recently released arsonist with racist tendencies –'

'I'm not a racist,' Renfrew shouted. 'Fucking hell, my gran's Belgian.'

'And how does she feel about your ENL membership?'

'She's dead.'

'She must be spinning in her grave,' Ferreira said. 'Or did you have her cremated?'

Renfrew glared but kept it together. 'The ENL is not a racist organisation. We're a political group opposed to the marginalisation of the English working class and the dilution of traditional English values.'

'You're not going to convert anyone here, Renfrew.'

Ferreira's mobile rang and she moved away to answer it.

'This is bollocks. I did what I did and I've served my time. You can't come round harassing me every time there's a fire in Peterborough.' He crushed the Coke can and threw it out onto the forecourt. 'You know why I burnt that place down. I told them when I was charged. The guy paid me. I've got no issue with the Portuguese or the fucking Slavs or anyone. It was a job. Place was supposed to be fucking empty.'

The other mechanics stood motionless and silent, watching Renfrew, and Zigic wondered if this was the first they'd heard of it.

Behind him Ferreira was talking in a hushed voice and all he caught was, 'Keep him there.'

'Now, I've got work to do,' Renfrew said, taking a pair of latex gloves from the pocket of his overalls. 'Unless you want to caution me and repeat this conversation with my solicitor present.'

'Don't leave town, Mr Renfrew.'

The compressor screeched again and the sound hit Zigic like a heart punch as he left the garage. Ferreira was in the car already, behind the wheel, and her hand was open when he climbed in the passenger side.

'Keys, quick.' She grabbed them. 'Maloney's got our tattooed man.'

21

Fintan Maloney was at his usual corner table, playing dominoes two-handed against an emaciated old man with a shock of white hair standing at strange angles from his head. There was a bottle between them and their glasses held stiff measures, but he caught sight of Zigic and Ferreira the second they walked into the pub.

The lunchtime crowd was merging into the afternoon one and Zigic noticed a few suits among the regulars, English he thought, stopping off for a quick drink and a blow job before they returned home. The background chatter was a mix of Polish, Lithuanian and Latvian, though, and the natives looked like they knew they were out of place.

A young blond guy in a Tesco's uniform slipped out of the door marked Staff Only, followed by one of the waitresses, who gestured at his half-zipped fly before she returned to the bar, all smiles for the people waiting to be served.

Maloney came over to them, hoicking the waistband of his jeans up under his wrecking-ball gut. His nose was glowing from the drink and he moved with the exaggerated steadiness of a man who knew he'd had a few too many.

'Your boy's over the end of the bar there.'

'Which one?'

'In the black Puffa jacket,' Maloney said. 'Talking to Olga.'

He was leaning across the bar, one foot resting on the brass rail, a pale young man barely out of his teens. Olga poured him a vodka and when he shot it back Zigic caught a glimpse of blue ink on the side of his neck, the tattooed bird soaring and swooping as his Adam's apple bobbed.

'Let's do this then.'

Zigic headed for the far end of the bar, aware of Ferreira peeling off to his left, taking a slower, circuitous route through the groups of people drinking where they stood and the waitresses bringing out plates from the kitchen.

The man ordered another vodka and said something to the barmaid which made her frown. He tapped his foot against the brass rail and nodded to himself.

Zigic could feel ripples coming off him, a spiky, unpredictable energy. The couple next to him inched away, the woman moving so that her boyfriend was shielding her.

Ferreira stole up to the bar, two stools down from the man, hidden behind a couple of painters in heavily spattered work gear.

The man paid for his drink and necked it, slammed the shot glass on the counter as Zigic reached the bar. The man glanced at him, his expression neutral, and called to Olga for another drink. She was serving someone else, pulling a pint of Guinness with a slow, practised hand, and ignored him.

He tapped his glass on the bar, once, twice, impatient or nervous or maybe he was just the kind of arsehole who liked making noise.

'Heard you're looking for Jaan Stepulov,' Zigic said.

'Sorry. No English,' the man said.

'Did you find him?'

'No English,' he said again, giving Zigic a leery smile, big teeth packed crooked in his mouth.

The painters moved away and Ferreira stepped up close to the man's back, ready to restrain him if he tried to run.

'Stepulov's dead.'

The shot glass skittered away from his fingers and smashed on the floor behind the bar.

'Dead? How is he dead?'

'He was murdered.'

The man dropped heavily onto a bar stool and buried his face in his hands. It wasn't the reaction Zigic was expecting.

'How did you know him?'

'His daughter, she is my wife.' He rubbed his face, bringing some blood to the surface of his milk-white cheeks. 'Why does nobody tell us he is dead? I have been here, looking for him – weeks now – nobody tells me this.'

'It happened yesterday morning, we've been trying to locate his next of kin,' Zigic said. 'What's your name?'

'Tomas Raadik.'

'Is Jaan's family living over here, Mr Raadik?'

He jumped off the stool. 'I have to tell them.'

Zigic grabbed his elbow and steered him down again. 'Where are they?'

'We live in Spalding.'

'So why was Jaan in Peterborough?'

'He came to find his brother,' Raadik said.

'Viktor?'

'Yes.'

'And did he find him?'

'No.'

'Then why did he stay?'

Raadik looked away. 'This is what we think. He does not come home for three month. Why not?'

Behind the bar a young blonde woman was clearing up the broken glass with a dustpan and brush, taking her time about it, and Zigic waited until she moved away before he continued.

'You went to the hostel where Jaan was staying – that's right, isn't it?' Raadik nodded. 'But he didn't want to speak to you. He ran off.' Another nod and his eyes stayed fixed on the polished wood counter. 'Why did he do that?'

'I do not know.'

'Has there been an argument between you?'

'No,' Raadik said sharply. 'We wanted him to come home. That

124

is all. Arina is scared he is living badly. She wanted me to bring her papa back.' Raadik closed his eyes and mumbled something which sounded like a prayer. 'Now I have to tell her he is dead.'

'We haven't positively identified the body yet,' Zigic said.

Raadik's eyes widened for moment but the hope was short-lived and he crumpled where he sat. 'How did he die?'

'The shed he was sleeping in was set fire to.'

'Then it must be Jaan.'

'You went there, didn't you?'

'I asked him to come home with me. He would not leave.'

'Why?'

'He said he must find his brother. It is a matter of family. I tell him he has family who need him but he will not leave.' Raadik shook his head. 'We are having baby, next month is due, now he will never see his grandchild.'

22

Zigic drove, Raadik next to him, silent and increasingly tense, Ferreira in the back. He glanced in the rear-view mirror a couple of times and saw her staring out across the sprawling black fenland, thousands of acres of uniformly flat ground punctuated by an occasional farmhouse or a bank of wind turbines turning much slower than the wind buffeting the car suggested that they should. She was chewing on her knuckle and he couldn't decide if it was nicotine withdrawal or a reluctance to return to a place she'd told him she loathed on more occasions than he could count.

There was something oppressive about the magnitude of the landscape. It made you feel small and inconsequential to be surrounded by so much empty space, that massive unending sky reaching away to a distant horizon. In Zigic's memory it was always summer here, the sky perfectly blue, not a shred of cloud for weeks on end and the sound of irrigators snickering all around them as they worked. To a boy who grew up in a terraced house, with a handkerchief of back garden and neighbours on every side, it had felt like freedom.

Today though he could see why Ferreira hated it. Ahead the sky was pregnant with rain, sheets of it strafing the farmland where the workers were no more than dots, moving up and down the rows, the waiting lorries toy-looking. To the north the clouds were almost black, huge, rolling boulders closing in on the town.

Zigic slowed as a crosswind slammed the car, forcing it onto the verge. The dykes here were steeply cut and deep enough to swallow them up. He felt Ferreira's knee hit his seat and wrestled the car back into the middle of the road, narrowly missing a van coming the other way. It swerved but didn't slow and the driver threw his hand up in disgust.

He made the rest of the journey at forty miles an hour, gathering a long line of traffic behind him until they reached the edge of Spalding. Raadik directed him in a weak voice, up here, turn left, the house with the white car on the drive, then they were climbing out, the smell of rotten earth and rain on the air, and a few spots hit Zigic's face as he stood on the front doorstep, waiting for Raadik to find his keys.

The door opened as he fumbled them out of his pocket.

Arina Raadik was sharper than her husband. She knew they were police instantly and she faltered where she stood, hanging onto the door just long enough for Tomas to catch her under the arms and keep her upright. It was an awkward manoeuvre, hampered by her belly, which looked further along than eight months, stretching her floral tunic to its limit.

'You have found Papa?'

'I'm sorry, Mrs Raadik –'

'He is dead, Arina,' Tomas said.

She fell against her husband and cried into his chest, pulling at his T-shirt and thumping his shoulder with her small fist, trying to punch her grief out into him. Finally Tomas guided her into the living room, eased her onto the sofa. There was a bowl of chocolate ice cream left balanced precariously on the arm. Tomas moved it away and she shouted at him to leave it.

'I'll go and make some tea,' Ferreira said, escaping into the kitchen.

Arina snatched a handful of tissues out of a box on a side table and dried her eyes. She had her father's hard-boned face, softened slightly by baby weight but the lines were the same, high cheek-bones and a pronounced jaw, the same striking blue eyes big with tears.

'Was it an accident?'

'He was murdered,' Tomas said.

She pressed the tissues to her mouth and cried for a few minutes, while Tomas stroked her hair and cupped her belly, speaking to her quietly, words Zigic couldn't understand. He should have brought a translator but it would have taken time and he felt the case slipping away from them already, didn't want to waste another hour.

He looked around the small, bright living room, trying to picture Jaan Stepulov in it, this man who'd been dossing at a hostel then finally in the Barlows' garden shed, a beggar and a petty thief, a drunk and a gambler. Had he chosen the bright acidic green on the walls? Had he and Tomas taken a day off to paint the room while the women kept them supplied with tea and sandwiches? He tried to imagine the man who had broken Andrus Tombak's wrist pushing an uncooperative trolley around Ikea, picking out the floating shelves and the paper floor lamps, arguing with his wife over which prints would look best behind the sofa.

The two lives seemed impossibly remote from each other.

Zigic went to the fireplace, a gas flame dancing over white pebbles, and picked up a framed photograph standing pride of place at the centre of the wooden mantel, Arina and Tomas outside a registry office, a heavy-set woman who must be her mother on one side and on the other Jaan Stepulov in a smart grey suit, his hair barbered and his cheeks clean-shaven, the picture of respectability.

That man had refused to come home when his family begged him?

Zigic sat down in a wicker armchair, a snapped strand poking into the back of his thigh. Ferreira was clattering around in the kitchen, opening and closing cupboard doors as the kettle came to a boil.

Outside half a dozen children were playing in the cul-de-sac, kicking a ball about, going into the open front gardens to retrieve it when they lost it. Their voices were distant and high-pitched, an occasional scream breaking through the front window.

'How did he die?' Arina asked.

'There was a fire –'

128

'That man on the news? That is Papa?'

Zigic nodded. 'At least we think so. We're still waiting for the DNA results, they should be through in the next forty-eight hours, but we think so, yes. I'm sorry.'

'Why would anyone do that?'

'We were hoping you could help us with that,' Zigic said. 'Your father was in Peterborough looking for his brother. How long has Viktor been missing?'

'Since November. Papa thought something bad had happened to him.'

'Maybe he went back to Estonia,' Zigic suggested.

Arina's face darkened. 'He would not leave without telling us.'

'When did you last hear from Viktor?'

'He was to come to our wedding in August but he did not arrive. Papa phoned him and he said they would not let him have time off from work. Two or three weeks after this he came to the house and after that we did not see him again. Papa called him and he did not answer his phone.'

'Where was Viktor living at that point?' Zigic asked.

'In Peterborough, in a house with some other men.'

'Did he mention a man named Andrus Tombak?'

She nodded. 'Uncle Viktor was working for this Tombak. He is a gangmaster.'

'Jaan knew him too,' Tomas said. 'He went to Tombak's house to look for Viktor but he was gone.'

Arina turned to her husband. 'Why did you not tell me this?'

Tomas squirmed where he sat, inching away from her, and when he answered he directed it at Zigic. 'Jaan thought Tombak knew where Viktor was. When he was here the last time Viktor said he was going to start a new job. A big money job he said.'

'Where?'

'I do not know.'

Ferreira came into the living room carrying a wooden tray with white mugs filled to the brim and a plate of sugar-glazed biscuits which looked home-made. She set it down on the coffee table and retreated to an armchair in the window with her cup. Nobody else touched theirs.

Zigic shifted his weight in the uncomfortable chair, a second strand of snapped wicker spiking his buttock.

'If your father was so concerned about Viktor why didn't he call us and report him missing?'

'Papa does not trust the police,' Arina said.

'This isn't Estonia, Mrs Raadik.'

'You would look for him? Some immigrant?'

'If there was evidence he was in danger, yes, of course we would.' The heat from the fire was burning across his face, and he felt stifled inside his parka suddenly. 'From what we know of how Jaan was living he doesn't seem to have been looking for Viktor very hard.'

'Of course he was looking,' Arina said. 'Why else would he not come home to his family? He must have found something to stay there for so many months.'

She was very young, Zigic realised. Despite the wedding ring and the coming baby, she was still a child who couldn't accept her father as an individual distinct from his family. Was Stepulov acting like a man on a mission? Drinking all day, shoplifting and begging, bringing a woman to the Barlows' shed?

'Did you or your mother go and try to convince him to come home?'

'No,' she said, her eyes dropping to her belly. 'Maybe if we had he would be alive now.'

The letter box snapped and something hit the mat. Through the window Zigic saw a teenaged boy with a fluorescent-orange bag cut across to next door, delivering the local free paper.

'Do you have a recent photograph of Viktor?' Zigic asked.

Arina nodded to Tomas and he got up from the sofa, went over to the bookshelves which were lined with candy-coloured paperbacks and a few dozen DVDs. He took down a small floral box and started to sort through the photographs inside.

'Had your father made any progress? Did he say anything about where he thought Viktor might be?'

'No.'

'Tomas?'

'He would not talk about it.'

'Doesn't that seem strange to you?'

'Of course, that is why we argued. I wanted him to come home – Arina does not need this worry with the baby. Here, this is from the last time he visited.'

Tomas handed Zigic a photograph which had been printed off a phone or a digital camera and he wondered why they had specifically selected this one to preserve. Viktor Stepulov standing at a small portable barbecue with a long-handled fork in one hand and a bottle of beer in the other, smiling broadly, all white teeth and crow's feet. He was shorter than his brother, heavier and darker, and if he'd been asked Zigic wouldn't have said they were brothers.

A car pulled onto the driveway then and Arina struggled to her feet, pushing Tomas aside as he tried to stop her. Ferreira went for the door and Zigic gestured for her to hang back, this was family business and even though they needed to observe he saw no reason to interfere further.

Mrs Stepulov came in and threw her handbag over the newel post, taking in the scene with a calm eye. Then Arina started crying again and she put her arms around her, shushed her and smoothed her hair.

Finally, when she had settled Arina, she fixed Zigic with a firm look and told him to help her in the kitchen.

She reminded him of his own mother, fifteen years younger at least, but they shared an imperious air, a tone which would brook no argument. In the kitchen she offered him a vodka and when he refused poured a heavy shot into a mug and threw it down.

'This is Viktor's doing,' she said, her hand going to the bottle again, wedding ring chiming against the glass. 'He is no good that man. I tell Jaan, if he is in trouble I do not want it at my door but he goes, like a dog, he follows him. Ever since they were boys it was that way. Viktor makes fuck-up, Jaan takes the blame.'

She pointed at him with a wavering finger. 'You will find who killed my husband.'

'We're trying, Mrs Stepulov, but you have to understand, how Jaan was living, it's very difficult to get a clear picture of events.'

'What does this mean?' she snapped. 'You are not trying hard enough.'

DCS Riggott could learn a thing or two from her, Zigic thought, feeling his face flush, a knot twisting in his gut. He wasn't used to this. The victim's family was usually shell-shocked, too brittle to answer the most basic questions. He was used to coaxing people round, a soft voice, a gentle approach. That wasn't going to cut it here.

'What was Viktor involved in?'

'I do not know. But it will be bad. Whatever he was doing.'

'But Jaan thought he was in trouble. Why?'

'The night before Jaan left Viktor phoned here, he said he was in danger.' She looked into her cup, a deep frown on her face. 'I begged Jaan to stay. He said he would not go after him but when I woke up the next morning he was gone. I tried to call Viktor's mobile phone and there was no answer, only this woman's voice saying the number was no longer available.'

The bottle of vodka on the worktop looked tempting suddenly.

'I need you to tell me everything Viktor said to your husband.'

'He tells me nothing. Jaan was a secretive man. We have been married twenty-one years and I never know what he is thinking.' Her eyes lost focus. 'I did not want to come here. Viktor says there is opportunity in England so Jaan decides we will come here too. He said we would work hard, save money, go home and buy business. But he would not work. The agency, they find him job, he went one, two days, is told to leave. Next job is the same.' Her mouth set into a hard line. 'We are better off without him.'

'Did he tell you about Andrus Tombak?'

'Tombak, yes. Viktor said when he was here that this man has a lot of money. He joked that he could rob him and start a new life somewhere.'

'Maybe he wasn't joking. Your husband got into a fight with Tombak just before Christmas,' Zigic said. 'He broke Tombak's wrist. We think it was over Viktor.'

Mrs Stepulov slammed the cup down. 'Then you arrest him. He killed Jaan.'

'We have arrested him but there are twenty people who say he was at home when Jaan died.'

'So he paid someone to kill him,' she said. 'What kind of police are you? This is obvious.'

There was a cool head behind Stepulov's death, Zigic thought. The lock on the door, the smashed window and the lighter fuel. Not exactly an execution, but it showed a level of care which suggested forward planning, a familiarity with Stepulov's routine. He could imagine Tombak scoping out the situation and handing over instructions with a wad of cash.

It was elaborate though. A quick knife to the ribs would look more natural. They saw it often enough, put it down to quick tempers and too much drink. Those cases had a way of drifting into oblivion unsolved. An arson like this raised questions which demanded to be answered.

But Stepulov was a big man, seasoned and tough. Maybe Tombak wasn't sure his hired thug would come out on the right side of a fight. He'd failed after all, even with a baseball bat in his hands. Who was to say a knife would be enough to fell Stepulov?

23

'How long are you going to stay in there?' Gemma asked, her voice muffled by the bathroom's heavy oak door. 'Phil, come on, that water must be cold by now.'

'I'll be out in a minute.'

The floorboard creaked as she shifted her weight.

'Your tea's ready,' she said.

'You eat, I'm alright.'

The handle turned but he'd locked the door and she rattled it sharply.

'Phil. What're you doing in there?'

'For fuck's sake, woman, leave me be, will you?'

A few seconds later he heard her going downstairs and he sighed at the ceiling, sinking lower into the tepid water, knowing that there would be an argument when he got out now, all for the sake of nothing.

He should have gone down to have dinner, sat across the table from her, forced the food into his mouth, forced himself to swallow it, while she watched him with the newly shrewd eye she'd developed, waiting for him to say something he knew she didn't really want to hear.

She thought he was guilty.

She hadn't asked and she wouldn't accuse him, but she believed he'd murdered Stepulov.

He should have said something the minute they got home from the police station but he was tired and flat and all he wanted was a cup of tea and some silence to order his thoughts in. Now the moment was passed and any denial would sound like a lie.

The evening yawned ahead of him, stilted conversation and television programmes they would both look at but not watch. She'd offer to make tea, he'd drink it. They'd sit at opposite ends of the sofa with the dead man's ghost filling the empty cushion between them. That's how it was last night and that's how it would be tomorrow. They would move further and further apart until the police charged someone and by then the damage would be done.

How could you love a woman who thought you were a murderer?

Last night he lay in bed watching the red numbers on his alarm clock changing, aware of Gemma awake next to him, not talking, hardly breathing, and every time his foot touched her leg she drew away. He wanted her to say something, anything, but she didn't, and when he finally spoke to her, she only mumbled and told him to go back to sleep.

Phil pulled the plug out of the bath and the greyish water drained slowly, exposing his goose-pimpled body to the chilled air. The radiator in here had never worked properly. A cheap thing from Wickes he'd filched off a job. Gemma had been moaning at him to replace it for eighteen months.

Tomorrow he'd pick up a new one. She'd appreciate that.

He climbed out of the empty bath and towelled off, avoiding his reflection in the mirror over the sink. One night's sleep missed and he looked like an old man, all jowls and eye bags and broken veins around his nose.

In the bedroom he pulled on a pair of jeans and long-sleeved T-shirt, shoved his feet into his second-best trainers and sat down on the blanket box to tie them. The room still smelled of smoke from the shed. Not as strong as yesterday but enough that he could still detect it under the plug-in air-freshener Gemma had moved up here from the living room. It smelled in there too. The whole house was permeated by it and he doubted they would ever shift it from the curtains.

At the weekend he'd take her to Dunelm for some new ones. She always bitched that he wouldn't go in there with her, it would make her happy for a while at least, get her out of this fucking house.

As he headed for the stairs he noticed the door to Craig's bedroom was open. Gemma had been in, tidied up the clothes he'd left on the floor, turned back the covers to air the bed ready for his next visit.

Kerry wouldn't let him come over this weekend, not after what had happened. She'd say she didn't want him upsetting. He was too young to deal with something like this. And if he argued she'd lose her temper, tell him Craig wouldn't be safe there. It was just the excuse she needed to stop him seeing his boy.

In the kitchen Gemma was sitting smoking at the table, staring into middle distance with a frown between her eyes.

'What's for tea, love?'

'Love, is it now?'

'I'm sorry.' He put his hands on her shoulders and kissed the top of her head. 'You know I never meant it. I'm just a bit – I dunno – shell-shocked.'

'That makes two of us then.'

He pulled a chair up close to her. 'We're alright, aren't we?'

'Yeah.' She stood abruptly and went to the oven. 'We're fine.'

He got a beer out of the fridge and drank it at the worktop, looking at the burnt-out hulk of the shed, just a darker shade of black against the unlit garden. Gemma moved briskly behind him, slamming down the cutlery and banging the spatula against the tray as she dished up their fish fingers and chips.

'Can I do anything?'

'No.'

She threw the tray in the sink and something broke in the scummy water.

They sat opposite one another at the table and tried to make conversation. She asked how work was with an edge in her voice. She hadn't wanted him to go in today and he could feel her spoiling for an argument. He told her it had been fine, didn't mention that his boss had given him the third degree about the fire, acting amazed that they'd let him out already. Then she talked about Jeremy Kyle and *This Morning*, faking lightness and laughing with her mouth too wide, as if she was on the verge of tears.

This would be his evening, Gemma play-acting normality until it was respectable to turn in. Then another long night without sleep, the conversation they needed to have running through both their minds as the silence boomed in the bedroom.

As she was scraping the uneaten food into the bin he found his wallet and tucked it into his pocket.

'Where do you think you're going?'

'Fancy a pint,' he said. 'Don't mind, do you?'

She smiled thinly. 'No. You go. Go and enjoy yourself.'

'I'm only going over the road.'

'You don't need to explain yourself to me, Phil.'

'I'll stay here if you want.'

There were tears in her eyes. 'I can't take much more of this.'

'It won't be like this forever.'

'Won't it? Everyone thinks we're guilty,' she said, her hands clawing the air next to her head. 'My mum phoned today and told me to leave you. She begged me to come home.'

'That bitch never liked me.'

'Is that all you've got to say?'

He sighed. 'You know what she's like. Take no notice of her.'

'Don't you care what people think of us? My own mother thinks you're a murderer for Christ's sake.'

His gut felt hollow suddenly. 'I only care what you think.'

She closed her eyes.

'You know I didn't do it, Gem. Look at me.' He grabbed her arms, fighting the urge to shake her. 'For fuck's sake, look at me when I'm talking to you.'

She opened her eyes; they were small and bloodshot.

'I know you didn't do it,' she said quietly. 'You've not got the arsehole.'

He stormed out of the house, slamming the front door after him, and the cool night air hit him like a slap around the face. He was relieved and furious all at once. Part of him wanted her to think he did it, have a bit of respect for him.

He crossed Highbury Street and went into the Hand & Heart. A skinny ginger mongrel was tied up just inside the front door, a bowl of stout on the floor next to it. The dog was asleep, back leg kicking as it dreamed.

The bar was busy for a Thursday night, a handful of regulars lost among a crowd of fat, bearded men all wearing the same red CAMRA T-shirts. The pub was famous on the real ale circuit for its original art-deco interior and every now and again a gang of aficionados would descend on it.

He was grateful for the cover, didn't feel like talking to anyone.

The landlord clocked him through the bodies crowding the bar, smiled and pointed and started to sing,

'*He's a firestarter. Twisted firestarter.*'

A couple of the regulars chuckled and Phil dug deep to find a smile that made his cheeks ache.

'Usual?'

'Yeah.'

'Just messing with you, Phil lad.' The landlord took a pint glass down and started to pour his Guinness. 'How's the missus holding up?'

'She's a bit – you know?'

'Fucking shock for you, I bet.'

'Yeah.'

He took his pint to a table under the window and tried to close himself off from the chatter around him. Two blokes at the next table talking about Syria like they'd just wandered in from a NATO summit, a group on the other side of him dissecting last night's Champions League game, saying how Barça's tactics had been hacked now and they were beatable.

He knew he was being watched but he ignored it. Sipped his pint and tried to think of something to say to Gemma when he went home. Maybe the best course was to pretend nothing had been said and keep going like before. She needed time to recover. That's all. A few more days to remember what a regular life felt like.

It would be easier once the remains of the shed were gone. Having it there waiting for you every time you looked out of the window . . . how could they hope to move on?

His face was prickling. He kept ignoring it.

They were curious. Some of them thought he was guilty and he couldn't change that. He shouldn't have come in. Not so soon. But did they really believe he would saunter over for a pint if he'd killed a man? Who did that?

Before he knew it his glass was empty and the landlord asked if he'd have another, on the house.

Why not? It was early still.

He put his glass on the bar and went to the Gents.

The door opened as he was zipping up at the urinal and he felt that stinging sensation at the base of his neck.

'Alright, Phil, long time no see.'

Clinton Renfrew was standing between him and the door, older and thinner than Phil remembered, but how long had it been? Ten years, twelve. Before him and Gemma. Renfrew had been inside, he saw it in the paper. Arson.

'How you doing, mate?'

'Not as well as you,' Renfrew said. He reached out and weighed the gold chain hanging outside Phil's T-shirt. 'The building's still paying.'

'It's fucking slack.'

'What d'you expect, all these immigrants about?'

Phil stepped around him, washed his hands quickly and dried them on a fistful of paper towels. Renfrew moved as well, still blocking off the door.

'Had a visit today,' he said. 'Couple of coppers come to see me at work.'

'Yeah?'

'Wanted to know if you paid me to torch your shed.'

The floor lurched under him and he gripped the edge of the sink to stay upright. 'What did you say?'

'Told them to get fucked, didn't I?' Renfrew took a step closer. He reeked of dirty clothes and diesel. 'Now, what I wanna know is why you sent them after me.'

'I didn't.'

'Don't treat me like a cunt, Phil. They've let you go, you gave them something.'

'Why would I say anything about you?'

'Cos you're shit up.'

Phil pushed away from the sink, tried to get around him, but Renfrew grabbed the front of his T-shirt and shoved him back so hard he slammed into the edge of a cubicle.

'Look, Clint, I never said anything.' He heard the tremble in his voice. 'I swear to God.'

'Don't do me much good now, does it?' Renfrew shoved his face close. 'I lost my fucking job. You ever tried getting fixed up when you've been inside?'

'No.'

'You'll see what it's like. If you survive it. Which you won't.'

'I'm sorry, Clint.'

'Fuck your sorries.'

'I don't know what else to say, mate.'

Renfrew smiled. 'I know what to say. Tomorrow morning I'm going down to that cop shop and I'm telling them you gave me five hundred quid to torch your shed.'

'They won't believe you.'

'You wanna bet on it?' Renfrew said, a crazed fervour in his eyes. 'They're already sure you did it. All they need's a push.'

'You'll go down too.'

'Think I give a shite? What've I got out here to worry about? No job, no money, I'm living with my brother and his cunt of a girlfriend, kids all over the place. I've got nothing to lose.'

140

'You can't –'

'Fucking watch me, fat lad.'

'Please, Clint, don't do this. You know I never did it.'

Renfrew laughed. 'So what? Place is full of blokes never did what they're in for.'

Phil felt the room closing in on him, a deep-buried claustrophobia making the walls curve and bend over him. He felt his chest tighten, thinking of Gemma, but more of himself. Banged up, trapped with men like Renfrew and worse.

'Less you wanna help me out.'

'OK, alright, yeah,' Phil said, mind racing. 'Look, you need a job, yeah? Why don't you come and work with me? You're pretty handy, aren't you?'

Renfrew nodded. 'Nice of you to offer, Phil. Always said you were a gent.'

The walls snapped back into place.

'Gonna need a sub on my wages though,' Renfrew said. 'This bling should cover it.'

Phil smiled uneasily. 'What? No, come on, don't fuck about.'

'Do I look like I'm fucking about? All of it. Now.'

'Clint. Mate –'

'Keep it if you like. But they'll take it off you when they arrest you.'

He was serious.

Phil undid the clasp on his chain with shaking fingers and dropped it into Renfrew's waiting hand.

'And the rest.'

'Come on, Gemma bought me these.'

'I'm being polite, Phil. Don't push me.'

He removed his sovereigns and the onyx pinkie ring Gemma had bought for their fifth anniversary. He remembered sitting up in bed opening it, the small velvet box wrapped in gold paper with spirals of ribbon and a big plastic bow. What had he bought her? His mind was blank, there was only Renfrew smiling at him with a chipped front tooth and an old scar twisting his philtrum.

'Can I keep my wedding ring?'

'Course you can, mate.'

Renfrew shoved the jewellery into the pocket of his denim jacket, closed the stud over it as he headed for the door. He turned back.

'I'll be in touch about the job.'

Phil walked out of the pub on weak legs, the pavement tilting beneath his feet, and he crossed Highbury Street without looking, only distantly aware of a car horn sounding. It could have been miles away.

His hand was shaking as he tried to fit the key in the lock and finally Gemma opened up, the verbal assault she looked ready to launch dying on her lips as he pushed past her.

'Phil, what's happened? Where's your rings gone?'

'Got mugged.'

'What?'

'Two blokes. They mugged me as I was coming out the pub.'

'We've got to call the police.'

'No. I don't want any fuss.'

'Did they hurt you?'

'I'm fine.'

Her hands were on his face, checking for damage.

'Were they foreign?'

'Yeah. No. Yeah, I think so.'

'I'm calling the police. They're not getting away with this.'

'Just leave it.'

'But –'

'I said leave it,' he shouted.

She shrank back, her hand at her throat.

He couldn't look at her any more. He ran upstairs and locked himself in the bathroom, didn't even bother turning on the light.

24

Andrus Tombak knew his rights. The minute he set foot in the interview room he demanded a drink and something to eat, said he wouldn't answer any questions without his solicitor present and gave them a number he had committed to memory, rattled it off like machine-gun fire.

Forty-five minutes later the solicitor arrived. Gone six but Mr Ahmal looked fresh as the proverbial in a sharp black suit and a white shirt with French cuffs pinned by bullet-shaped gold links. Despite Zigic's warning, Pickman Nye had come through for Tombak, sending someone from the firm on Priestgate they used. Not one of the partners, he wasn't that important, but there was a sharkish vibe around the young man which suggested he knew full well where the money to pay his bills was coming from and didn't much care if there was blood on it.

He asked for some time alone with his client and Zigic let him have it. No option either way.

In the office Wahlia was going through the paperwork from Pickman Nye, trying to piece together the Stepulov brothers' employment history – processing then packing then cleaning, no one job lasting very long, the usual story. Ferreira sat at her desk, one foot up on an open drawer, just waiting.

Zigic went into his office and called Anna, told her he'd be home late and that she should eat without him. He found a Mars bar squashed almost flat under the paperwork in his out tray and ate it over the bin, broken pieces of chocolate falling away from it. They should have stopped for food in Spalding but when he suggested it Ferreira said there was nowhere good and it was late and shouldn't they take a stab at Tombak straight away; did everything short of reach over and stamp down on the accelerator herself.

He threw the wrapper in the bin and went to get a Coke from the vending machine along the hall. If he put enough sugar in his system it would get him over the slump. He didn't need much, just an hour's energy to deal with Tombak, then he could go home, curl up on the sofa and sleep.

In the office he returned to Jaan Stepulov's board. The Barlows' pictures had taken on an opacity since yesterday and he felt he could safely remove them from the suspects column; underneath them Clinton Renfrew glowered out of his mugshot, more attitude than guilt, and only Andrus Tombak looked right for the position. Zigic untacked his photo and moved it to the top of the board.

'If Stepulov was so hell-bent on finding his brother, why's no one mentioned it?' Ferreira said, coming to stand next to him. 'Wouldn't he have told them at Fern House? They'd have helped him.'

'You'd have thought so.'

'I mean, I know we didn't ask them, but come on, it's a big deal, isn't it?'

'You think they're withholding?'

'Why would they?' She planted her hands on her hips. 'Maloney might know more than he let on, though.'

Zigic drank the last mouthful of his Coke and dropped the can in the bin. 'I don't think he was looking anything like as hard as the family think. He's been in Peterborough for three months; the city's not that big. And the woman Barlow saw him with, who was she?'

'A girlfriend. A prostitute maybe.'

'And he didn't even go home for Christmas. Who does that?'

'Someone who's left his wife,' Ferreira said. 'It's a bus ride away but he didn't go home for the holidays. He wasn't interested in seeing his daughter when she's about to drop a baby. That's family problems. I don't care what they say about the brother, that's something between them.'

Zigic thought of Mrs Stepulov standing dry-eyed in the kitchen,

144

knocking back the vodka and assassinating her brother-in-law's character. It could have been shock, she could be weeping for her husband now, wailing and rending her garments, pulling out her hair in clumps, but somehow he doubted it. She was emotionally detached already. Three months' estrangement would do it, he imagined, the tension of a Christmas celebrated without him.

'We need to find the brother,' he said. 'If Mrs Stepulov was telling the truth, and he was in fear of his life, then it has to be linked.'

'I've checked the records, November and December were quiet.'

'There's nothing suitable-looking?'

'No. A couple of domestics, arrests made, confessions stumped up. There's a double shooting in Bretton but that was almost definitely gang-related – CID know who they want but he's skipped the country. English guy, they think he's in Cyprus. They've got witnesses, DNA, the whole nine yards.'

Zigic heaved a sigh. The forty-eight-hour mark was coming up and it felt like they'd made no progress at all, just added another layer of impossible complication to the case.

'Bobby, have you found anything in Pickman Nye's paperwork?'

'It's a load of nothing,' Wahlia said. He looked tired out, purple shadows under his eyes and his usually perfect hair lying flat against his head. 'Tombak's had close to a hundred men through the house in the last year; some of them are still on with the agency but over half have dropped off the map.'

'Any of them in the system?'

'Couple of minor offences, drink-driving, driving uninsured. One of them's doing two years in Ashton for sexual assault but he was locked up months ago.'

'No wonder Harrington was so easy-going about handing it over.'

'Yeah, that should have tipped you off,' Ferreira said. She perched on the corner of her desk. 'Course, we could be looking in totally the wrong place. Raadik knew where Stepulov was, there's friction between them. Maybe he likes being the man of the house.'

145

'I think Mama Stepulov holds that position,' Zigic said. 'Did you check his prints?'

'Yeah, no match to the partials on the padlock, but we've already established how meaningless that is, haven't we?'

Zigic checked his watch; almost seven. Anna would be bathing the boys now, their pyjamas warming on the radiator while they soaked the bathroom floor. They'd be in bed by the time he got home, another evening he wouldn't see them and he felt a swell of resentment towards Jaan Stepulov for keeping him here.

'Alright, let's talk to Tombak if we're going to.'

The air in interview room 2 was thick with the brash, metallic scent of the solicitor's cologne. Ahmal had taken off his jacket and Zigic noted with vague distaste the stays he wore around his biceps, an old-school affectation which made him look exactly the kind of spiv he was. Tombak sat next to him, crumpled and bearded, picking at the remains of his chicken dinner, which bled grease through the cardboard container. He stuffed a limp chip in his mouth and grinned at Zigic as he closed the door.

'I hope this won't take very long, Inspector,' Ahmal said. 'My client has an early start tomorrow. And I'm sure you'd like to get home to your family.'

'Your client isn't going anywhere,' Zigic told him. 'He's assaulted a police officer and he's going to be charged with that.'

'My understanding was that your officer launched an unprovoked attack on Mr Tombak, despite his evident injuries.'

As if on cue Tombak rubbed the flesh above his cast.

'You entered his home without a warrant, I believe.'

'One of the residents invited us in,' Zigic said. 'Good luck proving otherwise.'

Ahmal smirked at him. All just a game; some rules you adhered to but most you could bend, and the only question was how far until they snapped and you had to invoke another one to get you out of trouble. Eighteen months ago one of Pickman Nye's drivers ran down a woman on a pedestrian crossing in the city centre, over the limit and using his mobile phone. The woman was paralysed from the waist down, her face shredded by the tarmac, but the arresting officer wasn't as careful with the paperwork as he should have been and Ahmal found enough to stop the CPS from prosecuting.

Ferreira set up the tapes and Ahmal uncapped his Mont Blanc, held it poised over a yellow legal pad, ready for action. Outside a rising wind buffeted the side of the building, throwing waves of rain against the obscure glass window high above their heads. Droplets found their way around the corroded metal frame and they dripped intermittently like an elaborate torture.

'Tell us about Jaan Stepulov,' Zigic said.

'Mr Tombak is more than happy to answer any questions you have,' Ahmal said, his hand coming down on the table. 'Questions, Inspector. Not vague statements.'

'Why didn't you want to press charges when Stepulov attacked you?'

'It was fair fight,' Tombak said, going for another chip.

'Which you came off second-best in.'

He shrugged.

'You must have felt pretty pathetic, getting beaten up so badly.'

Another shrug.

'Generally when someone refuses to press charges it's because they're intending to deal with the person themselves,' Zigic said. 'Or find someone to do it for them.'

'That isn't a question, Inspector.'

'Who did you pay to kill Stepulov?'

Tombak grinned at him, food between his teeth.

'You find them. You say I do this. Find them.'

Mr Ahmal cleared his throat noisily and Tombak's smile died. He was going off the agreed script, Zigic thought. Too arrogant and self-assured to listen to anyone's advice.

'Is joke,' Tombak said. 'You English like jokes.'

'Not when they're about murder.'

'Stepulov is dead. I am not sorry about this, but is nothing to do with me.'

'I find that rather hard to believe.'

'Until you have any evidence to the contrary you'll have to,' Mr Ahmal said. 'And from your questions I doubt you do have any evidence.'

Zigic brought out the photograph of Viktor Stepulov and pushed it across the scarred white tabletop.

'What is this?' Tombak asked.

'He's one of your former workers.'

Tombak picked up the photograph with greasy fingers and brought it close to his face, squinting slightly.

'I do not know him.'

'We've seen the records from Pickman Nye and we've spoken to the men at your house. This man was working for you and living with you. So there's no point denying it.'

Tombak glanced at Mr Ahmal and he gave the merest of nods.

'What is his name?'

'Viktor Stepulov.'

'He is this other one's brother?'

'That's right.'

Tombak peered at the photograph again, a ruminative expression on his face.

'Yes. Last year he worked for me. Only for few weeks.'

'Why did he leave?'

'He is greedy. Very arrogant man, always wanting more money, complaining that I do not find him good job.' Tombak threw the photograph down. 'What can I do? He is useless. He speaks no English. Ignorant Valga peasant.'

'Where did he go?'

'He did not tell me. He says he has found good job, I tell him go, you find idiot to pay you big money, go fuck yourself.'

'When was this?'

Tombak took another chip. 'You have records. You check. I cannot remember every man I am employing.'

'It was the beginning of October,' Zigic said.

'Why ask, you know already?'

'And nobody's seen Viktor since he left your house.'

Mr Ahmal spoke up then. 'We seem to have wandered off-topic, Inspector.'

'No, we're getting down to the heart of the matter now,' Zigic said. 'Jaan came to you because he was looking for Viktor. Viktor called him and said he was in fear of his life.'

'He is lying.'

'We have one brother murdered and another missing and the only connection was that they were working for you.'

'The only connection you know of,' Ahmal said.

Tombak looked sick suddenly and he couldn't meet Zigic's eye.

'It's a transient population,' Ahmal said, sounding less certain. 'You know how these men live, Inspector. They come and go on a whim.'

'What happened to Viktor?'

Tombak rubbed the skin above his cast, didn't reply.

'Did you fight with him too? Maybe you got the better of that brother.'

Tombak glared at him. 'I tell you, he went to new job.'

'Is that what you and Jaan were arguing over? He thought you'd killed Viktor?'

'No. He says nothing about Viktor.'

'But you knew they were related,' Zigic said, pressing on. 'Stepulov's not a common name. You knew they were brothers.'

'No.'

'Viktor calls home, frantic, terrified, so Jaan comes looking for him at your house but he's gone. What did you tell him about Viktor?'

'He asked nothing.'

'You're lying.'

Tombak turned to his solicitor. 'He cannot talk to me like this.'

'I think we've reached the point where I tell you to charge Mr Tombak or release him,' Ahmal said, recapping his fountain pen. 'And from the sound of things you don't actually have enough to charge him, so that only leaves one course of action, doesn't it?'

25

The last customer left just after 3 a.m, rolled out onto Westgate and promptly threw up in the gutter. A few minutes later Emilia heard him shouting and saw him arguing with a couple of taxi drivers from the rank across the road. The men shoved him roughly away, kicked him up the arse as he was going. He turned back to fight his corner but seemed to think better of it and walked off, still shouting, gesturing from a safe distance.

It had been that kind of evening. Two fights, one knife pulled, and a lot of broken glass to be cleaned up.

Emilia was numb to it all. She kept thinking of how close the police had been to her, that young woman and the tall Slavic man who must be her boss. Only the bar had been between them and she thought she would faint when he mentioned Jaan's name. She actually gasped when the young man said he was Jaan's son-in-law but the police seemed as surprised as she was and didn't notice. She was just another invisible East European cleaning up somebody else's mess, no need to worry about her.

Now her feet ached and her back hurt and she kicked off her heels while she finished clearing up. Maloney had gone to bed already and she noticed Olga had excused herself from duties, slipped off upstairs to attend to more important ones, leaving Sofia to lock up.

Somehow she got through the next half an hour and then she was pulling on her coat and fitting her feet back into her shoes, saying her goodnights and getting half-hearted responses.

Outside the air was crisp with coming frost and her breath bloomed in front of her when she released the sigh she'd been holding in her chest for what felt like hours.

A few people were out on the street, hanging around the kebab shop on the corner of Lincoln Road, a gang of men playing at fighting, throwing one another into the path of oncoming cabs from the rank outside John Lewis's back doors. Two girls, clinging to each other on their high spiked heels, came along Westgate, shivering without coats. A lone man, walking with his head tucked into his chest and his hands thrust in his pockets, followed them towards the locked-down bus station near the shopping centre.

Emilia's mobile rang as she climbed into the taxi and she gave the driver her address before she answered it.

'Where are you?' Skinner asked. 'Need some stuff off of you.'

'I have just left work.'

'Good, I'll come round yours.'

'No.'

'Look, love, you don't want me to come to the pub, you don't want me to come to your place. Frankly, I'm starting to feel a bit insulted, you know what I mean?' A lighter snickered at his end and she remembered the smell of tobacco on Skinner's breath as he moved on top of her, panting, gurning, his fingers in her hair. 'So, what d'you wanna do?'

She swallowed her revulsion.

'Come to mine,' she said and told him her address.

'Be half hour. Got a bit of business to finish up here.'

The cab dropped her at Rivergate. Most of the other flats were in darkness, and the corridor felt still and haunted as she let herself in. She switched on every light, chasing the ghosts out of the rooms, turned on the television, needing voices around her.

She threw her clothes in the hamper and showered quickly. The heat of the water started her thumb throbbing. There was something in there, stinging close to the cuticle. She examined it under the light above the bathroom mirror, could see nothing, but when she probed it with the tip of her tweezers she found a sliver of glass.

She gritted her teeth and pulled the glass out. Blood welled and she stuck her thumb in her mouth, tasting copper and soap.

She opened the medicine cabinet for a plaster and froze, looking at the bottles of cologne arranged neatly on the top shelf, more of them than any one man needed, his razor and shaving soap and the brush which was losing its bristles; not that he would ever use it again. His toothbrush was still in the holder above the sink, nestled close to hers, and she snatched it up suddenly and threw it in the bin.

His things were everywhere in the flat.

Emilia opened the wardrobe and his clothes confronted her like so many shed skins.

They would have to go, she thought, but as she ran her hand down the sleeve of his favourite blue-striped shirt, she wondered if that was such a good idea. Only a guilty person would throw his things out. If she was innocent she would be wearing one of his big sweatshirts, grieving over the smell of him.

She pulled on jeans and a thick jumper with a polo neck, not wanting Skinner to get any ideas, and went into the kitchen.

The intercom buzzed as she was pouring a stiff shot of vodka. She hit the button to let him in and necked her drink.

He was leaning against the wall when she opened up and he pushed his hoodie back off his bald head, straightened to his full five six and strolled in like he owned the place, looking through the open doors, nodding to himself.

'Nice set-up you got here, girl. Not what I was expecting. Not what I was expecting at all.' He sat down on the sofa, placed his messenger bag on the low glass coffee table and took out his laptop. 'Get us a drink, will you?'

'Beer or vodka?'

'You got Bud?'

Like she was at work.

'Yes.'

'That'll do.'

Emilia fetched it and put it on the table, retreated to the armchair near the window. Skinner had switched the television off and the room was so quiet she could hear her neighbour snoring through the paper-thin wall.

'What do we do?' she asked.

'Straight down to business, hey?' Skinner took a long drink of his beer. 'I need a photograph.'

She flipped through the menus on her mobile, found the one she wanted.

'This one.'

He looked at it for a couple of seconds, smiled, showing small, back-slanting teeth.

'Very attractive.'

He took a cable out of his bag and hooked her phone up to his laptop.

'This is going to cost you,' he said, as his fingers poked at the keyboard.

'I know this.'

'Two thousand.'

'I have it.'

'In cash.'

'What else would I pay with?' Immediately she regretted the question, seeing him leer at her across the top of the computer. 'When will it be ready?'

'You can have it Tuesday.'

'This is too long.'

'Try the passport office if you like,' Skinner said, going for his beer again. 'They can do it in twenty-four hours if you explain the rush. They're very accommodating.'

Emilia curled up in the armchair, pulled her cuffs over her knuckles.

'No, that's what I thought.'

He uncoupled her mobile and closed his laptop, stowed it away in the leather messenger bag again. He made no move to leave though, grabbed his beer and settled back in the sofa.

'You going home?' he asked.

'Yes.'

She thought of the little flat overlooking the chemical works. Her old bedroom with its ikons and faded floral wallpaper. Was her sister still there? Sleeping in the narrow wooden bed pushed under the eaves? She would be fifteen now and Emilia hoped Yulia was more sensible than her, stayed where she was safe. She hadn't spoken to her family for four years. The men who brought her over took her phone and kept her captive and she had an excuse not to contact them then. But she had been free a long time and the only reason not to call home was the fear that they would not want her back.

They had warned her not to come here. Her mother had told her what happened to girls who came to England to be waitresses. The cousin of a woman she worked with had lost her daughter that way, only found out what happened to her when the London police rang one morning, out of the blue, to tell them their girl had been found with her throat cut in a park.

The girl deserved it, Emilia's mother had said, for living how she had.

'Maloney won't be happy you're leaving,' Skinner said.

'He will find another girl.'

Skinner unbuckled his belt one-handed and started to pop the studs on his flies.

'Come on then,' he said. 'Might as well, since I'm here.'

FRIDAY

26

The building was taking shape now. Massive steel girders sticking up along two walls, a skeleton waiting to be filled in with heavy grey blocks and corrugated cladding. Paolo had worked on these places before but he didn't know what they became. Storage perhaps, or processing plants like the one he worked at in Spalding, standing at a conveyor belt in a refrigerated section, packing salad into bags destined for supermarkets and fast-food restaurants, inhaling the metal smell of the chemicals sprayed on them, his fingers numb in the thin plastic gloves which irritated his skin.

He had thought it was the worst job in the world back then, didn't last a week before the gangmaster had him pulled off and sent home again. Now he would do the job for nothing if it got him away from this hellhole.

They climbed out of the vans and stood around in loose groups, waiting for instructions.

The English were in a huddle around the boss's car, while he shouted at someone on the other end of his mobile.

One of the Chinese offered Paolo a cigarette and he hesitated a moment before accepting. But the man nodded, gestured at him with the packet and he took one, leaned in for the man to light it and thanked him in English, hoping he had picked up that word at least.

'You speak English?'

The Chinese man made a 'little' sign with his hand, said, 'How long you?'

'Six month,' Paolo said, showing him six fingers.

The man put his hand on his chest. 'Xin Gao.'

'Paolo.' He nodded to the other Chinese man. 'Your friend?'

'No. Malay. Not friend.'

'You came with another man,' Paolo said.

'He go today.'

'He left?'

'No. Go other men.'

They'd separated them then, Paolo thought. It was something the bosses did to stop you talking, sharing information. There was another Portuguese man on the site but Paolo had never worked on the same job as him.

Divide and conquer.

'When pay?' Xin Gao asked.

The English started towards them and Paolo shook his head slightly, telling Xin Gao not to speak any more, and he caught on, stepped away. They divided up the work with hand gestures and shoves, shouting at anyone who didn't move fast enough. It was unnecessary – they had been on the job for weeks, knew the procedure – but the English liked the sound of their own voices.

Paolo started loading out the long stretch of footing on the north side of the building, piling blocks into a barrow, a dozen at a time. He wheeled it from the loading bay to the wall where four men were working, bending over awkwardly, holding the heavy blocks two-handed and dropping them in place. Every now and again one of them would straighten up to stretch and a shout of 'back to work' would ring across the site from the boss, who was leaning against the front of his four-track, smoking and playing with his mobile phone.

On the other side of the building, two hundred feet away, he saw Xin Gao climb out of the trench, his clothes spattered with concrete.

That side of the building was still in the earth, steel spikes sticking up at regular intervals. Paolo had been put on that section originally and it was back-breaking work, driving the steels in with a weighty hammer, then fixing horizontal pieces over the tops, weaving it all together to make a mesh cage they would pour

160

concrete into later. He didn't have the strength in his arms and shoulders for it and he doubted Xin Gao would last the day. He was small and underweight, no muscle on his body.

They were the wrong kind of men for this work.

A concrete lorry arrived and parked on an area of hard standing a hundred metres away. Jakub and another man were dispatched to handle the hose, an awkward fat snake which they unfurled across the site and dropped into the footing where the steels were. The pump started up and the footing began to slowly fill, one of the English supervising.

They did little but that was one job they didn't trust to anyone else.

Paolo continued loading out. A couple of times the barrow tipped in the rutted black earth, spilling its blocks. The boss shouted at him to pick them up and he did it, thinking how satisfying it would be to take one of them and break it over his head, see him drop in a pool of blood.

The thought stilled his hands for a moment, so alien to him that it felt like another man's voice whispering in his head. He wasn't violent, had never been in a fight in his life, always the one to step in and play peacemaker. This job was changing him, reducing him to a set of animal impulses, sleep, eat, fight, and he added that to the list of reasons why he hated it.

The digger trundled past, one of the English driving it – another job they wouldn't trust to anyone else – and collected a beam from the stack in the loading bay. It hung precariously over the edges of the forked bucket and Paolo felt his whole body clench as it passed him, convinced it would drop and crush him. Part of him wanted it to but relief washed over him once it was gone, and he threw his weight behind the barrow.

Across the footing Xin Gao and the Malaysian man were dragging the concrete along the trench with long-handled rakes. The pump droned on, the sound of it drilling through Paolo's skull and making his eyes throb.

A shout went up and he saw Xin Gao standing with empty hands suddenly, looking into the footing where he must have dropped the rake. One of the English stormed over and Xin Gao shrank back. The man cuffed him around the head and Xin Gao gave a low bow, gesturing to the trench. The man hit him again and pointed away towards the loading bay.

Paolo quickly emptied the blocks and pushed the empty barrow across the quagmire, reaching the loading bay a few seconds after Xin Gao.

'You OK?'

He nodded but his eyes were shining with tears. There was a red mark on the side of his face.

'Where?' He mimed raking, not looking at Paolo.

'Here, look.' Paolo went over to the storage shed and found another rake for him.

Xin Gao mumbled a thank you and hurried away.

Paolo slammed the blocks into the barrow.

The unfairness burned him. They worked hard, they did everything they were told to, and yet they were treated with such disrespect. The English were animals. Not just these ones. They were making money from their behaviour, it was to be expected that they would act like tyrants, but the others, the ones who knew this went on and did nothing to stop it, they were no better. They wanted their old and their sick looking after, their offices cleaned and their factories building, but they wouldn't work like this.

He turned the barrow round and froze, seeing Xin Gao walk in front of the digger. He tried to shout but no sound came out.

The beam fell in slow motion, seeming to take forever to land, and he saw the end of it strike Xin Gao on the back, driving him into the mud.

Then he was running, screaming in English for someone to help.

The driver jumped down from the digger and the English converged on Xin Gao, while the rest of the men stood dumbly watching, tools in their hands, faces blank with shock.

'Get back to work,' the boss shouted.

Nobody moved.

Xin Gao was face down in the black earth, arms and legs splayed, the rake a few inches away from his hand. The beam lay across his lower back and Paolo retched at the sight of his flattened torso, bone sticking through his thin shirt, blood welling out of him, flowing fast and seeping into the ground.

'He's still alive.'

One of the English, a bald, fat one who wore gold rings like knuckle-dusters, grabbed the front of Paolo's jumper and shoved him away.

'Work. Now.'

'He needs hospital.'

'He's dead, you stupid cunt.'

Xin Gao's foot twitched.

'You take him to hospital.'

The man threw a short, straight punch at Paolo's face and blinding pain exploded in his head. He stumbled back and fell, tasting blood in his mouth, running down his throat. He tried to stand but his knees had turned to water.

Two of the English lifted the beam off Xin Gao's back and dropped it a few feet away from Paolo. They were going to help him, it was OK, it would be OK. He shouted to Xin Gao, told him they were taking him to hospital.

The English picked Xin Gao up, one taking his arms, the other his feet, and started to carry him towards the trench.

'On three.'

Paolo got to his knees. 'No!'

'One.'

They swung Xin Gao's body.

'Two.'

They couldn't do this.

'Three.'

They let go of him and Xin Gao landed in the wet concrete with a dull splash.

Paolo forced himself up, the world lurching and blurring as he stumbled over to the trench. There were hands on him but they didn't hold him back. The bald man grabbed the scruff of his neck and dragged him over to the edge of the footing.

'You see that?'

Xin Gao was sinking, impossibly slowly, into the concrete, his face submerged but the back of his head still visible.

'You wanna go in there with your boyfriend?'

Paolo's knees buckled and he was shoved to the ground. The man picked up the rake and pressed it against the back of Xin Gao's neck, forcing his head under the concrete, then his shoulders and his back.

The heels of Xin Gao's work boots sank into oblivion and Paolo heard himself praying softly. The bald man threw the rake into the trench and pulled Paolo to his feet.

'Now. You wanna go back to work or you wanna go in there? Your fucking choice.'

Paolo stared at him. Their faces were inches apart and he had never been so close to the man before, this thug, this murderer who controlled all of their lives and now decided on their deaths too. He looked ordinary, like a million other men, bald and pale-skinned, heavy around the jowls and with bags under his eyes. His breath smelled of tobacco and coffee and one of his front teeth was chipped. There were broken veins around his nose, a few long hairs poking from his nostrils. He had just murdered Xin Gao but his expression was neutral, his voice perfectly even.

'Well? What's it to be, big man?'

'Work,' Paolo stammered.

'Get to it then.'

The man pushed him away and turned a slow circle, aware that he still had an audience. 'Any of you other fuckers got summat to say?'

They couldn't understand him. Not the words, but the gesture required no translation. Heads dropped, feet shuffled in the dirt, and one by one the men went back to their tasks.

'That's what I thought.'

Somehow Paolo walked away, his feet taking him back across the ridged ground to the loading bay where the barrow full of blocks was waiting for him. There was blood in his mouth, but he swallowed it, and his hands moved of their own volition, lifted the barrow and pushed it ahead of him.

Why did nobody do anything? Why was he the only one to act?

There were five English and twenty of them. What were they so scared of that they were content to stand by and watch one of their own murdered?

They were broken. He knew that. Knew that he was broken too or he would have gone to the storage shed and taken out one of the big lump hammers they used to drive in the steels and hit the bald English with the cold blue eyes. He couldn't trust the others to follow him though.

When he returned to the loading bay he didn't even look at the shed. He just got on with his job, numbly placed more heavy, grey blocks in the barrow, deaf to the sound of them slamming down, not even feeling their rough texture any more. The site had fallen silent to his ears and everything look flat and unreal, the colour bleached out of every surface, the air sluggish and so thick he could hardly breathe.

Around him the other men kept their heads down. He was marked now and they didn't want the taint on them too.

The bald man could have pushed him into the wet concrete and held him down with the rake until he drowned and nobody would have helped. He would have died unmourned among strangers.

Tomorrow it might happen. Or the day after that.

He had to get out.

165

27

Zigic was up just after six, needing to clear another fitful night's sleep out of his head before the day began. He stretched his calves against the low stone wall in front of the house, taking deep lungfuls of icy dawn air, feeling the chill sharpening him already.

He stuck in his earphones and selected a Radio Moscow playlist the right length for the route he would take around Castor Hanglands – fifty minutes if he ran it flat out. The groin pull which had been plaguing him for months had eased in the last couple of days; Anna took the credit, said it was her healing hands, nothing to do with the stretches his physio had recommended.

Behind him it was still dark but the sky was lightening across the fens and he ran towards it, out of the village along the Helpston Road where a few houses showed life already, commuters who had to make the six twenty train into King's Cross, light sleepers or night workers getting ready to turn in.

At the edge of the village he passed a girl walking a vicious little Jack Russell which yapped at him as he ran past; she yanked on its lead and tugged it after her, in no mood to be up so early, Zigic thought, judging by the pyjamas she wore under her brown tweed coat.

Half a mile ahead of him, on the straightest stretch of Heath Road, he saw another runner, a flash of white gone round a curve within seconds.

He caught sight of her again as he crossed the strip of grassland towards Wild Boar Coppice and wondered how any woman could plunge into that isolated tangle alone, at this time of morning, and not worry about her safety.

The Hanglands were notorious for attacks during the seventies and eighties and Zigic knew they had a dozen or so unsolved ones on the books still. They'd arrested a man last autumn for the murder of a young woman whose body had been found in the spinney he was running through now. A shallow grave and thirty years with no resolution for her family.

Zigic pushed on. The track was soft and yielding from last night's rain and it dragged at his feet, making his muscles burn. He focused on his breathing, the music in his ears and the woman's white top pulling away from him.

In a few weeks the Hanglands would be thick and green but for now it was a mass of knotted brown hedgerows with a sparse dressing of last year's dead leaves clinging tenaciously on. There were buds on the hawthorn trees, he noticed, and the buck-thorns were tinged green here and there. He might bring Stefan up to pick sloes this autumn if the crop was good. He'd gone at that age, dragged out by his grandfather. He remembered hating every second of it but Stefan was a different kind of kid to how he'd been, always out in the garden, elbow-deep in the compost pile.

He crossed a clearing where half a dozen ewes were penned off waiting to give birth. He'd wanted to take the boys to Sacrewell Farm to see the lambing but Anna had vetoed that, sure it would warp them in some deep and irrevocable way.

The woman in front of him was getting nearer and he decided he was catching up rather than her dropping back.

They went through Lady Wood, the water tower standing ominously to the north, grey and monolithic, the pair of them in step now, the distance between them stabilised at eighty yards. Zigic checked his watch, behind time but doing well, and no pain in his groin yet.

The track would split off soon and he decided that whatever way she went he would follow, a feeling in his gut that they might not be the only people out there this morning.

She went on straight, taking the longest route, leading him

through another clearing, sprays of snowdrops and wood anemones in the long grass, dozens of felled trees with their branches stripped stacked in neat piles, and Zigic caught the briefest glimpse of a roe deer as it sprang out from behind one, a blur of rust-red hide before it disappeared into the undergrowth.

His mobile vibrated in his pocket and he slowed to a jog to work it out.

'Yeah?'

'Have I called at an inopportune moment?' Ferreira asked. 'You sound a bit breathy.'

'Running. What is it?'

'I think we've got a lead on Vlktor Stepulov.'

'Great. Where is he?'

'Hinchingbrooke mortuary. I got a – the photograph –'

'You're breaking up, Mel.'

' – like him –'

'The signal here's rubbish. Are you at the station?'

'No, I'm –'

The call cut dead and he swore at his handset and the trees and the lack of mobile phone masts. Everyone complained about them in the countryside but where were they when you needed one?

He cut across a clearing on Ailsworth Heath, went over a fence into a section of field where a few sheep were penned up, a ram among them, but he sprinted off before it decided to charge him and vaulted the fence at the other side, getting onto the track alongside the old Roman road which took him back down to the main drag within ten minutes.

It was busier now and he saw a couple of cars parked up near the entrance to Wild Boar Coppice, people out dog walking, seven o'clock approaching, the day starting for real.

Home, he stripped off his sweaty running gear off and jumped in the shower, starting to build a plan of action in his head. Someone would need to go to the mortuary, they would have to get a positive

ID – how did Hinchingbrooke even know that was Viktor Stepulov? Bloody cranky phone signal.

Anna opened the shower door and stepped in with him. He protested, told her he didn't have time and he was knackered from the run, but she just smiled and kissed him, one hand in his hair and the other on his cock, found an energy reserve he didn't know he had and charmed it out of him.

Afterwards she went down to make breakfast and by the time he was dressed the boys were at the kitchen table, squabbling over their boiled eggs and soldiers, and he grabbed a quick slice of toast which he ate while he drove, listening to the local news on the radio; no mention of Stepulov's death now. There would be another spike of interest when they formally identified him but no one was much bothered about a dead migrant worker.

In the office he cleaned the coffee machine, dumped yesterday's filter in the bin and started a fresh pot with the last few spoons left in the bag. Ferreira arrived as the final drops came through, tired-looking, her hair scraped into a greasy ponytail and a too-bright lipstick which dulled her tan skin.

'Rough night?'

'A late one,' she said.

He handed her a coffee and asked what she had on Viktor Stepulov.

'I sent his details out to the local hospitals, thought maybe he'd had an accident or something. Hinchingbrooke got back first thing – and I mean first thing – they've got an unclaimed corpse that matches his description.'

'Did he have ID on him?'

'No. Nothing. They're waiting on a copy of the photograph we got from the family.' She booted up her computer, the start music jangling. 'I'll send it now, should have an answer pretty quick.'

'How long have they had him?'

'Twelve weeks.'

'No wonder Stepulov couldn't find him.'

Ferreira stabbed at the keyboard for a minute, then sat back, holding her cup between her hands, inhaling the steam.

'You want to guess how he died?'

'A fire?'

She shook her head. 'He was hit by a train. The body's in pieces apparently. They've got most of them, which is something I guess, but he was spread along half a mile of track. The head was undamaged though. Weird how that happens.'

Zigic dropped into a chair on the other side of the desk, a sudden weariness coming over him. They needed Viktor alive. Whatever Jaan Stepulov was killed over seemed inextricably linked with his brother and now there would be no information from that quarter. Last night, lying in bed, staring at a shaft of moonlight cutting up the ceiling, he had begun to wonder if Jaan had found Viktor after all. And the idea had taken hold, a sinuous voice in the darkness, persuading him that Viktor was the nub of this, Viktor who didn't want to be found, who had always been trouble, always looking for a quick way to make money, dirty or clean. Wasn't it possible that Jaan had found him and they argued, over something or nothing the way brothers did, and maybe Viktor was their murderer?

This morning he was going to add him to the suspects column. So much for that idea.

'Where did they find the body?'

Ferreira was rolling a cigarette and she plucked a strand of tobacco from her tongue before she answered. 'One of the crossings on Holme Fen.'

'What was he doing out there? It's the back end of beyond.'

Holme Fen was a desolate spread of black farmland, thousands of acres cut by narrow, winding roads, with deep ditches on either side, fringed by bulrushes, and isolated farmhouses surrounded by crumbling outbuildings and paddocks where a few mangy horses waited for the end. There was a village with around a hundred homes, but it wasn't the kind of place many migrant workers washed up in, and the pub near the main railway crossing was all farmers and shooting parties; someone like Viktor Stepulov would have been made instantly unwelcome, Zigic guessed.

The second crossing was buried deep in the fen, off the main roads, in a patch of ancient woodland. There was a farm nearby, he thought, but was sure it was derelict. Why would Viktor be there? Miles away from Peterborough. December; not much to be done in the fields, cutting celery perhaps.

'He must have been working around there somewhere.'

'The nearest site I can think of's in Gidding,' Ferreira said.

They'd investigated a stabbing there a couple of years ago and Zigic remembered the ramshackle farmhouse the gangmaster lived in, a dozen caravans in the field next to it, dirty, broken-looking things up on breeze blocks, net curtains at the windows and washing lines strung between them. When they arrived the gangmaster had their murderer locked up in an old outhouse, badly beaten and covered in the dead man's blood.

Ferreira's computer pinged and she flicked her cigarette out of the window quickly, came back to check her email.

A wide smile cracked her face.

'Got him.'

28

Zigic offered to collect Mrs Stepulov from home but she insisted she would drive herself, there was no point him coming all the way over to Spalding to go all the way back, she said. Her voice betrayed nothing when he told her they needed her to formally identify her brother-in-law's body and when he met her in the cafeteria at Hinchingbrooke hospital he found her calmly flicking through a magazine, a cup of tea on the table in front of her.

'How did he die?' she asked, as they rode the lift down to the basement.

'He was hit by a train.'

'Drunk again. Stupid man.'

The doors opened onto a chilly white corridor with lino the colour of offal and strip lights encased in mottled Perspex. A moth was trapped inside one of them, batting furiously against the heat of the bulb, the sound very loud in the hush. The scent of pine cleaning fluid was sharp in the air and Mrs Stepulov wrinkled her nose at it.

'Did Jaan know about this?'

'No,' Zigic said. 'He couldn't have.'

Their footsteps echoed along the corridor and Zigic became aware of her pace slowing as they approached the silver swing doors. She switched her handbag from one shoulder to the other and straightened her quilted jacket. She wore a light pink uniform underneath, a name tag on her chest from the nursing home at which she worked. In the cafeteria she had said they'd told her to take as long as she needed. They weren't paying her to be away, what did they care?

'Last night I think Viktor maybe . . .' She stopped dead.

'What, Mrs Stepulov?'

She shook her hair out of her eyes. 'I think maybe he kill Jaan.'

'That's not possible. Viktor's been dead three months.'

She looked at her feet, pressed her lips together and for a few long seconds her face held an unreadable expression. It would have been an unpleasant explanation, but understandable, and Zigic imagined she was stuck now, between relief and fresh uncertainty. Everyone wanted closure in these situations, no matter what the immediate emotional cost.

'I am ready,' she said finally.

There was a small lounge next to the mortuary, pale green walls and a two-seater sofa with hard cushions, a low coffee table with a vase of plastic flowers and an empty tissue box in front of it. A flat screen hung on the opposite wall. It could have been anywhere if it wasn't for the atmosphere, a strange, airless quality created by all of those moments of held breath and hope and then the screen would come to life and you would see a corpse on it, breaking the thin illusion of normality.

'Could you wait here please, Mrs Stepulov?'

'We are not going to see Viktor?'

'The identification is done on-screen,' Zigic said. 'You don't have to see the body. If you want to you can, but there's no need.'

'I want to see.'

He nodded. 'If you could wait though, I have to talk to the attendant first.'

She perched on the edge of the sofa, handbag clasped on her knees, back very straight.

Zigic went into the mortuary. It was still and empty, the same pine scent so thick he could taste it, but there was another smell here, stronger than it could mask, meat and shit and chemicals, and Zigic was half convinced he was imagining it because the bodies were all stowed away and every surface was sparkling clean.

He went to the office, the door standing open.

The attendant was a gangly young man with red hair standing spiked on his head and heavily freckled skin. He had his earphones in, bleeding tinny music while he played some game on his computer, entirely absorbed by it.

Zigic rapped on the door. Nothing.

You probably shouldn't sneak up on people who worked in mortuaries, he thought, and pounded the door again, hard enough to get attention this time.

The young man swivelled away from his desk and pulled out his earphones. He was wearing a T-shirt with 'Capitalism Kills' printed across the front.

'What can I do you for?'

'Detective Zigic. You spoke to my colleague earlier.'

'You're here for the train man?' He stood up, stuck his hand out. 'Chris. We've been wondering when someone would come for him. Real mess. Mess like you wouldn't believe. But you step in front of a train it's not going to be pretty, is it?'

'The sister-in-law wants to see the body.'

'Why?' He went over to the bank of stainless-steel drawers, twenty of them, humming softly and chilling the air. 'Does she want to make sure he's dead or something?'

'You better tone this shit down when she comes in.'

'Alright, I'm a professional, you know.'

'Act like one then.'

He opened one of the drawers, pulled it halfway out. Viktor Stepulov made an odd shape inside the body bag, flattened and incomplete-looking.

'How much of him's in there?'

'Everything they managed to scrape up. The head's totally intact, you'd never guess what happened to him. You want to take a look before you bring her in?'

Zigic gestured for him to open it up and braced himself for the worst. He'd seen the result of enough car crashes to know the human body didn't come out of them well, and despite what Chris said he was expecting damage. Mortuary workers were a sadistic breed.

'See what I mean?'

Viktor Stepulov's head was almost untouched. His skin had taken on the usual waxy cast and his eyelids were held closed with tape but if that was all he'd seen Zigic would have guessed he'd died without violence. Then he looked lower, saw a right shoulder but not a left one and the abrupt termination below his collarbone, the wound raw and uneven, a mess of purple and red and very white bones splintered and shattered.

'Let's see the rest of him.'

Chris pulled the drawer out further, unzipped the bag the rest of the way.

Viktor Stepulov had been reassembled as far as possible but there were gaps and his body reminded Zigic of a skeleton in an anatomy class, hung together but disconnected. The rest of his right arm was there, the left one cleanly severed, wiry black hair on it, an old scar above the elbow. Most of his torso was missing and what they'd recovered of his hips and stomach was badly damaged, twisted and cracked, pulp held together by skin, coils of slick intestines. His legs were relatively unscathed though, thick and powerful-looking until you reached the left shin. The bone was broken and it stuck out through his skin at a forty-five-degree angle, somehow more painful-looking than everything else. The flesh around it was swollen up and tinged with incipient bruising.

'This didn't happen when the train hit him,' Zigic said. 'The bruising looks hours old.'

'That's probably why he couldn't get out of the way. Breaks his leg, drags it after him . . . you're not going anywhere very fast like that.'

'What did the pathologist make of it?'

'He's not been PM'd,' Chris said. 'He was hit by a train.'

'Well, what about the coroner's report?'

'Off the top of my head? Are you serious?'

Zigic swore under his breath, took a final look at the break in Viktor Stepulov's leg, wondering how that got overlooked.

'Alright, make this presentable. I'll fetch Mrs Stepulov.'

He returned to the small green lounge and she gathered herself slowly. She had removed her quilted jacket in the overheated room, and she folded it carefully over her arm before she left, walking with a firm step and a hard expression on her face, steeled for what was to come.

Zigic paused with one hand on the door. 'I should warn you, Viktor's body is – it isn't complete, do you understand?'

'He is hit by train, of course I understand. I am nurse, you think I don't see these things?'

She shoved through the doors and went straight to the open drawer. Viktor's head was the only thing visible now, the body bag zipped tight up to his jaw.

'Yes. This is Viktor.' She turned to Zigic. 'Why is he here? Where did he die?'

'On Holme Fen.'

'Where is this?'

'A few miles outside Peterborough,' Zigic said. 'Did he know people there?'

'I do not know.'

'Did he mention a job there maybe? Did Jaan?'

She shook her head. 'We do not know this place.'

There was paperwork to sign and she signed it in a flowing hand, businesslike and unquestioning, but as they left she asked to see Viktor one more time and when the bag was unzipped she hesitated for moment, then placed her hand on his forehead and gently kissed his eyes.

29

It was the quietest Ferreira had ever seen Maloney's. Quarter past ten and only a few of the tables were taken, men who looked like they'd just got off a coach, drinking beers and eating fry-ups off massive oval plates. The smell of bacon and sausages filled the place, good enough to make her think she could force something down herself.

Maloney was sitting alone at his regular corner table, studying a copy of the *Racing Post*, a pot of coffee on a tray in front of him and a cigarette smoking itself on a saucer. So much for the ban.

The girls were doing all of the work, shuttling between the kitchen and the customers, clearing away plates and wiping down the tables, a couple of them restocking the fridges behind the bar while a third, a new girl she thought, dusted the rows of optics, making sure they sparkled.

Maloney glanced up as a fruit machine paid out in a riot of clank and jangle, a look of annoyance flitting across his face. He noticed Ferreira then and waved her over.

'Got any tips for me?' she asked, pointing at his paper.

'You don't want to get started on this game, Sergeant. She'll bleed you white.' He closed the paper and folded it neatly in half, took off his gold-rimmed reading glasses. 'Any news on Stepi?'

'We're getting there.' Ferreira sat down on one of the blue velveteen stools.

Maloney whistled sharply. 'Olga, bring the sergeant a cup, there's a good girl. I heard you arrested Andrus Tombak.'

'Is there anything you don't hear, Maloney?'

'We're the centre of Peterborough society,' he said, that infuriating glimmer in his eye. 'Tombak's a piece of work, wouldn't be at all surprised if he was behind it. Wouldn't get his hands dirty of course, man hasn't got the graft in him to kill someone. Be one of his workers.'

'You want to give me a name?'

'Just speculating.'

They were running the records of Tombak's tenants, but it was slow going, foreign police forces to deal with, obscure protocols and strange working hours, the language barrier not so much of an issue as they feared, but the list was long and already Wahlia had identified two men who were in England on stolen passports, the original owners still in the old country, minding their own business, when Stepulov was murdered.

Olga came over and placed a cup and saucer on the table, poured coffee from the pot without being told and asked Maloney if there was anything else, an edge in her voice which made him grin. Then he slapped her on the backside and told her to put the big screen on.

'She's a diamond that one,' he said, watching her walk away. 'Grandmother sold her to a couple of Kosovans – you imagine such a thing? Old mare wanted a few more acres of land to graze her goats on and these fellas said they'd see her right. Fourteen years old she was, a child.'

'Where did you find her?' Ferreira asked.

'Your lot cleared her out of a whorehouse in Paston year before last. She came in here after a job.' He picked up his cigarette, knocked ash off the tip. 'I took one look at those big blue eyes . . . what was I going to do? Couldn't see her out on the street. Five minutes she'd be in the same state with some evil bastard or other. Peterborough's a veritable Sodom and Gomorrah these days.'

Ferreira almost managed it. She took a mouthful of coffee to try and scald the words off her tongue, swallowed it, reminding herself that she needed Maloney, she couldn't afford to antagonise him. In her head she heard Zigic telling her to stay quiet.

The cup chimed against the saucer.

'So, she's not whoring here?'

Maloney took a long draw on his cigarette, squinted at her through the smoke. 'She is when she wants to. But that's between her and the clients. I don't take a penny off her, or any of them, since you're asking.'

'That's a very enlightened approach.'

'I'm a safe haven, Sergeant. It might not sound like much to you but these girls appreciate it.' He leaned back in his chair and the wood creaked, his gut bulging against the candy-striped shirt which was too young for him.

Ferreira wondered if one of his girls had chosen it, pictured him trailing around John Lewis behind Olga, while she picked things off the racks and held them up to him, telling him how handsome he would look, that blue really suited him. In Olga's position what would she do? In a heartbeat she knew the answer, exactly the same thing. Maloney would extract his payment but he was good value in comparison to what the girls were used to. And how often could he manage it now anyway? Pushing sixty, overweight, it would be touch and go every time, whether he came or had a stroke.

'I'm sorry.'

Maloney waved it away. 'You wouldn't be doing your job if you didn't disapprove. The world's a cold place though, never forget that.' He offered her a cigarette and when she declined took one for himself. 'Tombak, then? Don't know what I can tell you you won't already have gathered.'

'I'm not here about Tombak.' Ferreira slid the photograph of Viktor Stepulov across the table. 'Do you recognise him?'

Maloney put his reading glasses back on and studied the photo-graph with his chin tucked into his neck. 'Rare-looking fella.'

'It's Jaan's brother.'

'I couldn't swear to it but I reckon he came in here now and again. Kept to himself.' He put the photograph down again, went for his cigarette. 'Are you after arresting him?'

'Jaan was looking for him, he'd disappeared,' Ferreira said. 'He didn't mention this to you?'

'We didn't have that sort of conversation. The football, the weather. He played a hand or two of dominoes with us, there were no heart-to-hearts.'

'But you're the centre of Peterborough society,' Ferreira said. 'When I'm looking for someone I come and ask you. Jaan must have realised his brother might come in.'

'Might be why he spent so much time in here. Do you want to see if the girls recognise him?'

Before Ferreira could answer Maloney called them over and as they formed a cluster near the table she realised how similar they looked, eight pale, petite blondes of various nationalities, none above twenty-five, none above nine stone, all with the same watchful expression in their over-made-up eyes. These were women who'd been under the boot, alive to every slight shift in a man's temperament and aware of the price of misreading them.

'Sergeant Ferreira wants you to look at this photograph.' He passed it to Olga.

'His name's Viktor Stepulov,' Ferreira said, watching the photo move between their hands, cheap rings and gleaming nail polish. 'He might have been calling himself something else. Do any of you recognise him?'

Quiet 'nos', head shaking, disinterest.

'He's Estonian, from Tallinn. Are any of you Estonian?'

Maloney answered for them. 'Emilia is.'

The girl holding the photograph looked quickly between Maloney and Ferreira, then dropped her gaze, nodded. She looked about eighteen, sharp features and a gamine haircut, barely five foot tall in her black patent hooker heels.

The others strode back to their work and Ferreira asked Emilia to sit down.

'You mind, Maloney?'

'Go and call my bookie.' He picked up his *Racing Post*. Emilia, you answer Sergeant Ferreira's questions, no silly business now, you hear.'

Ferreira waited until he was out of earshot before she spoke.

'How well did you know Viktor?'

'He came to see me a few times.' Emilia recrossed her legs, turned her body away, arms folded over her boyish chest. 'I think he is lonely. We talk about home.'

'What about work?'

'Sometime yes. He tells me I am too good for this place.'

'And his work?'

'He is angry that there is no good jobs here. He is – what is word? With wood? He make things with wood?'

'A carpenter.'

She nodded. 'He tell them at agency he can do this and they give him work in factory packing salad. It is not a good job. Very bad pay. Many chemicals you breathe.'

'When was the last time you saw Viktor?'

Her gaze slid across the table, the lip-stained cups and the coffee pot, the ashtray overflowing with butts. 'I have not seen since in last year. He come here, want to go up to room but when we go and I ask him for money he says he has none.'

'Did you still sleep with him?' Ferreira asked.

'I am not girlfriend. I tell him this and he is sad, he says he is going to start new job and he will be gone for some months. He says he will miss me.' Emilia looked down at her fingers, started to pick at the ink-blue varnish on her thumbnail. 'He tells me when he comes back he will pay.'

'But you've heard that one before?'

Emilia smiled with faint humour. 'He is nice. Gentle. I give him handjob as goodbye.'

A group of Englishmen in suits and ties came into the pub, their voices crashing ahead of them, all fake bonhomie and work-speak, trailing a metallic-tinged cloud of aftershave and body spray. They beelined for the bar and Emilia glanced over nervously, shifting on the stool to get up.

'I should help.'

'We're nearly done,' Ferreira said. 'Where was Viktor's new job?'

'London. He was going to build the Olympics.'

The words sprang up like a brick wall. It was the kind of lie a man like Viktor would tell, especially to Emilia, self-aggrandising and vague at the same time. Either that or he was making a very long commute from Holme Fen. Not impossible, but unlikely.

'Did he get the job through an agency?' Ferreira asked.

'No. He has a friend who is looking for good workers.'

'From back home?'

'No, an Englishman,' Emilia said. Again she looked to the bar and Ferreira realised why she was so impatient, watching the suity boys jangling their change, eyeing the other girls; Emilia saw revenue going elsewhere. 'What has Viktor done?'

'He died just over a month ago. Hit by a train.'

'That is very sad,' Emilia said flatly. 'He was nice man.'

Ferreira wondered if they would find anyone who cared that he was dead. What was it about the Stepulov brothers which provoked such cold ambivalence?

She took the photograph of Jaan out of her pocket. 'This is Viktor's brother. Jaan. He drank in here quite regularly . . .'

'Yes.'

'He's dead too.'

'Yes, I hear this.'

'And you don't find that strange?' Ferreira asked. 'Two brothers, dying so close together?'

Emilia shrugged. 'People die.'

'Jaan was looking for Viktor when he was murdered. He came in here looking for him. He must have asked you girls if you'd seen him?'

'No.'

'You're Estonian though, he would have asked you even if he didn't talk to the others.'

182

'No.'

Ferreira decided to wing it. 'A young woman matching your description was seen visiting Jaan a few days before he died.'

'It was not me.'

'Jaan was squatting in a shed on Highbury Street.'

'I tell you. I do not know him.' Emilia stood up and smoothed her hands over her hips, straightening her short black skirt. 'Can I go?'

'Jaan and Viktor were involved with very bad people, Emilia. Now they're both dead. If you know something you'd do well to tell me.'

'I tell you all I know.'

For a second they looked at each other and Ferreira scrutinised her face, but it was locked down and implacable, an expression honed over the course of a hard life. Finally she told her to go and watched her return to the bar. Emilia found a professional smile for the men waving notes at her, poured their drinks and took their compliments, and when she glanced back at Ferreira, some minutes later, there was only the vaguest trace of unease around her mouth.

30

How long would the policewoman sit there watching her?

Emilia held her hand steady as she pulled a pint of bitter for the loud Englishman in the cheap suit, eyes lowered, focusing on the pump like she had never done it before. She felt a flush creep up her cheeks and hoped her foundation would hide it.

'Ah, you're blushing,' the man said, laughter in his voice, proud that he'd got a reaction from her. 'But you are, I'm serious, you're really pretty. You should be a model.'

'Thank you.' She dug deep and found a smile, one of the fake, plastic ones men like him couldn't tell from the real thing.

She wondered if any woman had ever been genuinely delighted by him. This ugly man with his bad skin and receding hairline, so full of himself to think she should be flattered by his approval.

She placed his pint on the bar.

'Three pounds eighty.'

He placed four coins in her hand. 'Keep the change, sweetheart.'

Emilia went to the till, her movements automatic, all the while watching the policewoman out of the corner of her eye, seeing her sip her coffee, looking to the bar across the rim of the cup. She slammed the drawer back harder than she meant to, making the glasses near it jingle against each other.

'Who is next?'

She served more customers, concentrating on the sound of their voices, wanting to appear unshaken as she drained vodka from the optics and opened bottles of beer. She pulled pints and made coffee and took orders for all-day breakfasts, enquired after the health of the regulars and smiled through more stupid, repetitive compliments, and when she finally looked back to Maloney's regular table the policewoman was gone and he was back in his rightful place, reading the newspaper.

Very bad people, she had said. As if she knew what those words meant.

Had she been burned with cigarettes and bitten until she bled, fucked so hard she couldn't walk for a day? Did she spend her seventeenth birthday servicing men old enough to be her grandfather on a stained mattress in a locked room in a country she wished she'd never come to?

No. She knew nothing of *very bad people.*

Olga tapped her on the shoulder. 'Clear the tables.'

Emilia went out onto the floor and began gathering empties, trying to avoid the places where people's mouths had been. Not wanting their spit on her fingers. She filled one tray and placed it on the bar, filled a second, feeling eyes moving over her, appraising her.

She could appraise them too; that bull-necked Latvian with the baby dick, the Bulgarian who could only get it up with the light switched off. If they knew how the girls laughed about them they would never dare to show their faces.

Viktor she didn't joke about with the others. He was the gentlest man she'd ever been with and she hated herself for speaking of him so dismissively to the policewoman. But what alternative did she have? She couldn't tell her the truth.

Emilia felt her eyes beginning to prickle.

Not now, not here. She couldn't let them see her crying.

The pub was getting busier, lunch hour drawing closer, the crowd thickening. Through the glass wall at the back she saw a coach pull into the car park and knew she would be expected to go upstairs soon. The men came in flush with the cash they had saved to get themselves set up, but the journey was a long one and their balls spoke louder than their brains, demanding to be emptied before they could concentrate on finding their contacts in this strange, new city.

Viktor had come in like that, one day last spring, crumpled from the bus, all enthusiasm, and every day for the last four months she expected him to come in again. At some point the expectation gave way to dim hope and finally she realised she would never see him again.

And then there was Jaan.

She put another tray of empties on the bar.

'Emilia, love,' Maloney shouted. 'A drink when you're ready.'

Meaning now.

She went behind the bar and poured him a whiskey from his special bottle, took it over to his table and placed it on a beer mat. He caught her wrist as she moved away.

'What did the sergeant want?'

'Nothing.'

'Come on now, she never talked to you all that time over nothing.'

'She thinks I know these dead men.'

'But you told her you didn't.' His grip tightened on her wrist. 'If you've gone and gotten yourself involved in something you shouldn't . . .'

'I fuck them,' she said, making her voice hard and cold. 'What else am I good for?'

Maloney let go of her, picked up his glass.

'Clean your face, darling, you look like something the cat threw up.'

Emilia strode away quickly, through the door marked Staff Only and up the back stairs to the rooms above the bar where they brought their clients. Behind a closed door she heard a man grunting, the girl he was with encouraging him on, trying to talk him into coming quickly.

She went into the bathroom and locked the door. She could still feel Maloney's fingers on her wrist and she rubbed the red marks, tears springing into her eyes.

Viktor was dead, and crying would change nothing.

She had to think of herself now.

Somehow they knew she was involved. She had suspected as much and now she knew for certain. She needed to get away before they worked out just how deeply.

She took her mobile out of her tabard and dialled, listening for footsteps in the hallway. All she could hear was the couple in the room opposite and the sound of music from the bar pounding up through the floorboards.

'Yeah?'

'It is Emilia.'

'I told you it wouldn't be ready until Tuesday,' Skinner said. 'I don't just pull this stuff out my arse, you know? There're protocols.'

'But I need it today.'

'No can do,' he said.

In the background she could hear screaming; he was watching a film, she realised. Nobody screamed like that in real life, no matter what happened to them.

'And the price has gone up.'

'What? No, we agree price,' she said. 'You cannot do this.'

'Think you'll find I just did.'

'Why?'

'You know full fucking well why, so don't come the innocent,' he said. 'It's Tuesday and it's five hundred extra.'

Emilia fell against the door. 'I do not have five hundred.'

'Why don't you ask your boyfriend for it?' Skinner said, and she could see that shark smile.

'I have no boyfriend.'

'Better get back to work then, hadn't you?'

He killed the call.

31

Glebe Farm sat huddled in a shallow basin at the western edge of Great Gidding, far enough from the village that no one would complain about the caravans or the bright orange shipping containers which looked fit for the scrapyard.

Zigic turned off the main road onto a rough track peppered with waterlogged potholes, slowing to five miles an hour to save the car's suspension. The fields on either side of him lay fallow, a couple of forlorn shire horses in one, a dozen mangy sheep in another, no cover for them to shelter from the rain, which drilled down relentlessly, threatening to become hail.

He heard guns going off at a distance and wondered who would be out in such filthy weather.

The bottom end of the track was blocked off with a solid metal gate hanging from stone posts. A new addition since he'd been there last. He swore as he got out of the car, hunched his shoulders against the rain and hit the intercom.

'What?'

'Is that Mr Drake?'

'Who wants to know?'

'DI Zigic. Need a word with you.'

'Hold on, I'll buzz you in.'

Zigic jumped back in the car, banging his knee on the steering column and cursed Bob Drake for his paranoia. As if anyone would come to Glebe Farm on the rob. He had a lot of expensive plant but there were dogs prowling and a couple of dozen men living on site who wouldn't be slow to ask what the fuck you thought you were doing.

188

The gates closed behind him with a weighty thunk, reminding him of a prison yard. Or a cult compound. It was more like the latter, he decided, as a bald-headed man crossed the track in front of him, swinging a brace of pheasants in one hand, a rifle in the other, heading for the caravans lined up forty yards from the house.

There were more than last time Zigic was there. He counted eighteen, set out in two long rows, mismatched things bought cheap and patched up, some better than others but none of them good enough to make the grade at a commercial site. A few bore homely touches, a wind chime outside one, a pot of herbs near the steps of another, but these weren't homes, they were somewhere to sleep and eat as cheaply as possible, save money to send back to the family or hoard it for an eventual return.

Inside they would be cold and grey, he imagined, and the rain battering down would drive you mad for the first few nights, until you learned to tune it out.

He pulled up outside the house, next to Bob Drake's Mitsubishi pickup. The flatbed was empty, except for a rolled-up tarpaulin and a spray of broken plastic from one of the lights mounted on the cab. The side panel was neatly sign-written in understated lettering – Drake Engineering Ltd – and anyone who saw it would probably imagine it returned to a well-run yard at night, not somewhere like this. There were four transporters parked alongside it, no company logos on them, and they looked right at home.

The house wasn't in a much better state than the caravans. A Victorian place tilting with subsidence, smoke billowing blackly from the chimneys. The gutter was leaking under the rain, and water poured out down the front of the house, following a well-worn route, the bricks streaked green with algae.

As he got out of the car Zigic glanced towards the outbuildings, a long run of brick and block barns which had once housed livestock; now they were tumbling down, with broken windows and rotting doors. The one on the end, where Bob Drake had locked up a murderer for them, had collapsed in the last two years, revealing the corroded skeletons of old farm machinery.

Next to the barns a new tractor shed had been erected, a huge corrugated building with CCTV cameras mounted above the doors and an alarm box which flashed blue and red. Drake had early form for ringing plant and Zigic could only smile at his security precautions – nobody had a better system than a thief.

The front door opened as he reached the house. Bob Drake, short and wide, stood with his arms folded across his chest, an inch of bare gut showing under the bagged-out hem of his Fair Isle jumper.

'Summat I can do for you, Inspector?'

'Invite me in.'

'Depends what you're after.'

A drop of rain found the gap between Zigic's collar and his neck and he felt it run down his spine like a slick finger.

'We've got a dead migrant worker on Holme Fen. Wondered if he's one of yours.'

Drake stepped back. 'Come you on in then.'

The house was stuck in a time warp, striped wallpaper to the dado rail, sponged paintwork above in the same deep burgundy as the carpet. Zigic followed Drake through a dining room with a china cabinet full of Royal Worcester and then a dark oak kitchen where an old brown Rayburn was chugging away, something simmering which smelled just as brown and past its sell-by date.

'You not working today?' Zigic asked.

'Waiting on floor beams. Should ha' been there day afore yesterday. Agent never bothered to ring us and let us know, so me and the lads went down there for nun't. Just got in half-hour back.'

'Where're you working?'

'North London,' Drake said. 'Spent three hours driving and never earned a penny.'

They went into Drake's office. It was another new addition, lit by a single naked bulb, the concrete floor not yet carpeted, but there were two desks fully kitted out with phones and computers and the pink plaster walls were covered with maps and charts, work rotas and lists of phone numbers. On a corkboard he had passport photographs of his workers, their names underneath.

The room reeked of wet dog and as he moved to take the seat Drake offered, Zigic noticed an old grey lurcher curled up on a cushion behind Drake's desk. It fixed Zigic with an intent yellow stare for a few seconds, then pushed its face into the cushion and went back to sleep.

'What's with the ramped-up security all of a sudden?' Zigic asked.

'A lot of unsavoury characters round this way of late,' Drake said, and if he was being ironic he was very subtle about it. 'Got a lot of money's worth of machinery out there.'

'You've got a lot of blokes too. That'd put off most people.'

'At night it would, but my Davina's here on her own all day. You want your missus out in the middle of nowhere like this?'

'How's she doing now?'

'She's alright. Knocked her sideways it did, young Marius getting killed.' Drake frowned behind his beard. 'She's like a mother to 'em. Always fussing.'

Zigic remembered her at the trial, spitting at Marius's murderer as the guard led him down to the cells. She was fined for contempt of court and asked the judge if he'd take cash since she didn't have her chequebook on her.

'So,' Drake said, 'what's to do with this dead fella?'

'Name's Viktor Stepulov,' Zigic said, taking the photograph out of his jacket. 'We think he must have been working around here somewhere. Or maybe just dossing local.'

Bob Drake shook his head over the photo. 'No, not one of ours.'

'When you let me in I got the impression you thought he might be.'

'Week before last a few of the old boys went into Peterborough clubbing,' Drake said. 'They get cabin fever stuck out here.'

'And?'

'Ferdi never come back. Went off with some old gel and we in't seen hide nor hair of him since.'

'Have you called him?'

'Soft bugger left his mobile here,' Drake said. 'Last time they went out he got it nicked so he wouldn't take it. Gel took it out his pocket while she were giving him a blow job.'

'Have you reported him missing?'

'He'll be shagging himself silly.'

'Or he's had an accident?'

'Hospital would've phoned us if he did.'

'How would they know to call you?' Zigic said.

'Reckon he'd tell them, less he's in a coma or summat, and if he's in a coma we couldn't do much for him, could we?'

The dog barked sharply and woke itself up, looked accusingly at Zigic.

'Davina called PDH and City General, told them she were looking for her son. They hadn't had anyone come in.' The dog nosed at Drake and he scratched it behind the ear. 'He'll have fallen on his feet with some old scrubber. He's a handsome-looking young lad, good luck to him I say.'

'Why don't you give me his details?' Zigic said, taking out his notepad. 'I can make some inquiries.'

'Don't be daft.'

'He might have been arrested.'

'Well, I'm not bailing him out if he has,' Drake said, forced amusement around his mouth, but it didn't reach his eyes. 'He'll find his way back when he's ready.'

'Indulge me.'

Drake sighed heavily and raised his bulk from the chair, pushing the dog away with a big, flat hand. It slunk around the desk, all wiry grey fur and a muzzle like a werewolf, and started to sniff Zigic's leg.

Drake slid open a filing cabinet. 'Just smack him on the nose if he's bothering you.'

'He's fine. Do you hunt with him?'

'Few rabbits.' Drake flipped through the files and finally found the one he wanted, dropped it on the desk in front of Zigic. 'There you go. Ferdinand Kulic.'

Drake's paperwork was more comprehensive than the stuff he'd been given by Pickman Nye. There was a large, glossy photograph of Kulic and underneath it a copy of his passport and his work permit – he was a Croatian national and Zigic recognised the name of the Dalmatian tourist resort he came from; Milan was conceived there, in the shadowed doorway of a baker's two minutes away from their hotel. At least that's what Anna said. It could have been the hotel room or the beach or the back seat of the hire car they drove out into the countryside one afternoon. She preferred that story though.

'Why did he come over here to work? They're building like mad where he's from.'

'But the local builders are all using Indian and Pakistani labour. Said he couldn't get on a job over there.'

Everyone moved west, endlessly, Zigic thought.

Kulic's bank account details were in the file, his tax number and the address of the doctor's surgery in Sawtry where he was registered. Next of kin in Croatia and another in London.

'You keep good records.'

'Davina's very particular about it,' Drake said.

He rocked back in his chair, hands closed around his gut, sovereign rings on three fingers but he wore a cheap plastic watch which couldn't have cost him a fiver. He was a strange one, Zigic thought, twenty or thirty men working for him, making better than decent money with his civil engineering projects and shiny new plant, but he lived like he was on the point of poverty.

He thought of Andrus Tombak in his cramped semi, living cheek by jowl with his men to keep them in line, and wondered if Drake was any different. He was polite and open but maybe he was just intelligent enough to realise it was good business to act that way with the police.

'This fella, was he murdered?' Drake asked.

'Too early to say. His body was found on the train tracks at Holme Fen.'

Drake grimaced behind his beard. 'But you don't reckon he found his own way there?'

'His leg was badly broken,' Zigic said. 'It looks unlikely he walked there himself.'

'I've heard of unscrupulous gangers getting shot of injured workers that way,' Drake said. 'Bit public when you could drop him in a dyke.'

'Is that what you'd do?'

'Now you listen to me, I run a fully legit operation here, Inspector,' Drake said. 'We're doing work for the MoD, the Church – you unnerstand? I've got health and safety up my arse every two minutes, right footwear, wear goggles, walk here, don't walk there. I've got five millions pounds' worth of public liability for fuck's sake. I don't go dumping my boys on train tracks if they get bashed up, I take them to a hospital where they belong. You go out there and ask them yourself you want confirmation.'

'Mr Drake –'

'And on Holme Fen and all,' he said, the colour rising in his weather-worn cheeks. 'You reckon I'd be soft enough to leave some bugger ten minutes away from my house? We haven't had a job round here for nigh on four years, you reckon I'd drive some old boy all the way home from north London and leave him on Holme Fen?'

'No, Mr Drake, I don't, but someone left him there and I want to find them.' The dog shoved its muzzle into Zigic's hand and he felt the sharp points of its canines against his fingers, heat and drool on his skin.

'Cassius, come here.'

The dog paid no notice.

'Cassius. Here. Now.'

'He's fine,' Zigic said, drying his hand on the dog's matted grey fur. 'Whoever did this is local. Or they're on a job nearby.'

Drake shook his head dismissively. 'I don't know. There're a lot of new boys set themselves up the last coupla years.'

'Like who?'

'I don't keep track of them,' Drake said. 'Every farm round this way's got migrant workers on for them. Could be anyone.'

Drake wasn't going to grass anyone up, Zigic realised. He'd help as much as it suited him but now they were getting into territory he felt uncomfortable with and Zigic was sure shouting and threatening wouldn't shift a man like Drake. He was too old-school for that.

He saw Zigic back out to his car, the dog loping along behind them, until it spotted a rabbit on the grass, then it bolted, crossing the ground quicker than Zigic thought was possible, its long stride closing in on the rabbit in a few seconds. The rabbit froze and Cassius pounced on it. There was a weak cry and a shake and Cassius returned to his master with the animal clamped in his massive jaw.

Zigic drove away with the image stuck in his mind, picturing the small bones in the rabbit's neck snapped and splintered.

32

Wahlia and Ferreira were eating lunch when Zigic got back to the office, fatly stuffed ciabatta rolls from the Italian deli on Queen's Street filling the room with the smell of toasted bread and garlic, an antiseptic hit of thyme.

'Yours is on your desk,' Ferreira said, going for her Coke.

He shook the rain out of his parka before he hung it up and went into his office, found the brown paper bag sitting squarely at the centre of his desk, stapled closed and oozing olive oil onto a sheet of paper covered in doodles of chain link and cross-hatched bars.

Next to it was a copy of the coroner's report into Viktor Stepulov's death and he took both out into the main office, sat down at one of the spare desks and opened up his lunch. Parma ham and artichoke hearts, slivers of pecorino.

Ferreira and Wahlia were talking about some fight his cousins were doing security for on Saturday, debating going, but it was in Manchester and they couldn't seem to sort out the logistics to their liking. Ferreira didn't want to drive because it meant not drinking, Wahlia suggested they train it, leave early enough to catch the full undercard. Was it worth the haul though? A northern area title fight? Even for ringside seats?

Zigic took a bite of his sandwich and started on the coroner's report.

There wasn't much to it.

'Have you looked at this?'

Wahlia nodded. 'Half-arsed, right?'

'Is there anything on the system?'

'DI Hawkes was dealing with it,' Wahlia said.

Zigic remembered the whip-round and the Get Well Soon card he'd signed for the man he hardly knew. How long ago was that? A month or more. They were cut off from CID up in Hate Crimes and he'd heard nothing of Hawkes's progress since.

'I'll talk to Riggott about it.'

He took another bite of his sandwich, felt something gritty between his back teeth but swallowed it, and returned to the scant findings in the report.

Viktor Stepulov's body was found by a farmer and his labourer working in the field next to the railway tracks. They were clearing away lumps of bog oak which had risen to the surface over the autumn, pulling them out with chains and stacking them to be burned. The farmer's spaniels were running around while they worked and their barking alerted him to the arm lying in the long grass. A few yards further along he saw the torso and a leg.

The emergency services found Viktor Stepulov's head in a clump of nettles.

They had a vague time of death, a seventeen-hour window between the farmer's discovery and the reports of a line main-tenance team which had been through the day before, checking rivets and making repairs, but it wasn't much to go on.

Sometime between 4 p.m. on Sunday, the eighteenth of November, and 9 a.m. on Monday the nineteenth, a train drove through Viktor Stepulov. The drivers who worked the route had been questioned but none reported seeing him, or being aware of hitting someone. Of course. They would have reported it if they had.

Zigic imagined Viktor stumbling onto the line in the pitch black of a winter evening, breathing frost, disorientated, maybe drunk, maybe hurt already, feeling the line shudder underfoot . . . wouldn't he have moved? Thrown himself out of the way of the lights bearing down on him?

No.

He thought of the break in his shin. Viktor hadn't walked

197

anywhere. He definitely hadn't walked onto a train track in the back end of beyond on a Sunday night.

'We need him post-morteming,' Zigic said. 'Bobby, get it sorted, quick as possible. And get Irwin to do it. They've fucked up over there once already, I want it doing properly this time.'

'Yes, boss.'

Wahlia picked up the phone and started to dial.

'What did Drake say?' Ferreira asked.

'He was cagey but I don't think Viktor was working there,' Zigic admitted. 'I'm not saying he'd be above doing it but he knows we'd go to him first, he'd have been more careful where he dumped the body.'

Ferreira opened a fresh pouch of tobacco and began to shred it into the tin, pulling apart the damp clumps.

'Maybe whoever did it liked the idea of implicating him.'

'A rival gangmaster?'

'It's a cut-throat business,' she said.

He thought of what Drake told him, that they hadn't worked locally for years, and wondered who was taking the jobs from under his nose. Groundwork was lucrative, heavy and dirty but largely unskilled, more about brute force and the right plant than anything else. It attracted criminals too. Always had. For years it had been locked up by firms loosely affiliated to Irish paramilitaries and their gangster offshoots, a good way of cleaning up money and getting rid of bodies. There was a reason why people joked about putting someone under a motorway, why they said flyovers were full of men who'd forgotten who their friends were.

Drake was a small-time operator really but still big enough to be worth fitting up.

'Did you get anything in town?' he asked.

'There's a girl working at Maloney's who knew Viktor. I think she's hiding something.' Ferreira licked the edge of her cigarette paper and deftly sealed it. 'He told her he'd got a building job down in London. Some English guy set it up.'

'Another agency?'

'I've made some calls,' she said. 'You want me to go outside with this?'

'No. Have you got anywhere?'

She went and opened a window, sat on the sill to light up.

'Pickman Nye no longer handle the construction sector apparently, but I've been in touch with some of the smaller firms. No one knows him, but what else are they going to say without a warrant?' She took a deep drag. 'I'll tell you something I find really strange though – Maloney reckons Jaan didn't ask about Viktor. And when I dropped by Fern House they said the same thing. Not only did he not mention a brother, he told them he didn't have any family in England at all.'

'Jaan wasn't looking for him,' Zigic said.

'Then why was he here?'

'I think he just wanted out and Viktor was the excuse. Mrs Stepulov said he hated working, he wasn't pulling his weight with the bills and she strikes me as the kind of woman who would have made it clear that was unacceptable.' He thought of her ambivalence when they informed her of Jaan's death; she'd grieved for him already, got it all out of the way once she realised he'd walked out on them and didn't want to come back. He'd made his choice and if it got him killed that was his own fault. 'What's happening with the call logs from the Stepulov house?'

'Bobby was handling it.'

Wahlia glanced up at the mention of his name.

'We need to know where Viktor called them from.'

Wahlia nodded.

Viktor had told them he was in danger back in October and six weeks later he was dead. It had to be work-related, didn't it? Migrant labourers were mistreated and disrespected, routinely ripped off, but it was par for the course and most of them knuckled down under the pressure.

Was Viktor the type to fight back, though? Jaan had argued with

Andrus Tombak and maybe that got him killed. It wasn't unrealistic to assume Viktor had a similar streak of obstinacy in him, enough to annoy his new bosses. But if he believed he was in danger why did he hang around? The money couldn't be that good. Nobody's was.

Zigic closed the coroner's report, slapped it on the desk.

'Start a board, Mel.'

'Yes, sir.'

Upstairs CID was quiet, a handful of people working diligently at their computers, or doing a good impression of working. Phones rang, keyboards clattered and Zigic felt a surge of envy at the industrious mood. He knew they were probably running into brick walls of their own but the one he faced felt insurmountable, and a niggling, negative voice in the back of his mind told him that even if he managed to scramble over it he would discover another one waiting, taller and wider and with a deep pit on the other side of it.

He pushed away the voice and found a smile for Riggott's secretary when she glanced up from her typing. She wore a powder-blue twin set and her blonde hair was drawn into an impossibly neat bun. Riggott would appreciate that, he thought, the vintage look, and wondered if there was something going on between them.

'Is he in?'

'He's having lunch,' she said. 'Is it important?'

She was like a doctor's receptionist, weighing the calls on her boss's time, deciding which ones he could ignore. Zigic forced the smile to stay put, told her it was, and she debated for a moment before announcing him.

He went in, closed the door behind him.

'You got good news for me, Ziggy?'

'Depends on your definition of good.'

Riggott was eating a steak sandwich, cuffs turned back, two napkins tucked into the neck of his crisp white shirt and his silk tie thrown over his shoulder. He leaned forward as he took a bite, drops of blood spotting the newspaper on his desk. Reading upside down Zigic saw the article was about some American actress who'd been on a very public bender, and felt a little of his respect for Riggott slip away.

'You want something,' he said, around a mouthful of meat and bread.

'We've found Stepulov's brother.'

'And?'

'He's dead too.'

'Popular boys, those two.' Riggott put his sandwich down and wiped his mouth with a paper napkin. 'I take it he didn't pass quietly in his sleep.'

Zigic filled him in on what they knew.

'And you're assuming it's linked with your case?'

'It's got to be more than a coincidence.'

'Who's dealing with it?'

'Hawkes was.'

Riggott's face twisted briefly, annoyance or sympathy. 'Well, he won't be back for a good while yet.'

'How's he doing?'

'Last I heard they were running more tests.'

He didn't really know, Zigic suspected. While you were in the station, at the centre of things, you were important, but the second you slipped, through illness or stress or suspension, you were as good as dead. If Hawkes did make it back Riggott would shake his hand, drag him into a bear hug like they were long-lost brothers; if not, he'd stick fifty quid in the collection for the wreath and get on with his day.

The phone on Riggott's desk began to ring and he gave it a cursory glance, just long enough to check it wasn't coming from up the ladder, and let it go.

'Alright, Ziggy. You take this one, but keep me informed.' He picked up his sandwich again and gestured at Zigic with it. 'Closely informed, right?'

'Yes, sir.'

33

Kate Jenkins was fighting the vending machine in the corridor outside the lab, pounding it with the heel of her hand. She was five foot four and slightly built; Zigic didn't fancy her chances against it.

'Bloody thing's robbed me again.' She squatted down in front of it, her corkscrew red hair falling across her face. 'Don't look, Ziggy, you won't approve.'

She slipped her hand into the tray at the bottom and Zigic winced as her arm disappeared after it, watching her twist and huff, snaking up into the rows of chocolate bars and cans, wiggling her fingertips.

'Why don't I get you something from downstairs?'

She grunted. 'It's not beating me.'

'You'll need cutting out of it the way you're going.'

'I'm nearly there.' She slammed her body into the curved plastic front and swore under her breath. 'Come on, you bastard.'

'Just take something from the bottom row.'

'No. I want a KitKat. I've paid for a KitKat.' Her middle finger hooked one and she made a final push, flexing to tip it out from its holder. It hit the tray with a thunk and she grinned at him.

'Shit.' The smile died on her face.

She tried to pull her arm out but it wouldn't budge.

'Shit, I can't –'

'Just relax,' Zigic said. He dropped the bag with Viktor Stepulov's clothes in but didn't know what to do next, stood stupidly looking at her. 'Alright . . . OK . . . don't tense up. Just let me think.'

'I'm scared.'

'I'll call maintenance, they can take the front off or something.'

'No, pull me out.'

'It'll break your arm.'

She pressed her face against the machine. Closed her eyes. 'I don't want to lose my arm.'

'You won't.' Zigic crouched next to her, took hold of her free hand. 'You're going to be alright, I promise.'

'I need it. This is the hand I hit my kids with.'

He straightened up as Jenkins laughed at him.

'Nice, Kate.'

She disengaged her arm from the vending machine, came up brandishing the KitKat.

'What are you, five?' Zigic snatched at the bag of clothes.

'It's been a slow morning.' She unwrapped her chocolate and offered him half of it. 'To the hero the spoils.'

'No, you earned it.'

Jenkins nodded at the bag, her nose twitching. 'That for me, is it?'

'Don't say I never bring you anything.'

They went into the lab, a large, square room with stark white walls and blue lino floor scrubbed almost to its underlay, bleached in places and stained in others, the damage worst around the pair of long, stainless-steel tables which dominated the space. They reminded him of the mortuary he'd just come from, but where there would have been a body a set of clothes was laid out, arranged as they would have been worn, a woman's grey pinstripe suit, the jacket at the top, then a shirt, then the pencil skirt with a splash of red wine down the front, tights ripped at the knees and a pair of shoes with uncomfortably high heels and sweat-smudged inners.

'What happened to her?' Zigic asked.

'Her boyfriend happened. She got in a bit later than he liked so he strangled her,' Jenkins said. 'Put the bag down there, I'll just fetch some gloves.'

'Is she dead?'

'No. She's in a bad way apparently but she'll survive.' She came out of her office with her hair scraped back into a ponytail, pulling on a pair of gloves, a clipboard tucked under her arm. 'Have we got a name?'

'Viktor Stepulov.'

'Any relation?'

'Brother.'

'Your case just got complicated, Ziggy.'

'Tell me about it.'

Jenkins put the clipboard aside.

'Alright, let's see what smells so bad in there, shall we?'

She opened the blue plastic bag and rolled it down to get at the contents. The smell bloomed into their faces and Zigic turned away from it. He'd brought a faint echo of it with him from the mortuary, the odour of Viktor's chilled corpse lingering in his hair and on his clothes, and that was OK, he could ignore it. This though, a full, deep blast, was more than he wanted in his lungs.

'Do we know how he died?'

'He was hit by a train,' Zigic said.

'Explains this then.' Jenkins took out a bundle of shredded fabric, blue check cotton tangled up with the remains of a grey sweatshirt and pieces of bright red nylon which had been a waterproof jacket. His combat trousers had been cut off his body, the legs slit from hem to waistband.

She checked the pockets, turned each one inside out, finding nothing more useful than fluff and crumbs. Zigic would have liked a detailed map or a business card with a mobile number scrawled on the back, but he was past expecting such things.

Jenkins started jigsawing the pieces together on the stainless-steel counter. The annihilating white lights brought out every stain and snag, blood dried brown and blobs of purple and black from his minced organs. The cuffs of Viktor Stepulov's shirt were frayed and there were barbs in the fabric of his sweater, vicious grey hooks which looked like thistles. The thick cotton of his trousers was ripped low on the left leg where his shin bone had broken through, first the skin and then the fabric, and the sight of it put a sick knot in Zigic's stomach.

Jenkins kept rearranging the pieces, intense concentration on her face, her mouth set in a firm line, and finally, when she had them assembled to her satisfaction, she took half a step back from the table and looked at Zigic, one slender brow flicked up.

'Well?'

'What?'

'Tell me what's missing,' she said.

'His shoes.'

'They're still in the bag. Tell me what's missing from the clothes.'

Zigic looked at the ragged costume laid out in front of him, like something stripped from a scarecrow. He put Viktor's body back inside it, seeing how the tears matched the terrible jumble of limbs in that tray at Hinchingbrooke mortuary, thinking of the nauseating pile of intestines and pulped organs.

'There isn't enough blood,' he said.

'Nothing like enough. Did you see the body?' Zigic nodded. 'And it was in pieces, I imagine?'

'Cut in half pretty much, right across the torso, under the breastbone approximately.'

'OK,' Jenkins said, picking up her clipboard, writing quickly. 'That fits. But the deposits on here aren't consistent with that kind of trauma. If he'd been alive this lot would be totally saturated. We've got some . . . internal matter here and there, but the only place he's bled heavily from is his left leg.'

'His shin was broken. It looked like a pre-mortem injury to me. Not that I'm an expert, but there was heavy bruising, a lot of swelling.'

'Sounds like you're right then. When's the PM scheduled?'

'I'm hoping Monday,' Zigic said. 'But if you can get anything for me before that . . .'

Jenkins looked at him expectantly.

'I will be very grateful.'

34

The afternoon ticked down in a grey torpor and Zigic stood at the window for a long time watching the clouds darken over Peterborough, the rain which had followed him from Huntingdon to Great Gidding and back to the station becoming finer but heavier, settling in for the weekend.

Typical. He was planning to take the boys down to Ferry Meadows tomorrow morning, cycle around Gunwale Lake then stop at the cafeteria for milkshakes and chips. They'd bought Stefan a new trike for his birthday and Anna was getting annoyed with him riding it around their small back garden, tearing up the turf and running over the edges of her flower beds. He needed more space but she didn't like the playing field in the village as much as she did when they moved in, too many big dogs running off their leads and kids hanging around getting stoned at the weekends. She didn't want Stefan and Milan seeing that kind of behaviour.

If the rain didn't lift it would have to be the cinema again. He made a mental note to check the listings later, thinking about taking them to Stamford Arts Centre rather than the multiplex on Eastern Industrial Estate, it was smaller and quiet, and he thought Anna might enjoy a couple of hours to herself, wandering around those chichi boutiques she liked so much.

She seemed frazzled lately and he knew she wasn't coping with Stefan as well as she had with Milan when he was that age. He was inquisitive and demanding, wouldn't focus on anything for more than ten minutes at a time, and Zigic could understand how exhausting it was for her.

She wanted girls. That was part of the problem too, even

though she would never admit it. Every time Stefan brought a handful of worms into the kitchen or fell off the rabbit hutch she'd be thinking how different life would have been but for the sake of that single chromosome.

They'd discussed having another baby over Christmas and agreed to wait until Stefan started school, but the way she'd been on at him lately made him suspect she had other ideas. Not that he minded. He'd always pictured himself with a big family, some leftover from childhood when they'd been to visit his cousins in Somerset, a dozen kids all running wild around the family's farm, staying out in the orchard until it got dark, coming home to a long table on the veranda, food piled up end to end, drinking watered-down wine and stealing sips of imported slivovitz that tasted of metal and fire. They lived like they were still in the old country and it appealed to him, spoke to something deep in his bones.

It was a fantasy though. He knew that.

Anna didn't get on with his family and he had never been accepted by hers. There would be no warm gatherings at the Zigic homestead.

He folded his arms across his chest and watched the beginnings of the evening rush on the parkway below. Friday night and people wanted to get home. Freed from the shackles for forty-eight hours they drove more aggressively than usual, recklessly cutting lanes and hanging on each other's bumpers. They were desperate to get in and wash the day off, grab a drink then another one, vegetate in front of the TV, or dress up as a different, more alluring person and try their luck in town.

He envied them the ability to shut out work for a couple of days. It was a luxury he hadn't enjoyed for years.

He knew some coppers said they could forget the job the moment they walked out of the station but he didn't believe them. You didn't choose this occupation if you didn't care. Even the most politically motivated officers were consumed by cases, not to avenge the victims or console their families, but because any slip would blot their record and threaten the carefully plotted trajectory of their career. They had it worse, he guessed.

A patrol car pulled off the road, blue lights strobing but no siren, and when it stopped the uniforms hauled a man out of the back. He made his body a dead weight and they struggled to get him off the tarmac. Zigic remembered that manoeuvre, trying to get a belligerent suspect into the station without damaging them. They did it to provoke you, wanting to push you into using a non-approved method of restraint they could complain to their solicitor about later.

He'd done less than a year in uniform and almost quit the job. It was an endless grind of verbal abuse and senseless violence, glassings and stabbings on the weekend shift, neighbour disputes and antisocial behaviour, one domestic after another ending unresolved.

That year he'd seen parts of Peterborough he never knew existed despite living here all his life.

He could deal with that though, chalk it all up to experience; he didn't want to be one of those university-educated detectives the old school hated, unconnected and soft. What almost finished him was the locker-room atmosphere of the uniform section. It didn't take long to realise the people he was supposed to stand shoulder to shoulder with were no better than the ones they were facing down.

His first week he was given a crash course in how to keep his fucking mouth shut from a forty-something PC with two marriages behind him and a catalogue of disciplinary issues. He watched PC Galton shake down shopkeepers, carried the boxes of beer they were 'gifted' out to the patrol car, saw him take freebies from prostitutes working the Triangle and bribes from motorists who couldn't afford another three points on their licence. Galton fancied himself a Wild West sheriff and at first Zigic thought it was a joke, but as the weeks went on and Galton opened up he realised it wasn't. Galton's world was sharply polarised, decent people and scum, and as it transpired almost everyone fell into the latter category. Not just the criminals they arrested, but their families and their neighbours; their victims too more often than not.

Zigic wondered what he would make of the Stepulov brothers.

Even back then Peterborough had a substantial migrant population and Galton wasn't shy about showing his disapproval, always going on about how much better it was back in the seventies, 'were a few Pakis and that but they knew their fucking place'.

Galton retired soon after Zigic made sergeant, sold his council house and took his pension over to Spain, where he was probably still playing golf and shouting at waiters in his broad fen accent, complaining to anyone who'd listen about the amount of African immigrants over there, telling them it was much better back in the early noughties when the only foreigners were English.

If he knew his old station now had a dedicated Hate Crimes Unit he'd probably stroke out into his fry-up, Zigic thought, smiling to himself.

Knowing the mess they were in would probably perk him up, though.

Zigic turned away from the window, feeling a weighty fatigue settle across his shoulders. He could blame it on the early start and the long run, tell himself he'd had too much coffee and not enough food today, but none of those things would matter if they were making progress. Seventy-two hours after Jaan Stepulov was murdered they had nothing. No reliable witnesses, no clear motive, no solid evidence. The suspects they'd stuck to the board looked increasingly untouchable too. How was he supposed to charge anyone under these conditions?

And now there was Viktor.

Ferreira was standing at his board, transcribing the information from DI Hawkes's embryonic investigation, and he noticed her writing was larger than usual, as if she wanted to fill that massive white space at any cost.

It challenged you, the emptiness, shoved your failure at

you every time you walked by; a metaphor for every question you didn't know to ask and every line of inquiry you hadn't yet identified.

Wahlia sat hunched over his desk, hair pulled about, shirt tails hanging out the back of his designer jeans, staring with a blank expression at the monitor as he played through the CCTV footage from the crossing on Holme Fen near where Viktor's body was found. Hawkes had got as far as requesting it but they didn't know if he'd had anyone check it.

Zigic wondered how the case had fallen through the cracks when Riggott reassigned Hawkes's workload. He could have asked but knew there was nothing to gain by raising the subject. CID were understaffed, Hawkes off on sick leave and Lawrence on maternity, they'd taken a hit in last year's budget cuts too. No one had been sacked but the money for cover wasn't there any more, and he guessed that didn't help. Things got overlooked, priorities changed. A possible accident involving a corpse with no ID was easy to ignore.

Wahlia straightened with a grunt.

'Got something?'

Zigic went over as he was winding the footage back. On the screen it was night, the train tracks bathed in a pinky-orange glow, the rails glowing silver against the dark swathes of gravel and the rough shape of the verge. Where the rails cut through the road the tarmac bore a slick sheen and when Wahlia started to run the footage again at normal speed the rain was visible, coming down in sheets, like streaks of neon close to the security lights.

The time code at the bottom of the screen showed 9.32 p.m. Sunday, 16 December.

'Any minute,' Wahlia said, shifting nervously in his seat.

Zigic leaned on the desk, feeling a stirring excitement in his gut. This was it. This could be the break they needed. Any second.

Ferreira came over and braced her hands on the back of Wahlia's chair.

'What is it?'

'Just wait,' he said. 'OK, here they come . . .'

Two cones of white light appeared at the top of the screen, they seemed high off the ground but the vehicle stopped before its front bumper entered the shot.

A stiff wind rattled the barrier where it stood, bolt upright, and Zigic half expected it to come down but it didn't, just kept rattling, the collapsed skirts chiming against the barriers as one car door opened and slammed shut, then a second, then the distinctive grating whoosh of a van's side panel shooting back.

Ten seconds passed and the rain lashed down.

'What's taking them so long?' Ferreira said.

'Just wait, will you?'

The first man was tall and broad, even with the foreshortening effect of the lens. He shuffled into shot, back bent under the weight of Viktor Stepulov's shoulders. The second man was smaller, whippet-looking inside a white Adidas tracksuit already plastered to his body by the rain. Both had their faces covered, balaclavas or scarves under dark-coloured knitted hats, Zigic couldn't tell.

'Can the techies do something with this?' Ferreira asked.

'Technology's come a long way but it can't uncover their faces.'

'Yeah, thanks, Bobby, I was thinking of getting a better view of that bracelet.'

'What bracelet?' Zigic asked.

'The skinny guy, he's wearing a bracelet – you can just see it between his glove and his cuff.'

Zigic hadn't noticed.

The men made slow progress onto the train tracks, the smaller one losing his grip at one point and dropping Stepulov's legs. He squatted down and tried another approach, hooked the legs under the thighs, holding his part of the load high around his own hips. He looked more comfortable with the weight then, but it restricted his movement and he duck-walked away out of the right-hand side of the shot, Viktor Stepulov disappearing with him, feet first, never to be seen whole again.

'Please tell me they drive away over the crossing,' Zigic said.

'I don't know, I haven't watched that far yet.'

The tape kept rolling and they let it play in real time, the rain swirling in the light as the wind changed direction, the barrier pinging quietly to itself. A rat darted into shot and out again, just a dark blur through the shadows.

Suddenly the barrier juddered and began to drop. The alarm sounded. The warning lights flashed red.

A few seconds later the men reappeared, the skinny one running at full pelt until he came to the barrier and he vaulted it like a world-class athlete, landing smartly on the other side. His partner followed close on his heels, jacket flapping around his body. He ducked under, the skirts dragging his beanie off his head, revealing dark hair in a ponytail. He was a couple of steps away when he realised he'd lost it and he turned to retrieve it as the lights of the oncoming train washed the tracks. Too late.

The train trundled through. A goods vehicle, slow and heavy, dozens of containers passing the camera, their sides printed with the names of shipping companies, bodies ancient and rusted. Zigic held his breath, willing them to stop coming, hoping the men were waiting to cross, sitting stunned in the front of their vehicle with their hearts pounding, scared still for a few minutes by their close escape.

'Is this on a loop?' Ferreira asked. 'Wind it on, Bobby.'

'Let it play,' Zigic said.

As the tracks finally cleared, the headlights retreated and Zigic swore into his fist – they were backing up, leaving the way they came. They weren't stupid, they knew the crossing had security cameras. That's why they'd parked at a distance and covered their faces. He turned away, stretched his neck and looked up at the ceiling, a humourless smile twisting his face.

'Idiots,' Ferreira said.

He looked back just in time to see the rear bumper of the vehicle come into shot, brake lights flashing, white paintwork and there, smeared with mud which had been partially washed away by the rain, a number plate.

MONDAY

35

Lindsay hated driving at night. She knew the statistics on this stretch of road, twelve fatalities last year, four people dead in a single accident, when a car full of teenagers skidded on a patch of black ice and plunged into a waterlogged dyke.

She was working in A&E when they were brought in, two stick-thin girls in tiny dresses and spiky heels who had survived the initial impact but died eventually of hypothermia, trapped and pinned in the twisted wreck of the car with their boyfriends' corpses for six hours, waiting for someone to come along and call an ambulance. The boys had been luckier, dead on impact; one went through the windscreen, severing his jugular, the other sustaining massive head trauma, the damage compounded by the cocaine and alcohol in his system.

She thought of her own girls, eleven and thirteen, knowing that they'd soon be getting into cars with their friends, driving this same dark and winding road, going into Peterborough for the clubs, and it made her blood run cold, imagining the nights she was going to spend sitting by the phone until 3 a.m., waiting for them to get in, convinced as the minutes ticked by that something terrible was happening.

A motorbike screamed past her, doing at least eighty, and she glanced in her rear-view mirror, saw the rider take the next corner without slowing.

There was a sign warning bikers about the bends but rather than putting them off it encouraged them to come in from all over the county and ride the black route, like skiers wanting to test themselves against a tough run.

One had come in tonight, a few minutes before her shift was due to end, his skin stripped off the right side of his body where he'd been dragged along the tarmac as his bike went out from under him. He had broken bones in his arms and legs, internal bleeding, ruptured organs. It looked unlikely he would walk again. If he survived.

Lindsay yawned into the back of her hand.

She wanted her bed but home was twenty minutes away still and the dog would need to be fed when she got in, the washing machine loading and the dryer emptying. Half past six now; by the time she'd done all that Martin would be getting up, banging around their bedroom, and she just knew the shirt he'd want would need ironing and then the girls would be out of bed, fighting over the bathroom mirror and screaming for their gym kits or money for lunch, and once that was sorted the dog would be whining by the back door, needing to be walked.

She'd be lucky if she was in bed before nine.

How much longer could she do this for? Since they'd moved out of Peterborough the drive was killing her. A two-hour round trip after a twelve-hour shift, longer if she was bullied into covering for someone. Yes, the house was nicer than their old place in Paston and the garden was bigger, but was it worth this constant bone-tiredness?

She cracked the window and cold air trickled across her face, sharpening her focus on the road ahead of her.

The sky was tinged grey on the horizon but it still felt like night, a starless sky filled with clouds, nothing but darkness all around her.

She put on the stereo and music pounded out of the speakers, some cheesy pop on Lite FM. She shoved the CD in. Martin had been promising to sort out the dock for her iPod for weeks but it was still sitting in the box on the kitchen worktop. Amy Winehouse's voice filled the car and she sang along, trying to keep herself alert.

Another yawn shuddered out of her, making her eyelids drop,

and when she opened them again she saw a figure darting across the verge.

She stamped on the brakes. The tyres squealed against the tarmac.

'Please, God.'

There was a thud and the car stopped. The music kept playing but she could hardly hear it, blood pounding in her ears.

She could see a body in the headlights.

She reached for her mobile but there was no signal. She had to get out and check if he was alive.

But she didn't move. Where had he come from? There were no houses around here, nothing but fields for miles in every direction.

Lindsay climbed out of the car, and the wind blowing across the fields whipped the door back on its hinges. Her knees were weak as she walked towards the man. She told herself it was just like work, assess the situation and deal with it professionally.

'Can you hear me?'

She stopped a few steps away from the man. He rolled over and she saw his face was badly damaged above a thick black beard, blood on the front of his grey T-shirt.

'I'm a nurse, I'm going to help you.'

He groaned and kicked his legs weakly. 'Please.'

Lindsay moved closer. The wind tore at her hair, snapped her coat around her body.

'We need to get you to hospital.'

'Help me.' He reached out to her. 'Please, help me. They're coming.'

'Who?'

'Please.' He was crying. 'I don't want to die.'

His accent was foreign, thickened by the tears and his broken nose. Lindsay took his hand and he got to his feet, bracing himself against the car. He was bleeding heavily and she saw a ragged wound high on his chest.

Had he been shot?

Fear gripped her spine.

'What happened?'

'There are men coming.'

'What have you done?'

'I –' He froze. 'We must go. Now. They are coming.'

He pointed into the darkness and Lindsay saw headlights jumping over a field, heard the rumble of a throaty engine.

He stumbled away from her, making for the passenger side of her car, but she was rooted to the spot, watching the lights come closer, the engine growling. A shot rang out and she ducked instinctively.

This wasn't real. This didn't happen.

'Please. They will kill you.' He opened the door and got into her car. She saw his face, bloodied and beaten, skin very white under the interior light.

Lindsay threw herself behind the wheel again and started the engine.

A horn sounded to her right and she saw the headlights, fifty or sixty yards away, bearing down on them.

'Go!'

She backed up quickly on the grass verge, saw the lights in her rear-view mirror, seconds away from them, and accelerated off. The CD was still playing and she stabbed at it, one hand on the wheel, eyes on the road, focusing now on getting them away.

'They shot you.'

'Yes.'

'Why?'

'They killed my friend,' the man said. 'They are bad people.'

Lindsay glanced at him, saw his fingers coming away bloody from the wound in his shoulder.

'You need to put pressure on it.' She took hold of his hand and pressed it onto the gunshot. 'Like this. Press it hard. You need to stop the bleeding.'

'You will take me to hospital?'

'Yes,' she snapped.

The other vehicle was on the road now, headlights sitting high and another set of lamps a few feet above it. A truck of some kind, she thought. Slower than her car, but they had guns and if they had shot at her once they would do it again.

She shifted gears, put her foot down, accelerating away from them on the long stretch of open road. They were coming up to a village. In a few minutes they would be among civilisation but she realised there would be no point stopping.

What would she do? Knock on random doors at this time of morning and hope some kind soul opened up? And what if someone did? Was she prepared to draw armed men to a stranger's house?

'What is your name?' the man asked.

'Lindsay.'

'Thank you, Lindsay. You have saved me.'

Her hands tightened around the steering wheel and she felt tears pricking her eyes, thinking of Martin at home, her girls sleeping safely in their beds, dreaming of shoes and boys and fame, and prayed to the God she didn't believe in that this man wouldn't get her killed.

36

Zigic was awake before the alarm sounded, lying on his back with Anna snuggled up close to him, her head under his chin. Her breaths came slow and even against his skin, her face perfectly placid in the dim light from the hallway. He always envied her ability to sleep soundly no matter what was happening. She just shut it out, closed her eyes and drifted away. It didn't seem to bother her that the same troubles would be waiting when she woke up.

Carefully he removed her arm from his chest and slipped out of bed. He pulled on his dressing gown and went to look in on the boys.

A night light was glowing softly next to Milan's bed, where he was curled up small under the covers. His thumb was stuck firmly in his mouth and Zigic pulled it out, tucked his hand under his pillow. It was a habit they'd thought he was finally growing out of but he'd returned to it since starting school last autumn and the teacher had sent a note home twice now, advising them to talk to their doctor about it. As if it was some aberrant behaviour pattern akin to torturing cats.

Milan was a sensitive boy. Shy around strangers, quiet even with his friends, and Stefan tyrannised him despite being two years younger, always bossing him around, but Milan took it with grace, gave his little brother the toy he wanted, didn't fight back when he stole food from his plate.

Zigic feared what would happen if he didn't toughen up. The village primary was a calm, safe environment but what about after that? In a few years he would move up, and Anna was talking about sending him to Stamford Boys, as if the money wasn't an issue. He was intelligent enough to get into King's, a couple of years ahead of his peers already, but even twenty years ago, when Zigic was there, the school had its fair share of bullying, and the area around it was rough, blighted by street crime, often targeted at the pupils who made easy marks in their dark blue blazers.

Anna's father had suggested they send him to a martial arts class, said it would make a man of him. Their five-year-old boy. He was a reactionary old bastard. Ex-Air Force, still played rugby at fifty-four, did Ironman triathlons. To his mind every problem in the world could be solved with the reintroduction of conscription and corporal punishment.

He was delighted when he found out Anna was dating a policeman, but the initial flush passed quickly and Zigic still cringed at the memory of their first meeting. A pub in Elton with dark beams and horse brasses on the wall, neutral ground. They shook hands, all smiles, and then he asked Zigic where he was from. Peterborough wouldn't do – 'But where are your people from?'

Zigic told him and they spent the remainder of the afternoon listening to war stories from his tours in Bosnia and Kosovo, what he'd seen in a Sarajevo, the places he'd bombed. Anna kept squeezing his hand under the table and Zigic forced down the urge to take his steak knife and stab her old man, confirm all of his racist opinions about Serbs.

They saw her parents only a couple of times a year now. They came down for Anna's birthday and Boxing Day, spent the majority of their visits talking about how well their son was getting on in Saudi, where he worked as an engineer. Anna was drifting away from them and Zigic was secretly glad of it, didn't want their influence to spread to his boys. They'd done enough damage to their own kids.

He stepped over the toys littering the floor and picked up the duvet cover Stefan had kicked off in the night, drew it up to his chin and kissed him on the head before he crept out again, pulling the door shut behind him.

Downstairs he switched the radio to the World Service and started a pot of espresso on the stove, listened to distant horrors with half an ear while he thought of the more immediate ones he had to deal with.

Viktor Stepulov's post-mortem was scheduled for ten. He didn't expect much from it. The body was in pieces, it had been left out overnight to be gnawed at by animals and rained on. So the chances of DNA transfer from the men who'd dumped him were slight.

On Saturday morning he'd led a hastily convened search of the area along the train tracks on Holme Fen. Riggott insisted their budget wouldn't run to extra bodies or overtime so it had been him, Ferreira and Wahlia – the two of them hung-over and bleary-eyed, reeking of the club they'd rolled out of a couple of hours before. Kate Jenkins agreed to come along in exchange for lunch and admitted, as they walked the line, eyes down, that she was happy to escape the birthday party she was supposed to be taking her daughter to.

It was a long shot. Twelve weeks after the event, but they found what they were looking for, the man's brown woollen hat which he'd lost in the rush to escape the oncoming train. It was sodden and filthy, sitting snagged in buddleia bush a hundred yards away from the crossing, dragged along in a slipstream.

Zigic knew that if it ever came to court the hairs Jenkins recovered from it would be considered dubious evidence. They couldn't conclusively prove how or when it got there, but if the owner was in the system it would be a start at least.

They'd been arrogant, dumping Viktor on railway tracks which they must have known were covered by security cameras. Arrogant or stupid, and both possibilities boded well. They would have made mistakes elsewhere. Once they'd been identified better evidence would follow, he felt sure of it.

If the hat's owner was in the system.

They'd identified the make of van used to transport Viktor's body to the railway crossing. A Citroën Berlingo, 05 model, but the number plates were stolen or cloned, registered to an identical vehicle scrapped last year after a pile-up on the A1 just south of Grantham. The owner was a family florist's in Rutland, the driver dead.

Wahlia had called around the local scrapyards to see if a white Berlingo had come in some time during the last month, but so far no joy.

The coffee bubbled up into the top of the pot and Zigic whipped it off the heat before it burned, took down a white espresso cup from the shelf and poured a double shot he sugared and splashed with cream.

He drank it standing at the kitchen window, looking out across the empty road to the allotments opposite, a patchwork of black and green and the rotting yellow of last year's crops which hadn't been cleared yet, clumps of rhubarb insulated with straw and lines of old plastic bottles being used as cloches. It would be built on eventually and he would miss the view. There was something reassuring about seeing the old men from the village working away there on a Sunday morning, the few young mums who'd taken plots showing their kids how to grow vegetables.

Zigic cut a slice of rye bread from the loaf in the tin and drank another espresso while it toasted, feeling the caffeine start to stir his system. He felt like he could run this morning, but the twinge in his groin had reasserted itself over the weekend and he knew he should rest it.

Half an hour later the boys were up and he made their breakfast – toast with honey for Stefan, cereal for Milan – while they chattered across the kitchen table, talking about wrestlers and who could beat up who. He put cartoons on the television for them and went upstairs to get ready for work.

There was a thin layer of frost on the windscreen when he went out to the car, ice on the gravel and on the leaves of the clipped buxus either side of the front door. He ran the heater at full blast as he drove through the village, overtaking a pair of women on horses riding two abreast up the steep climb of Loves Hill, thinking about the coming autopsy and listening to the bulletin on Hereward FM. A shooting in the early hours of the morning being reported with more gusto than solid information. An unidentified man. A country road.

They were appealing for the good Samaritan who left the man at A&E to come forward and rule himself out of their inquiries. Translation – we know you were involved, you bastard.

It would keep Riggott busy at least, something so high profile, and give them some much needed breathing space.

Ferreira was in the office already when he arrived, sitting at her desk with a coffee and a cigarette, going through old case notes. She was uncharacteristically smart today, a slim black trouser suit and white shirt, her hair pulled into a sleek ponytail.

Zigic tried to remember the last time he'd put a suit on for work. He had a wardrobe full of ones he never wore and by the time he needed them again, promotion or the ongoing threat of the department's closure driving him back to CID, they would be too dated.

Some mornings he wanted to put one on, needing to feel armoured against the coming day, but the dress code in Hate Crimes was strictly casual, and the suits stayed where they were, sealed up in nylon body bags.

'Are you in court today?'

She glanced up from her notes. 'Ten thirty. It's that boy who got beaten up outside the Polish club in Fletton last year. You remember?'

'No.'

'No. It's kind of fuzzy for me too,' she admitted. 'I hate this part so much. They always make you feel like an idiot.'

'Just try not to get rattled.'

'I always wonder what kind of person goes into criminal law. They know their clients are guilty most of the time and they stand there in court ripping into us, trying to break the victims.'

'Someone has to do it,' Zigic said, going over to Viktor Stepulov's board.

226

He did it every time he walked into the office. As if a magical pixie would have cracked the case in his absence and left the evidence for him. They never did.

'They're worse than the people they defend,' Ferreira said. 'Scumbags.'

She shook the coffee pot at him.

'No, thanks. I've had about six cups already.'

He went into his office to check his messages. Nothing new there either. The cleaners had been in, emptied the bin, wiped the dust off his computer screen, leaving a faint whiff of lemon-scented polish behind them. They'd moved the photographs of Anna and the boys and he returned them to their proper alignment near his in tray; Anna barefoot and brown on the beach in Novi Sad, Milan and Stefan posed on the bench in his parents' back garden. He remembered the day it was taken, didn't recall them being so well behaved.

'Have you heard about the shooting?' Ferreira said.

'It was on the radio. What's the story?'

'Adams has caught it. He's got it down as a gang thing. The guy's in surgery apparently, they're waiting for him to come round so they can question him. Doesn't look serious, shoulder wound.' She shrugged. 'Wouldn't mind something easy like that, would you?'

'Right now I'd take a non-fatal gunshot to get rid of this case.'

Ferreira smiled. 'We've got a dirty old hat to go on, what more do you want?'

37

In the corridor outside Court 4 Ferreira went through her notes again, not wanting to have to refer to them while she was questioned. It looked stronger to answer from memory, as if the defendant's guilt was so obvious you didn't need to check a single detail. She wanted the jury to see that.

If they were paying attention.

When she was called, twenty minutes later, she saw that they weren't. Eight men, four women, all bored-looking and slumped in their seats, except for an old guy in a tweed jacket who sat ramrod-straight, a notepad resting on the ledge in front of him.

She stepped up into the witness box, feeling a flush creep across her cheeks as the eyes of the court turned on her, and she swore the oath with her shirt sticking to her back and dampness under her arms suddenly.

The prosecutor, a thin, young man with rimless glasses and a receding hairline, asked her the questions they had already rehearsed and she answered them smoothly, heard her voice coming out strong and certain.

When she walked out ten minutes later she couldn't remember anything she'd said to the defence lawyer. She knew she'd spoken, knew as well that she'd begun to stumble around the answers even before her mobile phone rang, prompting a wave of stifled laughter and a verbal lashing from the judge.

After that was a blank.

She went into the Ladies and splashed cold water on her face. Her cheeks still burned. She patted her face dry with a handful of paper towels and swore at her reflection in the mirror.

She didn't wait for the verdict.

Outside she switched her mobile on again and saw two missed calls from an unfamiliar number. She threw her phone back into her handbag; whoever it was they could wait, the bastards, showing her up like that.

A chrome burger van was parked up outside the magistrates' court, two women in red uniforms and hairnets slinging junk food for passing shoppers and the gathering throngs of people waiting for their appearances. The smell of frying meat and onions just beginning to singe filled the air, bludgeoning the exhaust fumes and the rotten brown odour of the River Nene thirty yards away.

Ferreira ordered a sausage butty and a Coke, ate quickly at one of the aluminium cafe tables set up on the pavement, needing to put something on top of the angry nausea which was making her stomach roil. An elderly couple, heavily insulated against the cold and weighed down with bags from the supermarket in Rivergate, joined her at the table, started talking about their sick cat, glancing at her as if they expected her to have an opinion.

She rolled a cigarette, hiding behind her sunglasses, and said she was more of a dog person.

After a few deep drags she started to feel calmer. It would be a story to tell if nothing else, one more inopportune phone moment to add to the list.

Nearby a voice barked out and the couple at the table threw disapproving looks towards the burger van.

'I gave you a twenty.'

'It was a ten, sir.'

'It was a fucking twenty.'

Ferreira turned to see Clinton Renfrew up on the balls of his feet, holding a hot dog smothered in toxic yellow mustard.

'I'm sorry –'

'Gimme my change or I'll come up there and get it myself.'

The other people in the queue were finding the pavement and the surrounding buildings fascinating suddenly, all frozen silent. Behind the counter the two women were conferring, trying to decide whether it was worth the hassle, if he looked like the kind of bloke who would kick the side door in.

'Well, what's it to be?' Renfrew asked.

The older woman went to the till and returned with a handful of change she slammed down on the counter, asked who was next.

Renfrew strutted away from the burger van, head held high as he took a bite of his hot dog. As he walked past, Ferreira clocked the label on his jeans and the logo on the side of his wrap-around sunglasses. The combined price was more than he would earn in a week at the garage and she wondered why he wasn't under a car right now. Monday mornings were busy, all of those clanks and rattles which emerged over the weekend to deal with.

Maybe they'd sacked him.

Maybe he'd come into some money and quit.

At the table the old man started to complain about falling standards and how the schools were to blame, his wife agreeing as she blew on her tea.

Ferreira gave Renfrew five seconds' head start then hitched her handbag onto her shoulder and went after him, seeing the swagger in his walk, a bolt of added confidence from the small scam he'd just pulled. He stopped at the traffic lights where Bridge Street crossed Bourges Boulevard, four lanes dividing the edge of the Woodston suburbs from the city centre proper, standing behind a woman in a grey skirt suit, so close that she took a step forward, almost moving into the road.

The lights changed and Ferreira let get him fifteen feet ahead of her. He blended into the crowd of shoppers ambling down the broad, tree-lined street, just another average-looking, middle-aged bloke with a shaved head. Only the wings tattooed across the back of his neck marked him out.

It was a crisp, bright morning and Bridge Street was bustling with people brought out by the weather and the mid-season sales, New Look's window screaming 70 per cent off, M&S 50. Renfrew stopped to check out the display at a small menswear boutique and Ferreira swerved away to lose herself between the metal benches and market stalls which ran up the centre of the street, skirting a railed-off section of seating outside Deli France, where women were sitting talking over their lattes, wrapped in coats and sunglasses, smiling into the unseasonal sunshine.

Renfrew threw the rest of his hot dog to the ground and moved off again.

Where was he going?

A straight line through the centre of town would take him to the Barlows' house but Ferreira didn't think she was that lucky.

She kept him in view as they passed the town hall, a small anti-cuts protest clustered around the main doors, their ringleader talking to an ageing security guard who'd probably had his hours and wages slashed. One of the protesters had sloped off to the Costa nearby, was sitting out front with an espresso and a panini, his placard leaning against the wall behind him.

It was no way to start a revolution, Ferreira thought.

The cathedral bells rang the hour as Renfrew crossed the main square and Ferreira fell in step behind him, a dozen people between them as they moved up Long Causeway, passing a coffee wagon and a flower stall which filled the air with pollen, making her nose twitch. The road gave way to flat grey cobbles, more cafe tables on the pavement and a *Big Issue* seller outside the back entrance of Queensgate shopping centre, fighting for spare change with a busker playing an inevitable Bob Dylan cover.

A Securicor van was parked in front of Halifax and Renfrew gave it a speculative look as he walked past. He probably thought he could take it, tough guy like him.

As they crossed Westgate, Ferreira realised Renfrew was likely going to sign on. If he'd been sacked Friday this was his first opportunity to get in there and demand some money, but he kept going, walking faster now, hands tucked into his pockets, a new determination squaring his shoulders.

The crowd was thinning out as they headed north, fewer shops this far up and still too early for the big chain pubs which were strung along both sides of the street. Their doors were open, wafting out the spilt beer and stale body smell of the night before, a few diehards already in. Ferreira expected Renfrew to head inside Yates's or the College Arms, but he passed both of them without even a sideways glance and kept going.

Another three hundred yards and they would be out of the city centre. Fern House was a couple of streets away, a five-minute walk. The Barlows' house five minutes further on, and Ferreira couldn't imagine what else there was to interest Renfrew in New England. Somehow she couldn't see him frequenting any of the Polish cafes or Bangladeshi grocers.

A group of students came out of the library, lost in conversation, and Renfrew barged through them, sending one of them flying into a parked car. They looked up the street after him but seemed to think better of it. As she walked past, Ferreira heard one of them murmur 'psycho' and almost told them how right they were.

Then she lost him.

She quickened her pace, swearing at herself. No side streets, no doorways.

Where was he?

She stopped and scanned the street; two Asian men outside Domino's, a woman smoking in the doorway of a hairdresser's, an old guy leaning on a stick, a young one shouting into his phone, Renfrew emerging from behind a UPS van, crossing the road, heading for a hole-in-the-wall jeweller's opposite. She started to follow but as her foot hit the road she decided against it. Renfrew knew his rights, he would be combative and awkward. Best to wait.

She rolled a cigarette while she watched the door, smoked it quickly, wanting to move, get in there and find out what Renfrew was up to. She wanted to stop him when he came out, provoke him into losing it so she could drop him hard to the pavement. But she wouldn't. It was the chase talking, that aggro thrill of tailing someone to their destination.

Her mobile phone rang and she fished it out of her bag – *DI Adams*.

'Hey, Mel, you busy right now?'

'Ish, yeah.'

'Do me a favour? I've got a guy here doesn't speak any English and it's a time-is-of-the-essence type of thing, don't want to wait for a translator.'

Renfrew emerged from the jeweller's and Ferreira ducked behind the UPS van, out of his eyeline. He wasn't looking anywhere but dead ahead though, going back into the city centre.

'Where are you?'

'City Hospital,' Adams said.

'Has your unidentified man identified himself?'

'Something like that.'

'Alright, I'm on my way.'

'Put your foot down, would you, darling? He looks a bit peaky.'

Ferreira went into the jeweller's, a buzzer sounding over the door as she entered.

The shop was dark and poky under a low ceiling, display cases lining three walls, old wooden things with antiquated locks, crammed with a lot of new silver jewellery and photo frames, christening sets and watches with high street names on their faces, nothing of any value.

The owner looked up from what he was doing, scribbling away behind the counter. 'I'll be with you in just a minute, madam.'

She eyed the security camera mounted high in the corner, another antique, and thought how easy it would be to rob the place. The owner was a dainty little guy, couldn't have weighed more than a hundred pounds, and he looked like a bleeder with that near-albino colouring.

Maybe he had a sawn-off shotgun holstered under the cash register, but she doubted it.

He tidied away his paperwork and clapped his hands together, a toothy smile splitting his face.

'Now, what can I do for you?'

Ferreira showed him her warrant card and the smiled closed to a moue.

'Bloke just came in here,' she said. 'Was he buying or selling?'

'I really couldn't –'

'There's no fence/mugger privilege, sir. So you really can and you'd really better.'

'He was selling.'

'I want to see it.'

He went out the back and returned a moment later with a few pieces of jewellery in a stainless-steel tray, placed it on the counter in front of her. Two battered sovereign rings made for thick fingers and an onyx pinkie ring, scuffed up and misshapen from wear, the gold band worn thin.

'How much did you give him?'

'Two hundred and ten.'

'They're a bit shabby,' Ferreira said, inspecting the sovereigns closer.

'That was the scrap value.'

'Where did he say they came from?'

'They're just some old pieces he doesn't wear any more.'

'Course they are.'

Ferreira picked up the onyx ring and turned it to the light. Despite the wear to the stone the words etched inside it were still clear, *To my big bear, love Gemma.*

She smiled.

'I'm going to need to take these with me.'

38

There was building work in progress at the hospital and half of the car park was cordoned off behind high wire fences, men in viz vests and hard hats wandering about, a few in suits with clipboards monitoring them, making sure to keep their white wellington boots pristine, staying well away from the rubble and dust.

Ferreira found a space and went to get a ticket, swearing at the machine as it spat out the same pound coin three times in a row, finally taking it, along with another four, in exchange for an hour's grace from the clamp.

As she crossed the road she saw DI Adams standing with the other smokers under the wide blue canopy outside reception. He was his usual dapper self, in a black suit and narrow charcoal overcoat with the collar turned up against the wind.

They'd slept together two and a half times, their last encounter a drunken fumble at the Christmas party which was hastily aborted when his then-girlfriend tracked them down to the ladies' toilets. He'd called a couple of times and suggested a drink but neither of them were that invested in the idea.

He didn't look bad today though, she thought, watching him bend to give a light to an old man in a wheelchair.

He smiled as he saw her, slipped off his sunglasses.

'Very smart.'

'In court,' she said.

'What were you up for? Slap a suspect again?'

'Used non-approved method of restraint.'

'Yeah, I know how much you like them.'

She looked at her shoes, bit back the smile before it spread too wide, remembering him shouting at her as he sat naked on his living-room floor, handcuffed to the radiator.

'Ziggy's alright without you for a bit, is he?'

'He'll have to be.'

'You give him lip like that in the office?' Adams asked.

'He's an enlightened boss.'

'I'll square it with him when we're done. Say I threw my rank at you.' Adams flicked his cigarette away into the road. 'Shall we do this?'

They went into the aqueous grey-blue gloom of reception, a hubbub of voices coming from the cafeteria, all low and serious, passed a jumble sale for a local hospice, tables piled with third hand paperbacks and children's toys, two elderly women with fake smiles plastered on their faces for the patients who picked things up and put them down again, their attention elsewhere as they tried to distract themselves with the dusty tat.

'Heard you've taken over one of Hawkes's cases,' Adams said, as they entered the stairwell. 'That thing on Holme Fen. Why did Riggott give you it?'

'The dead guy's brother's one of ours,' Ferreira told him.

'You getting anywhere with it?'

'Nobody wants to talk, you know how it is.'

Adams opened the door onto Ward 7 and she went in ahead of him, the smell of disinfectant barely masking the shit it had recently cleaned up. There was a large sign warning of norovirus in the area and she wondered why they'd put someone with a gunshot in an infected ward.

A fat nurse in blue scrubs stepped in front of them.

'Hands.'

'Excuse me?'

'We ask all visitors to disinfect their hands before entering the ward.'

'Yes, that's what I thought you meant,' Ferreira said.

The nurse watched as they pumped pink goo from a canister and finally cleared their path when she was satisfied her instructions had been carried out.

Adams shot Ferreira an amused look.

'What? Manners don't cost anything.'

'I'm not arguing. Wouldn't dare.'

A consultant was doing his rounds as they passed the bays, a young guy dressed fogeyish in grey flannel trousers and a striped shirt, a bow tie at his neck. He led a gaggle of students behind him, more women than men, all watching him rapt as he reduced the patients to slabs of diseased meat, speaking as if they weren't there.

Ferreira could still hear his voice as they reached a private room at the far end of the ward, rich, round vowels projecting the full length of the corridor, talking about a colonoscopy like he was giving a soliloquy from *Hamlet*.

The PC outside the room snapped to attention, his right hand twitching like he was going to salute Adams.

'At ease, soldier.'

The room was dimly lit and warm, machines humming and pinging, tubes snaking in and out of the man lying propped in the bed, with the bars pulled up either side of him. He was sleeping or sedated, didn't notice them enter, but his visitor stood as the door opened.

'Sergeant Ferreira, you are here.'

'You two know each other?' Adams asked.

'Yes,' she said slowly, cogs turning; the steamy kitchen in Andrus Tombak's dosshouse, the procession of close-lipped men and fruitless conversations. It felt like months had passed, although it had only been five days. 'Mr Perez was helping with our inquiries into the Stepulov murder.'

She slipped into Portuguese as he took her hand between both of his.

'What are you doing here, Mr Perez? How do you know this man?'

'He is my cousin,' he said, eyes bright. 'Paolo.'

'Your cousin who was missing?'

He nodded. 'Yes, look, he is alive.'

Barely, Ferreira thought, looking at the man's broken nose and blacked eyes, the seeping gunshot wound high on his chest. They had bandaged him and cleaned him up, but he'd evidently suffered for a long time before that injury was inflicted. His ribcage showed through his tan skin and his collarbones stood sharply out, shadows pooled behind them.

His eyes were open now though, haunted and watchful.

'How did you know he was here?'

'A nurse phoned me this morning,' Perez said. 'Paolo gave them my number. I thank God I didn't change my mobile or I would never have known he was here.'

'Has he talked to anyone yet?' she asked Adams.

'We got a few words out of him earlier, in Portuguese – I don't know what he said, God knows how he got them to make that phone call. They sedated him while I nipped out to check with the office. The doctor reckoned he was getting pretty worked up about something or other. She wanted him to rest for a bit.'

'He doesn't look like he's up to being questioned.'

'I need anything you can get, Mel. This is serious shit now.'

'Has he spoken to you?' she asked Perez.

He shook his head. 'He keeps talking about Maria – his girlfriend – but he wasn't making any sense.'

'Just give it a go, will you?' Adams said.

Ferreira inched past Marco Perez and sat down in the visitor's chair pulled up close to the bed, placed her hand lightly on Paolo's arm and switched to Portuguese.

'Paolo, my name's Mel, we need to ask you a few questions about what happened. Is that OK?'

His head rolled towards her on the pillow and he blinked slowly, giving the merest nod.

'He speaks English very well,' Perez said. 'He worked in bars back home, his English is perfect.'

She told Adams.

'We've tried that, he doesn't answer. The doctor said it happens sometimes when people have experienced trauma, they revert to their first language.' He folded his arms. 'I wouldn't have dragged you over here if it wasn't necessary, would I? Just ask him if he knows who shot him.'

She squeezed Paolo's arm lightly, drawing his attention back to her.

'Paolo, do you know who did this to you?'

'The English.'

'I need you to tell me their names.'

'No names.'

'You're safe here, Paolo. There's a policeman outside the door, nobody can get to you, you don't need to be afraid of them. Tell us who they are and we'll lock them up. OK? Just tell us and we'll get them.'

'I do not know names.' His foot twitched under the tightly drawn covers. 'They tell us nothing.'

'What's he saying?' Adams asked.

Ferreira ignored him.

'Where were you when it happened?'

'I do not know. There are fields and a road.' He lifted his hand from his stomach, made a vague gesture in the air. 'I cannot remember. Black fields, big.'

'On the fens?'

'I don't know where.'

'Were you working there?'

He nodded, closed his eyes and swallowed.

'Did the people you were working for do this to you, Paolo?'

'They are animals.' He gripped her hand suddenly and she felt how rough his skin was, calloused and worn like it had been scraped with sandpaper. 'They killed my friend. You must find them.'

'When did this happen?'

'It was Saturday. I think. What is today?'

'It's Monday.'

'What month?'

'It's still February, Paolo, you were only unconscious for a few hours.' His fingers tightened around hers. 'What did they do to him?'

'There was an accident,' he said, his voice thickening. He closed his eyes again and when he spoke every word looked like it hurt. 'He was injured and I told the English they must take him to hospital but they wouldn't. They threw him into the concrete and he was still alive. One of them pushed him down with a rake. They killed him.'

He pulled his hand free and covered his eyes. The heart monitor was beeping faster and when Ferreira glanced at it she saw his pulse racing, climbing above ninety beats, then a hundred. He groaned low in his throat and turned away from her.

'For Christ's sake, Mel, what's he saying?'

Paolo let out a string of prayers and curses and his heart rate kept rising.

'Stop now,' Perez said. 'He cannot do this.'

Adams leaned across the bed. 'Mel.'

'I get nurse.' Perez bolted for the door and she heard him calling out to someone in the corridor. 'Please, he is dying. Help him.'

Ferreira rose from the chair and within a couple of seconds the room was full of bodies, pulling her aside, telling Adams to move, then they were on the ward again and the door was closed on them. Perez stood with his hands clasped around the back of his neck, looking through the window as a nurse dropped the bars on the side of Paolo's bed.

Adams drew her away, his face stony.

'What the hell was that?'

'He's terrified.'

'Yeah, I got that. What did he tell you?'

'He said he doesn't know who shot him.'

'Bollocks he doesn't.'

'He couldn't give me a name or a location or anything.'

Adams shoved his fingers back through his hair, blew out a long, controlled breath. 'He told you something. He didn't freak out like that for no reason.'

'You've got another murder, that's what he said.'

39

By midday Viktor Stepulov's board was beginning to look chaotic, the morning's yawning white spaces colonised with information coming in from the teams Zigic had deployed to canvas the farms and nurseries scattered across Holme Fen. A quick audience with DCS Riggott had got him four fresh bodies for the day and he was told to use them wisely.

He drew a ten-mile radius around the dump site on the railway crossing and divided it in half, the area taking in twelve villages, dozens of farms, four nurseries and another two accommodation sites beside Bob Drake's. Three had been ruled out already, nobody knew Viktor Stepulov, he had never been there. He struck them through as the news came in, aware that the teams would be lied to if they hit the right place, but what else could he do other than trust the instincts of the officers Riggott had given him?

They were good people, there was no reason to think they would miss the hints, but the idea that he should be doing their job himself gnawed at him as he paced the office, unable to rest for more than a few seconds in one place.

It wasn't usually like this. They were working in a vacuum with the Stepulov brothers. These men were transient and cut off from their families, with no friends to speak of and no solid work-places to investigate, no laptops to sift through, no definite phone lines or bank accounts to interrogate.

He wondered now how previous generations of coppers ever solved a crime. When you removed all the electronic ephemera of modern lives, what were you left with but that hitch in your gut that told you something was amiss?

He felt that hitch now.

In the office his computer gave out a two-tone ping and he went to check his emails, cleared some space on his desk to get at the keyboard. Dr Irwin with the post-mortem results, photos attached but he wasn't interested in seeing them unless it was absolutely necessary.

He knew plenty of DIs who papered their walls with the goriest images they could find, spurred on by them, but it always seemed wilfully macabre to him, just another pissing contest – look what I can handle.

He scanned quickly through the report, knowing what he wanted to see.

'. . . *signs of malnutrition . . . no alcohol in his system . . . X-rays reveal hairline fractures to cheekbone, fully healed . . . four broken molars on the same side, consistent with impact injury . . . massive trauma to the chest and abdomen . . .*'

'Understatement of the year,' he said to the empty office.

'. . . *break to the tibia occurred approx four hours prior to death . . .*'

'Cause of death . . .'

'. . . *inconclusive . . .*'

Zigic dialled Irwin's office number, waited five rings for an answer and was met with a mumbling hello.

'Have I caught you in the middle of something?'

'Lunch.'

'Look, quick question? Was he dead before the train hit him or not?'

Irwin swallowed audibly. 'It's all in the report, Ziggy.'

'You said inconclusive.'

'I can't tell you what killed him, no. If you'd like me to speculate I'd say there was a fatal wound somewhere on his torso and placing him across the train tracks was a deliberate attempt to obliterate any evidence we might have recovered from said wound – that is purely speculation though, so don't quote me.' Irwin broke off to drink a mouthful of something. 'He was definitely dead when the train went over him, though.'

'Can I quote that?'

'Anywhere you like.'

Zigic thanked him and rang off, went back into the main office with the findings swirling in his head. Malnutrition. No alcohol in his system. He thought of Mrs Stepulov walking the long dim corridor to the mortuary with him, implying that Viktor was always drunk, so she wasn't surprised he'd been hit by a train.

Drink was a curse and comfort blanket to migrant workers. Away from home, separated from everyone and everything you know, you had to drink. So why had Viktor given it up suddenly? Money was always a factor, but if he was as bad as Mrs Stepulov suggested he would buy vodka or beer before food.

She might have been lying about him.

The more Zigic thought about it the more convinced he became that she was. Viktor had no criminal record, here or in Estonia, and they had no evidence to suggest that he was a violent man.

Maybe she simply disliked him. For any of the thousand petty reasons people disliked their in-laws, and she was impugning his character out of habit.

'Bobby, where are you with the phone records?'

Wahlia had the sheets spread out across his desk, call logs from the Stepulov house and the family's mobile phones covered in pink highlighter.

'There's something weird here,' he said, scratching his eyebrow with his thumb. 'I've gone back to early August and the traffic's pretty much standard – they talk to each other a lot, there're a few calls a month back home – but the only thing that stands out is a call from a petrol station payphone in Wisbech. Evening of November the fifth, a Monday.'

'That could be Viktor. What time was it?'

'Eight ten,' Wahlia said. 'Lasted less than a minute.'

Zigic nodded. 'Why would he ring off like that? Mrs Stepulov said he didn't tell them where he was or what was going on.'

'But if he's in a petrol station why would he have to cut it short?'

'Maybe he ran out of money.' Zigic sat down at an empty desk, drummed his fingers against the top. 'We know where he was anyway. He could have been working there if he called at that time of night.'

'Or he stopped on the way home.'

'So, again, why ring off? Get in touch, check their employee records. And send someone over there with his photo. It might be his regular post-work stop-off.'

Zigic stood up again, paced to the window, saw Ferreira's car turn into the station, the stereo so loud he heard it three floors up.

'What about Jaan's phone?'

'Also weird,' Wahlia said. He turned away from the desk, swivelled in his chair. 'He's had no contact with the family since he left home nigh on three months back. Nothing at all – right? But we've got dozens of calls logged to this mobile number in the weeks before he died. All hours night and day, some very long conversations, half an hour, forty minutes, in the middle of the night.'

'A woman?'

'What I'm thinking, yeah.'

'And you've called it?'

'It's dead.'

'Naturally.'

Wahlia shoved his sleeves back to his elbows, getting down to it. 'The last call Jaan made to it was the night before he died, just gone ten.'

'A pay-as-you-go?'

'Wouldn't be anything else, would it?'

There should be no such thing as untraceable pay-as-you-go phones, Zigic thought. What kind of person had them? What did you use one for except no good? Crime and affairs. That was it.

'Run it down.'

'Sure thing, boss.'

He poured a cup of coffee from the machine, stood stirring sugar into it for a few seconds, thinking about the woman Gemma Barlow said she saw coming to visit Jaan Stepulov in their shed.

What kind of woman got involved with a man in his situation? Gemma assumed she was a prostitute but that was more about her prejudices than anything else. The kind that Jaan could afford wouldn't make house calls very often, and if they did they definitely wouldn't make them to sheds. It was too dangerous for one thing.

Surely it wouldn't be an affair either.

No. More likely that last late-night call was to the person who killed him.

Ferreira came into the office with a broad smile on her face, walked straight over to Jaan Stepulov's board and moved Clinton Renfrew's mugshot to the top of the suspects column, stood next to it looking very pleased with herself.

'How'd it go at the hospital?' Zigic asked.

'Adams has got problems,' she said. 'We, on the other hand, have solutions.'

Zigic crossed his arms. 'Intrigued. Go on.'

She took an evidence bag out of her jacket pocket and held it up in front of him. Three gold rings inside.

'I saw Renfrew in town.'

'And you mugged him?' Zigic took the bag from her and shook the rings out into his palm. 'What's the significance?'

'They're Phil Barlow's. Check out the inscription on the pinkie ring.'

He read it, thinking nobody would give away something so sentimental without good reason.

'How did you get them?'

'I followed Renfrew down to that little jeweller's near the university –'

'Have you arrested him?'

Ferreira perched on the edge of her desk, fists thrust down into her jacket pockets. 'No. He doesn't know we're on to him. I thought they'd be more useful as leverage with the Barlows.'

Zigic slipped the rings back into the evidence bag.

'What're you thinking? Blackmail or payment?'

'What's the difference?' Ferreira said. 'They're guilty either way.'

He weighed the rings in his palm. 'Renfrew's working cheap if this is all he got. There can't be more than three hundred quid's worth here.'

'Two-ten, but we've got to assume there's more, haven't we?' Ferreira said. 'Barlow was loaded with chains and shit when we interviewed him. And it explains why we've not seen any lump sums go out of their back accounts.'

'Have they got lump sums?'

Ferreira nodded. 'They're ticking over, lot of credit card debt, but there's a Post Office savings account with four grand in it. Joint names but it's mostly Gemma's wages in there.'

'Probably a holiday fund,' Zigic said.

'They're not stupid. They realised we'd find out if they used that to pay Renfrew off.' Ferreira straightened away from her desk and buttoned her suit jacket up. 'You want me to bring them in?'

Zigic's mobile vibrated – Jenkins, *more good news*.

'Hold on for ten minutes, Mel.'

She planted her fists on her hips. 'This is what we've been waiting for.'

'And we can wait ten minutes longer.'

40

Kate Jenkins was at her desk in the small glass-walled office attached to the lab, working with her earphones in, singing along in a tone-deaf voice, provoking amused looks from her assistants as they pored over a set of tattered, bloodstained clothing on the other bench. DI Adams's case, he guessed, seeing one of them poke a gloved finger through a bullet hole in the shapeless black cotton T-shirt.

Zigic knocked on the open door.

'Kate.'

She belted out another line, nodding along, fingers skipping across the keyboard.

'Kate.'

He went up behind her and hooked out one of the white buds. She turned sharply.

'I was just getting to the good bit.'

'I heard,' he said. 'I think the whole station heard actually.'

She whipped out the other earphone and the music kept running from it, a man's voice, high and screechy. 'Why weren't you at the PM?'

'Had some extra troops to marshal.'

'Aw, and I said it was because you were delicate.'

'What have you got for me?'

She pulled a Manila folder out from the stack on her desk. 'Let's wait for Adams, OK, I don't want to have to go through it all twice.'

'What's it got to do with him?'

'There's been a development.' She picked up a bag of Skittles. 'Want one?'

'Kate.'

'No, he'll be here in a second.'

Zigic took a couple of sweets. They tasted plastic and saccharine.

Jenkins put her feet up on her desk, pink Crocs spattered with God knows what, and rocked back lightly in her chair. The music kept bleeding out of her earphones like white noise waiting for the voices of the dead to come through.

Zigic looked at the postcards arranged across the corkboard above her desk, small reproductions of Impressionist landscapes and still lifes, Pissarro street scenes and Cézanne apples. Bland, safe art to resettle her eye after hours staring at blood-spatter patterns and body parts disrupted from their natural arrangement.

She tossed a yellow Skittle in the air and caught it in her mouth.

'How's the family?' Zigic asked.

'Good. Yours?'

'Yeah, good.'

She flicked another Skittle up in the air and a hand snatched it as it began to drop.

Adams popped the sweet in his mouth. 'What've you got for me, red?'

'Same thing I've got for Ziggy.'

They nodded to each other and Zigic realised Adams was as happy with the development as he was. Nobody liked sharing a case.

'Come on then.'

Jenkins went back out into the lab, taking the file with her, and they danced around each other for a moment, an excess of good manners which Adams managed to turn into a pantomime, a stupid smile on his face as he half bowed and ushered Zigic out of the door.

He was supposed to be an excellent detective, vicious and intuitive by turns, and rumour was he'd be replacing DCS Riggott within the next five years, but Zigic couldn't see it, dreaded the idea of having him as a superior. Not that he didn't like the man. They'd been sergeants at the same time, worked on several major cases together, and Adams struck him as capable, but he treated the job like a game, glided through it seemingly unconcerned with the victims or their families, unless he was trying to screw one of them.

Zigic suspected he was completely amoral.

'Right then, gents, to business.'

Jenkins stood at the head of one of the long stainless-steel tables, the file open in front of her, a rack of test tubes to her left, sealed evidence bags to her right, clothing inside them, just rags.

'Ziggy, we recovered this from the tread of Viktor Stepulov's work boots.' She held up a test tube with some black dust in it.

'What is it?'

'Dried mortar. Very unusual stuff. They only use it for laying black engineering bricks.'

She handed it over and he glanced at it.

'OK.'

'Billy.' She gave another test tube to Adams. 'That came out of the turn-up of Paolo Perez's jeans.'

Adams rattled the test tube, a small black nugget inside it.

'So, it's the same mortar?'

'Yes.'

'So what? They must use it tons of places.'

Jenkins took the samples off them and fitted them back into the slots in the Perspex rack. 'Actually they don't. But you're sceptical, that's fine. It's your job to think nobody knows anything but you.'

'Where was Perez working?' Zigic asked.

'We can't get a straight answer out of him right now,' Adams said. 'He told Mel he was on a building site, though. Where was your guy?'

'We don't know. The Olympic redevelopment was mentioned but that seems unlikely given where his body turned up.'

'We got peat from his boots too,' Jenkins said. 'So he was out on the fens somewhere. The same with Perez.'

'Can you narrow it down a bit?' Adams asked.

'Forensic science has come a long way, Billy, but unfortunately, no, I can't give you an exact grid reference for soil.'

'*CSI* lied to me.'

'Yeah, you can't trust anything those bastards say.'

Zigic pulled the sleeves of his jumper up, crossed his arms. 'Is this really enough to suggest the two crimes are linked? We're in the middle of fenland and there are thousands of migrant workers in the building trade.'

'It's my job to supply the information,' Jenkins said. 'You two can draw your own conclusions. But we've found the same grey fibres on both men's clothing – they're from a Volkswagen transporter van. Which is a popular model, I'll grant you that. Except these fibres went out of production in '04.'

Zigic thought of the vans parked up in the dirt outside Bob Drake's house in Great Gidding, trying to remember what make they were. He'd run in quickly to get out of the rain and hadn't paid as much attention as he should. He made a mental note to have the DVLA records checked out when he returned to the office.

He still couldn't believe Drake would dump Viktor so close to his home.

He couldn't believe he'd shoot Paolo Perez either but that was just a gut instinct about the man with no basis in fact. He seemed well set up and happy to cooperate. Too happy, perhaps. One of those elaborate displays of innocence the guilty sometimes managed to pull off.

The image of the bald man with the hunting rifle came back to him.

Maybe Drake wasn't involved. He had thirty men there, what if an argument blew up between Viktor and one of the other workers? How far would they go to dump his body? A few miles? Drake said they went out clubbing, they weren't captives. It was possible.

'I need to talk to Perez,' Zigic said.

Adams checked his watch. 'Brief Mel. I'll take her with me. Want to try and have another go at him today anyway.'

Jenkins looked between them and Zigic knew she was waiting for an argument. This was where they'd traditionally whip their dicks out to decide who was in charge, but he had enough to worry about with Jaan Stepulov's case stalling; Adams could take the extra stress and if there was a pat on the head from Riggott at the end of it he was welcome to take that too.

He'd prefer to talk to Gemma Barlow without Ferreira anyway.

'OK. She's all yours.'

Adams smiled. 'I won't keep her out too late. Scout's honour.'

41

Gemma Barlow was still in her pyjamas when she opened the front door, her hair flat on one side, tangled on the other, and from the state of her eyes Zigic guessed she'd spent a fair part of the day in tears.

She stepped back to let him inside, mumbled something about tea and retreated to the kitchen, leaving him to close the door.

There was a pall hanging over the house, curtains drawn, the air smoky and stale as if the windows hadn't been opened for days, and even in the living room, where the lights and the television were both on, it felt sombre and grey. He noticed a bottle of white wine, almost drained, on the coffee table.

In the kitchen Gemma was banging around, a little unsteady on her feet, and when she tried to fit the kettle back down onto its pad she struggled to line it up.

'Is Phil at work?'

'Yeah.'

She leaned against the counter and combed her fingers through her hair, suddenly aware of how she looked. But she lost interest in that quickly.

'What do you want him for?'

'It's you I need to talk to.'

She crossed her arms. 'Why?'

'We think we've identified the man who killed Mr Stepulov,' Zigic said, and saw her face soften instantly, an insinuation of a smile at the corners of her mouth. 'But I need you to come in and take a look at his photo, then hopefully give us a statement.'

'OK, that's great. I'll just get changed.'

Gemma went upstairs and he heard her walking around in the bedroom overhead, the one which looked out across the garden, which they couldn't possibly have missed the fire from, and he moved to the back door, saw that one of the shed's side walls had collapsed since he was last there, exposing the tangled wreckage of the sunlounger which Jaan Stepulov had died on.

She hadn't asked who the man was and he guessed he could put any photograph he liked in front of her and get a positive ID.

He went into the living room and switched off the television. There were used tissues wadded against the arm of the sofa, a boxful at least. He wondered what conversations this room had seen during the last couple of days, accusations and recriminations, denials and pleading. Had they sat here with their bank statements spread across the coffee table, trying to work out where the money to pay off Renfrew would come from?

Or maybe they were just blundering along, holding their fears to themselves, not wanting to voice the possibility that they wouldn't get away with it. The same things could be said only so many times before they became meaningless, the hollow reassurances and comforting lies – *if we just stick to our story they can't touch us.*

Zigic looked at the family photographs ranged across the shelves, thinking how genuinely happy Phil and Gemma appeared. There was no strain around the eyes, no too-wide smiles or lopsided body language. There were a few of Gemma with Phil's teenaged son and even they seemed comfortable together.

It didn't take much to disrupt the pattern of people's lives.

One night Jaan Stepulov wanders down Highbury Street, drunk maybe, needing shelter, and they were unlucky enough to be the ones who hadn't locked their shed. A simple oversight and everything changed.

Gemma came downstairs again, hair tidied, make-up done. She took her car keys off the heart-shaped hook above the telephone table.

'Ready when you are then.'

'I think it's best if I drive,' Zigic said and made himself smile. 'Don't want you getting pulled over for the breathalyser, do we?'

In the car she was quiet and Zigic let the silence stretch out as they passed through the centre of the city, noticed her turn to look at the Crown Court as it loomed up on their left, a cold, grey building standing squat and ugly next to the river. Her hands tightened around the straps of her bag.

The traffic was thick along Bourges Boulevard, the end of the working day drawing close, the offices throwing out suited men and women who filled the paths and bus stops, a few late shoppers and early drinkers among them, moving with different levels of determination. Phil would be heading home soon, Zigic thought, and he might worry when he found the house empty, but they'd be back for him later.

He crossed the Crescent Bridge onto Thorpe Road, passing Peterborough General Hospital, a 1970s eyesore eight storeys high, then one new block of apartment buildings after another filled the road, upscale, exclusive developments where four small rooms cost more than a family home elsewhere in the city. There were a few halfway houses and hostels tucked between them but you wouldn't know that until you moved in.

The traffic was all heading in the same direction, out of the centre and home towards the suburbs or the ring of nice, quiet villages beyond where nobody had ever been burned to death in a locked shed. It was major news in Ailsworth if one of Zigic's neighbours lost a few hand tools from theirs, created a sense of unease which would last for weeks and have the Neighbourhood Watch out in force as darkness fell.

At the station Gemma Barlow went docilely up to the interview room and when he asked if she'd like a cup of tea or something she said she just wanted to get finished quickly so she could be home in time for Phil. He hated coming in to an empty house.

It might be the last evening that happened for a while, Zigic thought, as he collected what he needed from the office.

Gemma sat up straighter when he returned to the interview room, gave her name for the tape in a confident voice very different to the one she'd used last time she was in there. He couldn't tell if it was the drink giving her courage or the prospect of this finally being over.

Her composure cracked when Zigic slid the photograph of Clinton Renfrew across the table.

'Have you seen him before, Gemma?'

'Yes.'

'Who is he?'

'Did he burn our shed down?'

'I asked first,' Zigic said. 'Who is he?'

She pressed her lips tight together and looked away to her left, stared at the door she was regretting walking through.

Zigic brought out the evidence bag with Phil's rings inside and placed them on the table. The noise drew Gemma's attention back and her eyes widened.

'Where did you get those?'

'You recognise them then?'

'No,' she said quickly. 'I don't know what you're talking about.'

Zigic took out the onyx pinkie ring. 'You had this one engraved, Gemma. You must remember doing that. What was it, Phil's birthday?'

'Our anniversary. Five years.'

'It's very nice. Phil must have cherished it.'

Her bottom lip quivered.

'You wanted to know where we got it,' he said. 'This man – Clinton Renfrew – sold it to a jeweller in town earlier today, along with a couple of Phil's sovereign rings, for two hundred quid. Now, what I'm wondering is how he came to have them in the first place.'

Gemma stared at the ring, her mouth open slightly but nothing came out.

Zigic waited, the clock ticking softly in the quiet, hearing muffled voices from the next room, angry but indistinct, then the sound of a chair falling.

256

'Phil was mugged,' Gemma said finally. 'Thursday night, he went over the pub for a pint and he was mugged on the way back by two big blokes. They took everything, all his jewellery.'

'Why didn't he report it?'

'I told him he should but he thought with all this going on you wouldn't care.'

'But it's a lot of money's worth,' Zigic said. 'And it's important, I mean sentimentally – you lose an anniversary present like this, you want to try and get it back. If I lost my wedding ring –'

'They didn't take his wedding ring.'

'That was decent of them.'

'He couldn't get it off,' she said, snapping out the reply so quickly he was sure she was lying. 'He's put on weight, he needs a new one really but he won't change it. He's superstitious like that.'

Zigic nodded. 'Understandable. So what did these blokes look like?'

'Polish or something. Big.'

'And how do you think Clinton Renfrew came to have what they stole?'

'I don't know. Maybe he bought them off the blokes and then sold them on. I don't know how thieving bastards like that work.'

Zigic put the ring back in the bag, Gemma watching him.

'Where do you know Renfrew from?'

'I don't.'

'Gemma, be sensible now, you just told me you recognised him.' Zigic leaned across the table. 'Him and Phil are friends, we already know that.'

'They're not friends,' she said sharply. 'Phil hates him.'

'Why?'

'He's a piece of shit.'

'But they go way back.'

Disgust contorted Gemma's face. 'Phil went out with his sister for a few months. Years back, before we met. He was on the rebound after his divorce, he wouldn't have touched that fucking skank otherwise.'

Zigic wondered if she realised what she was saying now, the implications she was creating and the connection she was admitting to so easily. The wine she'd drunk was still sloshing around in her system, making her cheeks flush through her make-up and loosening her tongue. She had days of emotional strain pent up in her chest and perhaps this was the tipping point.

This job was all luck, he thought, catching people at a low enough ebb to say something they'd regret.

'Has he seen Clinton lately?'

'Why would he?'

'Did you know Clinton's been inside?'

'No.'

'For arson.'

Gemma leaned back in her chair, hands on the table, and she looked again at the photograph. 'You reckon he did it?'

'Clinton burns down buildings for a living,' Zigic said. 'He fired a sandwich bar on Gladstone Street a few years ago – a man died in there too.'

Gemma buried her face in her hands. 'No. No, no, no.'

'And now he's somehow found himself in possession of Phil's jewellery. Do you see where I'm going with this, Gemma?'

'No.'

'Phil wants rid of Stepulov but he's not going to burn him out, he's not that kind of man, you said it yourself. Renfrew is, though. He wouldn't think twice about it. But he's going to want paying . . .'

'No.'

'Yes, Gemma.'

She shook her head, muttered more denials.

'The going rate is two or three thousand for a job like that,' Zigic said. 'So, how much do you think all Phil's chains and rings are worth?'

'He wouldn't do that.'

258

'I think he would. There's no other explanation.'

She snatched up the onyx ring, a wild look in her eyes. 'He wouldn't give him *this*. The rest of it maybe, but not *this*. He swore to me he'd never take it off as long as he lived.'

'So why is it here now instead of on his finger?'

She slammed it down. 'He was mugged.'

'I don't think so,' Zigic said. 'I think you'd had enough of Stepulov and Phil went to the only person he knew who could help. His old mate Clinton Renfrew.'

Gemma shook her head, tears springing into her eyes.

'Now's where you tell me the truth, Gemma. Before I talk to Renfrew.'

She sobbed into her hands.

'Because once he realises we're going to charge him he'll drop the pair of you in it to save himself.' Zigic slipped the rings away again, reminding her that they were evidence. 'That's what Renfrew does. He cuts deals to save his own skin.'

She wiped her eyes on the cuff of her cardigan.

'He will throw you to the wolves,' Zigic said. 'Both of you, unless you tell me what happened.'

'Ask Phil, he'll –' She stopped herself abruptly, lips pressed together so tightly that they almost disappeared.

'What, Gemma?' Zigic asked, trying to catch her eye. 'What's Phil going to tell me?'

A wobbly breath shuddered out of her but she didn't reply.

'Phil will tell me what really happened? Is that it?'

'I want to leave.' She stood up, gathering her handbag from under the chair.

'Do you know what happened, Gemma?'

She started for the door and he moved quickly to block her escape. Their faces were inches apart but she wouldn't look at him, fixed her eyes on the chrome door handle she didn't dare reach for.

'You're not helping Phil, do you understand that? The longer this goes on and the more you two lie, the worse it'll be when we charge you.'

She grabbed the handle but his fingers were already there.

'I want to go home,' she said, her voice breaking. 'Phil'll be worried where I am.'

'If Renfrew did this, you need to tell me right now.'

Finally she lifted her chin and met his gaze, and when she spoke the exertion was audible in every word,

'Arrest me or let me leave.'

Zigic waited for a couple of beats, seeing how fast she was breathing, hearing the squeak of her hand tightening around the strap of her shoulder bag. Then he opened the door and stepped aside.

'We'll speak again, Gemma, very soon.'

42

Visiting hours were almost over when Ferreira and Adams arrived at Ward 7, a few patients sitting upright in their beds, talking in quiet voices or eating the food their families had brought in for them. Most were alone, their people come and gone, or maybe they had no one, Ferreira thought.

A man in chinos and a check shirt was wandering around near the nurses' station, looking for someone to answer his questions, but there wasn't a staff member anywhere to be seen, except for a small Indonesian auxiliary pushing a cleaning trolley.

Ferreira hated this place.

Hated all hospitals.

Last year her mother had a cancer scare and she'd come with her for the appointment, sat in a waiting room in another part of the building, surrounded by grim-faced women dressed up for the occasion with their daughters and friends in tow. A few had brought their boyfriends or husbands for support and they looked trapped and bored as they waited, already planning their escape routes in case the news was bad.

Her mother had been terrified. Not of the cancer, she was strong enough to face that down and fight it, but of how her father would react to a mastectomy. In the car on the way over she had cried, looking down at her bust, saying she wouldn't blame him if he left her. What man would want her after that?

When she went in to see the specialist, a dour Germanic man with hair that looked like a toupee, Ferreira sat flicking through an old magazine, seeing nothing, rehearsing the talking-to she would give her father if the tests came back positive. She wanted to believe he was better than that. In the car she had found a smile for her mother and told her not to be ridiculous, he loved her, he would see her through it. But deep down she knew better.

They both knew what kind of man he was even if they'd never openly discussed it. They were that kind of family; too close for secrets, too Catholic for confrontation. He had affairs, Ferreira saw it in the way he behaved around women. She knew how to spot a man who would disregard his wedding ring when there was a sure fuck on offer, she'd been out with enough of them. Faced with a suddenly imperfect wife he would run to whichever whore he was seeing on the side.

It never came to that, though. The results were negative, just a benign fatty deposit, and everything went back to normal.

'Watch out.' Adams grabbed her elbow and pulled her aside as an obese man in an electric wheelchair cut along the corridor, scattering people left and right. 'Fucking idiot.'

'Do you want to chase him down and give him a ticket?'

'We could give him an on-the-spot fine and split it,' Adams smiled. 'I won't tell if you won't.'

'So that's how you afford such expensive suits.'

'They're not expensive, it's how I wear them.'

Ferreira nodded. 'Natural style?'

'You know it.'

They passed the last bay on the corridor, a large group around the bed nearest the window, where an emaciated Sikh man was being fed rice from a Tupperware container by a woman in a red sari. A heated discussion was going on around the foot of the bed, three young men, all with the same sharp profile, talking in a mix of English and Punjabi, the word negligence tossed between them.

Outside Paolo Perez's room a different PC was on guard, this one not so alert as his predecessor. He sat hunched over, thumbs swiping across his phone's touchscreen, eliciting cartoon sounds. He didn't notice them approach until Adams kicked his booted foot.

'That work, is it?'

'Sorry, sir.' He fumbled the phone as he stood and it dropped with a crack.

'Pick it up.'

He stooped to retrieve it.

'I see you fucking around like that again you'll be operating it with your prostate.'

'Yes, sir. Sorry, sir.'

They went into Paolo's room.

The television was on, showing the BBC News Channel, and among the debris of chocolate wrappers and coffee cups on the table pulled across his bed was a copy of today's *Evening Telegraph*; his shooting had made the front cover.

'How're you feeling?' Ferreira asked.

'A little better, thank you.'

'That's good. Has Marco been back?'

'Yes. He brought me some things.'

'I'm not sure you should be having coffee in your condition,' Ferreira said, seeing how tired he looked, hearing the listlessness in his speech.

She placed the file she'd brought with her on the table and slipped off her jacket. The room was stifling but Paolo had the covers pulled up to his waist and he'd acquired a pyjama top from somewhere. He had his good arm in it, the rest draped around his shot shoulder, and it swamped his thin form.

'You questioned me,' he said to Ferreira. 'This morning.'

'That's right.'

'Are you Portuguese?'

'Yes. From Lisbon. Where do you come from?'

'Carvoeiro. Do you know it?'

'No. I've been here since I was seven.'

'It is very beautiful. You should come there on holiday.'

Ferreira smiled. 'I might do that.'

Adams stood by the door, hands on his hips, a picture of

stressed impatience. Or maybe he just didn't like being shut out of the conversation, Ferreira thought.

'Is he up to being questioned, Mel?'

'I am, sir, yes.'

'Great, we'll do this in English then.'

'Are you OK with that, Paolo?' Ferreira asked.

'I think so.'

'Well, just switch when you need to. It's no big deal.'

Adams opened the door again and clicked his fingers at the PC, came back a moment later with the man's chair and placed it at the foot of the bed.

'Do your thing first, Mel, get it out of the way.'

She opened the file and found the photograph of Viktor Stepulov, handed it to Paolo.

'Do you recognise this man?'

He nodded quickly. 'Yes, he was at the same place as me.'

'Where you worked?'

'Yes. I did not know him but I saw him. He was there for some time then he was not. I thought he got out somehow. Why do you ask about him? He would not have shot me.'

'Three months ago someone took this man's dead body and put it on a set of train tracks just outside Peterborough.'

Paolo's hands curled into tight fists on his thighs, rucking the blanket. 'So he did not get out. They killed him and tried to make it look like an accident.'

'It appears so, yes.'

'There have been more then,' Paolo said. 'I thought Xin Gao was the first but now there is him too and I think the other men who disappeared from the site must have died also.'

'What other men?' Adams asked.

'Many. I don't know names. One day they are there in the van, at work, another day they are gone and nobody knows where.'

'Didn't you ask your ganger?'

Paolo scowled at Adams, the bruising pinched under his eyes.

'You do not ask questions there. If you ask once you are beaten. You do not make that mistake a second time.'

'Is that what happened to you?' Ferreira asked, softening her voice.

'No. I tried to stop them. I could see that they were going to throw him into the footing and I knew I had to do something. One of them punched me and then they picked Xin Gao up and – he was still alive when they threw him into the concrete, I swear it, I heard him moan.' Paolo looked up at the ceiling. The heart rate monitor pinged, faster and faster, and Ferreira saw a vein pulsing in the side of his neck. 'They made me watch while they pushed him under. They told me I would go in there next.'

'Where did this happen?' Adams asked.

Paolo shook his head. 'We were on a site somewhere – I do not know the place. They took us in vans. There were fields all around us.'

'What was nearby?'

'I do not know. We passed houses. These big –' he switched to Portuguese, looking at Ferreira – 'wind turbines. A lot of them.'

She told Adams.

'They're all over the place on the fens,' he said. 'We need to know where you were, Paolo. You want us to catch them, you need to give us something to go on.'

'Where were you living?' Ferreira asked him. 'Were you in Peterborough?'

'No. In the countryside.'

Adams shifted in his seat and Ferreira realised he was getting annoyed with Paolo. He thought they were being lied to, she'd seen that expression before, and she wondered why it wasn't obvious to him how scared Paolo was.

'Who shot you?'

'I don't know which one it was.'

'Didn't you see them?'

'I was running,' Paolo said. 'It was dark. I just wanted to get away from them.'

Ferreira pressed his hand. 'Paolo, we want to find these people and arrest them. And when we do they'll be going straight to prison, they won't be able to get at you. No matter what they've said, if they've threatened you or your family, I promise they won't be able to touch you. OK? But you need to tell us who they are.'

'I do not know,' he said angrily. 'They were English.'

Adams sighed. 'Alright, that's a start. Names?'

'They did not use names in front of us.'

'Never?'

'No.'

'In all the time you were there?'

'They did not speak to us. They ordered us about, told us what to do. That was all.'

'How did you get the job?' Ferreira asked.

'There was a man at the bus. He was waiting for some workers to arrive, I think. He started talking to me and asked how I was getting on here. I told him it was bad and I was going home. He told me he had a job if I wanted it. Easy work, but good money.'

'And you didn't think that sounded unlikely?' Adams asked.

'I am not an idiot,' Paolo said. 'I knew it would be hard work but I am not afraid of that.'

'Was the money good?'

'There was no money.' Paolo smiled bitterly. 'We were slaves. Do you understand? They paid us nothing. No money. Ever. If you asked about money you were beaten. If you complained they set a pack of dogs on you.'

'Why didn't you leave?' Adams asked.

Paolo pointed at the gunshot wound on his shoulder. 'This is what happened when I left. If that lady didn't stop I would be dead now and nobody would know.'

Adams sat up straighter in his chair. 'This lady –'

'I must thank her,' Paolo said. 'Can I speak to her?'

'We wouldn't mind speaking to her ourselves,' Adams said under his breath. 'She dumped you at A&E and did a runner. Nobody's seen her since.'

'Then you must find her. She might be in danger.'

'I'm sure she's fine,' Ferreira said.

But it did nothing to calm Paolo. His feet scissored under the covers and the fearful look, which never departed for more than a few seconds, came back into his eyes.

'What if they followed her?'

'Do you know what car she was driving?' Adams asked.

'A small one. Red. I did not notice the make,' Paolo said. 'Her name was Linda or Lindsay. Lindsay I think. She is a nurse, she was wearing a blue uniform like the nurses here wear.'

'How old was she?'

'Thirty-five maybe,' Paolo said. 'I don't remember very much. She had short hair, like a man. Very blonde, almost white.'

'OK. We'll see if we can find her.'

Adams got up and left the room, closing the door behind him.

Ferreira felt the heat from the radiator burning across her back and Paolo's rough fingers gripping her own so tightly that the ligaments stood out in his wrist.

'He does not believe me.'

'He does.'

'No. I can see. He thinks I am lying.'

'You need to tell him where they are, Paolo. You want this to stop, don't you? You don't want anyone else to die.'

'They didn't let us out. I don't know where we were.' He looked helpless. 'I didn't even know how long I'd been there until I saw the date on this newspaper. I thought it was years.'

Ferreira met his gaze, saw the fear filling his black eyes. 'How long was it?'

'Ten months.'

'How did you cope?'

'I didn't. It was hell,' he said, eyes dropping. 'I tried not to think about my family but there was nothing else to do but think. Marco says my girlfriend is getting married very soon.'

'I'm sorry.'

'I hoped she would wait but everyone thought I was dead. Why wait for a dead man?'

'She might feel differently when she sees you.'

'She wouldn't want me now. Look what they have done to me.'

'You'll recover, Paolo. A couple of weeks, some good food, plenty of rest.' Ferreira smiled. 'Shave that beard off maybe . . . you'll look fine.'

'I am not the man she loved any more. That man is gone.'

Adams came back in, clutching his mobile. Something had sent a bolt of energy through him, good news on the nurse or a verbal thrashing from Riggott, Ferreira thought.

Late-afternoon now and the DCS would want progress made before the hacks set up shop on the station steps at half past five.

'Right.' He took his car keys out of his jacket pocket and tossed them to Ferreira. 'Road map's in the glovebox. Let's see if we can't work out where these fuckers had Mr Perez interned, shall we?'

43

Zigic tried the garage on the Eastern Industrial Estate first, found out that Clinton Renfrew had called on Friday morning to let them know he'd been offered a better job. He didn't say what and the owner didn't push him, there were plenty of decent mechanics out there who'd be grateful for the work, especially the way things were. The man asked what Renfrew had done and Zigic walked away without answering.

He drove over to the brother's house in Old Fletton, arrived as Renfrew's sister-in-law was unloading her kids from the back of a people carrier, weighed down with gym bags and lunch boxes, shouting for her little girl to stay away from the road. The girl retreated from the kerb and climbed onto the pebble-dashed front wall, started pirouetting on the gatepost's broad concrete cap.

'What do you want?' she asked and looked away before he could answer. 'Keeley, get off there right now.'

The girl jumped down and landed in a heap on the front lawn.

'Is Clinton at home?' Zigic asked.

'No.'

'Where is he?'

'Fuck should I know?'

'He's quit his job at the garage.'

'More like they fired him.' She opened the front door and hustled the kids inside, threw their bags down at the foot of the stairs. 'Lazy bastard's not got a day's work in him. Been asking him to fix the tap in the kitchen since he got here, he ain't bothered.'

'He's come into some money recently,' Zigic said.

'Well, I've not seen any of it.' She put a sharp eye on him. 'What's he done? Second time you come round here, he's done something wrong.'

'I just need to talk to him.' Zigic gave her his card. 'How about you ring me when he gets home?'

She tapped the card against her fingernails, looked back into the house at her kids emerging from the kitchen with crisps and cans of drink, sliding across the laminate floor in their socks like they were skating. The boy, five or six, had a fresh bruise under his left eye, and maybe it was from a playground scuffle or the usual boisterous tumbling of kids that age, but Zigic could easily imagine Renfrew's temper getting the better of him.

'Was Clinton here Wednesday morning?'

'I told you already.'

A car pulled onto her neighbour's driveway, another woman bringing her kids home from school.

'Mrs Renfrew, please.'

'He was here, alright?' Her neighbour waved and she waved back, shot her a smile which might have passed for genuine at that distance, but Zigic saw the strain. 'What do you want me to say?'

Inside the kids started fighting and she went to deal with them without saying another word, slamming the door in Zigic's face.

When he got back to Thorpe Wood Station, the press pack was setting up in the car park, vans from *Look East* and *Anglia* blocking off the front steps, their side panels thrown back as their crews unloaded cameras and set up lamps, wires trailing out across the tarmac. They should have been in the press suite, everyone warm and settled, drinking bad coffee and talking shop, but obviously Riggott had decided that a brief statement would be enough. They were playing their cards close for now.

A couple of journalists from the local papers were standing smoking near the fire door, talking to a WPC who should have known better than to tell them anything. She was laughing though, and gesturing across to some distant point in the east.

'Clarke,' Zigic shouted. 'Over here.'

Her face froze and the hacks looked on with evident delight as she dropped her cigarette butt in a shower of sparks and walked over to him, puffing out her chest and rearranging her radio on her shoulder.

'Sir.'

'Has the PO briefed you on the official line?'

'No, sir.'

'And did she tell you to answer any stupid questions those jackals asked?'

'No, sir.'

'So get inside and keep your mouth shut.'

He followed her in through reception, where a couple of her fellow officers were trying to restrain a lanky young woman with heroin pallor and a black eye as she twisted and spat at them. The desk sergeant folded his arms across his ample gut and gave her a withering look, told her that kind of attitude wouldn't get her anywhere.

Zigic met Adams in the stairwell, the press officer walking in front of him, talking across her shoulder, her heavily made-up face drawn in the grey-blue light.

'Just don't let them sucker you, say what you've got to say and scarper. I'll deal with the rest.'

Adams stopped on the half-landing and the PO kept going, slamming the door into the stairwell wall.

'We got the woman who took Perez to A&E,' he said.

'Lucky break. Did she come forward or did you have to hunt her down?'

'Perez gave us a semi-solid ID. She works at City General, that's how come she managed to avoid the cameras, I guess, knows where the blind spots in the ambulance bay are.'

'Why didn't she go in with him?'

'Scared shitless,' Adams said. 'Can't blame her, can you? They chased her for about five miles, let a couple of shots off at her car.'

'Jesus.'

'Exactly.' He ran his fingers back through his hair, checking his reflection in the glass. He seemed to like what he saw. 'So we've got a location now.'

'Where was he?'

'A compound over on the Wisbech Road.'

'You going tonight?'

'*We're* going tomorrow. First light.' Adams grinned. 'Be good to kick some doors in, won't it?'

He took off down the stairs, almost running.

Zigic headed up to Hate Crimes. As he passed the CID floor he saw Ferreira standing in the middle of the office talking to Riggott, hands on her hips, giving the DCS hard eye contact while he spoke.

He kept walking, got a Coke out of the machine along the hall, took the last Mars bar left in the rack, thinking about Riggott trying to poach his officers back over into CID. He'd lost two of his team in last April's budget cuts. Wells moved down to Huntingdon, taking a place on their Domestic Terrorism Unit, Harris was promoted to sergeant and relocated to Cardiff, leaving his wife and young daughter in Peterborough. She had a job at the university she wasn't prepared to give up and when Harris laid down an ultimatum he didn't get the decision he was expecting. Zigic wondered if they'd managed to patch things up, imagined they hadn't. Harris was no loss. To his wife and daughter or the team, but Wells was a grafter.

If Ferreira went too, where did that leave them? Two people wasn't a department.

There were already rumours of more lay-offs, suggestions from on high that the administrative staff could be outsourced to private contractors. The uniform division was being slowly eroded, fully trained officers pensioned off in favour of civilian support, pointless, power-crazed wannabes who were nothing more than jumped-up security guards in high-visibility jackets.

Twenty per cent budget cuts. It didn't take a genius to work out where they would bite hardest. Anything voters didn't care about could go. Domestic violence, anti-stalking, hate crimes. Women and foreigners. They could be ignored without the world falling down around the council's ears.

In the office Wahlia was standing on his chair fiddling with the strip light over his desk.

'What are you doing?'

'Fucking thing keeps flickering, it's doing my head in.'

'I don't think tapping it's going to help,' Zigic said.

He popped his Coke and took a long drink, watching Wahlia overstretch, waiting for the chair to roll out from under him. Abruptly the light went dead.

'Result?'

'It's less irritating now anyway.'

Wahlia stepped down and the chair flew away from his heel, struck the empty desk behind him.

All of the desks were empty and there was a desolate feel to the office again.

'What happened to my fresh troops?'

'Riggott called them back to the fort. They've had a break in the shooting.'

'Yeah, I heard.'

'Adams is a lucky bastard,' Wahlia said, dragging his chair back and dropping heavily into it. 'We got nothing from the canvassing. Couple of sites looked a bit dodgy but no one knew Viktor.'

Zigic walked over to Viktor Stepulov's board, saw lines through the morning's avenues of inquiry. It didn't matter now, he reminded himself. Whoever shot Paolo was almost certainly linked to Viktor and it was just a matter of bringing them in and getting them to an interview room.

He went into his office and called Anna. She was a long time answering the phone and just as he was beginning to worry she picked up.

'Are you OK?'

'I was in the garden,' she said, a hint of annoyance in her voice.

'Stefan climbed over the fence into next door, he was standing in their pond talking to the bloody koi.'

'Are they in?'

'No, thank God. I don't know what I would have said to them if they were.'

'Is he alright?'

'He's fine.'

In the background he heard Stefan chattering away, telling her about Mr Fishy-Fish. Anna snapped at him and he stopped for about two seconds.

'You've got to talk to him, Dushan. Anything could have happened. He could have drowned.'

'I'll explain to him when I get home.'

'I don't even know how he got in there. One minute he was on the swing and the next he was just gone.' Her voice was trembling. 'What if he'd got out onto the road? He could have been knocked down or abducted or anything. We need to put a higher fence up. And we need to sort out the gate so he can't reach the latch.'

Zigic rubbed his eyes, they felt gritty and raw.

'I'll take care of it, OK, just calm down.'

'I am perfectly calm,' she said tersely.

He heard the fridge door open and a bottle rattling.

'Are you coming home? No, you're not, or you wouldn't be ringing me.'

'I'll be late,' he said. 'But I'll talk to him. I promise.'

She sighed heavily. 'OK.'

'I love you.'

'You'd better.' Stefan was still yammering away. 'I've got to go.'

She put the phone down and Zigic looked at the photographs on his desk, Anna and the boys all smiles. They were a lie. All family photographs were. He should replace them with one of Anna standing in the kitchen with a wine glass in her hand, Milan bent over a book and Stefan stationed on the naughty step trying to make himself cry. That would be more representative of what he was missing here nine hours a day.

He went back into the main office.

Ferreira was sitting at Wahlia's desk, smiling to herself as she watched him talking to someone on his mobile, out in the hallway for privacy, but he hadn't moved far enough and his voice was carrying.

'Baby, I can't tonight . . . no, I got this work thing I gotta do.'

'That's Bobby's sexy voice,' Ferreira said. 'The ladies love it.'

Wahlia glanced up and flipped her off.

'What did Riggott want?'

'He was just letting me know how much he valued my input.' She swivelled in the chair to face Jaan Stepulov's board. 'Speaking of which, I see you talked to Gemma already. Did she crack and give you a full confession?'

'No,' Zigic said. 'Do you think she would have if you'd been there too?'

'Maybe.'

She honestly believed it, he realised. She hadn't failed in enough cases yet, she still believed every suspect could be ground down by sheer force of will, verbally beaten into submission. She'd learn eventually that some people hardened the more you pushed them, and the louder you shouted the quieter they would become, until they finally stopped talking altogether. At least he hoped she'd learn.

'How did it go with Paolo?'

'The things he said . . .' Her face darkened. 'Do you know what they did when someone complained? They set a pack of dogs on them. Dogs. It's fucking barbaric.'

'We're going to get them, Mel.'

'You know, I was leaving the hospital and they're building the new wing there, right? And I suddenly realised Paolo and the others were working on jobs like that, there must have been delivery men and engineers coming onto the sites, why didn't they notice something was wrong?'

'Because they don't care to notice,' Zigic said.

She went round to her side of the desk and started to roll a cigarette, shredded tobacco onto the paper and packed it tight, rolling it between her fingers and thumbs, her face set in concentration which wasn't for the cigarette.

'They should have fought back.'

'It's not that simple.'

'Forty workers being held in slavery by five or six English. They'd got the numbers. They'd got tools in their hands. It *is* simple.' She licked the paper and sealed it. 'Paolo was the only one to speak up when they killed the Chinese guy. The rest just stood around watching. Then they went right back to work like nothing happened.'

'They were probably scared they'd be next,' Zigic said. 'It's impossible for us to understand what it feels like living under those conditions. Of course we think we'd fight back in that situation, but we wouldn't.'

'I would.'

She snatched up her lighter and headed for the door.

'You can smoke that here.'

'I need some air.'

Zigic went to the window and saw the press vans being repacked, the print hacks already leaving. They'd be back tomorrow morning, wanting something sensational for the lunchtime edition, and he wondered how much shock and outrage it would provoke when the full story emerged. Foreign workers kept as slaves a few minutes from the centre of Peterborough, the casual brutality and senseless murder.

He wanted to believe it would lead to change. Tighter controls on gangmasters, better enforcement. He wanted a groundswell of public outcry and questions in the House of Commons, but he knew, deep down, that it would cause nothing more significant than some brief hand-wringing from a minority of well-meaning but ineffectual people. An article in the *Guardian* perhaps, recommendations from a charity or two. The people with real power were profiting too much from the situation to want to improve it.

He picked up the coffee pot and put it down again. He wanted a proper drink. If he was the kind of copper who kept a bottle in his desk drawer he'd be in it now and that was purely why he didn't. There were too many moments like this.

There was a pub two minutes' drive away but it would be full of hacks and off-duty uniforms and he couldn't face the atmosphere of aggressive bonhomie.

He went back to Jaan Stepulov's board and thought of Gemma Barlow, home again now, waiting for Phil to get in so she could confront him or debrief him. Confrontation was more likely, Zigic thought. She was genuinely shocked about the jewellery and if she suspected Phil before that would have hardened into certainty this afternoon.

He remembered her almost admission and wondered if he should have pushed her more. Could she be pushed, though? She'd shut down so swiftly and completely that he doubted it, but the possibility that he'd lost a crucial new piece of information for the want of the right question was irritating as hell.

Ferreira came up behind him, hair blown about and smoke on her breath. She nodded towards the board,

'You think Phil's home from work yet?'

44

The house was empty when Phil Barlow got in.

He hated this, coming home to dark, deserted rooms, no kiss on the doorstep, no hot water in the tank to wash the day's filth off him. He dumped his keys on the hall table and checked the answer machine. One message, a reporter from the local paper wanting to speak to him. He hit the delete button and went into the kitchen for a beer.

It sloshed into his stomach, no food to absorb it. He'd thrown his sandwiches out for the birds at lunchtime, couldn't face eating them. He hadn't eaten properly for days, spent the weekend in front of the television with Sky Sports News playing the same dozen stories on an unending loop. He'd drunk himself to sleep on the sofa and woken up hearing sirens.

Upstairs he took a quick shower in lukewarm water, put on the clothes he'd left on the bedroom floor last night.

He went into the kitchen for another beer and took a look in the freezer, starting to feel a bit peckish. There was ice cream and frozen peas, one of Gemma's old Weight Watchers carbonaras that smelled like sick and tasted just as bad.

He called Domino's and ordered a twelve-inch and some potato wedges, then went back into the living room and watched *EastEnders*, seeing that Gemma had Sky-plussed it to watch when she got in. She'd be round her mum's then, curled up in her stuffy lounge, surrounded by cats and Capodimonte, on her third glass of wine. Her tongue would be loose from the drink and the stress, spilling secrets which had nothing to do with this situation but which her mother would store away for a later date. She'd been trying to break them up for years, telling Gemma he was too old, didn't earn enough, couldn't give her a baby. This would be a dream come true. *Do you want to be married to a murderer, Gem-Gem?*

As the end credits rolled he called her.

Her phone rang straight through to the message service.

'Hey, babe, it's me, call me when you get this. I love you.'

He flipped through his contacts and found her mother's home number. His thumb hovered over the call button, but he couldn't face talking to the old bitch, even for a minute.

The doorbell rang and he hauled himself up off the sofa, checking the time. The delivery guy had made it quick, no chance of arguing the cost.

He opened the front door and Clinton Renfrew was standing there with his hands tucked into his jeans pockets, chin thrown up like a challenge.

'Alright, Phil, mate? Mind if I come in?'

Renfrew muscled past him, eyes on everything. He was wearing a soft, black leather jacket over a khaki camouflage T-shirt and jeans stiff with newness, a pair of box-fresh white Pumas.

'Nice place you got here,' he said. 'Area's a bit downmarket these days but you wouldn't know it once you're inside, would you?'

He walked through to the living room, taking in the size of the television and black chandelier, nodding to himself, hands still in his pockets. He went over to the photographs on the bookshelves.

'This your lad?'

'Craig, yeah.'

'Got his mother's looks,' Renfrew said. 'Lucky for him.'

He didn't want Renfrew talking about his son. Didn't even want him to know Craig existed.

'How're your kids doing?' he asked.

'No fucking idea. I ain't seen them since I got out. Their ma's taken them back to Corby, don't even know her address.'

'I'm sorry.'

Renfrew shrugged and sat down on the sofa, pushed back like he was settling in for the evening, one foot tucked under himself.

'Offer us a drink then – where're your manners?'

'Beer?'

'Got anything stronger?'

'No.' He had.

'Beer it'll have to be then.'

Phil went into the kitchen, feeling trapped, certain he knew what Renfrew had come for and scared what he'd do when he told him he didn't have it. He took the last bottle of Stella out of the fridge and snapped the top off with the handle of a spoon. The opener was missing, somewhere in the murky dishwater.

'Where's your old woman?' Renfrew asked as he took his drink. 'Not left you, has she?'

'Gone to the gym. Yoga.'

The doorbell rang again but Phil just stood there, looking at Renfrew stretched out on his sofa, drinking his beer, dressed in clothes which had been paid for with the money from his jewellery.

'Think you better get that.'

The delivery guy asked him for the money in a thick accent, garbling the words. Phil emptied his wallet to pay for the food and found Renfrew hunched on the edge of the sofa when he returned to the living room.

'Smells good. Haven't had my tea yet.'

Phil dropped the pizza box on the table and Renfrew tore off the first slice, ate it in a couple of greedy bites, a blob of sauce hitting the floor between his feet. He was going for another when he gestured at Phil.

'Sit down then.'

He took the footstool on the other side of the table, watching Renfrew stuff a potato wedge into his mouth.

'You wanna eat this before it gets cold.'

He picked up a slice and made himself bite and swallow, not tasting it.

Renfrew wiped his greasy fingers on the arm of the sofa, went for the beer bottle he'd left shoved down between the seat cushions.

'Missed this when I was inside. Funny the stuff you want when you can't have it.'

Phil nodded, not knowing what to say.

He just wanted this to be over but he didn't know how to end it.

If he was a different kind of man he'd throw Renfrew out. He knew that wouldn't work though. Renfrew was lean and hard, always had been a fighter, ever since he'd known him, years back while he was dating his sister, a doll-like blonde with a volcanic temper. She started fights in pubs, men or women, she didn't care. He'd seen her beat a bloke twice her size for looking at her tits.

If he tried to play the tough guy with Renfrew he'd end up in hospital. Or worse.

'This about the job?' he asked, trying to sound relaxed, just two old friends talking.

Renfrew drained his Stella, Adam's apple bobbing.

'Don't reckon the building's my kind of thing. Out in the cold, dust up your arsehole all day long. That's not for me.'

He felt relief wash over him but it was short-lived.

'Bloke I know from up Hull's got something he wants me in on,' Renfrew said. 'Need some start-up capital though. Can't go in empty-handed.'

'What is it?' Phil asked.

'Best you don't know.' He shook the empty bottle at Phil. 'I'll have another.'

'None left.'

'Fuck me, your missus doesn't keep much of a house.'

Phil punched his fist into his palm, sat there with every muscle in his body clenched.

'What do you want from me, Clint?'

'That's not very friendly.'

'We're not friends. We were never friends. And you're blackmailing me. We both know it so let's just have it out now.'

'She due back?' Renfrew asked. 'You scared of her and all?'

'How much, Clint?'

'Couple of grand should do it.'

Phil stood sharply. 'I haven't got that kind of money.'

'Don't gimme that bollocks.'

'We're skint, man.'

'You own this place, don't you?'

'The banks owns it.'

'Getting it's your problem,' Renfrew said. 'Use some fucking initiative.'

'I can't manage two grand.'

'Look, I'm being decent about this cos we're mates. If you were anyone else it'd be five. Five's my usual price.'

'You didn't do anything,' Phil shouted.

'Not what I'll tell the police.'

'So tell them, see if I care.'

Renfrew was on him in a heartbeat and Phil tried to step back but there was nowhere to go. The hard edge of the mantel dug into his back as Renfrew pressed his face close, speaking in a low voice through his teeth.

'Don't try and bluff me, Phil. I've got nothing to lose. You think on that.'

Renfrew retreated less than a foot, still close enough to do some damage but Phil knew he wouldn't now. Nothing serious. He just wanted money. Money he didn't have to give him and couldn't hope to scrape together. They were at the limit of their overdraft, had six credit cards between them all maxed out and the only thing he owned of any value Renfrew had already taken.

There was the savings account. It was Gemma's more than his but she'd opened it in joint names, asked him to chip in whatever he could manage to make up the money from her little job at H&M. There must be a few thousand in there by now, he didn't know exactly, only that she didn't have enough for the next round of IVF yet.

She'd kill him if he touched it. Renfrew would kill him if he didn't.

'I need some time.'

'Friday,' Renfrew said, poking him in the chest. 'You don't have it by Friday you know what'll happen. And it won't just be you. I'll tell them your missus was involved and all. They'll send you both down.'

'Alright. I'll try.'

'Don't try. Get.'

'Alright,' Phil said. 'I'll get it. But after that –'

'What?'

Phil forced himself to meet Renfrew's eye.

'This has to be a one-off.'

Renfrew smiled, grease glistening on his lips, and turned away. He closed the lid on the pizza box and carried it off with him, balanced on his palm, well away from his fancy new leather jacket. He banged the front door home hard as he left and the sound shook through Phil's skull.

What did that mean, that smile?

He knew. Didn't want to admit it but the pressure in his chest and the gnawing pain in his stomach insisted. Renfrew wouldn't be bought off forever with a measly two grand. It might buy him a few weeks' peace but eventually there would be another knock at the door and another demand.

Renfrew owned him now.

Outside a car door slammed and he rushed to the front door, wanting to stop Renfrew talking to Gemma. A second door slammed before he could open up and he heard raised voices, Renfrew shouting and a woman replying.

He yanked the door open and saw Renfrew flat on his face on the front path, DS Ferreira with her knee in his back, snapping on the handcuffs. A squad car was parked at the kerb, blue lights bouncing between the houses and Phil clung to the door handle to stay upright.

Inspector Zigic gestured at the scene, perfectly placid. 'Now, you're not going to give us any trouble, are you, Mr Barlow?'

45

Clinton Renfrew waived the offer of a solicitor and Zigic wasn't sure if that was a positive sign or not. Either he was going to say absolutely nothing and let them waste their time or he knew he was so far in the shit that a solicitor wouldn't make any difference.

He asked for a cup of tea though and a packet of cigarettes, grinned when Ferreira refused.

'You don't trust me with a lighter, hey?'

She prepared the tapes while Renfrew went for his tea, holding it in his left hand, his right one was bandaged from where he cut it hitting the ground, landing on a shard of broken glass in the gravel between the slabs on the front path.

They'd decided to start with him. He knew the game, understood the benefit of trading honesty for leniency. Phil Barlow could wait. The longer he sat in a holding cell, alone with his thoughts and his fears, the more likely he was to cave. They'd found him out now, that was going to play on his mind.

'Last time we spoke you denied knowing Phil Barlow,' Zigic said. 'Why did you lie to us?'

'Didn't want to drop him in it.'

'How would admitting you know him do that?'

'Phil's an upstanding citizen,' Renfrew said, his voice laced with sarcasm. 'Wouldn't want you thinking he associated with ex-cons.'

'So how do you two know each other?'

'He went out with my sister for a bit. Till she got shot of him.'

'But you kept in touch?'

'Case you forgot, I've been away.'

'And you'll be going back soon,' Ferreira said. 'You must really have missed it. Out a couple of months and you set another fire. You having trouble adjusting, that it?'

Renfrew's mouth twisted into a smile but the look in his eyes suggested she'd hit a raw nerve. He scratched his tattooed neck, reddening the skin around his prison-issue Britannia.

'You celled with Lee Poulter, didn't you?' Ferreira said. 'Must have made you pretty important inside, being so tight with an ENL big dick.'

'What's that got to do with anything?'

'Depends,' she said. 'You've got fuck-all going for you out here, no job, no money, living with your brother and his family. Tough to go straight under those circumstances. But I imagine they'll welcome you with open arms when you get back to Littlehey. All your little fascist buddies.'

Renfrew turned his attention to Zigic. 'Usually the woman's the good cop. It works better that way because no matter how loud they fucking squawk they can't sell the bad-cop routine. Don't have the balls for it.'

'We thought you'd respond better to a sympathetic man,' Ferreira said. 'Given your . . . let's say, history.'

Renfrew laughed at her. 'Must try harder. Put that on her next performance report, Inspector.'

'You don't seem to understand the seriousness of this situation,' Zigic said.

'I understand better than you do.'

'Explain it to us then.'

He hunched forward in his seat, elbows on the table. The strip light, directly overhead, washed across his worn and stubbled face, hollowing out his cheeks and making shadows pool under his eyes.

'You've caught me coming out your prime suspect's house, so now you want to know if he paid me to set fire to his shed or if I just told him the best way to do it.'

'No,' Zigic said. 'We already know he paid you to do it. We're just wondering if you've got the common sense to admit it and take the goodwill we can give you.'

'That's what he usually does,' Ferreira said. 'You cut a good deal when you murdered that guy in the takeaway place.'

Renfrew stiffened. 'I didn't know he was in there. I said it a thousand times, I didn't fucking know.'

'Do you think the owner did?' she asked. 'What's his name?'

'Neves,' Renfrew said, spitting it out.

'Do you think Mr Neves knew?'

'I don't know.'

'I think it's likely he did,' Ferreira said. 'He let you go in there and fire that place knowing some poor kid was inside – because he was pretty much a kid.'

Renfrew couldn't look at her.

'He let you burn that place down and he didn't give a shit who was inside or what happened to you when it all came out.' She threw her hand up, muttered something in Portuguese that sounded like a curse. 'What's it matter to him? He gets on the first plane back to São Paolo and leaves you to take the fall.'

Renfrew stared into his tea.

'By rights he should have done ten years for that. Instead his daughter comes over and sells the property for a quarter of a mil and he's living it up back home in the sun.' She slapped the table. 'What did he pay you again?'

Renfrew stood sharply, kicked his chair away. 'You seem to know the rest of the fucking story.'

He paced into the corner of the room, his back turned to them, tight bunched muscles straining his khaki T-shirt.

Zigic touched Ferreira's arm, let her know that was enough. They'd found Renfrew's button, no need to pound it to destruction.

'Did you know Stepulov was in there?'

'I didn't set fire to that shed.'

'Then why did Phil need to pay you off?' Ferreira asked.

Renfrew cocked his head, smiled slightly. 'What?'

'This morning, Clinton, in town, I saw you go into that jeweller's.' She brought out the evidence bag with Barlow's rings inside, placed it on the table. 'You cashed in some of Phil's bling.'

Renfrew dropped back into his chair and hung his head, but the smile was still there, broader and more genuine than before, and when he looked up at them finally he was laughing to himself.

'That's it? That's what you've fucking got?'

'It's pretty damning,' Ferreira said.

'Do me a favour. You think I'd take a pile of his shitey jewellery for payment? I'm a professional. I take cash.'

'So why did you have his rings?'

'He gave them me.'

'Very generous of him,' Zigic said. 'Especially since one of them was an anniversary gift he swore he'd never take off.'

Renfrew shrugged.

'Why did he give you them?' Zigic asked again.

'You know why.'

'I want to hear you say it. For the tape, Mr Renfrew.'

He shook his head like he couldn't quite believe what he was going to do.

'I told him you'd come to see me at the garage and he started bricking it. He begged me not to let on we knew each other.' Renfrew smiled slightly. 'I said it'd cost him.'

'You're blackmailing him.'

'I wouldn't call it that.'

'I would,' Zigic said. 'And so will the CPS.'

Ten minutes later, back in the office with the sound of a vacuum cleaner droning in the corridor outside, Zigic amended Jaan Stepulov's board, thinking of how contained his murder had looked, right from the off. Phil and Gemma Barlow's photographs stared out at him, both of them wide-eyed in front of the camera, stunned by finding themselves in a situation they wouldn't have believed possible a month earlier.

'Renfrew knows what he's doing,' Ferreira said. 'He's copping to blackmail so we don't pursue him for the fire.'

'It's possible.'

'It's highly probable,' she said.

'He's got an alibi.'

'Family alibis shouldn't count.'

'The sister-in-law hates him.'

'But she'll do whatever her husband tells her.'

'You don't know that,' Zigic said. He rubbed his face, felt stubble against his palms; he'd been here far too long already. 'Just because you hate him it doesn't mean he's guilty.'

'That's got nothing to do with it.' She opened her desk drawer, dug out a tube of lip balm and sniffed it before she ran it over her mouth. 'I'll send a car out for Gemma. We can start on Phil straight away then.'

Zigic glanced at his watch; almost nine o'clock and they had to be back in at four to prepare for the raid at Knarrs End Drove. Neither of the Barlows would talk without a solicitor and that could take hours yet. By the time they were done it would be too late to go home.

'Let's leave them for tonight.'

Ferreira slammed her drawer shut. 'We should hit Phil while he's unbalanced.'

'You think a night in the cells is going to settle him down?' Zigic asked, already pulling on his coat. 'The longer he sits there, the more likely we are to get a confession.'

TUESDAY

46

At 5.30 a.m. the featureless dawn landscape of the fens was resolving under a grey sky heavy with coming rain, dark smudges in the distance marking small wooded areas, farmyards dominated by hulking tractor sheds and Nissen huts rotting and crumbling. A phalanx of vehicles rumbled along the Wisbech Road, passing transporter vans filled with workers and delivery lorries from the processing plants at Spalding heading into Peterborough.

Zigic shifted uncomfortably in his seat, the unfamiliar hard bulk of a handgun digging into his ribs. He'd taken firearms training years ago and never expected to use it. This was the first time he'd worn a gun on duty and he hated the way the steel felt, first ice cold through his shirt now warmed to body temperature as if it was a part of him.

Next to him Ferreira was tapping her feet against the floor, taking furious drags on her third cigarette, and the interior of Adams's car was close with the smoke. Adams had gone through a couple himself, complaining to Ferreira about how rough they were, but he was out and said right then he'd take his nicotine however it came.

In the passenger seat DC Carr was nervously rubbing his hands against the thighs of his jeans and every few minutes he tugged at the neck of his bulletproof vest.

It had been a while since Zigic wore one of those too and he wondered how the uniforms who put them on every day coped with them. Not the discomfort. That was nothing. But the knowledge that at any moment you might need it.

'These things are stupid,' Carr said. 'What if I get shot in the head?'

'It'll be over quickly and you'll get a hero's funeral,' Adams told him. 'Now shut up.'

Ferreira opened her window and pitched out the spent butt, immediately started to roll another cigarette, spilling strands of tobacco as they hit a pothole.

'For Christ's sake.'

'I didn't build the fucking road, Mel,' Adams said.

When she lit up he reached into the back of the car and she handed the cigarette over. He took a couple of drags and returned it a third smoked.

Zigic pressed his knuckles to his mouth and watched the fields whipping by, thinking of the boys, still sleeping soundly in their beds. He'd stood at the bedroom door watching them for a few minutes before he left the house, hadn't wanted to go in and risk waking them. Now he regretted the decision. Anna got up at three to make him breakfast he told her he didn't want and started to cry in the kitchen as she scraped the scrambled eggs into the bin.

He tried to laugh it off, told her how stupid she was being, it was perfectly safe, he'd be one of the last people to go in, and by the time he did the site would be secured. She asked if he'd have a gun and he lied, told her it wasn't necessary.

It was only as he was leaving the village that he realised why she was so upset. Her whole childhood had been spent watching war zones on television, knowing her father was in the thick of the action, and every time an unnamed soldier died she would wonder if it was him.

A helicopter crossed the road above them, the deep thwump of its blades banging through Zigic's head and then the car was slowing and he saw the vehicles ahead of them turning off onto a narrow drove, their headlights dimmed, a weighty black armoured van with a ram on the front of it, a tactical firearms unit behind it, then a van full of pumped-up uniforms.

'Here we go then,' Adams said under his breath, and swung down Knarrs End Drove.

The compound was two hundred yards away on the left, floodlit against the dim shapes of the surrounding countryside. It looked like any other travellers' site, four tracks and vans parked here and there, and everything surrounded by a high mesh fence topped with razor wire which glimmered viciously under the intense white light. The only anomaly was the L of Portakabins arranged along the perimeter.

Reconnaissance photos taken the previous afternoon showed eleven of them, shoved tight together, hardly a body's width between them, waste outlets running straight into a dyke, a mass of wiring strung haphazardly across the site to a pole on the verge which didn't look up to the job. Even in the photographs they looked half derelict, felt roofs peeling, damp climbing the prefabricated walls.

The caravans, by contrast, were at the luxury end of the market, three long, wide blocks of white cladding with bay windows and wooden verandas; business was good when you weren't paying wages.

Adams had tracked down the owners of the compound through a friend on the Lincolnshire force. The Gavin brothers leveraged the site off a local farmer in 1998, rolled onto it one bank holiday Monday and refused to leave. He tried to press criminal charges, got nowhere, tried civil, just the same. An ill-advised stab at clearing them out with a forklift truck put him on the wrong side of a compensation claim. Finally he agreed to sell them the land for market value, six grand an acre and they dropped their lawsuit as a gesture of goodwill.

Adams pulled up and they got out of the car.

Ahead of them dark figures emptied out of the vans and ran to take their positions as the driver of the armoured vehicle lined up to the compound's entrance and gunned the engine. It tore through the main gates and then everyone was moving at once. The tactical unit flooded the compound, calling to each other above the rising chorus of barking dogs. They moved in brisk formation, ignoring the cabins, focused on the mobile homes at the south of the site.

A haggard blonde woman in pink silk pyjamas was standing screaming on her veranda. Marie Gavin – two years for assault, eighteen months suspended for fraud.

Her place was the largest on the site, frilly curtains at the windows and hanging baskets on the cladding, but Zigic was looking at the cabins now. Up close they were filthy, buckled things, unfit for human habitation, and for a second he thought they'd made a mistake. People couldn't possibly be living in them. Then lights started coming on inside them, faces appearing behind the grilled windows and he noticed the padlocks fastened on the outside of the doors, just as Paolo had described.

A gunshot sounded above the chaos and a white pit bull dropped three feet away from one of the armed officers, twisted in the dirt and struggled to its feet again. As the man put a second bullet in it the rest of the pack emerged from the shadows between the cabins, scenting fresh blood. No barks now, just low growls as they advanced. Heads down, teeth bared.

Four more gunshots and the pack was neutralised.

A hefty man with thick black hair came out of another mobile home. Ken Gavin – eight years for aggravated burglary, six years for converting replica firearms.

'This about the TV licence?' he shouted.

'On the ground.'

'I paid it,' he said. 'On my mother's eyes.'

'Down on the ground. Now.'

Ken Gavin put his hands up but he was laughing. Kept laughing as he was surrounded and only stopped when a swift boot to the calf dropped him. Then he found some fight, lashing out with his elbows and feet as they tried to restrain him. One man drove a knee into his kidney and that stilled him long enough to get the cuffs on. Two uniforms dragged him across the ground towards the waiting van, dust blowing up from his heels.

'One down,' Adams said, standing with his hands on his hips, surveying the scene.

Marie Gavin was in the middle of the yard now, shouting as she was cuffed.

'You can't come in here without a warrant.'

'We've got one,' Adams told her.

'This is harassment, we've got rights.'

'Don't come the innocent, missus.'

'Don't you missus me, you shite.'

Adams laughed. 'Fucking charmer, this one.'

'If anything gets broken in my place you bastards are paying for it,' she shouted. 'And I know what's in there so keep your thieving fingers to yourself. That china's worth more than you earn in a year.'

They dragged her away as well, spitting and cursing them all to hell.

The point man went into her caravan, two of his team following, moving slowly, crab-stepping and hand-gesturing.

Her husband hadn't surfaced yet. Ray Gavin – fifteen years in Broadmoor, false imprisonment, torture, murder.

Shouts of 'clear' rang out then something smashed and a light flashed in a darkened window a split second before a shotgun blast ripped through the night. Black-clad figures piled into the caravan, their boots like thunder on the wooden veranda.

'What do we do?' Ferreira asked, her eyes huge and shining.

'Nothing,' Zigic told her, making it an order. 'This is their job. Not ours.'

She looked to Adams and he shook his head.

'Shouldn't we start opening the cabins up then? Get the men out.'

'Not until the site's clear.'

She was jittery and Zigic felt it too, the adrenalin pumping with nowhere to go while they waited in the deserted yard with the dead dogs and the faces of locked-up men looking out at them. There was no more noise from inside Marie Gavin's caravan but no movement either. The seconds leaked by with the helicopter circling overhead, its beam sweeping into the dark fields beyond the yard.

Then the floodlights shut down and Zigic was momentarily blind, negative impressions superimposed over the black, but his eyes adjusted quickly enough to catch a blur of movement as a man darted out from behind a four-track and bolted for the gates.

'Fuck. He's away,' Adams shouted.

But Zigic was already running. The helicopter banked sharply above him, isolating the man in a circle of light as he broke through the gate and hit the road, his footfalls fast and light.

Kelvin Gavin – a born runner. He'd run from foster homes and security guards and the police. Ten months ago he ran from the Serco team escorting him to court on a rape charge and hadn't been seen since.

Until now.

Zigic lengthened his stride, aware of Adams at his heels, the sound of more bodies joining the pursuit, and drove himself on, feet pounding the compacted dirt track.

Kelvin Gavin was becoming a smaller and smaller figure in the distance, the white stripes on his Adidas glowing. Suddenly he veered off the road and the helicopter lost him.

'Where is he?' Adams shouted.

Zigic slowed for a few seconds, heart hammering, and then the beam swept across a farmyard on the right side of the road, catching Kelvin as he vaulted the metal barrier closing off the gateway.

'He's heading for the barns.'

Zigic cleared the barrier and landed badly, pain shooting up into his groin. He pushed it away. Kept running. Kelvin Gavin was thirty feet ahead of him, tugging on the door of an old cattle shed with corrugated-tin walls.

Twenty feet.

The door slid open with a metal clang and Kelvin disappeared inside.

Zigic kept running, heard voices behind him, Adams telling the others to go round the back.

He slipped through the narrow opening and stopped dead. He

could see the hulking shapes of machinery, dark and indistinct to his left, and ahead of him a run of pigpens where a couple of dozen animals snuffled softly in the gloom, smelling of shit and straw.

'There's nowhere for you to go, Kelvin.' His voice echoed to the distant roof.

He heard something moving to his right, turned to face the noise.

'We've got the place surrounded. You might as well –'

A weight struck him between the shoulders and he hit the floor. Kelvin was on him, fists driving into his ribs and chest. A glancing blow split the skin above his left eye and the blood came quickly, blinding him. He threw a wild elbow and felt it connect. It slowed Kelvin for a second and Zigic moved fast, got astride his hips and punched him in the face. Cartilage snapped and he felt blood between his fingers when he hit him again. Kelvin squirmed, tried to kick out, but he had him pinned. He grabbed the collar of his sweatshirt and smashed his head into the barn floor, blinking through the blood running down his face.

Kelvin stopped moving and Zigic reached for the cuffs at the back of his belt, fingers brushing the holster and he realised too late that it was empty.

Kelvin jabbed the muzzle into his neck and black spots popped in front of Zigic's eyes.

'If you shoot me you'll never get out of here,' he said.

'Think I give a fuck?'

'We didn't come for you, Kelvin.'

'Get off me.'

Zigic climbed to his feet. His knees were liquid and he felt he might fall at any moment.

Kelvin kept the gun on him as he stood, none too solid himself.

'Just give me that thing and we can pretend this never happened.' Zigic held his hand out. 'We're not interested in you, Kelvin.'

He shoved the gun in Zigic's face. 'You know what they do to blokes who shoot coppers in the nick?'

'No.'

'Fucking nothing. We're kings.'

Zigic heard the gunshot and felt blood spray across his face and then he was falling through blackness, unable to see or breathe and the last thing he registered was the impact of the barn floor against the back of his head.

47

Ferreira sat on a desk at the back of CID, waiting for Adams to emerge from DCS Riggott's office and start the morning briefing. A young WPC, with blonde hair and black roots, brought her coffee and offered her a doughnut from a bright pink paper bag. That was Adams's style, cheap gimmicks to get people where he wanted them. He'd fill his team up with caffeine and sugar and then send them out onto the streets all hyped up to do his dirty work.

'Go on,' the woman said. 'They're custard.'

'I'm good.'

'There's nothing in them.' She shook the bag. 'You might as well.'

'Are you deaf?'

The WPC gave her a squinty-eyed look and Ferreira willed her to say something else. The mood she was in she could rip the woman's head off in front of everyone. But she only smiled and walked away, went over to a tight knot of people at the front of the room and whispered something which provoked a burst of harsh laughter.

Fuck her.

Ferreira sipped her coffee and tried to tune out the background noise.

It was too insistent though. Most of them were fresh in this morning, all perky as hell from a good eight hours and a proper breakfast. Only DC Carr had been on the raid and he was sitting as his desk a few feet away, working through a bacon sandwich, talking about POSH's home game at the weekend with an ancient sergeant in a bad suit and a claret tie whose accent was so thick Ferreira could barely penetrate it. Peterborough had won. She got that much.

Like she cared.

She'd been to see them play once, dragged along to London Road after drunkenly agreeing it might be fun. It wasn't. They'd been promoted since, got a new manager, but she doubted they were much better to watch. Bobby was a diehard, he'd had a season ticket since he was a kid and she told him he wouldn't know good football if it nutmegged him.

Around her the voices kept going, laughter breaking through the hum, and no one seemed to be talking about the raid or the men they'd broken out of those wretched cabins. It was all bullshit about films and last night's telly, what he'd like to do to that brunette on *Hollyoaks* and did you see that thing on 4 about the kid with the growth? *Oh my God . . . it was soooo sad.*

She saw Zigic on the barn floor. Motionless. Blood on his face. Adams squatting down next to him, pressing his fingers into his neck, searching for a pulse. She blinked it away.

Adams strode into the office, clapping his hands.

'Alright, you lot, bit of fucking hush.'

Riggott came in, wrapping up a conversation on his mobile, and trousered it as he slipped unobtrusively down to the back of the room. He gestured at Ferreira and she shuffled along the desk, giving him space to prop one buttock on the corner. He smelled of cigarettes and peppery cologne and she noticed a small nick from a razor low on his skinny neck.

Up front Adams launched into a debrief of the morning's raid, his voice stagy, his north London accent more pronounced than usual as he ran down the arrests made and outlined the plan of action for the rest of the day.

Ferreira took her tobacco tin out of her pocket and started on a cigarette, half listening to him, thinking about the men from the site, the expressions of disbelief and fear as the doors were smashed open to let them out into the cool morning air. A couple of them tried to run but they were caught quickly, not enough energy in their raddled and emaciated bodies to get beyond the gates. Several of them were illegals and Ferreira felt a deep stab of pity for them.

Once they'd given their statements they would be bussed to Oakington detention centre, where they would wait for a few days or a few weeks, in more comfort than they were used to, but still imprisoned. Then a van would come and they would be taken to Stansted airport, manhandled onto planes and sent home to countries where they still owed money to the gangsters who'd brought them over here.

For now they were being cleaned up and fed at Fern House. It was more than the Adus could cope with but when Ferreira suggested taking some of the men to the soup kitchen at St Mary's, Joseph wouldn't hear of it, insisted they would call in extra volunteers to help.

She licked the edge of the paper and sealed her rollie.

'You know you can buy them ready-made now,' Riggott said.

'I prefer them like this.'

He produced a gold Zippo from his pocket and held the flame out to her.

'Go on, I'm the boss.'

She leaned in and took the light, catching DC Carr smirking at her.

Fuck him too.

Adams was dispatching his officers in teams, ordering translators and people from social services to be sent to Fern House. He wanted statements from the Gavins' prisoners by the end of the day, everything neatly wrapped up and ready for the CPS.

It was open and shut now. No denying what they'd found at the site at Knarrs End Drove. There were unlicensed guns inside the vans, a couple of grand's worth of coke and weed, bundles of fake twenties wrapped in cling film and stowed in panels under the beds.

Nobody was talking though. The Gavins were on a group vow of silence, waiting for their solicitors.

'Mel.' Adams pointed at her. 'I want you to get Mr Perez out of City and find this building site where his mate's buried.'

Heads swivelled and she felt eyes on her.

'They're not going to let him out for that,' she said.

'So persuade them.'

He held her gaze until she nodded, then started giving orders to a couple of men standing near him, pointing at the sheet on the board.

She walked out of the office and went down to the car park, flicked her cigarette into the flower bed and got into the car. The radio blared when she started the engine and she turned it up higher, Left Lane Cruiser banging and wailing as she turned out onto the parkway.

She shouldn't be doing this.

The clock was ticking on Phil Barlow; twelve hours to go before they had to release or charge him, and he was still sitting in his cell, finishing his breakfast and building his strength for the coming day. She should have him sweating blood in an interview room right now, make him look her in the eye and admit that he'd burned Jaan Stepulov alive and then gone right back to his warm bed and slept like a baby.

Adams's case was the headline grabber though, and everything else stopped until he had a result worthy of the six o'clock news.

By the end of the second song she was pulling into City General.

On Ward 7 there wasn't a nurse in sight and the guard from Paolo's room had disappeared too, leaving a crumpled copy of the *Daily Mail* on the chair behind him. She knocked out of courtesy and went in.

Paolo was sitting up in bed, the remnants of his breakfast pushed aside on the high white table, toast crumbs on a plate and a mush of leftover cornflakes in a bowl. He'd had a shave since the last time she saw him and he looked younger without the grey-flecked beard, closer to his actual age but still older than thirty-one. It would be a while before he recovered, lost that gauntness and the weary expression he'd earned living under the Gavins' tyranny.

The sight of him pushed all thoughts of the Barlows out of her head.

'Good morning, Sergeant Ferreira.'

'You can call me, Mel,' she said. 'How're you feeling?'

'Very well, thank you.'

'Well enough to get up?'

He cocked his head. 'Am I going home?'

'What did your doctor say?'

'He doesn't speak to me,' Paolo said. 'But I feel strong enough to leave now. Marco has a place where he's staying. I will go with him.' He looked down at his chest. 'Unless you need me.'

'You'll have to come to the station and make a formal statement,' Ferreira told him. 'We've arrested the people who were holding you.'

His expression darkened and he tugged nervously at the blanket across his legs.

'They are in prison?'

'In custody, yes. Which is as good as.'

'But they will be given bail?'

'I don't know. It's possible.' She shoved her hands into the back pockets of her jeans, knowing it was more than possible, it was almost a certainty, and once they were out they were very likely to come looking for him. It was how people like the Gavins operated. Intimidation, murder, whatever it took to make charges go away.

'Look, if you're up to it, I've been asked to take you to find this place you were working when your friend died.'

'Xin Gao.'

She nodded. 'Are you up to it?'

He threw back the covers and swung his legs over the side of the bed, stood in front of her with his striped pyjama bottoms hanging on his hips, arms out to his sides like he'd just performed an elaborate tumbling trick.

The gunshot on his shoulder was well bandaged but the bruising had begun to come out and it spread beyond the tight binding and the gauze, blooming purple and red halfway across his sunken chest.

'I'd better go and find you some clothes.'

'Marco has brought me clothes,' he said, pointing to a plastic bag on the chair in the corner of the room.

'I'll give you some privacy.'

48

The roads all looked the same, flat black tarmac unravelling into the distance, fields on either side which he had never seen in daylight before. They drove out before dawn, came home after dark, and Paolo realised how little attention he'd paid to his surroundings on those journeys. Looking without seeing.

It seemed unimportant at the time.

How was he to know it would come to this?

He thought he would never escape that place, suspected he might die there.

It still felt unreal to him, being free. It felt like the man who ran across the fields, pursued by dogs and men with guns, was a completely different person. Then he would move and the hole in his shoulder would throb and he knew this wasn't just another dream.

Next to him Sergeant Ferreira drove with her eyes dead ahead, hands tight around the steering wheel. She was getting impatient. They'd been down this road before, turned around and double-backed.

He looked at her profile, the colour of her skin and the line of her nose so similar to Maria's that if he squinted he could convince himself he was with her. For a few seconds at least. She smelled different, wore a stronger perfume and a wreath of cigarette smoke, and when she turned her head he caught a hint of sickly sweet product on her long black hair.

Maria smelled of soap and vanilla and when he pressed his face into her skin there were spices and pepper. He wanted to phone her but he found he couldn't remember her number any more. He'd dialled it a thousand times, his thumb skipping over the keypad automatically. How was it possible to forget so quickly?

He'd been locked away in that place for ten months, he now knew. It shouldn't be long enough to forget.

'Does any of this look familiar?' Sergeant Ferreira asked.

They were a few miles away from the site on Knarrs End Drove, back where they had started twenty minutes earlier.

'We headed east.'

'We are heading east,' she said. 'You must have noticed things when you went through? Place names? A pub? Anything, Paolo. You've got to give me something to work with or we'll be out here all day.'

He trawled back through his memory as the car bounced over the uneven road, banging through potholes.

He remembered the small red cottages and bigger white ones with long gardens in front of them. Phone boxes and shops, paddocks full of horses and speed bumps on the road.

'There was the wind farm.'

'OK. A big one?'

'Twenty or thirty turbines, I think. I didn't count.'

She nodded to herself. 'What else?'

'A church. It was built from grey stone.'

'Alright, we're getting somewhere.'

She put her foot down and the car sped along the narrow road. She was a bad driver, erratic and dangerous, overtaking with the narrowest margin, like she didn't care if they arrived or not, and Paolo gripped the door handle to stop himself being thrown every time she took a corner too sharply.

They passed through a hamlet with a few houses standing close to the road and a large yard full of buses with missing wheels and smashed windscreens, their carcasses busted and rotten, dumped so long ago that a bush was growing through one of them.

He told her none of it looked familiar.

'It's OK, I know where we're going now. This is the quickest route.'

The sun was beginning to dip in the sky but it was clear and warm for a winter's day and it made him think of home. Marco said he had enough money put aside to get him a plane ticket; as soon as the police were finished with him they would leave. Marco had had enough too. The man he was working for was a bully and a thief – he kept half of what they earned and often didn't pay them at all, insisting he hadn't been paid either. As if they were stupid enough to believe that.

Or maybe he knew they didn't believe it but said it anyway, knowing they couldn't do anything about it.

'Being poor in the sun is better than being poor in the rain,' Marco said.

In the middle of nowhere they passed a large field, bordered by waterlogged ditches fringed with reeds, a couple of dozen workers bent double over rows of celery, knives in their hands, crates by their feet.

'How did you escape?' Sergeant Ferreira asked.

He looked at her but her eyes were fixed on the road.

He didn't want to talk about it, pretended he hadn't heard.

'The cabins were all locked from the outside,' she said. 'There were grilles over the windows. How did you manage to get out?'

His shoulder began to throb. The painkillers were wearing off already.

'Paolo.'

'They came for me,' he said. 'I don't remember exactly . . . one minute I was asleep and I heard voices and then someone hit me in the face and I must have passed out.' He ran his tongue across his broken molars and blood came into his mouth. 'I woke up in a barn.'

'The one near the site?'

'Yes. With the pigs.' He clenched his hands into tight fists to hide the tremble in his fingers. 'They were going to kill me. I heard them arguing about it outside. They were going to kill me and feed me to those animals.'

'So you ran.'

'I thought if I could just reach the road . . .'

'You were very lucky.'

At the edge of Spalding she pulled into a petrol station to fill up.

He stared out across the forecourt at the lorries lined up, waiting for their turn at the pumps, the names of supermarkets emblazoned across them, blown-up photographs of apples beaded with dew and carrots with lush green tops. He thought of the workers they had passed in the field and the ones in the packaging factories, an invisible army so far removed from society that they could go missing for months, years even, and nobody would come looking for them.

If he hadn't escaped the Gavins would be going about their business as usual today. He would be dead and Xin Gao would be lost forever under a building.

Sergeant Ferreira replaced the nozzle and told him to come in with her and get something to eat.

The shop was brightly lit and he felt disconcerted by the music and the hum of the air conditioning which blasted his face as he walked in. He followed her to the refrigerators at the back, feeling a stupid delight at the sight of so much choice, everything fresh and perfect. He chose a BLT and a can of Pepsi, noticing that the design had changed since he'd last had one.

This must be how people felt when they were released from prison. Finding the world the same but different. Everything louder and sharper than they expected.

He waited in the queue next to her, looking at the cigarettes.

'Do you want a pack?' she asked.

The woman behind the counter scanned his food.

'Marlboro Reds,' he told her.

Back in the car he lit one before he ate and the first hit of nicotine sang through his lungs. Sergeant Ferreira was fiddling with a tin of loose tobacco.

'You missed them, I bet.'

'Yes.' The second drag was duller and he took it deep, held onto it a long time, thinking of the rough cigarette Xin Gao had given him the morning he died. He was a kind man, too decent to have ended up where he was.

'Will you find Xin Gao's family?'

'If he was over here legally we probably could but there are almost no legal Chinese workers so I don't know. I doubt it.'

Her mobile phone rang as she was pulling out of the petrol station and she answered whoever was on the other end in brisk monosyllables, accelerating as she listened, like she wanted to get away from it.

'Near Gray's End Farm . . . It's on the outskirts of Spalding . . . No, not exactly, but how many options can there be? . . . Look, get them on the road and I'll call in when I've got a precise location.'

She threw her phone onto the dashboard and drove one-handed while she lit her cigarette, the car veering across the white lines. She pulled it back and put her foot down.

Paolo ate his sandwich, which didn't taste as good as it looked, and drank his Pepsi in a couple of long mouthfuls, spilling some down his chin when she took a corner too sharply. He should have got painkillers from the petrol station he realised. The ache in his shoulder was biting deeper.

He lit another cigarette, hoping that might take the edge off.

Fields went past in a blur. She was driving too quickly for the badly maintained road. When he glanced at the speedometer he saw the needle flickering around ninety and decided not to look again.

Then she was slowing, a warning sign flashing as they entered a village with a lot of quaint red-brick cottages and a large old pub standing on the broad, tree-lined green, where a man was letting two greyhounds run off their leads.

'I have been here before.'

'Good, we're on the right track then.'

A few minutes later they were back in open countryside and in the distance he saw wind turbines, their huge white blades standing still.

'That is the wind farm.'

'How close to it was the site?'

'We're almost there, I think.'

'Which direction?'

'It was on the right side of the van when we left in the morning.'

He scanned the landscape for something familiar, saw clumps of trees and an occasional farmhouse, miles away down dirt tracks.

They passed through another village.

'I remember that church.'

More fields. Polytunnels in rows. A house with fresh eggs for sale at the mouth of the gate.

Minutes passed and he leaned forward in his seat, eyes straining for the horizon. Then he saw it, half hidden by a sparse copse.

'There.'

The steels glinted under the midday sun, more of them than he remembered, sticking up high in the air.

'How do we get to it?'

'There is a turning along here,' he said. 'It is a long track, you can't see the building from the road.'

His heart was hammering in his chest, blood pounding in his ears. Suddenly he realised they might not have all of them. What if there were more English? On another site somewhere, and they had turned up for work this morning with no idea what had happened?

She turned off the road and drove more slowly along the bumpy dirt track. Ahead of them the track curved around a small wooded area which was so dense he couldn't see the site beyond it. He wanted to tell her to stop. Wait for more police. But his tongue was stuck to the roof of his mouth and he held his breath as she rounded the corner, only breathing again when he saw the broad metal gates still locked and the site deserted.

Sergeant Ferreira got out of the car and walked up to the gates,

310

tugged at them two-handed, then when they didn't budge, gave them a kick.

Paolo climbed out too, stood behind the open car door looking at the half-finished steel cage where Xin Gao's body was sealed in concrete. Three days ago now and it would be set. They would have to break him out.

Sergeant Ferreira was on the phone, giving directions to the man on the other end, telling him to get a move on.

Neither of them spoke until the vehicles arrived fifteen minutes later, two red vans and a silver car with a black-haired policeman inside who Paolo hadn't seen before. Not the one from the hospital. This one was younger, fresh-faced and expensively suited.

Another man, this one in scruffy clothes, worked quickly on the gate and then it was open and they were driving onto the site. Doors opened and slammed shut.

'OK, Paolo, can you remember where they threw him in?' Sergeant Ferreira asked.

They were all watching him now and he thought of how still and silent the other workers were as Xin Gao's body hit the wet concrete. He walked over to the spot, seeing ridged footsteps standing out sharply in the mud, a patch of brownish red which could only be Xin Gao's blood.

He pointed to the footing. 'There.'

Sergeant Ferreira squeezed his arm. 'You've done great, Paolo.'

Things happened quickly then and he stood near her car watching the other police pull blue plastic bodysuits on over their clothes, unloading equipment in silver cases. He didn't want to watch this. Seeing Xin Gao die was bad enough, he didn't think he could stand seeing the man's body brought out again.

Sergeant Ferreira was standing talking to the black-haired policeman. When he smiled she moved in close to him, her posture stiff with contained violence. Then her phone rang and she moved away.

Paolo heard her tone soften, saw her whole face change.

'What did they say? . . . Are they sure? . . . No, Bobby, I'll deal with it . . .' She glanced at her watch. 'Twenty minutes . . . this time of day it's twenty minutes . . . No, they don't need me here . . .' She grinned. 'Love you too.'

She came over, slipping her phone into her jeans pocket.

'Paolo, I've got to go back to the station.' She pushed her hair off her face. 'There's been a development in another case. I've got to deal with that.'

'I want to leave.'

'Get in then.'

49

Zigic's wife answered the door, the picture of domesticity with a floral apron over her clothes and full make-up on. Ferreira had met her briefly at one of the Christmas parties but she was drunk by then and had only the vaguest recollection of the woman, remembered a simple black dress and an air of carefully measured affability.

'It's Mel, isn't it?'

'Yes, hi. Can I come in?'

'Dushan's resting.'

'It'll only take a minute.'

She stepped back and let Ferreira into a hallway decorated in five shades of cream with blown-up sepia photographs of their kids framed on the walls and a console table carefully staged with a vase of stargazer lilies and a lot of white pillar candles which had never been lit. The door to the kitchen was open and baking smells wafted out, a warm fug of sugar and butter and cinnamon.

'Would you mind, Mel?' She pointed at Ferreira's feet. 'Cream carpets, they're a nightmare.'

Ferreira braced her hand against the wall and kicked off her boots. She was wearing mismatched socks with grubby toes and she half expected the woman to tell her to remove them too before she'd let her any further.

'You've been out in the wilds,' Anna said, eyeing the dirt on the floor.

'We've been looking for a body.'

'Did you find it?'

'Yeah. Eventually.'

A small boy with a mop of dark brown hair ran out of the kitchen and slid to a halt in front of Ferreira. He was holding a wooden dinosaur in one hand and a stuffed white rabbit in the other.

'This must be Milan.'

'Stefan,' Anna said.

He looked up at Ferreira with big green eyes full of sparky energy.

'Who are you?'

'This is Sergeant Ferreira, sweetheart. She works with Daddy.'

'Do you shoot people?'

'No.'

'Daddy got shot.'

Ferreira glanced at Anna. Her cheeks were flushed through her make-up and she ran a nervous hand over her hair, the strain of what-might-have-been momentarily closing her eyes.

'Your daddy's very brave,' Ferreira said.

Stefan shoved the wooden triceratops at her and she took it from him.

'Thanks.'

'His name's Max.'

'That's a good name for a dinosaur.'

'You don't need to be scared. He only eats plants.'

'OK.'

Stefan darted off and disappeared into the cupboard under the stairs, talking to himself in different voices which echoed in the small space.

'He's got a lot of imagination,' Ferreira said.

'Yes, he's very creative.'

Anna opened the door to the living room and went in ahead of her.

'Visitor for you, darling.'

The curtains were closed and the room was dimly lit by the glow from the flat screen in the corner, a bike race playing out on Eurosport. Zigic was lying on the brown leather chesterfield in his pyjamas, a hot-water bottle in a knitted cover clutched to his chest. The station doctor had sealed the cut above his left eye with a butterfly stitch but the skin was swollen and wet-looking now, giving him a slight squint when he smiled.

'Thought I heard you.'

'How're you feeling?'

'Like I've been shot in the chest.'

Anna switched a lamp on and Zigic blinked at the light.

'Can I get you a drink, Mel?'

'Coffee would be great, thanks.'

'I'll have another one,' Zigic said.

'Are you sure that's a good idea?'

'A small one.'

Ferreira sat down in an armchair opposite him. There was a half-eaten sandwich on the table, blister packs of pills and a book splayed cover up. Anna cleared the mess and took his hot-water bottle to refill in it, told him not to exert himself as she left the room.

'I see you met Stefan.'

Ferreira set the dinosaur down on the arm of the chair.

'He's a lovely kid.'

Zigic straightened carefully on the sofa, rearranging the pillows propped at his back.

'What's happening with Adams?'

'There's going to be an investigation,' Ferreira said. 'He seems to think it's just a formality.'

Zigic winced. 'It was my fault. He had no option but to shoot Kelvin. I don't even know how he managed to get my gun.'

'You shouldn't have gone in there on your own.'

'I wasn't thinking.'

'He's no great loss to the world,' Ferreira said, seeing it again, Kelvin Gavin face down on the barn floor in a pool of blood, Zigic a few feet away, trying to get up while Adams was unfastening his bulletproof vest, asking him where he'd been hit.

'I was stupid.'

'It could have happened to any of us,' Ferreira said. 'You just ran faster.'

Zigic pulled the remote control out from between the sofa cushions and turned the sound up loud enough to drown their conversation, a man's monotone voice droning over the action as a bunch of riders whipped through a flat landscape almost identical to the one she'd just come from. Ferreira looked at the fields and the farms and wondered what secrets were hidden a few yards from the bright blur of the race.

'Have you questioned the Barlows?'

'You told me to wait.'

He raised one thick, black eyebrow. 'I didn't expect you to take any notice. Especially since this.'

'I haven't had time anyway.'

The amusement went out of his face.

'What's happening, Mel?'

'There's been a development.' She placed the wooden dinosaur on the table, noticed his mobile hidden under the open book. 'Look, I can handle this, you don't have to come back in if you're not ready.'

'What's happened?'

She heard Anna bustling around in the kitchen, cups clinking, the fridge door opening and closing with a slam which sent the bottles inside rattling.

'The DNA results are back,' she said. 'It's not Stepulov in the shed.'

50

'Our deceased is Andy Hudson,' Zigic said, tapping his knuckles against the whiteboard, where the man's mugshot was now under the word 'victim'. Jaan Stepulov had been shifted ten inches to the bottom of the suspects column. It was getting cluttered there, Clinton Renfrew above him, Phil and Gemma Barlow at the top.

'Mr Hudson is well known to us.'

Six sets of eyes watched him, waiting for more. Ferreira and Wahlia at their desks, his extra troops, newly recalled, scattered about, cluttering the usually empty office. At the back of the room the press officer was tapping away on her BlackBerry, preparing a statement which he hoped wouldn't make them sound inept.

'Aggravated assault, intimidation, manslaughter – there's a high probability that he was asking for this but it doesn't alter the fact that he was brutally murdered and it's our job to find the culprit.'

He took half a step back and pointed to Jaan Stepulov's photograph.

'For those of you just joining us, Jaan Stepulov was originally believed to be our corpse . . .' He tailed off, looking at the crime-scene photos of the burnt-out shed, the charred body snagged in the twisted metal wreckage of a sunlounger. The smell came back to him, so strong and bitter he could taste it. Or was it just failure?

They'd made an assumption – *he'd* made an assumption – and it was wrong and now here they were a week later, starting from scratch, and Jaan Stepulov could be anywhere in the world.

'As of now our primary objective is to locate Stepulov and bring him in.'

He spread his hands wide, like it was simple, but he could see nobody was buying that. The new faces showed no enthusiasm, none of the usual energy which fired up the start of a case, and even Wahlia sat slumped in his chair, knees wide, cracking a pen lid between his teeth.

A hand went up, a black-haired DC in a pinstripe suit.

'Carr, yes?'

'What about the brother? Are we considering the murders linked?'

Zigic gestured at Ferreira. She put down her half-rolled cigarette, scattering strands of tobacco across the desk, and came over to the board with another photograph.

'This is what we've got from the CCTV at Holme Fen crossing.' She stuck it up. The man's broad back, his uncovered head where he'd lost his beanie and the dark comma of a ponytail at the nape of his neck.

Next to it the side profile from Andy Hudson's mugshots showed a similar configuration.

'It's not concrete,' she said. 'But there's a strong resemblance.'

'Our prime suspects are the householders, Phil and Gemma Barlow, but until we know for sure, it remains a solid maybe,' Zigic said. 'Hudson kills and dumps Viktor Stepulov and three months later he's murdered by Jaan . . . we can't ignore this line, but right now Jaan is a valuable witness and we need to bring him in.

'I want you – Carr – to get hold of CCTV from the train station, the bus terminal and the coach park on Bright Street.'

The DC's jaw tightened and he nodded.

'Greaves.' He pointed at a young woman with a severe blonde bob and the action sent a spike through his chest. 'Airports.'

She nodded.

'West and Parr, get me everything you can on Hudson. Tax records, bank accounts, known associates. We need to know what his link to Jaan Stepulov was.' He shoved his hands down into his pockets. 'DC Wahlia is coordinating, everything goes through him, right?'

Nods all around. A charge was stirring through the room now and he felt it too, movement, finally, in the case.

'Get to it then.' He turned to Ferreira. 'What's happening with Barlow's solicitor?'

'On her way.'

'Let's see what the widow Hudson has to tell us then.'

Ferreira pulled on her duffel coat, grabbed her keys.

'I'll drive,' Zigic said.

'You sure you should?'

'I'm not an invalid.'

There were roadworks on Bretton Parkway, one lane coned off where it bridged the River Nene through Ferry Meadows, but there were no workmen in sight, just a lot of annoyed motorists sitting tight on each other's bumpers, crawling along at ten miles an hour.

Zigic indicated and turned down onto the Oundle Road, passing a pub with a few people sitting out in the beer garden, togged up in coats while their kids played on the swings, their screams breaking across the traffic. A young woman was pushing a double buggy along the pavement, rushing towards the bus stop where a couple of schoolboys in grey uniforms were climbing into the waiting double decker, bags slung low, trousers lower, showing off the logos across the top of their pants.

'I still think the Barlows did it,' Ferreira said.

'You thought Renfrew did it last night.'

'He's too confident. I think he was telling the truth about blackmailing Phil. He saw his chance after we questioned him at the garage and he took it.' She turned on the heater, set it to full blast in the footwell. 'Phil did it. I don't know whether Gemma knows that, but he did. Why else pay up?'

'Blackmail doesn't actually require a guilty party, Mel.' Zigic slowed and flashed for a cyclist to come out of the Botolph Arms car park. 'Just a scared one.'

He thought of Phil Barlow, a big man but soft, not tough enough to stand up to Jaan Stepulov and throw him out on the street. How would he cope with Clinton Renfrew in his face, threatening to take away everything he'd worked for? He wouldn't dare call his bluff. Guilty or innocent, he'd pay up and hope that was the end of it.

Zigic cut across the Shrewsbury Avenue lights on amber, his chest twingeing as he turned the steering wheel, the pain so sudden that he almost ran into the back of a Royal Mail van stopped for no reason at the mouth of the business park to their left.

Ferreira's hands shot out for the dashboard.

'Are you sure you don't want me to drive?'

The van turned down towards the sorting office and Zigic pulled off again. He slipped on his sunglasses and that helped, blocked out some of the glare from the afternoon sun cutting in low across the blocky units sitting squat ahead of him.

'Do you think the Stepulovs know Jaan's still alive?'

'His daughter seemed properly distraught,' Zigic said. 'I don't think she does.'

'Do you want to send a couple of uniforms over to break the good news?' Ferreira asked.

'Best one of us does it.'

'So, me then?'

'You then.'

Hampton Vale sprawled towards the horizon as he came off the Serpentine Green roundabout, the shopping centre sitting on a plateau overlooking it, the only really solid piece of land there. The rest of it, where the houses and schools and health centres were built, was a rubbish dump ten years ago and rumour had it the place was sinking already.

Zigic drove through the first phase, red-brick cod-Georgian town houses with lead canopies and railings on the path, stone sills and busy facades. Quickly all the expensive ornamentation fell away and as they headed into the heart of the development things got brutal and utilitarian. Seventy per cent of the housing was council and the parts that weren't were slowly being gated, the private residents locking themselves away from their neighbours, the ones the local authority had built a battered women's refuge for and a drug rehabilitation centre, then a police station for when things got too serious to be handled by social workers.

'Where am I going?' Zigic asked. 'All these closes look the same.'

Ferreira had her mobile out, a map on the screen.

'Third left, then it spurs off right.'

He turned onto a short cul-de-sac of yellow-brick houses with white plastic windows and off-road parking, no fancy brickwork on the eaves here, just a lot of satellite dishes for decoration and the occasional flag in a window.

'Number 8,' Ferreira said.

There was a black people carrier in the driveway, its rear bumper overhanging the path when Zigic pulled up. Mid-afternoon and the neighbouring houses were all occupied, lights on, windows open, nobody working. Radio voices bled out into the close, arguing hotly, and the air smelled of frying food, but there was another odour coming up through the grass and the cracks in the tarmac, something black and rotten, a chemical base note.

Zigic rang the bell and started a dog yapping inside number 8. A woman shouted at it but the dog kept going, then it yelped and Tanya Hudson opened the door. She was petite and blonde, with a sharply pointed face that showed a lack of sleep and an excess of worry. She had form herself, a shoplifting career which dated back to her teens and a conviction for assault when she kicked a woman unconscious in a nightclub toilet for splashing water on her dress.

They must have made quite a couple, Zigic thought.

'Mrs Hudson, I'm DI Zigic.' He flashed his warrant card. 'This is DS Ferreira. We need to talk to you about your husband.'

She folded her arms. 'What's he done now?'

'Could we come in please?'

'You got a warrant?' she asked, but there was no force to the question, it was just a reflex, Zigic guessed, the kind you developed when you were married to a recidivist thug.

'I'm afraid we've got bad news, Mrs Hudson.'

'No. No, you're not giving me that shit,' she said, her voice dropping.

'Andy's dead. I'm very sorry.'

Her hands went to her chest. 'No. He can't be.'

'I'm very sorry.'

'When? What happened?'

'Maybe we should do this inside,' Zigic said softly, moving across the threshold.

She blocked him off, her body filling the narrow gap.

'No. Tell me what fucking happened to him.'

'He's been murdered. There was a fire.'

Her face was blank, eyes wide. 'Where? This doesn't make any sense.'

'On Highbury Street, he –'

'That shed?'

'Yes.'

'The news said it was a Pole or something.'

'We've just received the DNA results,' Zigic said. 'It's Andy. There's no question now.'

She moved away from the door with small, faltering steps, until she reached the stairs, where she sat down heavily, staring at the pile of shoes kicked off into the corner. The house was a mess, damp towels on the radiator and junk mail on the floor. The walls, painted a chilly blue, were scuffed black here and there, and the zebra-wood laminate was dented and gouged.

'What was he doing there?' Tanya Hudson asked.

Zigic closed the front door. 'We were hoping you might know.'

'We don't know anyone over there.'

'What about Andy's work?'

'What about it?' she snapped.

'Look, Tanya, we all know Andy wasn't exactly a saint –'

'Who the fuck are you to say that?' She jumped to her feet. 'My husband's been murdered and you come round here talking shit about him? Fuck you.'

'Tanya –'

'Mrs Hudson.'

'Mrs Hudson, it's too late to try and protect your husband's reputation. We know what he was up to and we've arrested the people he was working with.'

'Ask them then.'

'They don't care what happened to Andy,' Zigic said. 'Now, what was he doing for them?'

'Driving. That's all. He picked the blokes up from the site and took them to work, then he brought them back again. He wasn't involved with any of that other shit.'

'But he told you about it?'

She nodded. 'Tight-fisted bastards paid him eight quid an hour with what they were raking in.'

An alarm sounded and she pushed between them to get to the living room.

It was dimly lit and overheated, the gas fire blasting. Next to it, in an electric wheelchair, was a teenaged boy with Hudson's dark hair and square head, but the similarity to his father ended there. He was painfully thin and sickly-looking, the left side of his face drooped and immobile, his arm bent at an awkward angle, wrist turned back, fingers in a permanent splay. He watched his mother come towards him, spoke a few mangled words.

Tanya Hudson wiped his chin with a towel.

'It's OK, Jake, they're here to talk to Mummy.'

He threw his head to the right to look at them, more awareness in his bright blue eyes than Zigic expected. Gently, Tanya moved it back again, finding no resistance.

'Seen enough, have you?' she said.

They returned to the hallway and Zigic heard her ask the boy what he wanted on television, flicking through the channels until he told her to stop. She said she'd get his dinner in a minute, she just had to talk to Daddy's friends.

'What's wrong with him?' Ferreira whispered, hugging her arms around her body.

'I don't know, cerebral palsy maybe.'

Tanya Hudson came out of the living room, closed the door. There were tears in her eyes and Zigic wondered how long she would delay telling the boy about his father, whether she was already trying out the lines in her head, debating lying to save him the pain. *Daddy's had an accident, sweetheart, he's with the angels now.*

'Let's get this over with.'

'Wednesday morning,' Zigic said. 'Did Andy tell you where he was going?'

She sucked her bottom lip into her mouth, eyes closed. 'We haven't seen him since last weekend.'

'Why?'

'Why do you think?' she said, too loud, and glanced at the living-room door. 'He couldn't cope with Jake. Alright? He – we – we're still together but he works a lot of hours. We only see him at the weekend.'

'Where was he living when he wasn't here?'

'He never moved out, we were together,' she said again, less certainty in her tone. 'He dossed down where he was working.'

She was lying, or at least evading, Zigic thought. There would be another woman somewhere, another home, without a demanding child and all the problems which went along with caring. Hudson wasn't bad enough to cut and run, but not good enough to stay and help.

Tanya Hudson wiped a few tears away, set her face hard.

'I can't believe this.'

Zigic took the photographs of Jaan and Viktor Stepulov out of his coat pocket.

'Do you recognise either of these men?'

She gave them a cursory glance. 'No. Did one of them do it?'

'This man – Jaan Stepulov – was living in the shed where Andy was killed.'

'I don't understand.' She looked at the photograph again, boring into it, brows drawn down in concentration. 'What the hell am I going to tell Jake?'

Another transient, Zigic thought, as he got back into the car. What was wrong with these men? They had families but they weren't involved with them. They lived apart and unconnected and it didn't seem to bother them. There was no question of responsibility.

He knew he shouldn't be shocked, it was hardly uncommon, but it bothered him so much he hardly answered Ferreira as she sat speculating in the passenger seat, asking him if he thought Tanya was hiding something. She did, but she thought everyone was, all of the time. She had a streak of cynicism much wider than standard police issue and he guessed it came from how she was raised, living in a precarious situation, surrounded by strangers who came and went, different ones every month; that level of insecurity wasn't good for kids. You adopted mistrust as a default position.

'I need food,' she said. 'Can you pull into McDonald's?'

He did, thinking of Andy Hudson and Jaan Stepulov, wondering how they had come to know each other. Was Hudson really just a van driver? He thought Tanya was lying about that, it had seemed impossible that she was so ignorant, but that was before their marital arrangements were out in the open. Now he wasn't so sure.

There was a long queue at the drive-thru, white vans and fleet cars parked bumper to bumper, revving their engines impatiently. Ferreira went inside while he parked up but came out empty-handed two minutes later, dashed across the car park with her mobile clamped to her ear.

She slid into the passenger seat. 'We've got Hudson's bachelor pad.'

51

Emilia stood at the bedroom window, watching the River Nene glide by three floors below, murky and diseased-looking. She sipped her vodka, needing to feel the burn of it fill her chest, but it was refusing to comfort her today. It was just as fickle and unreliable as everything else, she realised, throwing the rest of it down.

She checked her phone again, no missed calls, no new messages. Only one person she wanted to hear from.

The waiting was the worst part.

She returned to the window and watched people crossing the Town Bridge, men and women in suits, hurrying into the city centre.

She always thought it would be nice to work in an office, have a computer and a telephone, wear a smart suit and eat her lunch at her desk like the women in adverts did. She wasn't sure what she would do in an office but she suspected many people who worked in them didn't know either, just moved pieces of paper around and played with their computers.

Then she thought of the Englishmen who came into Maloney's. They would be the kind of people she worked with, and if she couldn't stand them for a few minutes how would she manage eight hours?

It wasn't an issue now anyway.

Back home she would do bar work again or find a job in a shop.

She remembered a ladies' shoe shop on Vana-Viru when she was a girl. She never went in, only stood outside and looked in through the plate-glass window at the display, black stiletto heels and ballet flats with buckles on the toes, strappy sandals in the summer and leather boots in the winter; all placed just so on white boxes.

She would like to work somewhere like that.

Somewhere with no men to leer at her. She never wanted to be called love or darling or bitch ever again. Didn't want to hear another English voice as long as she lived.

She turned away from the window and went to count Skinner's money again. It was sitting on the bed in neat piles, two thousand five hundred pounds, tens and twenties separate from each other, a lot of fives.

The notes whispered through her fingers, sweaty and grubby, tainted by what she had done to earn them. She stuffed them into an envelope and sealed it. She wouldn't be sad to pass this money over and let somebody else take possession of its filthy history.

She went into the kitchen and washed her hands with antibacterial soap, came back to the bedroom and checked her phone again.

This waiting was hell.

Tuesday he said. And she thought Tuesday must mean first thing. Nine o'clock. So she called in sick, told Olga she had a bad stomach because it was the only illness which wouldn't be questioned. Olga said Maloney would not be happy but Emilia was past caring about what he thought.

She had worked her last shift and he didn't know where to find her, so let him rage and thunder, get all red in the face and smack one of the girls if he felt like it. He wouldn't lay a finger on her again.

She poured another vodka and took it into the bedroom, started to pack a bag. She would travel light. Enough to look like she was returning home rather than running away.

Her clothes were spread across the bed and she felt a painful twinge as she remembered packing her things the night before she left home, choosing the best clothes she had because she was going to England and she didn't want to look like a poor foreigner who didn't know how to dress.

She had a lot of English clothes, she knew what fashionable girls here wore because she bought their cast-offs from a woman on the market who had them sent over in bulk by a brother in London;

Topshop and Zara and River Island. She liked River Island the best and that night, sleeping with her bag stowed under her bed so her mother wouldn't see it, she had dreamed of walking around a huge, brightly lit shopping centre, gathering armfuls of clothes she would buy with her tips.

New clothes, still smelling of the factory, not second-hand things which came with odd receipts in the pockets and packs of gum, the odour of other women's bodies at the underarms and groins.

As she was folding a pair of skinny black jeans the phone rang.

'Yes?'

'It's ready,' Skinner said. 'You want me to come to the pub?'

'No. I will meet you.'

'Yours then?'

'My break is in twenty minutes,' she said and hoped he didn't realise that it was too quiet for her to be at Maloney's. She didn't want him here again under any circumstances. 'The Costa in Queensgate. I will meet you there.'

'Bit public, isn't it?' Skinner said. 'Best come to mine.'

'No.'

'Look, I'm not handing this over to you in the middle of a fucking shopping centre.' He muffled the phone and shouted at someone at his end. 'Right. This is what we're gonna do. I'll pull up round the back of Westgate House, you get it from me there. A black Golf. You know what they look like?'

'Yes.'

'Twenty minutes then.'

52

It took an hour to get a search warrant and another fifteen minutes to drag the letting agent out of his office on Cowgate to open up Andy Hudson's flat.

The agent – Damon – arrived in a black cashmere overcoat and a three-piece suit, half a pound of flashy Swiss engineering weighing down his wrist when he shook hands with Zigic and Ferreira. He punched a code into the entry system and proceeded to give them a run-down of the benefits of living so close to the centre of town, concentrating his attention on Ferreira, obviously figuring her for an upwardly mobile career woman who needed to be in the middle of things.

'This location is great for the clubs,' Damon said. 'You're a five-minute cab ride home. There's the supermarket of course but you look a bit more discerning than that.'

Ferreira rolled her eyes.

'There's a great little deli in the arcade,' he said, ploughing on. 'I use it all the time. Banging antipasti. And you're handy for the courthouses, which has got to be a bonus in your line of work.'

'How long's Hudson been renting the place?' Zigic asked.

'Coming up for a year.'

'Did you deal with him?'

'No. One of my colleagues did. I don't handle the properties in this price range.'

'Is there anyone else on the lease?'

'No. Just Mr Hudson.'

He took a key out of his pocket and unlocked the door, ushering them inside like he was showing the place.

'The views are stunning too.'

Zigic went in ahead and left Ferreira to deal with the formalities, get the key and hand over a receipt for it. He heard Damon still trying to reel her in, talking about a new development on Thorpe Park Road, executive apartments, very exclusive, another one overlooking the park which had just come in; he had a place there himself, maybe she'd like to see it . . .

The living room was decorated like a furnished let, sisal on the floor and a shaggy rug, a cheap brown leather sofa and a single armchair, shelves with nothing on them but a few knick-knacks, the kind you bought from Tesco or Dunelm to make a place look homely; wooden balls in clusters and little boxes covered in shells, every one of them empty when Zigic lifted their lids. There were no books or DVDs, and every photo frame still held the image which had been slipped into it at the factory.

In the kitchen he found a bottle of vodka standing on the drainer next to a lip-stained tumbler.

Hudson had been dead six days but someone had been here since. There were drops of water in the stainless-steel sink and when he opened the fridge he found fresh milk and a loaf of bread still soft to the touch. Someone had restocked since Wednesday.

The front door slammed shut.

'This place would be perfect for you,' Zigic said meeting Ferreira in the living room.

'Don't you start.'

'Are you going to see that apartment on the park?'

'He wishes.' She moved to the window. 'Stunning views . . . of the electricity substation and the railway line.'

Zigic went into the bedroom.

There were women's clothes thrown all over the double bed, some folded, most not, and a nylon holdall half packed already. The air smelled of perfume, sickly and vanilla-tinged.

'Someone's getting ready to bolt.'

'Looks like they got disturbed,' Ferreira said, going into the bathroom across the hall.

Zigic opened the bedside drawers, found hand cream and lube, a box of condoms and a hairbrush with congested teeth.

'Why wasn't he living at the Knarrs End site?' Ferreira said, her voice echoing against the tiled walls. 'Don't gypsies tend to stick close?'

'Some of them move into houses.'

The rail in the pine wardrobe was mostly empty, just a few shirts and pairs of jeans pushed up hard on the left-hand side, trainers underneath and a pair of brown suede desert boots. Clothes for Hudson's second life.

He wasn't just a van driver on eight pound an hour. That was a convenient lie to tell his wife and stop her asking for more money.

But what was he?

He was a charred corpse in a tray at City Hospital. Murdered in a shed whose regular occupant was now missing and with a girlfriend getting set to do a runner.

Where did the Stepulov brothers fit in this mess? Zigic thought, looking at the clothes strewn across the bed, white jeans and little vests with spangly fronts, short black skirts, sheer blouses, bras and stockings and thongs with swirling diamanté motifs.

There was only one good reason for her to run and that was guilt.

Ferreira came out of the bathroom holding a bottle of ink-blue nail varnish, a smile on her face.

'I know someone who wears this.'

'A lot of women wear it, don't they?'

'This one works at Maloney's and knew the Stepulovs,' Ferreira said. 'And last time I saw her I'm pretty sure she was wearing those tragic hooker-heels over there.'

In the lift Zigic gave Ferreira his car keys. The ache in his chest had spread to his shoulders and upper arms, something he'd been warned about but he didn't expect it to come on so swift and hard.

He dry-swallowed another codeine and told her to put her foot down.

When they reached Maloney's the man himself was nowhere to be seen. Two old Irish guys with nicotine-stained hair were playing dominoes at his usual table and when they enquired from the woman behind the bar she said Maloney had gone to see a man about a dog, the words spoken straight, as if she didn't know they were a euphemism.

Emilia Koppel wasn't there either, called in sick that morning.

Outside again Ferreira asked what he wanted to do and Zigic braced his hands against the roof of the car, remembering the young woman now, serving behind the bar when they caught up with Tomas Raadik, remembered her blue nails and her child's face and cursed himself for not reading her reaction at the time. She'd lingered and listened, as she swept up the broken glass, and he took it for the usual ghoulish interest, but now he knew better and she might have slipped through their fingers already.

He straightened slowly, the ache beginning to pound, and pushed the negative thoughts aside.

'Have a car stationed outside her flat. She's got to go back sometime.'

53

Andy Hudson's board showed a mess of activity when Zigic got back to the office. Within three hours lines of inquiry had been uncovered and dismissed, nothing from the CCTV at the bus terminal or the train station but they were still waiting on passenger records from the local airports. It was unlikely Jaan Stepulov would flee by plane. That took resources Zigic doubted the man had.

But if Stepulov flew at least he would have used his passport and they would get a destination. Even if they were forced to extradite him – even if Zigic had to go to Tallinn and drag him back by the scruff of his neck – they would have their man at last. Witness or suspect, they would have him.

He took a red marker pen from the ledge at the bottom of the board and added Emilia Koppel to the witness column, debated for a moment and added her to the suspects one too. The logistics made it unlikely but the connection to the Stepulov brothers meant she was a possible accomplice.

'We've cross-checked against Hudson's mobile logs,' Wahlia said, coming to the board. 'Whoever Jaan Stepulov's late-night caller was, they were also in frequent contact with Hudson and there're a couple of calls a week to Maloney's.'

'So it has to be her calling Jaan.'

'Looks like it.' Wahlia unwrapped a stick of gum and folded it into his mouth. 'Good old-fashioned love triangle, you think?'

'Stepulov was old enough to be her father.'

'Some girls don't mind that,' Ferreira said, chipping in from across the office.

'Usually there's a financial component.'

Wahlia shrugged. 'Maybe she was just homesick. It's nice to hear a familiar accent when you're miles away from where you want to be.'

Zigic turned the idea around. Hudson sets Emilia up in a swanky flat on Rivergate, buys her clothes, pays her bills . . . and she gets involved with a homeless man twice her age? It didn't sound right. Hudson was her way out of prostitution, if that's what she wanted from him, why would she jeopardise what little security she had?

Hudson was obviously more than an occasional visitor too. From the way the flat was set up and the details his wife had given them, it looked certain he lived there during the week. They slept next to each other, woke up together, ate breakfast, watched TV. Emilia was more girlfriend than mistress.

Zigic went over to Viktor Stepulov's board.

Andy Hudson was alone in the suspects column, staring out across the clatter and hum of the office with a hard expression.

Hudson kills Viktor. Jaan kills Hudson.

It was very neat.

'Mel, is Barlow's solicitor here yet?'

'No.' She came over and put a mug in his hand. 'Must be held up in court or something. Way she's going we're never going to get to question him.'

Zigic moved away towards Andy Hudson's board.

'Do you still fancy Phil for it?'

'He didn't know Hudson was inside instead of Jaan. So, yeah.'

'If Jaan's innocent he should have come forward.'

'He's probably scared of being falsely accused,' she said, going back to her desk where a half-eaten sandwich was waiting. 'In his position I'd run, wouldn't you?'

'No.'

'Liar.' She took a mouthful of her sandwich, said, 'Any money you like, Barlow's the one.'

'Even though Hudson and Jaan were seeing the same woman?'

'Yeah.'

Zigic threw his hand up in exasperation. 'You can't bend the evidence to suit your prejudices, Mel.'

'I'm not prejudiced,' she said sharply. 'The Barlows wanted rid of Stepulov, they had the opportunity and they took it. Then Phil paid off Renfrew when he threatened to make trouble for him. Innocent people don't do that.'

'They do if they're scared.'

'They should be scared.' She dumped the rest of her sandwich in the bin. 'For all we know they killed Jaan as well. Maybe he saw Phil torch the shed and he killed him to stop him talking. Did you think of that?'

Zigic took a mouthful of his coffee, tasting tobacco from her fingers on the rim of the cup. He had thought of that, briefly, and dismissed it as outlandish.

He still wasn't convinced Phil had it in him to set fire to the shed, definitely couldn't see him squaring up to a man in the open, killing him with whatever means he had to hand, then having the necessary cool to dispose of a body. And doing all of that between his neighbour raising the alarm and the fire engine arriving. It was logistically impossible never mind outlandish.

'Aren't you supposed to be somewhere, Mel?' She gave him a blank look. 'Mrs Stepulov should be home by now. Good news, remember?'

His mobile vibrated in his pocket and when he checked it he found a text from Anna reminding him it was time for a painkiller. She was right. He swallowed another codeine and went up to CID, took the stairs at a jog just to prove to himself that he wasn't completely crocked.

The office was deserted, a couple of uniformed officers manning desks to filter the information coming in from the field teams out taking witness statements from the Gavins' 'workers' and the ones still searching the site at Knarrs End Drove. He went over to the whiteboard where Paolo Perez's shooting was plotted out; everything enviably neat there.

Another board was pushed close to it, detailing the developing case against the Gavins for kidnapping and exploitation. The names in the victims column read like the guest list of an EU summit, thirty-two men all with families wondering why they had fallen out of contact. Some would have moved on, abandoned them for dead, and he guessed a few of the homecomings wouldn't be the joyful occasions the men were expecting.

Next to that a third board showed the embryonic investigation into Xin Gao's murder. His body had been disinterred already and Zigic grimaced at the photographs of his crushed torso and the chemical burns from the concrete which distorted his face. His mouth was open, packed with cement.

Adams came out of his office to shout at one of the uniforms, wanting to know where 'that facking ballistics report' was.

He looked frazzled, shirtsleeves folded back and his face lit with nervous energy.

'Aren't you supposed to be convalescing, Ziggy?'

'I'm recovered.'

'You're tough stock,' Adams said. He clicked his fingers at the uniform, who was sitting watching them. 'Jump to it then, I've not got all day.'

She picked up the phone on her desk and started to dial.

'What about you?' Zigic asked.

Adams made a dismissive gesture. 'Part of the job, isn't it?'

But it wasn't and Zigic remembered the panic in Adams's voice as he came round on the barn floor, remembered how his fingers were shaking as they probed at his neck for a pulse and how he walked away to throw up in the shadows a few minutes later.

'As long as I don't get charged, who gives a fuck? One less Kelvin Gavin on the planet . . .' Adams crossed his arms. 'Anyway, what's up?'

'I need to talk to your suspects,' Zigic said.

'Yeah, good luck with that.'

'No joy?'

'They're denying everything right now. Can't get one of the fuckers to crack.' He opened a blue patisserie box and picked out a chocolate-covered doughnut. 'That's the problem with these tinks, they're all related so they never break rank. On top of that a couple of the workers are denying they were held there against their will. They're fucking terrified what'll happen if they speak out now. God knows what they've been threatened with.' Adams shoved the rest of the doughnut in his mouth, licked chocolate off his thumb. 'What do you need them for?'

'We've just got the DNA results back from the shed fire,' Zigic said.

'And it's not your man Stepulov?'

'It's Andy Hudson. We think he was working for the Gavins.'

'Small world.'

'Minuscule.'

'Well, you're welcome to try,' Adams said. 'But I wouldn't expect too much. You want some advice, I'd say go for Marie, she's been the mouthiest of the lot.'

'Does she know what's happened to Kelvin?'

'No. And don't you say anything. We'll get fuck all from her once that's out.'

'You want to sit in?'

'Might as well,' Adams said.

Marie Gavin was still wearing the pink satin pyjamas she had on when she was arrested and a pair of Ugg boots trod down at the heels and crusted with dirt from the yard. She was younger than Zigic had thought, a badly weathered thirty, with coarse skin and dark rings under her hazel eyes. It was a tough life they lived. Not as tough as the one their workers endured but it left marks which no amount of hair dye and make-up could cover. She had four kids, all in care, and Ray Gavin was her second husband, the older brother of her first, who'd been killed in Littlehey while he was serving fifteen years for a double murder during a post office robbery.

Zigic would have felt sorry for her if he didn't know better.

'I told him already,' she said, pointing one French-manicured finger at Adams. 'I'm saying nothing.'

'Take a seat please, Mrs Gavin.'

She trudged over to the table and sat down.

'Can I get you anything? Cup of tea?'

'Don't fucking bother.'

Adams pulled out the seat next to the wall and set up the tapes. Marie Gavin watched him with a expression of pure contempt and Zigic wondered if he'd made a misjudgement bringing him in. They'd been in here together for hours already, banging heads, so she'd arrived on the defensive.

'Do you want your solicitor?' Zigic asked.

'Don't need him. I've said all I'm going to.'

'Just say if you change your mind.'

She smiled, thin lips drawing back from bleached teeth.

'You must think I'm a fucking idiot.'

Zigic opened the file he'd brought in with him and took out a photograph of Jaan Stepulov.

'Do you know this man, Mrs Gavin?'

'Are you retarded? I told you, I'm saying nothing.'

'Then listen,' Zigic said. 'We believe this man is responsible for the murder of your friend Andy Hudson. He beat him unconscious, then he locked him in a shed and set fire to it.' His words hung in the air for a moment. 'Did you know he was dead?'

'We're not close.'

Her eyes dropped to the photograph and Zigic went on.

'Look, I don't care what you were doing with those blokes on your site. From what I hear most of them were happy enough with the situation – that's not my problem – but I want to know why this Stepulov went after Andy and I want to arrest him. So if you know where he is –'

'I've never seen him before in my life.'

'He wasn't working for you?'

'I just said, didn't I?'

338

'When did you last see Andy?'

'I'm not his fucking keeper.'

'But he did work for you?'

'He worked for himself.'

'Doing what?'

She shook her head. 'It's nothing to do with us.'

'Look, Mrs Gavin, all I'm interested in is finding this man Stepulov. If you can help I'll be happy to say that you've cooperated with the investigation and make recommendations –'

She snorted. 'I don't need your recommendation.'

'We both know that's not true,' Adams said, his voice low and oily. 'Right now you're on a knife edge, you can go inside with the rest of your fucking brood or you can help us and stay out. I don't know, maybe you'll like it in nick, maybe you'll be queen-dyke and have your pick of the drug mules and baby-killers. That sound like something you'd enjoy, Marie?'

She glared at Adams and Zigic felt the rage radiating from her.

He took Viktor's photograph out of the file.

'You know this man,' Zigic said. 'He was working for you.'

'I'm saying nothing.'

'He's dead too. Andy and your nephew dumped his body on a railway line three months ago.'

'Nothing to do with me. Andy had his own stuff going on.'

'What stuff?'

'Like I cared.'

'You don't care that he involved Kelvin in it?'

'He's a big boy. He can make his own mistakes.'

Adams shifted in his chair, fiddled with his watch, straightening it on his wrist. Kelvin Gavin had made the last mistake he ever would.

'You see, Mrs Gavin, there are two options here,' Zigic said. 'Maybe Viktor died on one of your jobs and Andy was getting rid of his body to protect you –'

'You can't prove that.'

'We know he was working on that unit you're building. We have witnesses who can confirm that he was living at the site. It's only a matter of time before one of them tells us exactly how he died.'

'Probably be another industrial accident,' Adams said. 'You don't have a very good safety record.'

'He didn't die on a job,' Marie Gavin said, slapping her palm down on the table. 'You're not putting that on us. Hudson kicked the shit out of him.'

'Why?'

'Fucking why, I don't know.'

'We could ask him,' Adams said. 'Except we can't. Handy for you that.'

'Ask Kelvin.'

Adams stiffened.

'Kelvin isn't going to incriminate himself,' Zigic said. 'If you want his name to stay clean in this you have to tell us what happened.'

'I don't know. Alright? I heard a ruckus. I looked out the window and saw Hudson laying into this fella. I don't know what it was over. It could have been anything. Hudson couldn't control his temper.'

'Had there been trouble at work?'

'Not that I knew.'

'So it was personal?'

'Hudson didn't need a reason. If he felt like a fight he'd go and start one. You ask any of them.'

'We're asking you,' Adams said. 'Think on, Mrs Gavin, you need all the help you can get right now and Andy's already dead.'

She leaned back in the hard plastic chair, folded her arms over her ample chest and put the eye on Zigic. 'I want assurances, on paper, witnessed by my solicitor.'

He'd have given her them on vellum, in his own blood, if that was what it took.

'You have my word,' Zigic said, 'and you have it on tape, but we need to move quickly. Please, Mrs Gavin.'

She considered it for a long moment, scrutinising him like she could bore straight through his eyes into the deepest recesses of his soul, then she nodded.

'Like I say, Hudson started on this fella –'

'Viktor?'

'No, another fella, one of the Turks I think it was, and this one –' she tapped Viktor's photograph – 'he decided to be the big man and got in between them. Hudson knocked him about for a bit, just to let the others know who was boss – shut his leg in the van door, that sort of thing, you know? For show.'

Zigic thought of the broken bone sticking out, very white, through Viktor's skin, and how it had pierced the fabric of his grubby trousers. Imagined how he would have screamed and prayed to pass out from the pain, looking to the men around him for help and finding none.

'Then what did he do?'

'He was going to leave it at that, I reckon. He'd made his point. But this Viktor bit him and that set Hudson off again. He got a chisel out of the van and stabbed him.'

'A chisel?'

'Hudson kept one in the van door. Big thing,' Marie Gavin said, her hands eight inches apart in the air. 'He stabbed him in the chest with it.' She folded her hands in her lap. 'We didn't have any trouble for a good few weeks after that, I can tell you.'

That was why Hudson dumped Viktor on the train tracks then, he knew a chisel would leave a distinctive wound and he wanted all trace of it completely obliterated. In Hudson's line of work it would be to hand, Zigic guessed, something which wouldn't get him in trouble if he was pulled over for speeding, but which was capable of inflicting serious damage when necessary.

'And then what?' Zigic asked. 'You told him to get rid of the body?'

'It was Hudson's problem. Nobody told him nothing. He knew better than to let it come back to our door.'

'But it did.'

'Yeah, well, he always was a thick cunt.'

When Marie Gavin was on her way back down to the cells Adams put a call in to the search team at Knarrs End Drove, told them to look out for the murder weapon, but Zigic didn't hold out much hope of finding it. Not that it mattered now, victim and killer were both dead, there would be no trial.

54

Mrs Stepulov was unloading shopping bags from the boot of her car when Ferreira pulled up outside the house. She shuffled towards the open front door, weighed down with both hands full, sagging under the weight, and dropped her load in the hallway.

Was there a sensitive way do this? Ferreira wondered, seeing Arina looking out of the living-room window, arms wrapped around her swollen belly.

She'd never been very good at delivering bad news. She'd been on the training course, tried the tricks they suggested, knew to give people space, let them assimilate the information before starting on the questions. This was a very different situation though, not bad news but not quite good either.

Your husband isn't dead but we want to arrest him for murder. Don't suppose you know where he is?

Mrs Stepulov slammed down the boot and locked her car, turned to Ferreira as she walked onto the driveway.

'You have found who killed Jaan?'

'No, I –'

'Mama, what is wrong?' Arina asked, standing in the doorway now. 'What is happening?'

'Maybe we could do this inside,' Ferreira suggested.

The living room was overheated and stuffy from the electric fire, the smell of something cooking in the kitchen next door wafting in, rich and spicy. An ironing board stood in the centre of the room, an almost empty washing basket on the rug next to it and a pile of clothes neatly folded on the sofa. The television was playing quietly, the BBC News Channel reporting the fatal shooting by police at a travellers' site on the outskirts of Peterborough – *It is believed the dead man was armed at the time of the shooting. We are expecting a statement from Cambridgeshire Constabulary very soon.*

'I have some good news,' Ferreira said. Mrs Stepulov looked sceptical. 'We've just received the DNA results from the body we thought might be Jaan.'

Arina gasped. 'It is not Papa?'

'No.'

Arina reached for her mother's hands, began talking to her in Estonian, her voice high and bright, the relief lighting up her face. Mrs Stepulov smiled, squeezed her fingers, but her eyes remained hard as Arina hugged her.

'I must tell Tomas,' she said, breaking away to retrieve her mobile from the coffee table.

Mrs Stepulov waited until she'd left the room before she spoke.

'Where is he if he is not dead?'

'We were hoping you might know,' Ferreira said.

'He has not come home.' Mrs Stepulov slipped off her anorak and threw it into a chair. There were a few small spots of blood on the front of her pink tunic, just above her name tag. 'Who is this dead man you thought was Jaan?'

'His name was Andy Hudson,' Ferreira said, watching Mrs Stepulov closely for a reaction which didn't come. 'He worked for a local gangmaster, driving workers around.'

'You think Jaan killed this Hudson?'

'Right now we think it's more likely that Jaan witnessed something which scared him enough to run away,' Ferreira told her.

'I do not know where my husband is,' Mrs Stepulov said. 'I do not know and I do not care. You tell me he is alive. Why does he not come home to his family? If he is scared he should come to us.'

'Has he been in touch with you, at all, since we last spoke?'

'No.'

'Would you tell me if he had?'

Mrs Stepulov gave her a thin smile devoid of humour. 'No.'

Ferreira shifted her weight from one foot to the other, trying to decide whether that was arrogance or innocence. Arina was genuinely surprised to hear about her father, she was sure of that, and she couldn't believe Mrs Stepulov would let her daughter continue to suffer such crushing grief no matter what she felt about her estranged husband.

'We believe Andy Hudson murdered your brother-in-law,' Ferreira said.

'Viktor was hit by train. I saw his body.'

'His body was placed on the train tracks after he died.'

She went to the sofa and moved aside the stack of ironing to sit down, her face drawn into a thoughtful frown. 'You want to arrest Jaan for this Hudson's murder?'

'We just want to talk to him.'

'I tell you, I do not know where he is.'

The heat from the fire was giving Ferreira a headache, drying her throat. Behind her the television kept spieling.

'Would you know where he is if I told you he was seeing another woman?'

Mrs Stepulov glared at her. 'You are lying.'

'A waitress,' Ferreira said. 'She's about the same age as your daughter.'

'Who is the same age as me?' Arina asked, standing beaming in the doorway.

'Her name's Emilia Koppel, she's Estonian. Maybe Jaan knew her family back home,' Ferreira suggested, eyes on Mrs Stepulov.

'We do not know no Koppels.'

'She appears to've been involved with Andy Hudson. As well as Jaan.'

Mrs Stepulov's jaw flexed, biting down on her reply, and when her daughter began to speak she cut her off with a sharp burst of Estonian which stunned the girl into silence.

'Now you can see why we're eager to speak to Jaan,' Ferreira said. She took a card out of her pocket and placed it on the coffee table. 'If he gets in touch with you, I want you to call me. Any time, day or night, I'm on this number. And if he comes home –'

'I will keep him here,' Mrs Stepulov said darkly.

Ferreira left them to whatever conversation they were going to have about Jaan, hoping she wouldn't do too much damage to him if he returned to the bosom of his family.

As she got back into the car her mobile rang – Zigic.

'Any sign of Jaan?'

'No.' She could see them arguing through the living-room window already, Arina with her face in her hands. 'Any sign of Emilia?'

'She's on her way in now. You better put your foot down.'

55

Phil Barlow looked at his hands, the white marks on his fingers where his rings had been, wondering how much longer they were going to leave him down here.

He got up and paced the cell, three steps wide, back and forth, eyes on the green linoleum floor and the recently painted white walls which showed the ghosts of old graffiti, too faint for him to decipher without his reading glasses. If he wanted to read it, which he didn't. He wanted to be questioned, get it over with and done with.

He rolled his shoulder, aching from sleeping on the hard, metal bench and thought about Gemma, coming home to find a half-eaten pizza tossed away in the front garden and the house empty. Would she realise where he was? See the beer bottles in the living room and think he'd had company?

If she called the station they'd have to tell her he was here but that wouldn't ease her worry.

No. The police must have spoken to her by now. Told her about him and Renfrew.

He dug his fingers into the knot, high on his left shoulder blade, and looked up at the single bulb burning through a metal grille, dust on the cage and a dark speck where a moth had got trapped inside and scorched itself to death.

In the next cell someone was screaming and he closed his eyes, feeling what they were feeling, confined and scared and wanting out so badly he was considering smacking his head into the wall a few times just so they'd have to take him to the doctor.

How long had he been here?

The custody sergeant had taken his watch, along with his

belt and the laces out of his trainers. It was a precaution against suicide attempts, but he'd seen enough crime shows on television to realise you could hang yourself with your shirtsleeves or your trousers if you were determined enough. It was something they did so when you managed it they could say they'd made every effort to prevent you. Just arse-covering.

They should have questioned him by now.

The longer he waited the more he worried and part of him realised they were playing with him, letting him stew down here. They wanted him trembling and confused when they finally dragged him up to one of those small, white interview rooms.

He told himself that's all it was. Technique.

But no matter how many times he repeated it he didn't believe it. They weren't waiting, they were out there chasing down the truth. It started with Renfrew and where did it end?

He knew where.

Wasn't sure how they would have made the leap but the longer he sat, looking at the faded stains on the floor which could only be blood, he became more convinced that he knew exactly what was coming.

The slot in the door opened and a pair of wrinkled blue eyes appeared. The guard said nothing, snapped the slot shut again. It was the same one who had brought him breakfast, hours ago now, a leathery-faced old copper with dyed black hair and grey eyebrows who threw the food at him like he was an animal.

Four or five years ago Phil built a patio for him. He remembered the pretty limestone cottage in Elton, the prize-winning fuchsias and the vegetable patch at the end of the long, thin garden. The man's wife was dead, breast cancer, he'd told him, while they sat either side of a wooden picnic table eating fish and chips he'd bought from the village pub.

The man must have recognised him but he wouldn't acknowledge that link now. A line had been crossed and you could never go back over it.

348

Phil pressed his face into his hands and let out a muffled cry.

This would be his life. For the next ten or twelve years a cell like this, compact and sparse, reeking of bleach and other men's sweat. Twelve years with the walls closing in on him. He wouldn't make it. Ever since he was a boy he'd had a target on his back. It happened when you were big, every little bloke from miles around would come up to take a crack at you, wanting to prove themselves. Renfrew was right, he wasn't tough enough for prison.

And Gemma would talk. Sooner or later, given the right prompting, she would tell the police the truth. He'd begged her to lie and she'd done it, grudgingly, fearing the consequences of getting caught out. As the sirens blared in the street and the doorbell screamed in the house she stood in their bedroom begging him to come clean. She trusted a jury to be sympathetic. Or maybe she just didn't realise how much was at stake.

Another option occurred to him now, one which made tears spring into his eyes. Gemma didn't care about him as much as he cared about her.

56

Emilia Koppel sat tucked close to the wall in interview room 1, making her body as small as possible, arms and legs crossed and her chin tucked down into the collar of her cowl-neck jumper. There was a cup of tea on the table in front of her but she hadn't touched it.

She glanced up through her lashes as Zigic and Ferreira walked in and quickly dropped her gaze again.

She looked very young with her face scrubbed clean and her bottom lip bitten ragged. Nineteen years old but she could have passed for thirteen right then.

Zigic wondered how Maloney found her, suspected she'd got off the coach behind his pub and never moved on from it. Probably started as a waitress then was coerced into offering extras. Maloney acted the genial idiot but his connections were anything but inoffensive.

Or maybe he'd bought her from traffickers just like any other pimp. She had a lot of freedom if that was the case, though.

'Miss Koppel, I'm Detective Inspector Zigic, Sergeant Ferreira you already know.'

She nodded.

'Before we start, do you need a translator?'

'I speak English,' she said, a certain fierceness in her voice.

'And you understand that you're under caution?'

'I understand.'

'Would you like a solicitor?'

She shook her head.

'If at any time you change your mind, just say.'

'What good can they do me?' she said and looked away sharply.

Ferreira moved into the seat opposite her and started to set up the tapes.

Zigic pulled out the other chair and winced as pain shot into the centre of his chest. He needed another pill but they were making him woozy and clouding his thinking, something he couldn't afford just now.

Emilia Koppel stated her name for the tape, didn't look up as she spoke, only worried at the flaking, ink-blue varnish on her thumbnail.

'OK, Emilia, can you tell us what the nature of your relationship with Andy Hudson is?'

She still didn't look up. 'He pays for my apartment.'

'So you're his girlfriend?'

She bristled at the word. 'Yes.'

'How long have you two been together?'

'Almost one year.'

'And have you been living together all that time?'

'We do not live together. He comes sometime. Three nights maybe. Four.' She kept picking at her nail varnish. 'He has a wife. Sometime he is with her.'

'How did you two meet?'

She opened her eyes wide. They were dark green and unremarkable, except for the hardness which could only have come from living a life most young women would never know. Quickly she shut down the anger and they were blank, staring at Zigic across the table.

'He comes into Maloney's for a girl,' she said. 'First he is with Sofia, then Natasha, then he wants me.'

'And did you want him?'

'He is no different to the others.'

'But you moved in with him.'

She threw her chin up, gathered herself. 'He tells me he has this place I can live, if I see no other men. I do not want to live at the bar. So I go.'

'But you were seeing Jaan.'

'He did not know this.'

'What did Maloney think to you leaving?' Ferreira asked.

Emilia smiled with half her mouth. 'They make arrangement.'

'Hudson bought you?'

'What else does arrangement mean?'

She blinked slowly and turned away from Ferreira, back to Zigic who was watching her carefully, trying to decide if she knew Hudson was dead already. She would feel no grief, he guessed. She'd been traded like any other commodity, why would she care?

'When did you last see Andy?'

'Last week. I think Tuesday maybe.'

'Was he with you Tuesday night?'

She hesitated, looked between them again and there was a flicker of panic in her eyes.

'Maybe.'

Zigic sighed and the action made the muscles in his chest burn. The bruising was deep, not enough fat on his thin frame to absorb it. It went right down to his lungs and his heart. He took a couple of shallow breaths.

'What time did he leave?'

'Ask him.'

'We can't,' Zigic said. 'Andy's dead.'

She closed her eyes for a long few seconds.

'But you knew that already.'

'No.' It was a whisper in the hush of the interview room. 'I think he is with his wife and his son. I do not know he is dead.'

'So why are you leaving town?'

'I am not.'

'We've been inside your flat,' Zigic said. 'We've seen the bag you were packing. We saw everything.'

'I must go home to see my mother,' Emilia said, forcing herself to look up at him. She put a tremble in her voice. 'Mama is ill. She has problem with her heart. She needs me to be at home now.'

'What's your mother's number?' Ferreira asked.

Emilia stumbled, 'I cannot remember.'

'Is it in your phone?'

She nodded hesitantly.

'This phone?' Ferreira brought the mobile out of her jacket pocket, an old Nokia with a dented steel casing and scratched screen. 'The one which was in your handbag?'

Emilia made no move, said nothing.

'This is your phone, isn't it?'

Another bare nod.

In the office Zigic had rung the numbers, got Maloney's, then a gruff man with an Estuary accent who killed the call the moment he spoke. They were tracing that one. The final number rang straight through to a message service.

'Where's Jaan?'

'I do not know.'

'But you know he's still alive?'

She sighed, beaten now. 'Yes.'

'Then you know all about the fire,' Zigic said. 'You knew he was still alive when you spoke to Sergeant Ferreira. And you also knew that Andy was dead.'

Zigic opened the file he'd brought in with him, nothing inside it but a claret-coloured passport with a gold crest on the front. The words 'Euroopa Liit Eesti' were embossed at the top of it. They'd found it in her handbag, tucked into a brown envelope zipped away with her mobile and a wad of crumpled cash.

'Do you recognise this passport, Emilia?'

'Yes.'

He went to the photograph in the back of it, Jaan Stepulov clean-shaven and freshly bald, wearing a white shirt and pink tie. He looked a completely different man, some middle-aged semi-professional who you wouldn't give a second glance to. It was only the hard bones of his face and the striking, bright blue eyes which were the same.

Jaan Stepulov was now Ivo Kask.

Or at least he would have become that man if Emilia had gone straight to him rather than returning home.

'You were going to give him this. So you must know where he is.'

'No.'

'Do you know what the penalty is for aiding an offender?' Zigic asked. 'You'll go to prison, Emilia. And not for a couple of months. You'll be inside for years. Is he worth it?'

'He did not kill Andy.'

'What did he tell you?'

'He is not that type of man. He is kind.' A wistful smile lit her face and she brushed her fingertips across her bottom lip. 'One day we are together and there is a mouse in the room. Under the bed. I tell Jaan to kill it but he will not. He caught her and let her go in the hallway.' She looked at Zigic. 'Is that a man who will kill someone?'

'Maybe Andy started it,' he said. 'We know he is that kind of man. We know he murdered Viktor.'

Emilia turned to Ferreira. 'You said he was hit by train.'

'That's what it looked like initially,' Ferreira told her. 'But Viktor was murdered. We have witnesses who saw Andy do it. And we have footage of him dumping Viktor's body.'

'How did he die?' she asked. 'Why did Andy do this?'

'Viktor stepped in to protect someone Andy was beating up,' Zigic said. 'Andy turned on Viktor and stabbed him to death.'

Emilia buried her face in her hands. 'This is my fault. I sent him there.'

'You found him the job?' Ferreira asked.

'He said he is unhappy. He needs money to get home. We would go back together when he had enough. Start a new life.' She let out a long stream of Estonian, her voice hardening as if she was rebuking herself. 'I ask Andy to find him some work. It is my fault he is dead.'

'You and Viktor were a couple?'

'I loved him.'

'But you were screwing his brother,' Ferreira said.

'Viktor was gone.'

Zigic wondered what she would have done if Jaan had found Viktor and brought him back. Did she think neither of them would be jealous? She wasn't thinking at all, he guessed. She was lonely and sad and, by the time Jaan appeared, she would have grabbed any slim thread which could link her to Viktor again. The same tone whispering in a darkened room and she could pretend they were still together.

'How were you going to get the passport to Jaan?'

'I will not help you.'

'Then you'll go to prison,' Zigic said. 'And we'll catch Jaan anyway because at some point he'll go to your flat – he's waiting for this passport, he needs it – and we'll be waiting for him. For as long as it takes. But we will get him.'

'He did not kill Andy. Do you think I would help a man like that?' she demanded. 'He swore to me he did not do it.'

'Then he's a valuable witness and we need to speak to him.'

Emilia chewed on her bottom lip, fixing him with a penetrating stare, trying to decide what to do. Her judgement couldn't be very good, Zigic thought. She'd trusted the wrong people many times in her life or she wouldn't be sitting here now, she'd be back in Tallinn, studying still or working in a shop.

'If Jaan saw something – if he's scared to come forward and tell us, he doesn't need to be.' Zigic showed her the most reasonable face he could muster. 'We're not interested in blaming Jaan for something he didn't do. That's not how we work.'

'He is innocent.'

'Then he's got nothing to worry about.'

She stood sharply and paced away from the table, her arms folded across her boyish chest, looking at her feet as they moved across the linoleum floor.

Above her the clock was ticking.

If Jaan knew she was collecting his passport today he would

be wondering what the delay was. They would want to get away tonight, Zigic guessed.

Outside, evening was falling. They could get into her building under cover of darkness, hunker down and wait for him to come.

'Emilia.'

'No. I want a solicitor. Now.'

57

A stiff wind was rising as they crossed the Rivergate Apartments car park, heading for the front entrance, and Zigic felt the cold air seep through his shirt, making the muscles in his chest contract, finding the tender point over his heart.

Ferreira ran on ahead to catch the door as it swung closed, held it open for him.

'Don't want you pulling anything,' she said, smiling.

As they waited for the lift his mobile vibrated. A text from the press officer, telling him to keep her up to speed. She wanted progress made in time for the ten o'clock bulletin and charging Emilia Koppel with aiding an offender wouldn't cut it.

Riggott had said the same thing, less politely, as they left the station. Two shootings, one by a police officer, a slavery ring broken and a man burned to death, all in a single week; the DCS was getting heavy flack from above, Zigic imagined, and it was his right – his responsibility he'd say – to share that with his subordinates.

The lift doors opened and they stepped in, followed by a man in a grey three-piece suit, with a hands-free set stuck in his ear and an expensively branded messenger bag hanging from his shoulder.

Zigic wondered if Emilia Koppel had raised any suspicion among her neighbours. She was too young, too foreign, to be living in the same location as all these washed-out mid-level managers and low-end professionals. She kept strange hours, wore the wrong clothes, and Andy Hudson couldn't have blended in even if he bothered to try.

They probably thought she was a prostitute. It was the default insult when you saw a girl living outside her element.

He put his hand in his pocket and closed it around Emilia's mobile. At the office they spent twenty minutes trying to work out the best way to word a text message to Jaan. Did they use English or Estonian? Full words or text-speak? Finally they decided on a time and single x for a kiss; keep it simple.

It was five forty now. They'd told Jaan six.

He had to come. What choice did he have? He needed that passport.

As they stepped out onto the third-floor landing Ferreira dug the key out of her handbag, its small cardboard tag crumpled and smeared with a brown-red lipstick she must have left uncapped. There was a uniformed officer waiting outside Emilia's flat, his partner already ensconced in the one opposite.

Ferreira opened the door and they went in. Everything was just the same as it had been that afternoon, except the heating had come on and the flat was stifling hot and airless.

'You know what to do?' Zigic asked.

'I'm good.'

'Once he knocks, we'll be on him.'

'OK.'

'Don't open the door, Mel.'

'You don't need to tell me.'

'He could easily be armed.'

Ferreira's eyebrows made a jump for her hairline.

'Yeah, I know,' Zigic said. 'Learn from my mistakes then.'

He closed the door, another twinge in his chest as he twisted away. The PC in the corridor was nibbling on a hangnail and he dropped his hand abruptly, straightened up. He was tall and solidly built, just the kind of man they needed for the occasion.

'What's the neighbour's name?' Zigic asked.

'Laura.'

'Her surname.'

'Wise, sir. Ms.' PC Kent grinned. 'Reckon she's got a thing for blokes in uniform the way she dragged Jonesy in there.'

Zigic knocked on the door and it was answered by a curvy redhead in tight jeans and leopard-print jumper.

'I'm Detective Inspector Zigic.'

'Laura.' She put out a limp hand and he shook it, sending her bangles jingling. 'I've just made some tea. Would you like one?'

'Thank you.'

They followed her into a flat which mirrored Emilia Koppel's, the same layout flipped over. It was decorated the same too, right down to the brown leather sofa and the neutral carpet and the modular dark wood unit which was too big for the living room. This place was more homely though, framed photographs on the walls and a lot of shaggy cushions thrown around, the bookshelves crammed with black-spined crime novels and pastel chick lit.

PC Jones had settled himself in an armchair with a mug in one hand and a half-eaten cupcake in the other. He began to stand as Zigic walked in and he motioned him to stay where he was.

'Thank you for letting us use your flat, Ms Wise. It's greatly appreciated.'

'Just doing my civic duty,' she said, her tone loaded.

She was the kind of woman who could make anything sound suggestive, Zigic thought.

He directed PC Kent back to the door, left him with his face pressed to the spyhole, and went into the small cherrywood kitchen which overlooked the main car park and the cluttered hustle of Asda's service entry.

There was shopping still bagged on the worktop, next to a pile of mail and a copy of the *Evening Telegraph* with a photograph of Kelvin Gavin dominating the front page – MAN KILLED IN SLAVE RAID.

Zigic knew that the story carried over onto page 3, with a carefully worded statement by the press officer sandwiched between speculation and the most sensationalist facts. At the bottom was the photograph from his service file – *Detective Inspector Zigic is not believed to be seriously injured.*

He felt pretty seriously injured, the pain in his chest gnawing through the codeine.

'How do you take it?' Laura Wise asked.

'Black with one.'

She poured water into a Union Jack mug.

'Neal said she's a prostitute.'

PC Jones and his big mouth.

'She's a waitress.'

'A waitress couldn't afford the rent here.'

'What do you do?'

'HR. But I own the place.' She stirred in sugar. 'I got a very nice settlement after my divorce. And don't tell me I look too young to be divorced.'

She smiled as she handed over his tea.

'How well do you know Ms Koppel?'

'I don't. Not really. She took in a parcel for me a few months ago – I'm surprised she didn't keep it. You know what people are like.' Zigic nodded. 'She has visitors at all hours. That boyfriend of hers . . . I've seen him a couple of times. Not the kind you'd want to meet in a dark alley.' She leaned against the worktop, chest thrust forward in a push-up bra. 'Is that who you're here for?'

'Didn't Neal tell you?'

'He said it was strictly confidential.'

Zigic's mobile rang and he turned to the window as he answered it, saw a bald-headed man cross the car park.

'He's here, sir. He's heading for the main doors now.'

He slipped his phone away, feeling the adrenalin rising.

'Is this it?' Laura Wise asked.

'It is. You need to stay in here, Ms Wise.'

'But –'

'It's for your own safety. Please.'

She huffed but he was walking away already, calling to the others as he closed the kitchen door on her curiosity. Tomorrow at work she'd probably lie, say she saw the whole thing, embellish the story with details from one of the books on her shelf and enjoy a few hours' vicarious notoriety.

Zigic glanced at his watch. Stepulov was early. Impatient and desperate. He was liable to do anything.

'Get ready.'

PC Kent opened the door a crack. He was breathing heavily, the colour rising in his cheeks and his free hand clenching and unclenching, ready for action. Next to him Jones was silent, ashen-skinned as he took out his telescopic baton.

It seemed like an eternity they were waiting, three pairs of ears straining for the sound of Stepulov approaching. All Zigic could hear was the traffic rumbling across the Town Bridge and Laura Wise banging around in her kitchen.

Then the lift pinged and there were footsteps plodding along the thick carpet. Kent wrenched the door open and pelted across the hallway, throwing his full fourteen stone at Jaan Stepulov, driving him hard against the wall.

For a terrible moment Zigic thought it was the wrong man, just some suit coming home, then Stepulov started shouting in Estonian, thrashing and bucking as Kent wrestled him to the ground, one big forearm pressed across the back of his neck.

'No point fighting, sir.'

Stepulov twisted and kicked but he was going nowhere with Kent on him. He craned his neck to look at Zigic.

'What is this?' he snarled.

Ferreira opened the door of Emilia Koppel's flat and Stepulov turned to her.

'Where is Emilia?'

'At the station,' Ferreira said. 'She's given you up, Jaan.'

A soundless cry contorted his face and he stopped struggling finally, just lay with his cheek against the densely patterned carpet and let them cuff him.

58

Jaan Stepulov was silent in the car back to the station, staring out at the thinly peopled streets like a condemned man resigned to his fate. He went through processing without saying a single word more than he had to, sat where he was told, stood when he was asked, and it was only when he was shown into the interview room that he spoke up, asking for a solicitor in heavily accented English missing a lot of small words.

They should have celled him overnight and waited until tomorrow, but Zigic wanted this finishing.

Ferreira slammed her phone down.

'And Barlow's solicitor has finally decided to join us.'

'She can wait for us now,' Zigic said.

Ferreira glanced at her watch. 'Actually, we need to release him in . . . fourteen minutes. So we've really got to do this.'

He rubbed his temples, colours flaring behind his eyes when he closed them.

'Call Riggott, tell him we've been messed about by the solicitor and we need an extension.'

He went into his office and took another codeine with a mouthful of water from the bottle on his desk. It was rank and stale-tasting but he swallowed it and it was only as he was throwing the bottle in the bin that he realised he'd already taken his maximum dose for the day.

How dangerous could it be, though? He had a pounding headache from them and a low-level nausea that felt like nervous excitement. The side effects were worse than the pain they were treating.

He called Anna.

'You're going to be late again,' she said.

'We've arrested Stepulov.'

'Which one's he?'

She asked about work every night but she didn't really listen to the answers he gave, and he couldn't blame her, it was one small atrocity after another.

'It doesn't matter,' he said. 'What're you doing?'

'I'm just about to bath the boys. If I can get Stefan out from under the stairs. I don't understand the fascination with that bloody cupboard.'

'Kids like their dens. I had one when I was a bit older than him. It was in the old coal bunker at Mum and Dad's.'

'I can see where he gets it from then.'

'It's perfectly normal.'

She sighed. 'Shall I cook?'

'You eat, I don't know how long I'll be.'

'Are you sure you're up to this?'

'I'm not an invalid,' he said, his hand going to his chest. 'Just a bit tender.'

'Well, don't overdo it.'

They said their goodbyes and he leaned back in his chair, fiddling with the levers until it reclined, and put his feet up on the edge of the desk. He closed his eyes for a few minutes, listening to the road noise and the hum of the strip light, which was flickering above his desk, making the veins in his eyelids throb, thinking of Jaan and Viktor, Emilia and Hudson, trying to figure out how those four lives had clashed in such a way as to leave two of them dead.

He thought of Emilia Koppel, involved with all three men and yet the only one she seemed to care about was Viktor. So why risk her freedom for Jaan? Was it just because he was Viktor's brother or did she feel she owed him for something? Getting rid of Hudson maybe. She'd unwittingly set this in motion. She was at the heart of it.

He wondered if Viktor's death was a factor at all. How could Jaan or Emilia know Hudson had killed him for that to be a motive? Until Friday he was just an unnamed corpse on a cold tray at Hinchingbrooke mortuary. How could Jaan possibly have killed Hudson in revenge when the crime wasn't known about?

And the Barlows . . . there in the background, protesting their innocence but acting like guilty people.

He got up and began to pace the narrow channel behind his desk, trying to drive the fatigue out of his limbs.

Ferreira stuck her head round the door. 'They're ready now,' she said.

Interview room 1 was crowded with bodies. Jaan Stepulov sat at one end of the table in his second-hand suit, looking for all the world like any other office worker. At the other end, sat his solicitor, Ms Poole, her beige skirt suit rumpled and her make-up blurred by a long day. Zigic had dealt with her before, found her competent but uninterested.

The translator sat between them and a casual observer would have taken him for the suspect in the room. Dressed in jeans and a faded Radiohead T-shirt he looked like he'd been in the pub when the call came.

Zigic made the introductions and Stepulov sat sullen through them, eyes front as the translator spoke in a low voice, close to his ear.

Ferreira set the tapes up and the air in the room seemed to change, becoming charged suddenly. Ms Poole sat up straighter and tapped her pen against the notepad on her knee, eyes flicking from one side of the table to the other.

'Have you explained the benefit of cooperation to Mr Stepulov?' Zigic asked.

Ms Poole nodded, brushed a few strands of brown hair out of her eyes. 'Jaan understands the situation, Inspector. I think you'll find him receptive to questioning.'

Stepulov planted his elbows on the table and tucked his fists under his chin. There was a raw, red burn on his right cheek from where he'd hit the carpet, and now, seeing him up close, Zigic realised he wasn't quite as clean and neat as he'd first appeared. He had shaved badly, missing a patch of stubble near his left ear, and the skin on his neck was grubby enough to have dirtied the collar of his shirt.

'Where have you been the last week?' Zigic asked.

Stepulov cleared his throat and began to speak, echoed in English a few seconds later when the translator kicked in, speaking his words in a flat voice with a Birmingham accent.

'I have been sleeping down at the camp,' Stepulov said.

'What camp?'

'On the river.'

Zigic sighed, inwardly cursing himself for not canvassing the place. A collection of tents and ersatz shelters on the banks of the River Nene half a mile from the city centre, home to an ever-changing band of migrants, the ones who had failed to find work or accommodation but had no way to get home. It was a good place to hide. None of them would report him to the police even if they realised he was wanted.

'OK. Tell us what happened on Wednesday morning.'

'It was very early,' Stepulov said. 'I was asleep. A man came to where I was living and told me he was a friend of Emilia's. But before I could say anything he attacked me.'

Zigic placed Andy Hudson's mugshot on the table. 'Is this the man?'

Stepulov glanced at it. 'Yes, sir. He punched me and I fell back onto my bed. Then he reached for a bottle and I realised he meant to do me harm.'

'He must have said something to you. He didn't just lash out.'

Stepulov rubbed his palms together slowly. 'He told me he knew I was seeing Emilia.'

'What about Viktor?' Zigic asked.

'What has this got to do with him?'

'Hudson murdered your brother, Mr Stepulov.'

His eyes widened and he answered in halting English, thickly accented. 'No, Viktor is killed by train. Emilia tells me you tell her this. It was accident.'

'Emilia told you what we assumed to be the case at the time,' Zigic said. 'We later discovered that Hudson stabbed Viktor to death during a dispute at work.'

'Does Emilia know this?'

Zigic nodded.

'She loved Viktor.'

'And does she love you?'

He switched back to Estonian, as if retreating from the implications. 'She is with me because I remind her of him. She thinks I do not know this, but why else would she want me?' Stepulov folded his big hands together on the table.

'How did Hudson find out about you and Emilia?' Zigic asked.

'He came into Maloney's a few days before he attacked me. We were talking. Emilia was very sad about something a customer said to her, she was crying and I wanted to make her feel better. We did not notice Hudson until he was standing right next to us.'

'Did he say anything then?'

'No. He told Emilia to get him a drink and I left.'

Zigic wondered why Emilia hadn't mentioned it during her interview, realised she was so flustered over them discovering the passport that she probably wasn't thinking straight.

'Emilia said he is very jealous. She said he was rough with her afterwards. He does not like her being friendly with other men.'

Zigic leaned back in his chair. 'What happened next? After Hudson picked up the bottle?'

Stepulov took a deep breath and when he spoke again his voice was thick with emotion which didn't transfer into the translator's words.

'He tried to hit me with the bottle but I managed to get it out of his hand. I shouted for him to leave. I pushed him towards the

366

door.' Stepulov made a shoving motion across the table. 'He came at me again and punched me in the stomach. When I fell he kicked me. Here.'

Stepulov tugged his shirt out from the waistband of his trousers and held it high to show them the bruises planted across his stomach and ribcage. Hudson had landed half a dozen blows, expertly placed. Stepulov twisted in the chair and Zigic imagined him rolling into a ball to protect himself, only for Hudson to stamp on his back and dig at his kidneys. There was an odd, squarish bruise under his shoulder blade, like he'd fallen on something hard.

'I have been pissing blood for a week.'

'What made him stop?'

'His phone rang. He was distracted I think and I got up. I thought if I could get outside I could go to one of the houses for help. Call the police. But he was in front of the door and I could not get out. We wrestled. I realised then that he wanted to kill me and I had to defend myself. I don't know what happened. One moment we are standing up and the next he is on the floor.' Stepulov frowned. 'I did hit him. I do not deny that I hit him. But I did not kill him. I only wanted him to be still long enough for me to get away. I locked the door and I ran.'

'You locked the door? With the padlock?'

'Yes, sir. I wanted to stop him coming after me. I swear to you, he was alive when I left.' Stepulov stared at Zigic when he spoke, trying to force him to believe it.

But he didn't. Not now.

'Where did you go after that?'

'To Emilia.'

'Why not the hospital? Why not call the police and report Hudson for attacking you?'

'I was worried he'd hurt her,' Stepulov said. 'If he knew we were lovers he could have done something bad to her before he came looking for me.'

'So you put aside your own pain because you wanted to check she was OK?'

'Yes, sir. I only want to protect Emilia.'

'Well, you have protected her. Hudson won't touch her again now he's dead.'

'I did not kill him.'

'You had every reason to want to kill Hudson. He attacked you. There was every likelihood he'd attack Emilia later. And he killed your brother. Come on. Three motives and any one of them would be enough for most men to commit murder.'

'I did not know he killed Viktor.'

Zigic massaged his temples with his fingertips. The light in the room was too bright, too harsh. Was it usually like this? Like so many chrome splinters shooting through his eyeballs into the centre of his brain.

'If you're innocent why didn't you come forward?'

'I was scared,' Stepulov said. 'In my country the police are very corrupt. They would not believe me.'

'You're not in Estonia any more, Jaan, and you've had enough contact with the police to know how we operate. That isn't a reason.'

'You don't believe me. I tell you I am innocent and you think I am guilty. How are you any different to the police in Estonia?'

'You killed Hudson,' Zigic said and the pitch of his own voice was painful. 'We're doing you the courtesy of letting you explain yourself. If you had any sense you'd confess now. You'll be charged with manslaughter not murder and you'll be out of prison before Emilia hits twenty-five.'

'I am innocent,' Stepulov said again, rising in his chair.

'Sit down.'

'No. I tell you, he was alive when I left.' Stepulov planted his fists on the table, loomed over Zigic. 'I did not set fire to that shed. You ask the boy, he saw me leave and there was no fire.'

'What boy?' Zigic asked.

59

Ferreira replayed the conversation in her head, hands tight on the steering wheel, music thundering out of the speakers, loud enough to smother the sound of the engine and the heater turned up to full, burning her feet as they pumped the pedals. Kerry Barlow had been at work when she had called her and she had answered in clipped sentences, yes and no, not a single word more than necessary.

Should she have read fear in that?

She had put it down to the usual discomfort at receiving a call from the police, thought the woman was aware of being overheard by the people nearby and was picking her words carefully. There was no tremble in her voice, no telltale pauses.

At least that was how she remembered it now, vaguely, more mood than specifics. She remembered Kerry Barlow saying her son had been home with her all night. He only went to his father's at the weekends; Gemma didn't want him there any more often.

It sounded right at the time and nothing in the woman's account gave her reason to think otherwise.

Ahead of her the patrol car slowed as it reached the Boy's Head pub and turned off the main road. A small gang of men, smoking in the car park out front, jeered as they passed, threw up two-fingered salutes.

Ferreira flicked her indicator as she swung down Brewster Avenue and pulled onto the kerb fifty yards in. The uniforms were out already, standing under an orange street light looking towards Kerry Barlow's house. She'd brought Clarke for the matronly air, Jones for the bulk, but hopefully it wouldn't come to that.

Brewster Avenue was a quiet little cul-de-sac, red-brick and white-render semis with small front gardens and on-road parking which clogged the narrow road. At the far end there were a couple of larger houses divided into flats and the entrance to the local primary school, screened by bare-limbed trees. A security light blinked on as Ferreira climbed out of the car and she saw a figure come to the lit front window, bulky but indistinct, then the light went off and the curtains opened a crack, a second figure joining to watch.

That was how you judged an area, she thought. If people are curious about the arrival of a police car you know you're on a good street.

The door of Kerry Barlow's house opened and a man in shorts and a hoodie came out, waved across his shoulder and shouted goodbye as he headed for his vehicle. Kerry stood on the doorstep watching him, so distracted that she didn't notice the patrol car or Ferreira crossing the road, flanked by Clarke and Jones.

Ferreira was expecting her to be older, rougher, assuming Phil Barlow had traded up to Gemma, but his ex-wife had a lean, athletic figure and blonde hair feathered around a heart-shaped face.

'Ms Barlow?' Ferreira called.

'Is there a problem, Kes?' the man asked, standing with his car door open.

'It's fine, Graham,' she said. 'Go on, drive safely.'

'Boyfriend?' Ferreira asked.

'He's a client.'

'What sort of client?'

'I'm a physiotherapist. Why else would I be dressed like this?' Kerry shoved her hands into the pockets of her navy jogging bottoms. 'Is this about Phil?'

Ferreira nodded.

Kerry's gaze drifted past her, to Clarke and Jones standing on the path.

There was music playing inside the house, muffled by a closed door, all bass line, and Ferreira could smell food cooking, something spicy and salty, a late dinner for when Kerry had seen off her last client of the day.

'Is Craig at home?'

'Of course he's at home, I don't let him wander the streets at this time of night.'

'We need you both to come to the station, please.'

'Why?'

'We believe Craig saw our suspect leaving the scene of the crime. We need him to make an identification.'

'No,' Kerry said. 'He was at home all night, he couldn't have seen anything.'

She backed away as Ferreira crossed the threshold, her face frozen halfway between fear and incredulity, too stunned to protest for a couple of seconds. Then Ferreira was heading upstairs and the woman found her voice, shouted after her, 'You can't come into my house without a warrant.'

PC Clarke intervened, talking to her in a smooth voice, telling her not to worry, it was just some routine questions.

'You can't do this.'

Ferreira followed the music to a bedroom at the front of the house, a biohazard poster on the white panel door and few old stickers half scraped off, the remains of a marijuana leaf and a Spurs badge, like the boy had switched allegiance to more effective distractions.

She opened the door without knocking and the music boomed in her face, a black-metal voice raw and snarling over driving guitars. The room was a Lynx- and sweat-reeking pit, walls painted haematoma purple and covered with posters, so many clothes strewn across the floor that she couldn't see the carpet. Craig Barlow had his back to her, seated in a leather swivel chair at a desk pushed against the opposite wall, his attention fixed on the flat-screen monitor. He was playing some game, his character creeping along a shot-marked wall in a generic Middle Eastern war zone.

'I told you already, I'm not fucking hungry,' he said.

'And I'm not your fucking mother, so watch your mouth.'

He spun away from the computer but didn't get up. His feet did a nervous little dance against the floor and he started to chew on the ball of his thumb, looking at Ferreira like he was thinking of bolting for the door behind her. Pull some move he only knew how to execute on a keyboard.

He was his father's son, short-limbed and soft in the body, his face wrapped in puppy fat and dusted with freckles. He looked a very young fourteen.

'Put your shoes on,' Ferreira said.

'Where are we going?'

'The station.'

'I don't want to go.' His hands gripped the arms of his chair and he glanced back across his shoulder at the character on the screen, hunkered down and twitching, alert to attack. 'I'm in the middle of a game.'

Ferreira crossed the room in four quick steps. She stabbed the power button and the screen died.

'And now you're not.'

'You can't do that.'

'Grow the fuck up. A man's dead and you're a witness, I can do a hell of a lot more if you don't cooperate.'

Craig grabbed a hoodie from his unmade bed and shoved his feet into a pair of battered white trainers, stomped out of the room and down the stairs where his mother was waiting, bag on her shoulder, keys in her hand, and as Clarke took over, guiding Craig Barlow out to the patrol car, Kerry followed, shouted after him as she reached her own vehicle, 'Just tell them the truth, darling. Don't worry about your dad.'

60

A different guard brought Phil dinner, a woman this time, with bottle-red hair and a mannish jawline. She threw the tray down, weak tea sloshing over the rim of the cup, dousing the grey blanket.

He knew he should try and eat something but the limp chips and the dry chicken stuck to the roof of his mouth and every time he tried to swallow it felt like there was a pebble lodged in his throat. He gulped the tea, tasting a sour note from the almost spoiled milk, but the lump remained.

How long had he been here now? A day at least and they said they'd called his solicitor just after lunch, ready for questioning, but if that was true it would be over already.

Why were they keeping him waiting?

He got up from the bench and pounded on the cell door, the metal unyielding under his fist, banged until his bones ached and shouted for the guard.

She opened the eye-level slot in the door.

'What is it now, Mr Barlow? Dinner not to your liking?'

'I want to talk to Inspector Zigic,' he said, hearing how hoarse his voice had become. 'I need to tell him something.'

'He'll call for you when he's ready.'

'Is my solicitor here?'

'They will call for you when they are ready, Mr Barlow.'

She slammed the slot closed.

They were messing with his head.

He kept telling himself that. Knew he needed to stay strong, not buckle to the fears which had been plaguing him for the last twenty-four hours, trying to analyse what they were doing out there, poking around in his life, looking for something to hit him with.

There was only one thing he'd lied about and only Gemma could reveal it, but she would have done it by now if she was going to.

Unless they were working on her still, finding her more loyal than they expected.

He needed to talk to her. Just for a second. He didn't need to ask, he'd know the moment she said his name whether she was sticking by him or not.

They had to let him make a phone call. Wasn't that how it worked? You were entitled to let your family know where you were.

He banged on the door again, pulse throbbing through his hand with each fresh strike, imagining he was pounding his fist into Stepulov's face, knowing it was what he should have done that first day when he came out of the house to find him sitting in the open doorway of the shed.

If he'd been a man right then and made a stand, none of this would be happening. Maybe he'd have won the fight and been arrested for assault, maybe he'd have lost and suffered a beating, either way he would have been rid of Stepulov.

He kept hammering on the door, shouting for the guard.

Then there were feet in the corridor, more than one set, and he stepped back as the locks tumbled on the cell door.

The guard stood in front of him with her hands on her hips but whatever she said was lost on him as he saw Jaan Stepulov propelled along the corridor behind her, another guard holding him by the elbow. His head was shaved and his beard gone but it was Stepulov, definitely.

She followed his gaze, smiled.

'You look like you've seen a ghost, Mr Barlow.'

'How –'

'It's not my job to answer your questions. I'm sure Detective Inspector Zigic will explain everything in good time.'

Phil staggered where he stood, braced his hands against the

wall, seeing the pieces slotting together, the delay and the silence. There was only one explanation and only one course of action.

'Tell Inspector Zigic I want to make a full confession. You tell him that right fucking now.'

61

Zigic sat alone in the canteen, contemplating the vending machine sandwiches in front of him, the smell of sweaty ham making his stomach flip. He'd managed a Mars bar and a Coke, was already regretting taking on so much sugar.

He was going to feel like shit tomorrow.

A couple of WPCs from the night shift came in, their voices crackling around the deserted room, talking about some bloke they'd just pulled over, driving drunk and coked up, with a woman clamped on his dick. Their laughter was like shards of broken glass and it lingered for a few minutes after they left, an aftershock sparking across his brain.

He fingered the blister pack of codeine in his pocket, was debating taking another when his mobile vibrated against the table, screen flashing dementedly.

Ferreira – on her way back in with Craig Barlow.

He forced himself to eat one of the sandwiches, chewed and swallowed mechanically, barely tasting it. He threw the other one in the bin, hesitated for a moment and chucked the codeine in there too.

As he was leaving the canteen he ran into the custody sergeant. She was out of breath, flushed in the face.

'I've been looking everywhere for you,' she said. 'Barlow's kicking up a hell of racket. He says he wants to talk to you, he's ready to give you a confession.'

'The food's getting to him, is it?'

She smiled. There was lipstick on her teeth. 'He saw your prodigal corpse being taken down, it seemed to provoke him.'

'OK, thanks, Rita.'

'Would you like him bringing up?'

'Yes. No. Is Carr back with Mrs Barlow yet?'

'Just arrived.'

'I'll have a word with her first.'

She nodded, turned away smartly on her heel.

Ten minutes later she escorted Gemma into the interview room.

A long day alone, thinking about Phil locked in the cells, had left her crumpled and puffy-eyed. Her face still bore the traces of yesterday's make-up and her hair sat lank against her skull. Zigic was aware he probably didn't look much better, bruised and bearded, and he could smell the sharp tang of his own body odour as he sat down opposite her at the grey metal table.

'Why have you dragged me back here?' she asked. 'What're you doing to Phil?'

'I just need to ask you a few more questions, Gemma. I'm very sorry for the inconvenience.'

She let out a bitter laugh. 'This is harassment, you know that. When this is over I'm going to the best lawyer I can find and I'm going to sue you.'

'I'm only doing my job.'

'So do it then.' She nodded towards the tape recorder bolted to the wall. 'Come on. Ask me what you're going to.'

'Don't you want a solicitor?'

'I don't want to wait another minute in this fucking place.'

'She's downstairs,' Zigic said. 'She's on her way up now.'

Gemma crossed her arms. 'Fine.'

They sat in silence until Mrs Waites arrived and she didn't seem very amused about being kept hanging around either.

'Three hours, Inspector. Really, it's just not cricket.'

'I seem to remember we called you at one o'clock this afternoon,' he said. 'You kept us waiting for five hours. Now, if we're all ready . . .'

Mrs Waites settled herself next to Gemma as he set the tapes up, slipped off her burgundy suit jacket to reveal a creased white blouse with a tick of biro on the cuff. She pointed at Gemma's untouched cup of tea and asked if she was going to drink it, drained it in one long gulp when Gemma shook her head.

'First of all, you should know the man who died in your shed wasn't Jaan Stepulov.'

'What? Who was it then?'

'His name's Andy Hudson.' Zigic showed her the photograph, got a genuinely bemused expression in return. 'Do you know him?'

'No. What was he, a mate of Stepulov's?'

'Not a friend, no, but they knew each other.'

Gemma shook her head. 'So? What's the difference? We still didn't have anything to do with that fire.'

Zigic slipped the photograph away again, bunched his hands on the table and stared at Gemma, letting the silence stretch for a couple of seconds which felt like minutes, the clock ticking and the tapes turning. A fly had found its way into the room and it buzzed lazily around the table, drawn by the scent of unwashed hair and stale bodies.

'Phil wants to make a full confession.'

Gemma gasped, pressing her palms over her mouth.

'No. No, he can't, he didn't do it.'

'You can't protect him any more, Gemma. I can fully understand why you did it – he's your husband and you love him – but you need to think of yourself now.'

She covered her eyes and began to cry.

'I'm giving you a chance to retract your previous statements before this goes any further. Do you understand?'

Next to her Mrs Waites was examining something unpleasant she'd found under her thumbnail. 'I think I should speak to Mr Barlow,' she said.

Zigic ignored her. 'There are extenuating circumstances, a jury will be sympathetic to what Stepulov put you both through, but –'

'Oh my God, this isn't happening,' Gemma said. 'This can't be happening. What did he say?'

'You know how he's been suffering . . .'

She let out an anguished noise something between dark laughter and a cry of deep, soul-shattering despair. 'You have no idea. You've been picking away at him, haven't you? Bullying us and harassing us and you have no fucking idea.'

She got up from the table, paced into the corner of the room, arguing with herself in an undertone, dragging her fingers through her hair, pressing her palms to her cheeks, and Zigic waited it out, seeing that the battle she was fighting with herself was too big to be hurried to a conclusion by him.

He leaned back in the hard, plastic chair, his hand straying to his chest, feeling the points of his ribs throbbing, each one of them a distinct and special pain.

'No. I'm not having this.' She stomped back to her chair and drew it close, planted her hands defiantly on the table. 'You listen to me now. Whatever Phil said, he's lying. Alright? He's full of shit. You want to know what happened?'

Gemma didn't wait for him to answer. She took a deep breath, which made her shoulders shake, and spewed out the truth.

62

'I feel like I've been here for days,' Ferreira said, sitting on the radiator opposite the door to interview room 2.

'Tell me about it.'

Zigic was leaning against the wall, arms folded, head tipped back and his eyes closed, looking like he might slide down onto his heels and pass out at any moment.

'I could have handled this, you know. You didn't need to come in.'

He opened one eye, said nothing.

She wanted a cigarette but she'd smoked the last of her tobacco hours ago and there was no time to slip out to the garage in Bretton and get a fresh bag. She could smell it on her fingers and that was just making the craving worse.

Maybe there were enough loose strands scattered about on her desk for a very thin roll-up. The office was empty so no one would see her scraping them together from under the keyboard.

It was tempting.

She shifted where she sat, the ridges of the radiator digging into her backside through her jeans.

'We could just do this tomorrow,' she said.

'Lightweight.'

'Just saying.'

'I'm doing nothing tomorrow,' Zigic said. 'I don't care if mass riots break out and M&S gets looted by gangs of heavily armed pensioners, I'm staying in bed.'

'That's pretty unlikely. There's nothing worth looting in M&S.'

The door of the interview room opened and a thin blond guy in a grey suit poked his head out.

'Are you ready for us now, Mr Dean?'

'Yes, Inspector.'

Dean returned to his seat as they went in, smoothed his tie and straightened the crease in his trouser leg, ready for action. Next to him Craig Barlow looked even younger than he had at home; a child pulled out of his element and dropped down in an adult world he was ill-equipped for. He'd zipped his hoodie up to his chin, dragged the sleeves down over his knuckles, trying to disappear inside it like a turtle retreating into its shell.

Ferreira set up the tapes, aware of him watching her, a stunned expression on his face. It was getting real now, or maybe more unreal, the protocols so like something from television that he couldn't process it.

He stated his name for the tape, barely getting above a whisper, and when one of his trainers squeaked against the floor he mumbled an apology into his chest.

His mother put a protective arm around his shoulder but he quickly shrugged her off. Kerry placed her hands in her lap, fingers knitted tightly together, an expression of nauseous fear on her pointed features.

Zigic cleared his throat. 'OK, Craig, why don't you tell us what happened last Tuesday night when you were at your dad's?'

The boy shifted in his seat, glanced at his solicitor then his mother.

'I wasn't at Dad's last Tuesday.'

'Gemma told us everything, we know you were there.'

'She's lying.'

'Why would she do that?'

'I don't know.'

'We have another witness who places you at the house,' Zigic said, a hint of annoyance creeping into his voice. 'We know you were there, so let's not waste any more time with the denials.'

Craig was breathing heavily, eyes searching the tabletop. 'Nothing happened.'

'So how do you think that shed caught fire?'

Craig shrugged.

'Maybe your dad did it.'

'No.'

'Or Gemma.'

Craig tried to glare but there was too much fear in his small brown eyes to pull off the look. He didn't expect it to come to this, Ferreira thought. He was a kid, living in a world without consequences, coddled and lied for, and now there was nobody to protect him and all he had was his own wit to get him out of the situation. They'd done him no favours, Phil and Gemma and his mother, colluding so carefully to spirit him away from Highbury Street in the early hours of Wednesday morning.

Kerry had admitted that much during her own interview, the phone call just before six, Phil telling her there'd been a fire and he didn't want Craig caught up in it. Phil was the guilty party, there was no question in her mind. She was prepared to help him for her son's sake, but only up to a point, and that point had been passed.

Zigic opened the file he'd brought in with him and removed Jaan Stepulov's mugshot.

Craig blinked rapidly, then dropped his eyes.

'Look at him, Craig.' Zigic pushed the photograph across the table. 'This man was living in your dad's shed. On Tuesday night you went out into the garden and you threw a brick through the shed window while he was inside.'

Kerry inhaled sharply.

'I didn't,' Craig said.

'When he came out you threw another brick at him.'

'No.'

'Gemma saw you do it,' Zigic said. 'She told us everything.'

'No. She wouldn't do that.'

'It was a straight choice between you and Phil,' Ferreira said. 'He's down in the cells now screaming his head off, wanting to come in here and confess.'

Craig pulled his hood up, retreated a little further into himself.

'He's ready to do ten years for you.'

'It'll be more like fifteen,' Ferreira said. 'How does that make you feel, Craig, knowing your dad's prepared to go down for something you did?'

'I didn't.'

'Maybe you think he deserves it,' she said. 'Not much of a man, your dad, letting Stepulov push him around like that. Can't be much of a man to let someone punch you in the face and not retaliate.'

Kerry's shoulders squared. 'He's already told you he didn't do it.'

'Please, Ms Barlow, let Craig speak or I'll be forced to have you removed.'

'I didn't do anything,' Craig said.

'But you did.' Ferreira smiled at him. 'You stepped up where your dad couldn't. You went out there and confronted Stepulov – which was a pretty brave thing to do, given the size of him.'

He peeped out at her from under the shadow of his hoodie, a glimmer of pride in his face.

'Someone had to get him to leave,' Ferreira said.

'I only wanted to scare him.'

'Well, you succeeded. He left a few hours later, didn't he?'

'Yeah.'

'You saw him go?'

'I told him not to come back.'

'So you thought the shed was empty when you set fire to it?'

'I didn't.'

Zigic sighed and Ferreira saw him wince, press his hand to his chest for a second.

'Let me explain something to you, Craig. We have a very thorough statement from Gemma, we have your parents lying about your presence at the crime scene and now we have you admitting to attacking Stepulov. We also have a forensics team at your mother's house right now searching for the clothes you were wearing at the time.'

Craig's eyes widened and he turned towards his solicitor, looking for help which wasn't coming.

'Now, maybe you were clever enough to get rid of them but since you believed the shed was empty I doubt it. My guess is they're in the washing basket still, or if your mum's on the ball she's already washed them, which is meaningless because we will still be able to recover the material we need to prove you were there.'

Kerry squirmed in her seat.

'If you keep up this "I didn't do it" rubbish then we'll charge you and you'll go to court and you will be found guilty. I guarantee it.'

The boy's head dropped and tears sprang into his eyes. He tried to hold them down but they came anyway, despite his clenched jaw and the shame which burned across his cheeks.

'There was no way you could have known someone was inside that shed,' Zigic said softly. 'You saw Stepulov leave. You weren't to know he'd left an unconscious man locked in there. He's at fault as much as you are here.'

'I didn't know,' Craig said weakly.

'We realise that, believe me, we do.'

'I didn't want him coming back. I thought if I burned the shed he'd have to find somewhere else and Dad and Gemma wouldn't have to put up with him any more.'

'Alright, Craig.'

'I'm sorry.' He pressed his knuckles into his eye sockets, looking like an overgrown baby, swaddled in puppy fat and his big white hoodie, and when he spoke again each word was punctuated with a gulping sob, 'I didn't mean to hurt anyone. I'm so sorry.'

Craig wiped his face dry and Kerry rubbed her hand across his shoulder.

'Can I go home now?'

'There's a process,' Mr Dean told him.

Zigic placed his hands flat on the table. 'Craig Barlow, I am charging you with the manslaughter of Andy Hudson, do you understand the charge?'

'Yes.'

Ferreira stopped the tapes and Zigic began to explain the next stage in proceedings, statements to be signed, forms to be filled in which would release Craig into his mother's care until the trial. But Craig wasn't listening, he was whining and cajoling, desperation tightening his voice as he tried to get Kerry to do something which was out of her power.

Finally she shushed him. 'We'll be going home soon. Now be a big boy.'

Back in the corridor Zigic looked ready to pass out, slouching where he stood, eyelids beginning to droop. Whatever small reserve of energy he'd started the interrogation with was now exhausted.

'Do you want me to finish up here?' Ferreira asked.

He rubbed his face with both hands, yawned expansively. 'No, you've had as long a day as I have.'

'Actually you had a sofa break this morning.'

He smiled dozily. 'Yeah, I'm such a slacker. Look, I'll deal with Craig, you go and give Phil the good news.'

'My pleasure,' Ferreira said. 'What am I charging Mr Barlow with?'

'Conspiracy should just about cover it. Bail him, then you can get off.'

'And Gemma?'

He shook his head. 'Already dealt with.'

Ferreira went down to the custody suite, where a drunk was kicking up enough noise for two men his size, singing a pornographic version of 'Maggie May' at the top of his voice while a WPC tried to remove his belt.

She gestured to one of the guards, who was looking on grinning, and told him to bring Phil Barlow out.

A minute later he strode up to her, red-faced and furious.

'I want to confess. Right now. Take me up. I set fire to the shed.'

'It's too late for that, Mr Barlow. Craig came clean – he was very brave.'

A pained moan sounded low in his throat and he turned away from her, hands clamped around the back of his neck like a man preparing for a firing squad.

'But you can confess to covering for him if you like,' Ferreira said, when he was facing her again. 'It'll make life a lot easier and you can get home to Gemma tonight. I'm sure she's missed you.'

The fight was all drained out of him and he nodded once, eyes closed, in absolute surrender. She told the guard to get him a cup of strong tea and went to fetch the paperwork.

By the time she returned the drunk had been spirited away, his voice now muffled by two thick doors, and Phil Barlow was sitting in the corner of the room with his elbows on his knees and his head dropped into his hands. Seeing him like that she felt a vague sense of pity; he was only trying to protect his son, just like any father would.

She sat down next to him and ran through the charge. He nodded, gave short answers, his voice cracked and weak. That of a broken man. He signed where she told him to and took back his possessions from the custody sergeant, shoved his watch and shoelaces into his pocket, and it was only as he was slipping his wedding ring onto his finger that he asked if he would go to prison.

'I honestly don't know,' Ferreira told him. 'If you get a sympathetic judge, probably not.'

'What about Gemma? She only lied because I begged her.'

'I'm sorry, I couldn't say. It all depends on the judge.'

Ferreira called a patrol car to take him home and left him waiting in reception, between a prostitute in red thigh-high boots and a serial burglar who was checking her out, then headed back up to collect her things, thinking about dragging Bobby out of bed to hit the clubs. She was definitely getting her second wind now.

In the office she found Zigic struggling to get his parka on, one arm in it already but the other one kept flapping away from him and he winced as he stretched to reach for it.

'Do you want a hand with that?'

He pulled it off and threw it onto a chair. 'Not that cold out, is it?'

'No. Come on, I'll drive you home.'

Epilogue

Paolo was already at the crematorium when Ferreira pulled into the car park, standing out front under the fluted canopy with his cousin, Marco. They both wore dark suits, shirts and ties, and she felt a knee-jerk sense of pride towards them, her countrymen; as poor as they were they respected the occasion enough to spend money they didn't really have on clothes they would never wear again.

As she was locking the car Adams drew up next to her, managing to take up two spaces with his sleek black Audi. He climbed out and pitched his cigarette butt into a narrow flower bed planted with stunted rose bushes just coming into bud, small copper plaques dotted between them bearing the names of the deceased.

'What're you doing here?' she asked.

'Thought it was the least I could do. Pay my respects, you know.' He took off his sunglasses, slipped them into his pocket. 'Poor fucker dies four thousand miles away from home, someone's got to be there to see him off, right?'

Ferreira nodded, thinking of Viktor Stepulov's funeral the week before. Arina and Tomas Raadik had turned out to see him off, no sign of Mrs Stepulov who Arina had insisted unconvincingly was at home with the new baby. Jaan and Emilia had stood on the other side of the grave, close together under an umbrella as the flimsy pine coffin was lowered into the ground. They had both been bailed, despite presenting a credible flight risk, and Ferreira had made a bet with herself right there that neither would show up for their hearings next month. It was easy to slip out of the country on a packed coach, half the time customs didn't even check for passports. Easier still to lose youself in the grey economy of another city.

A hearse swept past, slowing on the long curve towards the main doors. There was a single wreath on top of the pine coffin, a simple arrangement more foliage than flowers, just a few white lilies standing out against the green.

Adams crossed himself and looked expectantly to Ferreira when she didn't follow suit.

'You're Catholic, aren't you?'

'I was,' she said, starting across the car park. 'Then I grew up.'

A few fine drops of rain hit her face and she quickened her pace, reaching the main doors as the hearse came to a final stop. Paolo smiled, too warmly for the setting, and shook her hand, kissed her on both cheeks. He'd put on a few pounds since leaving hospital, had a haircut, and he looked a different man to the one she'd seen, close to death, only a couple of weeks earlier.

There was still that darkness in his eyes though, and she doubted if any amount of good food and sunshine would shift it.

'You look very well, Paolo.'

'Thank you.' He nodded to Adams. 'Xin Gao would be happy we are here.'

'Have you found his family?' Marco asked.

'We've been in touch with the consulate,' Adams said. 'But they've got no record of him. Chances are he was trafficked over here. They're making inquiries but it's a long process, lot of red tape.'

'The people who killed him, what is happening to them?' Marco asked.

'We've charged them with murder,' Adams said. 'They're in prison now, awaiting trial. I doubt they'll see the light of day for a good twenty-five years.'

'And what about the others?' Paolo asked. 'They were just as guilty.'

Adams frowned. 'We've got them on slavery, tax evasion, some weapons charges. They'll be punished, Paolo. Believe me, the courts will want to make an example of them to stop something like this happening again.'

They fell silent as four large men in matching suits came out to the hearse and unloaded the coffin, working quickly and precisely but still managing to maintain a posture of deference as they carried Xin Gao inside on their shoulders.

The minister, a short, waxy-skinned man with dyed black hair and thick glasses, ushered them through the high wooden doors into the chapel, where some dour music was playing softly. It was a cold, functional space, with rust-coloured carpet and lacquered pine pews, bare white walls and a lectern where there should have been an altar.

There were no hymns for Xin Gao, no speeches from his family members, no tears, just a single person who had briefly met him, shared a quick cigarette, and three who knew him as nothing but a murder victim. Paolo got up and said a few words about the kindness Xin Gao had shown him, the goodness he'd sensed in the man, but he could say nothing more without resorting to lies or clichés, so he returned to the pew.

Ferreira found his hand and squeezed it quickly.

Then the minister was saying the Lord's Prayer and somewhere a button was pressed and Xin Gao's coffin slipped quietly away, disappearing behind a thick velvet curtain and into the flames.

A few minutes later they were outside again and it was like the whole thing never happened. Lapsed as she was Ferreira still thought it felt like a hollow sham. Death demanded candles and incense and wailing.

'We should send his ashes to the family,' Paolo said.

'I'll take care of it,' Ferreira told him, realising he hadn't really absorbed what Adams had told him. He'd come too close to suffering the same fate to accept the possibility that a man could die without his people knowing.

Xin Gao's remains would go into the ground in the garden of

remembrance and back home his family would continue with their lives, believing he had found something here which made them unimportant. Another woman maybe, a better life. That was what you came to England for after all.

'What are you doing now?' she asked.

'We fly home this afternoon,' Paolo said.

'They have a big party planned for him,' Marco said, and put his hand to his mouth. 'I have ruined the surprise.'

Paolo smiled vaguely, looking away across the lines of rotting floral displays, the car park where people were arriving for the next service, climbing out of cars and clinging to one another under umbrellas as the rain lashed down on them.

A taxi pulled up and the driver helped out an elderly woman in a black dress, her face hidden by a fine veil. She was clutching a rosary in a gnarled hand heavy with gold rings.

Marco called for the man to wait. 'We must go now. We will miss our plane.'

They said their goodbyes and Ferreira and Adams stood under the canopy, watching the taxi pull away, waiting until it disappeared out of the gate.

'We should go for a drink,' Adams said.

'Bit early, isn't it?'

He grinned at her. 'That's very English of you.'

'Just for that, you're buying.'

Acknowledgements

I owe a huge, gushing thank you to my agent Stan for his wisdom and guidance, and for taking that first big gamble on me. Equally effusive thanks to my wonderful editor Alison Hennessey, whose keen eye and good judgement refined the book I wrote into the one you now hold in your hands. I feel immensely privileged to be part of the Harvill Secker gang and am deeply grateful to the whole team for the hard work they have put into making this book happen.

Thanks also go to Luca Veste for being the best example an aspiring writer could have and a source of boundless optimism and moral support. The crime writing community contains some of the warmest, most generous people I've ever met, too many to thank by name, but you know who you are and that there's always a drink behind the bar for you.

Finally to my family; my long suffering, endlessly patient, constantly encouraging family – thank you for always believing that 'author' was a perfectly reasonable career choice and for never letting me give up on my dream.